C0-AQA-953

SECRETS OF THE HEART

JUDITH LUKE

ROMANTIC SUSPENSE

JUDITH LUKE

Copyright © 2022 Judith Luke

ROMANTIC SUSPENSE

JUDITH LUKE

All rights reserved. By payment of the required fees, you have been granted the non-exclusive, non-transferrable right to access and read the text of this book. No part of this text may be reproduced, transmitted, down-loaded, decompiled, reverse engineered, or stored in or introduced into any information storage and retrieval system, in any form or by any means, whether electronic or mechanical, now known or hereinafter invented, without the express written permission of the publisher.

All characters in this book have no existence outside the imagination of the author and have no relation whatsoever to anyone bearing the same name or names. The author also acknowledges the use of various trademark names.

Secrets Of The Heart

*A Hightower
Mountain
Novel*

JUDITH LUKE

Secrets Of The Heart

*A Hightower
Mountain
Novel*

JUDITH LUKE

ACKNOWLEDGMENTS

Special thanks to some important people. First, my husband Don for his support and his male point of view. And my critique partners Nora and Jennifer who tell me when something is missing or needs a touch up. And my creative book cover artist, Patti Roberts for taking my vision and putting in picture form.

CONTENTS

Chapter 1	1
Chapter 2	12
Chapter 3	19
Chapter 4	25
Chapter 5	37
Chapter 6	54
Chapter 7	63
Chapter 8	83
Chapter 9	95
Chapter 10	109
Chapter 11	121
Chapter 12	142
Chapter 13	155
Chapter 14	170
Chapter 15	184
Chapter 16	199
Chapter 17	210
Chapter 18	228
Chapter 19	243
Chapter 20	256
Chapter 21	266
Chapter 22	275
Chapter 23	287
Chapter 24	310
Chapter 25	327
Chapter 26	345
Chapter 27	357
Chapter 28	371

Chapter 29 382

Chapter 30 392

About the Author 413

CHAPTER ONE

*B*rooke downshifted the white Mercedes convertible and came to a stop at the Montgomery Ranch Road. A warm glow flowed through her as she gazed at the wrought-iron gate with a giant 'M' in its center. She tapped in the code her father had sent her and watched the large gate swing open. After eight long years, she was finally home.

The road was a red ribbon of clay, snaking its way down the natural grade to the house and barns. Beyond the ranch buildings, the lush valley was bordered with snow tipped mountains. Before her lay the vastness of her family's Wyoming homestead. Her heart warmed with the view.

Nearly a century ago, her grandfather had built the large two-story colonial home for her southern-belle grandmother. The brick exterior was enhanced with white trim and glossy black shutters. Blue spruce stood on each corner like stalwart soldiers. Cottonwoods lined the drive, spaced evenly like sentinels. Just past the house was the original barn. On the right, was the new arena and larger horse barns.

"This is your home. You're always welcome." Her father replied when Brooke spoke of her plans to return to the ranch. Over the years she had visited only a couple times for a few permitted days. Did she imagine an indulgent voice, as though he was forcing his enthusiasm?

Her mother died when she was barely five. From that moment on, Joe Montgomery kept her at arm's length, giving her everything she wanted and needed but not enough of himself. Could it be he really didn't want her to come back to live on the ranch?

Or was he still angry about her choice to stay in Los Angeles and marry a man he didn't choose? Well, she hadn't come to love Mike either. But he was dead, and she was finally free. Brooke pinched the bridge of her nose and closed her eyes. So many wasted years. A few tears escaped and slipped down her cheek, and she quickly wiped them away.

She shifted into first gear. Gripping the wheel, she breathed out a fortifying breath and headed down the drive. The gate automatically closed behind her. She parked her car adjacent to the brick walk that would lead to the back door. Before her was the original horse barn. The doors on both ends were open for a fresh breeze to pass through. Euphoria filled her as she stretched her limbs and breathed in the crisp mountain air. After a quick glance around, she opened the trunk to remove her suitcase.

Through the lilacs, she recognized the familiar horse trotting toward her from the arena. Brooke hurried to greet her father, but the pointy toe of her spindle-heeled boots clipped the ridge of the cement curb. She stumbled and careened across the drive into a lush lilac bush. She slid off the branches, landing face down on the recently watered lawn and wet gravel.

Embarrassed, she rose and looked around to see if anyone saw her flight into the bushes. She felt childish and clumsy—and now stained and dust covered. She rubbed her hands to ease the scrapes and tried to brush away the wet grass and pebbles sticking to her silk shirt. An errant leaf stuck to a button.

Brooke turned with the sound of footsteps and found herself staring into the smiling face of a much taller and more muscular man than her father—Adam Tower.

"Adam." She could hardly raise her voice above a whisper. A thread of confusion led her eyes past him toward the new arena. "I expected my father."

She swept the grass and dirt from the knees of her designer jeans and white silk shirt. She wanted to look nice on this first day home—at least look like she still had some money.

A deep chuckle rolled out of Adam. He tied the beautiful, sorrel mare to an antique hitching post positioned along the drive. Coming to stand near her, he picked grass bits from her sleeve and hair.

Adam was more stunningly virile than she remembered. The unwanted thought made her edgy. Tall, dark, rangy. She didn't want to think of Adam in those terms. They had known each other their entire lives. His family owned the ranch next to theirs, the Hightower Ranch.

"Have a good *trip*?" His pun came with a grin.

"Nothing like a grand entrance." She grinned reluctantly and continued to remove the small, wet pebbles from her shirt. Unprepared for this encounter, her face flushed. This was Adam. But the potent sexual package, picking grass from her long blonde hair and making her heart race, was not the memory she held of him.

Adam was thirty-five, six years her senior. As children, he enjoyed provoking and devilling her. She always took the bait, she recalled. Play slapping, pushing, and laughter usually ended the event. The smell of a freshly washed shirt with horsy overtones was a key to those memories. They wrapped around her like a warm blanket.

Towering over her, his frame was barely confined in the denim he wore so well. His self-assured mannerisms exasperated her own insecurities. Knowing who he was and what he wanted from life, he always made his own decisions, requesting nothing of others except honesty— even from her.

"Welcome home, Princess." Adam smiled as he slid a pebble from her hair.

Princess, his pet name for her when they were children—usually in a derogatory way.

He could so unnerve her. But she remembered the constant contention between them—their relentless competition to win the prize, a coveted belt buckle, a trophy, a new saddle, the last chocolate cookie. Not this sexual magnetism flaring through her now. No, he was just Adam, part of her past life.

After the financial traumas related to Mike's estate, not to mention years of spousal abuse, she wanted to fold herself into his solid body, have him hold her in those strong arms, and tell her she was going to be fine. Just like in the past. Just like when he held her while she cried over the death of her favorite horse. Just like he did at the county fair when he held her and told her the boy was no good, after flighty Kitty Jones walked off with her date. But they were not children anymore, and how could she admit to the terrible mistake she made?

"Where's Dad?" Annoyed with her clumsiness and her uncomfortable attraction to him, she swept her hair from her face.

"He'll be here shortly."

"Isn't that my mare, Sly?" The mare was her favorite from the time she was a small child when she watched the birth of a foal for the first time.

"Brooke, the mare is mine." His voice was casual as he claimed her horse.

She thought she detected regret as he searched her eyes and reached for her thoughts. She stared into those soft, brown eyes until he gave her a caressing wink.

Brooke turned and headed to her car. His long strides made it awkward for her to stay ahead of him, while her high-heeled boots found numerous soft spots and stones to stumble over.

"Be careful with those city boots."

His chuckle sent her spinning around to face him. "Don't you have anything to do?"

Caught off guard, he nearly walked into her and grabbed her elbows to keep her from falling. Her senses bloomed with the scent of horse and man. Besides the musky odor on his shirt, his dust-covered jeans told her he had been working. A ring of sweat stained his light-gray Stetson as his dark hair curled around the worn brim.

"Joe saw your car on the hill. He's with a customer and asked me to meet you. He'll be coming soon."

"Why are *you* here?" Her voice sounded blunt, rude to her own ears.

Adam took his hat off and ran his fingers through his dark curls. Slowly resetting his hat, his eyes caught and held hers. "I train your father's show horses. Joe must not have told you."

Fear rippled through her. Why would he be working on their ranch when he, his father, and brother owned twice the land they did? The Hightower Ranch was one of the largest in the county. The name came from a large rock formation, resembling a castle tower. As children they played at the site—knights to fire-breathing dragons. The Tower men competed in The American Paint Horse Association sponsored events and other national competitions, just as she and her father did. They had their own herd to train. Training your competitor's horses seemed like cheating.

What else hadn't she been told? Joe never included her in his decisions. But why hadn't he even mentioned that Adam worked for him? A primitive warning sounded in her brain.

She continued to her car. As she reached into the trunk for her suitcase, their hands collided. He pulled out the bag.

"I'll take this. I know Mary has your room ready."

"You said he was coming. How long will he be?"

Adam's eyes flashed a gentle tolerance. He grinned and nodded his head in the direction of the arena. "I believe he's coming now."

Joe and Hank, the assistant trainer on the ranch, loped up to where they stood. Joe dismounted with surprising spryness, handing the reins to Hank. He hurried over to embrace his only child.

"Oh, it's so good to have you back. How was your trip?" He held her at arm's length. "You look lovely, lovely. Doesn't she, Adam? You're a beautiful image of your mother."

7

Adam grinned. "Yes, she does … grass stains and all."

She sensed the teasing tone in Adam's words. Joe continued to keep his arm around her as if she was a spirit and would disappear before he had his fill. He seemed happy to see her, but she hoped it wasn't his same reaction as when she was younger. Yes, he would be happy to see her and hear about her day, and then he would go about his business.

"Your hair is so full and long again. But you look a bit weary."

"I'm fine. Spring is such a beautiful season." She wound her arm in his and gripped his hand as though it could tether her to the ranch. She wanted more from him now, more than a new horse or saddle.

Brooke extended her hand to her car. "I forgot what it's like on these gravel roads. I don't know if I'll ever get all the dust out of the leather seats."

"Now, don't go worrying about the car. I'll get someone to fix it up for you. Besides, I might take that beauty for a spin myself." He patted her hand.

Joe's six-foot frame seemed thinner than she remembered. His eyes, though evasive, glistened with tenderness and love. He's getting older, she thought as she noticed the gray highlights and graying mustache. He was over forty when she was born, and the hand covering hers was now worn and weathered. She talked to him on the phone periodically, but he never really told her anything—like she didn't tell him anything.

Going over to the horses, Brooke greeted Hank. He started working on the ranch when he was still in high school, a few years ahead of her. While holding the reins of both horses in one hand, he removed his hat. With a hug and a chaste kiss on the cheek, he smiled. "Good to have you back."

Joe turned to Hank. "Would you take care of the horses? Take Sly with you. Get Contender out and let him run free in the arena for a bit. We'll see you later."

Adam leaned his long frame against the door of her car, suitcase at his feet. He removed his hat and placed it on the hood. His presence rattled her emotions, making her feel like an adolescent again. Admittedly, Adam was the one who was always there for her, taking her to horse shows, bandaging up her scrapes, telling her no. Not her father.

Joe picked up Brooke's overstuffed bag.

"Joe, let me take it. For a small case it's heavy. She must have brought Los Angeles with her," Adam quickly offered.

"No, it's alright. I'm fine." Joe turned to his daughter in dismissal. "Is this all?"

Adam's overture to help sent off a warning signal. Something was wrong. Her father never needed help or asked for it. And now he was training their horses.

Brooke forced a smile. "Yes. Anything else is being shipped out from L.A. Should arrive in a few days—just a couple of boxes."

All my worldly goods, she mused. She thought

9

marrying Mike was so wonderful—a wealthy man. A wealthy man who needed a wife for display. Not for real love. A fixture like all his other possessions. Something to show off. Part of his image. And she quickly learned how to be that possession or suffer the consequences.

At the mudroom door, Brooke remembered her purse lay on the front seat of the car. Adam remained leaning on her car—somber, foxlike, watching. Reluctantly, she traveled the length of the brick walk, trying to avoid his stare.

"I forgot my purse. It's on the front seat."

He reached around and retrieved the small leather clutch. He continued to watch, looking more relaxed. An easy smile played at the corners of his mouth.

Pride and confusion churned within her as she tried to cool her thoughts. She put out a hand to take the purse.

"I seem to have been slighted—no hug, no kiss hello," he hinted, cradling her purse.

Brooke hesitated. She really hadn't greeted him with even a brief hug. They'd always been comfortable touching. Working together. Hugging for rewards of a job well done. Physical play. But the enduring game of cat and mouse played between them sparked a fire within her. She cradled his face with both hands and lightly pressed her lips to his.

"There, a kiss hello." Their eyes locked for a moment, and before any repercussions, she snatched up her purse and hurried to the door. Giving him one last glance before entering the house, she found Adam still leaning on her car, arms folded, eyes zeroed in on hers.

Brooke closed the mudroom door, shutting out the embarrassing silence. She had fallen all by herself on her 'city boots,' as Adam referred to them. She gritted her teeth. Instead of being pleasant, she had been rude, taking out on Adam her own mortifying tumble into the lilacs.

The fall wasn't what rattled her. No, it was her reaction to him. Adam was a well-seasoned man. Women, like their neighbor Kitty Jones, forever found him sexually enticing. But that little kiss set off a rush she hadn't felt for years.

And it was sparked by Adam Tower of all men.

CHAPTER TWO

Still flushed, Brooke stood in the mudroom, gathering her wits. She took a deep breath and let it out slowly. Why did she do that? And Adam didn't respond. What was he thinking while he watched her walk to the house?

She kicked off her boots and along with them her insecurities. She opened the door and stepped inside the kitchen to the loving reminders of home. Feelings of security and love were generated here, simple feelings she had missed the past few years. This constant, unchanging world was what she needed to get her life back on track.

She followed her father through the kitchen and into the main foyer. On her right was the open stairway to the bedrooms. The first set of stairs ended on a large landing. The rest of the stairs rose parallel to the first. The floor in the foyer was dark cherry, as well as all the doors and moldings in the house. A thick Persian rug was soft under her feet.

She glanced up through the white carved spindles. At the top on the left was a door to a large storage area. To the right was a long hall leading to four individual suites. The suitcase banged against a wall. "I should have helped him," she murmured to herself.

Why was Adam so eager to help? Secrets closed around her like a web. Was he really working for her father? And did her father really sell Sly to him?

The smell of the roast beef warmed her to better memories and carried her back to the kitchen with its white cabinets and black granite counters. There she found Mary, the long-time housekeeper, and probably her best friend.

"Hello," she whispered as she peeked around the doorway.

"Oh, Brooke." Mary's round face lit with joy as she came over for a hug. "I made your favorite chocolate chip cookies with extra walnuts. I had a hard time keeping them hidden away from your dad and Adam."

"You are going to spoil me all over again."

Her dark eyes twinkled. "You look a little thin. Nibble on these while I make tea."

Mary wore jeans and a bright pink blouse on her tall, slim frame. Moccasins of soft, tan leather were her favorite shoe. Fragments of her Cherokee family still lived in Oklahoma. She had a beautiful face, delicately carved with full lips. Her long hair had turned grey, and she wore it as usual, pulled back in a braid. On her ears silver and turquoise dangled. She was a gentle, generous soul with a strong inner strength and wisdom.

"I must have missed you when I came in with Dad."

"Oh, I was downstairs getting wine for dinner."

Mary put the water on to boil. She could have used the Keurig, but she always said tea tasted better from a boiling pot.

Brooke rested her folded hands on the oversized island. "Don't you ever tire of rambling around in this big house?" Awkwardly, she probed. "Haven't you ever wanted a family of your own?"

Mary glanced around the room and smiled. "No, I love this place. It's like a part of me. I guess after twenty some years, it kind of grew on me. When I came here, after your mom died, I didn't think I'd ever get the hang of taking care of a child, a house, the entertaining."

"Well," Brooke added, "I'm sure glad you did. Dad was always a perfectionist in everything from the horses to me. If he had his way I never would have been allowed out of a dress and patent leather shoes. I would have never been in jeans and boots if it wasn't for you."

Mary patted her on the shoulder. "Well, I'm sure glad I came, too. You're my family. Here, carry these cups and the cookies, and I'll bring the tray of tea."

Mary poured the tea in her favorite, china cups. "Is Joe going to join us? I'd hoped he would. He's always so busy. He's supposed to slow down, but you know how he is, has to have his say in everything. I'll get a mug for him."

"He won't be able to." Adam's deep, resonant voice carried from the doorway. He leaned one shoulder into the doorjamb of the mudroom. His voice was so unexpectcd. Brooke's heart skittered. "Why?" she queried, trying to rest the unwanted anxiety in her chest. His presence during this private time irritated her. Her eyes flicked away from the observant browns studying her.

"Joe is going into town with me. We have a shipping contract to sign and supplies to pick up." His usual cocksure attitude dared her to dispute his authority.

Mary interrupted. "Oh, I had wished you boys could stay and visit. After all, Brooke just got here. Would you like a sack of cookies to nibble on while you're driving? We'll sacrifice some."

"You must have been hiding these, Mary." Slipping off his boots, Adam strolled over to the table. "You can wrap some up for Joe. I'll have one here. They are fattening." Leaning over Brooke's shoulder, he took one of the large cookies from the blue china plate.

He moved into the work area of the kitchen, sniffing the preparations for dinner. She caught herself glancing at him surreptitiously, as she worried whether she was attracted to the powerful energy he gave off or to her new perspective of him. Before, he was just Adam, an old childhood friend, brotherly, nearly part of the family. Now, she felt a curious thump of her heart.

She looked out the multi-paned window. The view was one of her favorites. Down the hill, she could see the length of the original white barn and the runs, housing her father's registered horses. A large pasture opened from the runs for exercise and grazing.

During the spring new foals always brought fresh excitement. With paint horses every foal is a surprise as no two will be colored the same, even from the same stallion and mare. Those ready to foal were most likely kept under scrutiny in her own stall with an outside run for fresh air.

Brooke knew Joe would have someone watching round the clock until all the long-legged babies were breathing and suckling. She recalled the many nights she spent in that barn waiting for a new foal.

"Dad! Dad, wake up. It's coming. The foal." She pushed and pushed on her father's shoulder. Leaving the lights on in the barn, he had relaxed in a lawn chair next to the stall to be available in case the mare needed help. Joe had fallen asleep, but Brooke was too excited.

"Alright, alright. What's the ruckus, darling'," he replied softly.

Excitement bubbled out of her. She whispered, "The foal, the foal. I can see its little feet." She scurried back on her stool to watch through the bars of the stall.

"Well, then I guess we're going to have a baby," he whispered. "I'm sure glad you stayed awake, or we would have missed it. She looks all right for now. You go

in the tack room and bring the bucket with all the medicine and bring the towels."

"But, Dad, I already got them. They're here by your chair. Do something."

By then the mare had foaled alone, and it was time to clean up the wet newborn. When Joe felt it was safe, he allowed her just inside the stall and kept her busy with her own little towels. Later, while they watched the foal suckle on its own, they each drank hot chocolate from the thermos.

"You did a fine job, darlin'. What do you think we should name her?"

"She was pretty sly, coming when you fell asleep. We could call her Sly."

Joe picked her up and sat her on his lap. "I think that's a great name. Because you did such a good job, I'm going to give her to you as a present."

For awhile, she sat on his lap on the lawn chair, positioned next to the slightly opened stall door where they could view the newcomer, a sorrel filly with four white stockings.

Brooke remembered the night as though it had just happened. Out in the immediate pasture were older foals, playing in the sunshine while their mothers munched on the spring grass. She felt a pang of remorse for the years she missed. Her thoughts were interrupted when hands rested on her slim shoulders.

"Are you okay? You looked a bit sad," Joe asked.

"Oh, I was remembering when Sly was born. I really

miss the birth of a foal." She grinned with pleasure as she turned to look at him. *Had he really sold Sly to Adam?*

"Adam and I have to go to town on business you would probably find boring. So, I'm leaving you with Mary. I'm sure you two can find something to chat about." He reached over to steal one of the cookies and gave her a wink. "I'll see you later for dinner. By the way, Mary, Josh will be joining us for dinner, so set an extra place, please." Still smiling he went over to the mudroom to slip on his boots and retrieve his hat. "We'll be back around six, supper around seven."

Joe left with Adam through the mudroom door on the far side of the kitchen. She watched from the window as the two men ambled to the barn, and then headed out for town in the new white Ford pickup, the Montgomery brand adorning the door.

Brooke pondered why Adam would have time to work at their ranch. Hightower Ranch was enormous. Was he trying to add the Montgomery ranch to their holdings? Too soon, she thought, to begin questioning Dad on how he runs the ranch and who he hires.

CHAPTER THREE

*B*rooke knew that if Josh Tower was coming for dinner, then more than likely so was Adam, his oldest son. Josh was their nearest neighbor and her father's best friend. However, he did have the same dominating personality of the Tower men.

Steve, Adam's brother, was her bosom buddy during her childhood, a childhood filled with many adventures. In additions to being a rancher, he was also an artist who painted eagles in oils. Being three years older than her, she and Steve had more in common.

"Is Steve coming?"

After checking on the roast and fussing over the other delicacies, Mary sat at the end of the table. "Oh, Adam mentioned that Steve has been out of town on business for a couple of weeks. I don't know if it is for the ranch or his paintings." She wiped her hands on a dish towel and prepared her tea. "Did you have a good trip?"

"Yes. It didn't take as many days as I thought." Brooke took another cookie from the plate. So comforting. She held the bite in her mouth until it melted away.

Mary held her cup in both hands, rested her elbows on the table, and gazed at Brooke. "Have you made up your mind about what you are going to do now? Have you decided to stay?"

"I really don't know, Mary." No, she mused, she had nowhere else she wanted to be.

"Do you think you'll miss the city if you stay here?"

"No. I was never a city girl. I could find a job here in town, maybe at the bank. The thought of working in an office and living alone right now is not appealing." Brooke gazed out of the window pensively. She really wanted to be at the ranch and to feel safe. "I don't know. Being here brings back so many fond memories."

"Give it time, dear. It takes time to recover from the loss of a loved one." Mary patted Brooke's hand for encouragement. "Joe mourned for years after your mother died. But I sense the situations are different."

"Yes, very different." She wasn't sure if she had suffered a loss or been set free. Mike's control over her and finally his demise left her shaken. Wyoming seemed a paradise, a quiet, free-spirited paradise. "I really did miss the ruggedness of this open land." Her throat tightened. She whispered, "It seems everything has a place in life but me. I almost feel I am intruding in Dad's life."

"Don't you feel that way. He has missed your presence terribly. Since you agreed to come home, he has been happier than I can remember, except of course, when you beat those Tower boys in the youth rodeos. I think the competition between Joe and Josh was stronger than between you kids." Mary's smile became a chuckle. She poured them both another cup of tea. "There's always work to be done here. Joe will soon find enough for you to do. Maybe he can let you do some of the filing and charts in the office or help with the foals."

They continued to chat over town gossip, until Brooke's yawning became obvious.

"Go on up and get some rest. Take a bath, and I'll fix you one of my herb teas to help you sleep. You have a few hours before dinner, and the men won't be back real soon." Mary gently prodded Brooke toward the stairs.

"Please call me so I can help with the table. Don't forget." She didn't want to be treated like a guest. And she knew Mary would fuss over that night's dinner.

At the landing, Brooke stopped to gaze at the pictures displayed like an historical gallery. These aged photographs and portraits were her relatives, who over the past century had developed these ten-thousand acres into the ranch she called home. Her hand touched the portrait of her grandfather.

"Yes," she whispered, "maybe I do belong here."

At the top of the stairs was the guest room. As she passed by, she noticed a tray on the dresser, a comb and brush neatly placed alongside the bottles of aftershaves and colognes. A gray tweed blazer with matching suede elbow patches was thrown across the brown leather chair by the window. A used white towel hung on the doorknob to the private bath. She detected a familiar scent of aftershave.

A plane ticket on the edge of the dresser caught her eye. She paused, and then with overwhelming curiosity, hurried across the room and furtively opened the envelope. Adam had returned from Oregon. The ticket, however, did not explain the clothes, hanging in the walk-in closet. He worked here, he told her. Did he also live in the house?

Placing the envelope back as she had found it, she headed to her own room, foreboding washing over her.

Her bedroom was next to the guest room. Everything was the same as when she left. Sea foam green carpet and cream-colored walls were an invitation to serenity. The bedspread was a patchwork of cream satin and velvet, handmade by Mary as a sixteenth birthday present. The loveseat sat at an angle to the long, casement windows.

She curled up on the soft pillowed support. Relaxing in the privacy of her old bedroom, she recalled the fond memories of her childhood and the freedom from adult decisions.

On the many roundups over the years Brooke had ridden a paint pony no bigger than the cows she tried to move. The county and state fairs allowed her to display her skill on a horse. A few times she beat Steve and

Adam in competition, but they were such sweet victories. Life seemed less complicated then.

She turned on the water and added the lavender bath oil Mary had left for her. Getting out of her clothes, she viewed herself in the completely mirrored wall. Her five-foot six frame carried her weight well. However, she would have to do some exercising before she spent too much time in the saddle, she reasoned. Winding her flaxen hair into a bun, she slid into the suds and relished the warmth of the water on her weary body.

Later, on her bedside table she found a covered teapot filled with herb tea. She sipped a cup of chamomile. The solid brass bed faced the windows. Fluffing the pillows behind her head, Brooke relaxed and stretched out in comfort. She watched two robins making a nest in the old cottonwood tree outside her windows.

"A new beginning for you and for me," she murmured before sleep overtook her.

A whistle shattered the quiet. Sheer black fright swept through her. Her heart drummed as she blinked several times to shake off the lead weights of sleep. She turned to scan the clock on the bedside table. Adam. He lounged in the doorway, one hand on the door jam. His face held an animated smile, not unlike a child who had pulled a prank.

"You made that noise?" Fear turned to anger—and relief—as she glared at him.

He shrugged a brawny shoulder and grinned with

amusement. "I knocked, but you didn't answer. Mary asked me to wake you. It's almost time for dinner."

She looked away from his brown, taunting eyes, those lips she had kissed. She stood up quickly. Not quite awake, she finger-combed the mane of hair spilling over her face.

"Tell her I'll be right down." His nearness made her head spin with unsettling thoughts.

Instead of leaving, he was next to her in two strides. Her heart skipped. Fearing some form of retaliation for her *welcome-home* kiss, she clutched his wrists. His hands gently adjusted the overlapping edges of her robe. His warm fingers negligently contacted her bare skin.

"Relax." His eyes were hooded. He tied the sash in a bow. "You almost had no secrets."

Brooke moved away from the bed and sat on the love seat. A tense silence invaded the room. She could still feel the warmth of his fingers on her skin. Why didn't she feel as comfortable around him as he did her? How many times did they go swimming in their underwear and think nothing of it?

Her voice was shakier than she would have liked. "I'll be down soon."

He stood by her bed watching her, his hand resting on the rumpled covers. She could easily get caught up in the way he looked at her.

His voice was soft. "Welcome home, Princess." He left her room, closing the door.

CHAPTER FOUR

*B*rooke dressed in jeans and a lavender camp shirt. With gold-tone combs, she secured her hair behind each ear. Eyebrow pencil and eyeliner accented her bright-blue eyes.

She padded down the stairs. On her left was the office. The door was closed, just the murmur of voices came from within. She turned and headed down the hall to the kitchen and observed Mary at the island tearing lettuce. "Aren't the men here?"

"Yes, dear, they're in the office, talking business. Have a nice nap?"

"Yes, I did. Here, let me help." She took the green head from Mary.

Adam's appearance at her door still bothered her. Why would Mary send him up to wake her? Unless he did live in the house.

"You look refreshed." Mary patted her shoulder as

she went on to her cooking. "I'll mash these potatoes while you're making the salad. The table is all set. Adam helped while your father was busy on the phone. So, we're about ready."

Macho Adam doing anything domestic seemed totally out of character.

Joe entered the kitchen and smiled. He came over to Brooke and gave her a loving hug. "There's my girl. How was your nap?"

"Very restful."

"Hello, Brooke." A familiar voice from the doorway caught her attention. Josh Tower and his sons had an extraordinary resemblance to one another. Except for his weathered skin and white hair, he was the image of the younger Tower, coming in behind him.

Wiping her hands on a clean towel, she went over to receive a welcome peck on the cheek. "Hello, Josh. How have you been?"

He held her at arm's length as he gazed at her. "Well, you look wonderful."

"Thank you." Her voice was a polite whisper.

During the meal, the men chatted about business, upcoming horse shows, and the going price for cattle, as well as the rustling plaguing everyone. Brooke tried to avoid Adam. However, her eyes seemed to zero in on him of their own free will, and there he would be, observing her.

"Is Uncle Dan here? I noticed the front guest room is being used?" She directed the question to her father.

Joe put his fork down and blotted his lips. He seemed momentarily confused. "Dan? No, he isn't here. I talked to him the other day though. He'll be out to judge a horse show sometime this summer."

"I believe, Brooke, you're referring to my room, the one at the top of the stairs?" Adam interjected. His dark eyes never left hers for an instant.

"You mean you occasionally use the room when you need to?" she pressed.

"No, Brooke, I live here." His face was sober, sincere.

Joe cleared his throat. "Adam has been living here for nearly three years. Since he manages the physical aspects of the ranch, it's better if he stays here."

The room at the top of the stairs was Adam's. The room right next to hers. No wonder he felt so at home. A blanket of silence covered the table. Everyone attended to their plates as though the meal was vitally important, avoiding her, except Adam, who watched in quiet contemplation.

She tried to appear to be listening while inside she burned with rage. Was Adam after the ranch? She sensed the changes since her arrival. A dire warning whispered in her head. As their eyes met, she felt a shock run through her. Fearful images filled her mind. She fiddled with her napkin before she responded. "Yes, I suppose it would be. Excuse me. I'll help with these dishes."

At the kitchen sink she closed her eyes but distancing

herself didn't stop the flow of discomfort. This was a change she hadn't considered.

Why? Why would her father let him into their lives, into their home? She had visited three times when her husband allowed her to with a grim warning about returning. The last visit was more than five years ago. This was more than she expected.

Joe had always spoken well of Adam, even when they were children, but she shrugged the praises off, thinking he was the closest Joe would come to having a son. Adam probably had some notion of getting her family's ranch. The Tower men had acquired several ranches between the father and two sons, nearly forty thousand acres including oil and gas wells. They were not going to get hers.

Nor would she allow another man to rule her life.

Tomorrow she would get down to business. Her father wasn't a young man anymore, and she did have an accounting degree, waiting for some use. She would learn as much as possible, as fast as possible, and then have the pleasure of moving Adam out of the house and back to Hightower.

Brooke awoke, invigorated with emotions she had not experienced in years. She was a now a free woman, educated, and healthy. Girding herself with resolve, she threw her covers off. If she could get down to the kitchen early, maybe she could talk to her father, get him to see her as a partner in the ranch.

Dressed in faded jeans and a worn tee shirt, she was downstairs having coffee before anyone else stirred. The belt, surrounding her waist, held a large silver buckle. She won it at the Western Stock Show in Denver. She rode Sly and out-roped Steve Tower in their youth heading and heeling classes. Her heart welled up with the memory, recalling how jubilant she was, but remembering also Steve's graciousness in his loss—he insisted on presenting the buckle to her along with a red rose.

How different these two brothers were, she mused. Both had a head of thick wavy hair, but Adam shadowed Steve's slighter build. Adam was always strong minded and hardworking. Steve, an artist in his own right with western paintings in various galleries, also worked their ranch, but he enjoyed the finer, lighter aspects of life.

Brooke recalled with a smile the many times she and Steve found trouble while their families were on roundups, when they would find some frivolous fun rather than stay on task. And Adam was always assigned to round them up and keep them working.

She reached down to caress the buckle. The buckle gave her strength, a determination to reconstruct her life. The last years seemed too unproductive, wasted time, wasted dreams. Now she had a purpose. She felt compelled to do something worthwhile, no more sitting around as a captive ornament to a well-to-do, abusive man. She was home, comfortable. In her heart, she was a rancher's daughter.

Brooke looked out the large window as she sipped her sweet, cream-laced coffee. She took a deep breath and released it slowly, thinking how fortunate she was, she could return to a place like this. However, dealing with Adam wouldn't be easy.

A niggling fear in the pit of her stomach kept reminding her of the formidable strength of the man, always the competitor, always setting goals. Brooke's back stiffened when she heard footsteps coming from the stairs.

"What are you doing up? Didn't you sleep well?" Joe questioned as he came over to place his hands on her shoulders.

She took his hand in hers. Relieved it was not Adam, she brightened. "Oh, like a log, nothing like clean mountain air. I haven't slept this well since the last time I was here."

"You should have stayed in bed, relaxed some. No need for you to be up so early." He sat down at the table and cradled her hand.

"Actually, I got up, so I could talk to you before the others were up and about."

"Well, Mary doesn't get up until later. We fix something quick to eat before we go down to the barns. Sometimes Adam is the only one banging around this early."

Joe gazed at his daughter's big, blue eyes. "What is so important you had to get down here before dawn?"

She poured him a cup of coffee and refilled her own. She came back to the table. Eyeing her father nervously, she assembled in her mind what she wanted to tell him.

"I can put a sweet roll in the microwave if you want."

"No. Thank you anyway. Mary over feeds me as it is." He grinned.

"When did you start to drink decaffeinated coffee?"

"A few years ago. Now darlin', what is it you want to talk about?" Joe's affection and patient curiosity showed in his posture.

"I've had a lot of time to think. After Mike's death, I had nothing but time. Since I left California, I've been contemplating what I might do. Being here has helped."

Brooke leaned over from her seat and took her father's leathery hand in hers. She watched his face for any unwanted responses. "I belong here on the ranch, here with you and Mary, and all the work. I feel like I've put on a well-fitting pair of boots. Am I making any sense?"

"Yes." He patted her hand. "It's the same way I felt when I came home to stay. I'd thought, when I was a young buck, ranch life was not for me. I'd pictured some glamour job with no manure and mud." He chuckled softly. "Yes, my dear, I understand. I'm surprised, though. Really didn't think you had any interest in the ranch, or for that matter, coming back at all."

"I've always been interested in the ranch. The horses were my love. You never seemed to want me to be involved." Her voice grew rapid as she tried to make him understand. "You shut me out from the business. Now you can't. The degree you paid for should be of some help, and even the physical work would almost be fun at this point."

Joe caressed her hand with his leathery thumb. His voice was soft and reminiscent when he spoke. "I did shut you out when you were young, when you were growing up. You were such a little thing. I wasn't sure how your mother would have wanted her daughter raised. Many times, I thought you were too much of a tomboy, always competing with Josh's boys." He pointed to her buckle. "Remember when you won that?" His eyes glazed with unshed tears.

"Yes," she whispered, "Seems like yesterday, doesn't it?"

"It sure does. And you have turned in to such a beautiful woman, just like your mother." He took a large breath and sipped his coffee. "Now, what did you have in mind?"

Brooke spoke with quiet, but determined, firmness. She had to make him understand. "What I want is to become your partner. You know, taking some responsibility, being in on some decisions. Learning all you never taught me before."

"Well, it all takes time. Learning how to run a ranch of this size is a tall order, can't be acquired overnight. Lots of planning. Adam is here because he is one of the best managers around." He hesitated. "You really don't have to learn anything. You can feel secure the rest of your life … However, I realize you're going through a difficult period, and you need something to occupy your time."

He was sidestepping her idea. "Why is Adam here anyway? He has ranches to tend to. After all, the Tower' holdings are not small. It takes a small army to manage it all." She blurted out her feelings.

Adam's voice penetrated their private talk. "I'm here because your father wants me to be here. Someone has to help out on a ranch this size."

Barefooted, he sauntered over to the coffee pot and poured himself a cup. A pair of white socks hung on his shoulder. His chambray shirt was open and loose over his well-worn jeans.

Brooke sighed with irritation, blushing with embarrassment. Damn him.

Adam padded to the table. He sat across from her, blocking her view of the barn and the horses. She could not avoid looking at him without moving from her seat, allowing him another win in this battle of wills. Dark curling hair peeked out from his open shirt. Her eyes seemed to wander there of their own accord.

"Do you always pussyfoot around?" His presence ruined her privacy with her father and cut short the discussion she found essential to her existence. She felt like a kid again. Under his steady scrutiny, she tried to keep her fragile control.

As Adam sipped his coffee, he stared at her. "Actually, I'm up because I have a full day ahead of me." Placing his cup on the blue woven placemat, he stood and padded to the pantry for cereal and milk.

Joe cleared his throat. He picked up his cup. "Adam and our hands, Josh's outfit, and Kit's employees are riding out to the communal valley to bring in a herd of cows and calves to separate and doctor. Josh is moving his to another site. Kit will probably be selling off a good portion of hers."

Joe paused, glancing at Adam. "Brooke wants to become involved in the ranch, more than she has been in the past, kind of like learning from the bottom up." His voice was noncommittal, almost patronizing.

Adam returned with his breakfast and resumed the seat across from her. He glanced her way, but his expressive eyes grew pensive.

"Maybe that's where you could start, dear. We've lost a couple of hands this month and one is leaving for college next week. I'm sure Adam could use an extra rider."

Adam's eyes never left her face. She found it difficult to remain passive under his probing stare. She wasn't surprised Kitty was along. Kitty always arranged a way to be with Adam. Maybe, she reflected, they were still a hot item.

She had nowhere to look without his massive chest being in the way, or his dark penetrating eyes. Staring back at him with feigned bravado, she replied, "Yes, I've decided to stay, learn the ranch. I may as well get started."

Silence blanketed the table. Joe sipped his coffee. Adam dropped his eyes from hers and worked over his cereal flakes as though he was trying to pulverize them.

She was not indifferent to the hotblooded man who dared her. His lusty, good looks, dark from the sun, still wore sleep lines. The open shirt front invited her to explore the wispy curls. Brawny biceps nearly filled the chambray shirt sleeves. She knew why women found him attractive. She pulled her drifting thoughts back together.

"Well?"

A curious look passed between her father and Adam before she was given an answer. "I am shorthanded. I suppose I can find something you can do as long as you follow directions. Otherwise, it's back home with you."

Joe patted her hand. "Don't get overtired though."

Adam growled with sudden impatience. "If she is going to be part of the group, she will have to stay with it." He pointed his spoon at her. "No favors, my dear, among the crew. You will have to keep up, understand?" His bare feet collided with hers as he stretched his long legs, assessing her over his cup of coffee.

"Don't worry, Adam, I'm not a quitter." She rose from the table, angry and frustrated. He was ruining everything—and her enthusiasm. She wanted to get away from his presence, particularly his naked feet, rocking like a cat's tail under her chair.

Banging around in the mudroom, she found a pair of her old boots in a storage chest. She left them while she filled a canteen with ice and lemonade. With stiff dignity, she walked over to the table and planted a kiss on Joe's balding head. "I'll see you later."

"Don't overdo it, hear me? Adam will find a mount for you. I think your saddle is still in the tack room."

"You can ride Buddy." Adam rose from his seat and placed his dishes in the sink.

"Buddy?" He was giving her a childproof horse to ride, a babysitter.

"Yes. He's twelve, but I won't have to worry about you on him. He was your horse, right?" Adam's stare challenged her to refute his authority.

"Yes, he was mine." She knew what his motives were. Buddy was a trusty gelding she rode for ranch work. He could work cows, trail ride, and pony babies. He was loyal and easygoing. However, he was not as fast as the roping horses and wouldn't be as much fun to ride.

"Then I see no problem."

"Well, then, I'll use Sly."

"No. Your father sold Sly to me. She's older and now she is only used to pony babies."

Joe remained silent, so she had to believe what Adam said was true. She wouldn't want to harm the mare. But it was the heartbreak of knowing she had been sold. Her mind spun with negative thoughts. Secrets permeated the house. What else had he sold to Adam?

CHAPTER FIVE

*B*rooke hurried to the main barn ahead of Adam, ignoring the steady crunch of his boots behind her. The personal tack room was just inside the overhead barn door on the right. Large and roomy, it held all their saddles and halters, and included a leather couch and a small table. A refrigerator stored pharmaceutical items and ice packs. She looked around for her own saddle.

Adam stopped to talk to Hank for a moment. She heard him tell Hank of the 'new help' he was bringing along and instructed him to bring Buddy to the outside arena where they would gather.

Her saddle had been wrapped in clear plastic and stored up high. Noticing her plight, Adam took it down for her, and with a considerate gesture, he carried it out to the corral. Brooke toted a grooming bucket, a padded saddle blanket, and a hackamore that he had handed to her. His free hand lightly rested on the small of her back as he escorted her though the maze of white fences to the waiting cowboys.

As she brushed the gelding, she let her hands slide down the satin coat. The smell of horse warmed her heart. She thought how beautiful the day would be. Although it was chilly from the cool breeze sliding off the mountains, she knew the day would soon be warm enough to remove her windbreaker. Mornings like this she remembered with fondness—riding out with her father to check cattle, fix fence, or to give a young colt a pleasant ride way from the arenas. She was tightening the cinch when a voice from the past burst her bubble of pleasant memories.

"Hello, Brooke." The silky voice of Kitty Jones was nearly next to her. "I didn't realize you were home." Kitty was beautiful with a creamy, flawless complexion, and a tall willowy body. She attracted men like flies to manure, Joe often remarked about her.

"Yesterday." She continued to brush and stroke the horse.

"I'm amazed you would be ready to tackle a day such as this," she crooned. "I, for one, am going in to have my hair and nails done while Adam and the boys take care of the cattle. It's much too dusty and dirty for me."

She stared at Brooke as she spoke, her red hair piled atop her head loosely, her face painted to perfection so early in the morning. Her clothes were an expensive blend of designer western wear. A form fitting red silk shirt and a pair of too tight jeans, bunched up on the toe of her snakeskin boots, showed off her voluptuous curves. "I see you're dressed for the day."

Brooke tried to be social with this local tart, but it was difficult. "I'm surprised to see you still in the valley. I would have thought you would have moved into the city long ago."

Kitty always had the best of everything, including men. Older than Brooke, she dated Adam frequently. Many believed she would eventually be Mrs. Tower.

"Well, you know daddy left me everything," she crooned. "And Adam has been so helpful, I decided to stay and try to keep the ranch. I really do like the house and all. It's great for parties—large and small."

"Adam seems to have everyone gathered. I'd better get going. Nice to see you again." Brooke turned back to saddling Buddy. Irritation poured through her. Why did she always feel like yesterday's breakfast toast when she was around Kitty?

"Maybe lunch sometime." Kitty strolled over to speak to one of the men on horseback. In her normal flirtatious manner, she placed a hand on his knee as she spoke with him. The man wore a full dark beard and reflective sunglasses. His cowboy hat looked new, along with his shiny boots. Was this her newest intimate?

Adam lingered toward the back, waiting for her to catch up. "What were you and Kit talking about? You two used to hate each other."

"She was telling me what a great help you are. I guess she was talking about cattle?"

He huffed and continued down the road. Deciding she would try not to argue with him, she urged the gelding to the front to ride with Hank.

They moved within sight of the long valley. Brooke noticed how lush everything looked. The aroma of spring wafted up to her as the horses plodded though the new growth. The winter snows provided a run-off of much needed water, so she was sure the calves this year would be quality animals.

When they reached the top of the hill, she was seized with a sudden bout of nostalgia. Before her were hundreds of cows and calves, feeding on the grass in the valley below, a postcard scene with the snowy peaks in the distance.

Hank stopped alongside her while the rest of the men caught up. His palomino glistened like polished gold in the sunlight. "I was surprised to hear you would be coming today." He gave her an uncomfortable smile and looked away.

"I've always liked spring roundups. Of course, his majesty wasn't too thrilled with the idea." She gazed down the hill toward Adam.

Hank turned back at her. "It's nice to see Buddy out working."

"Well, it was Adam's suggestion to ride him, or should I say order." She let out a sigh of unconcealed anger as she shifted her weight forward once more.

"Adam is the boss," Hank replied.

Looking back, she saw the boss, loping up the hill toward them, paying acute attention to guiding the young horse he was riding. She forgot what an imposing figure Adam presented. He sat deep in the saddle, his rangy body moving naturally with the motion of the horse.

Hank raised an inquisitive eyebrow at her remark. She decided to change the subject. "Rustlers were mentioned during our dinner last night. Have many ranches been hit?"

"A few. Over thirty head are missing."

"Is anyone doing anything about it? A loss of a herd is a lot of money."

Hank gazed at the cows below them. "Well, Josh is furious. He's lost quite a few. They seem to hit open ranges, and they are very quick, very professional, using four wheelers and motorbikes. One of Josh's men was wounded by gunfire when he came across them while checking fence. He's all right now. Kitty has lost the most." Hank shifted in his saddle.

"Well, how do they know exactly where the cattle are?" she persisted.

"Don't know." Hank shrugged his shoulders and fiddled with his reins. "For years only the Montgomery and Tower cattle grazed together here. Somehow Kitty's cows got mixed in."

While she digested the information, she revisited the land around them. The mountain was a remnant of glacial days, leaving a long, narrow valley, bordered on both sides by steep, jagged ridges. Bald Mountain was one of those ridges. The valley below was divided by a smooth, running stream, providing clear, snow run-off for the many cows and calves.

Adam gently reined in Contender, her father's young, roping stallion and dismounted. While he adjusted his saddle, he gave Hank instructions. "Divide the men up and work the cattle down from the north ridge. Brooke and I will keep them together at first. You and the men know the routine. When we have them gathered, we'll break for lunch. We should have a count of about two hundred cows and calves."

"Will do." Hank turned his gelding toward the group and waved for them to follow.

Saddle leather creaked comfortably beneath her as she turned the horse around. "I would have preferred to work the ridge with the men. It's not like I haven't done this before," she said with more emotion than she wanted.

Adam finished adjusting the saddle and looked up at her from over the horse. "I don't want you on the ridge." His eyes dared her to question his orders.

"I know you don't want me here, but you don't have to treat me like an apprentice in front of all the men."

"Your father wanted you to learn from the bottom up." he quipped in a cool tone. He looked at the silver buckle she wore. "Yes, you could ride, and you used to rope as well as me. Sometimes you were better. But this is not a kids rodeo."

He settled his worn Stetson on his head. He mounted the stallion and side passed close to her gelding.

"I don't want any favors," she said, determined to have her own way. "My father never singled me out for special assignments."

He seized her elbow and caused her to turn in his direction. She grabbed the saddle horn to remain balanced. "You are out here because I said you could be here. As for singling you out, I'm more concerned about bringing you back, slung over Buddy, and then explaining to Joe what a fool his daughter was."

Piqued by his big brother attitude, she wanted to retaliate. She turned Buddy and sidled up to Contender, head to tail, and ran her hand down his bicep provocatively.

"Well, the men might believe you decided to ride with me for other reasons, if you know what I mean?" A taunting spark lit her eyes.

His stiffened jaw and thinned lips told her she had hit a mark. He grinned. "You think too highly of yourself, Princess. They probably think I'm babysitting." He chuckled and moved his horse down the hill toward his men.

For the rest of the morning, he voided her except to give her instructions or to indicate where he wanted her positioned. Most of the men worked with her as an equal, joking and laughing with her as they rode.

· · ·

Adam monitored Brooke as he rode nearby. Some cows were wild, having sustained noticeable scars from mountain lions or bears. He and his father chose a short-horned Hereford cross to pasture in the valley, hoping they would be able to provide some protection from bears and cougars. Among the herd were about thirty of Kit's. How hers became mixed here on this pasture one could only suspect.

He paused a moment to wipe his brow and to take a survey of the valley. He pulled his binoculars from his saddlebag. When he spotted Brooke, he maintained his surveillance of her for a short time. She was obviously having a good time, laughing and high-fiving Hank. She worked as hard as the men. She seemed to know how to handle any situation without anyone coming to her aid.

Watching her, he felt a warm glow build. He had never found a woman who gave him so much pleasure. When he woke her from her nap, he wanted to go over and hold her, run his fingers through that thick hair, and take the wary fear from her eyes. His feelings for her had nothing to do with reason. He had always loved her. Soon she would hate him. Damn secrets. Joe was going to have to tell her the truth soon. He sighed and squeezed his horse into a trot.

The sun passed its noon apex. The animals were gathered into one group. The crew stopped only for short breaks to stretch their legs and wash the dust from their mouths. About halfway to the ranch at the canyon's entrance, Adam signaled a lunch break. As the cows settled and were grazing contently once again, the men relaxed. A few rode to keep the herd together.

Brooke must have forgotten that the lunches for the ranch hands were prepared by Mary the night before and placed in the refrigerator in the main barn. Each man took his bag to pack in his saddlebag. She didn't complain. He surreptitiously watched as she took her canteen of lemonade and relaxed against a fat cottonwood. After removing her boots, she slowly extended her stiff legs. Tiny curls escaped around her face, pink from sunburn. With her head back against the tree she slept …

"Wake up sleepy head. You've been asleep for half an hour, and as much as I'd like to let you continue with your nap, we must get the cattle home before dark. You forgot one thing." He was down on one knee nearly eye-to-eye with her. "Since Mary packs two of everything for me, I saved back a sandwich and an apple, but I'm not giving up the brownies."

"Thank you, Adam," she said between yawns.

"If you want to take a hike into the trees, I'll watch over your lunch. Most of the men have left," he hinted. "I'll wait for you."

Brooke returned a few moments later. He was still waiting by the tree as he promised. "Thanks, Adam. I think I'll put the sandwich and apple in my saddlebags and eat while I ride. I don't want to hold up the drive."

Feeling like tight rubber bands, she was sure her thighs would snap if she were to ride much longer. But she asked, pleaded, for this day, and Adam was watching. Determined not to let him see her pain, she walked as naturally as she could, her muscles screaming in protest.

Buddy and Contender were the only mounts left. She placed the sandwich and apple in the saddlebag. She set the reins and tried to mount the older horse.

The gelding danced sideways and seemed edgy. She thought his behavior odd, but since she hadn't been acquainted with the animal for quite some time, she felt he was as tired as she and refused to go on. With determination, and Adam watching, she forced her aching body into the saddle.

Buddy refused to move.

Feeling foolish, she tapped her heels into his soft sides. Without warning, he began to buck, and then he would bolt and buck again. Brooke held onto the saddle horn as well as she could, but the pounding of the saddle and the force of the jolts weakened her stamina.

She felt something pop, and the saddle slid to her left. Like an airborne blur of rust-colored saddle and blue denim, she landed on the edge of an old stream gully, and then tumbled down the slight embankment and into the mud and water below.

A cowboy came trotting up to her. Before he could dismount to help her, Adam brought Contender to a splashing stop right before her in the stream. Frustrated with this first beginning, she pounded her fists into the water.

"Are you all right? Buddy's never done anything like that before." Helping her up on the rocky embankment, he ordered, "Sit up here in a dry spot for a moment. Just sit."

Adam checked her hands and arms for anything broken. His gentleness was vaguely comforting. He examined each limb and even bared her back to check for bruising.

"You didn't want me to come today," she accused, trying to readjust her tangled clothing and to keep the well of tears from overflowing.

He cupped her face with his hand. "I would never intentionally hurt you, Brooke. You should know that."

His sincerity broke her bravado. Covering her face with her hands, she tried for control and to blot out the sensitivity, showing in his eyes.

He eased her fingers away from her face and applied a cold wet handkerchief to her smudged cheeks. "There. Now if you're sure nothing's broken maybe you could hold Contender while I see what set Buddy off." He helped her to her feet. After walking Contender out of the stream, he handed her the reins.

Hank caught up with Buddy and led him back to Adam. They spoke for a moment, pointing and prodding the animals right side. Then he led the horse over to Brooke.

"He has quite a gash on his side. He's also limping."

As Adam examined the saddle, she saw a cloud of rage cross his face. Not only was the horse injured, but a handful of cockleburs were scattered in the fleece of the saddle pad and in the cinch. This was no accident. Someone on the trail drive wanted her hurt.

"Looks like the cords on this cinch broke, maybe it was old," he murmured to her. "However, you may not be broken, but your saddle will never see the back of a horse again. I'm afraid I'll have to buy you a new one." He smiled, but his smile never reached his eyes. "But that's not the worst of it." He walked over to where she was standing, carrying something behind his back. "Your sandwich also took a beating." He handed her the white blob, still wrapped in plastic, feigning intense worry. "The apple is more sauce than apple." He smiled like he used to when she was young.

"Oh, dear, I was so looking forward to eating it." Brooke wiped away the residual tears. "I'll have to come out with a four-wheeler and pick up the saddle."

"I'll send someone out to pick it up."

Her heart turned over at his kindness. He could have been as surly as he was earlier. Instead, he was trying to make this fiasco go a bit lighter. She walked over to the gelding to examine the wound. She realized the injury was not a cut but a three-inch gash along the horse's side where the cinch would press. Maybe the cords of the cinch were severed.

She looked up and found Adam still and somber. When their eyes connected, they both knew this was not an accident. Had he contrived to get her back to the house? Did he have someone else maim this wonderful animal? Confusion enveloped her as she tried to gather her feelings and determine which Adam to believe, the one who rants and raves or the kind one. In her heart she knew he would not hurt an animal for spite.

She spoke in a whisper. "Is the path through the woods still open?"

"Yes, it's a bit grown over, but it's passable. Do you want me to go with you? I'd double up, but this young stallion isn't ready for that."

"No, you better get back to work. Some of those rangy calves are being a problem. Besides, the barn is only about a mile through the trees." She turned from him, not wanting to talk anymore. As she began to walk away, Adam stopped her.

"Look, I'm sorry this happened. I know how much you wanted to have a good time, and you did a great job this morning—really!" He took her face in his hands and kissed her forehead lightly. He wiped away the residual tears with his thumbs. Sliding his hands to her elbows, he said, "Take my handgun in case you need it."

The gentle hold on her arm belied the greater strength of the man. The smell of horse sweat, mingled with his masculine aftershave, tormented her senses.

"If you run into any trouble, at least you can give off a shot. Are you sure you don't want someone to go with you?"

"No, I'll be fine. You know I can use it." She tried

not to let her own insecurities show. "Besides, from the rodeo out there, they need you more than I do." She saw cattle wandering away from the herd.

Adam unbuckled the holster and handed it to her. She re-buckled the strap and looped it over her shoulder. Without another look back, she walked toward the looming pines, trailing the injured horse behind her.

The walk home was pleasant. The land was very fruitful this year. Shrubs and wildflowers showed new growth everywhere. The area was dense with aspen groves, pine, and various ground covers.

As a child she would play in these treed hills and valleys. Often as not, Adam or Steve would be with her. They were so close then, kindred in mind. Now she was not sure who to trust. Was the real Adam the blustery man she knew so well, or the sensitive one she glimpsed today?

Even her father gave her reason to feel uneasy. The curious looks at breakfast more confused than angered her. She felt like an outsider, and maybe she was. It was twelve years since she left for Los Angeles to attend college and come home on breaks. But it had been eight years since she married Mike Boyle with only a few allowed quick trips to the ranch. She had been left out of the loop of daily routines. Had she been left out of their plans, too?

A rustle of a choke cherry bush directly behind her broke the spell. She was reminded of Adam's curious warning and remembered Hank's talk of rustlers. But the only intruder was a small raccoon who came to feed on the berry bushes. Buddy seemed unperturbed.

However, the frantic beating of her heart let her know she was not as brave as she thought she should be. She knew someone wanted her out of the way—probably Kitty. Maybe her cowboy peppered her pad with cockleburs. With outward calm, she took the lead rope and continued homeward. The sooner she got the old horse in the barn and tended to, the better she would feel. As she neared the barns, she put her less than confident thoughts behind her to seek out Abe, the in-house veterinarian, horseshoer, and general sage of the ranch.

Brooke always loved the old man, coming toward her. Abe's curly hair was now pure white. His dark skin shined with a healthy glow, but he seemed to walk with more stiffness than she remembered. His face melted into a loving smile. Abe helped raise her after her mother died. Her first saddle was a gift from him, and so, too, was her first real riding lesson. He taught her how to rope steers when her father refused, thinking she should do girly things. With his coaching she beat the boys, and the memory welled in her vividly.

Brooke walked up to Abe, beaming with love for this old man. She threw her arms around his neck and kissed his cheek. He squeezed her, lifting her off the ground.

"You're a sight for these old eyes. Whatcha doin' walking, and where's the saddle?" he questioned as he held her at arm's length.

"Buddy has a terrible cut on his side, and the saddle is ruined, and I'm sore."

"Are you banged up bad?"

"No." She sniffed on his shoulder. She could be free with Abe. "Buddy needs some attention."

Abe had come from Mississippi decades ago. No family. He never married. He took care of all the wounds and illnesses not requiring a licensed vet. Brooke sat in an armed, captain's chair outside the tack room while he ministered to the horse. He clucked and fussed as he worked, first administering a mild tranquilizer, and then stitching up the wound. He wrapped Buddy's front leg to give the tendon support.

"Are you still living on the ten acres my grandfather gave you, or have you decided to come in and live with the rest of us?"

"Yep, just down the road, in my little cabin in the woods. Got my animals to take care of. Course I really only have a few hens for eggs and a couple of steers I plan to sell soon." He put the horse in the first stall and opened the door to the outside run. "I'll leave Buddy here for a spell until I know he's healin' fine. Then I'll return him to the pasture in a few weeks."

"Are you still cleaning stalls or has Dad finally retired you?" Brooke stretched her aching legs out before her as she sat on the ground.

"I jest clean the stalls in this main barn where the mares foal or we have a sick one like Buddy here. Adam keeps Contender in the stallion wing of the new arena, and all the other show horses are in other wing. Adam has a few young men helping, sometimes tacking horses, lunging young ones, or jest cleanin' up. They bunk in the double-wide next to Hank's."

Brooke smiled at this gentle old man. "Are you ever going to retire?"

"Thought about it, but I kind of like it here. Don't know nothin' else. Besides your dad said I was part of the family and had a place here as long as I want. And Adam's been good to work with, real kind man." Then he paused and said, "Besides, I've been waiting for a grandchild to teach to ride and rope." He gave her a wide smile.

Dismissing his hint, Brooke went over to the stall and gazed at Buddy. "Do you think he will be okay?"

At her worried tone Abe stopped straightening out his medical kit and came to stand near her. "Yes, Sugar, he'll be good as new in a few weeks. We'll have to wait." He patted her shoulder.

The smell of wood chips in the fresh stall was pleasant, but the disturbing smell of blood and disinfectant lingered. She walked over to the open barn door for some fresh air and gazed up at the house. At the large window of the breakfast room, Mary stood, looking down on them.

CHAPTER SIX

*M*ary's worried expression met her at the door, probing for an answer. "Looks like your day ended early."

"I took a spill and Buddy has a bad cut and a limp, so we came home through the woods." Her heart ached for the animal. Someone injured him to get at her. Not acceptable.

Did Kitty tell her overdressed cowboy to get her away from Adam?

"You are mud from head to toe."

"I fell into the stream. I think I'll go up and sit in a hot bath." She didn't want to go into any explanations about the saddle and her suspicions. Mary would fuss over the incident if she related what happened in detail. Besides, she was still too frightened to explain it once more. Who would have hurt an animal to get to her? Was it meant to get her out of the way?

"I bet more than your bones are sore. You'll probably have some bad bruising, too." Mary took a sip from her coffee cup. She turned back to Brooke. "Would you like a sandwich or something? A snack, maybe? Cup of tea?"

"No, thank you. I ate a sandwich on the way here, so I should be fine until dinner." She grinned, thinking of the white blob she ate. She pulled off her dusty boots. "I think I need to get cleaned up."

"One good thing happened today." Mary smiled, but her eyes still exhibited worry. "Your boxes arrived. Abe put them in your room."

"Great. I only packed a small amount for the trip. I'll see you in a bit."

Brooke went over to the refrigerator, took out a bottle of orange juice, and headed down the hall toward the stairs. She thought about the boxes in her room. Four, filled with clothes and shoes, those she had personally purchased. The gaudy styles Mike chose for her, she left at a secondhand store. The only other clothes she owned were those still upstairs in her dresser and closet from eight years ago.

Soaking in a warm, perfumed bath to ease the pain in her legs, she pondered Buddy's injury. She reflected time and again the places she rode and the ranch hands. Had she said anything to make one of them want her injured? Her thoughts, again, moved to Adam who preferred not to have her along. He was very clear about that. But deep down she knew Adam would never cause an animal misery to spite her. He would simply tell her to go home.

Wouldn't he? Paranoia reined as she worried with building concern the act was intended to harm her, to get her out of the way. Was there something she wasn't supposed to see?

With little satisfaction, she viciously threw the bath sponge, but felt no real comfort as it hit the tiled wall with a splashing thud.

As she dried off, she realized Buddy was not the only one to sustain an injury. Her left hip and thigh were a dark shade of blue and were swollen where she landed on the rocky ridge of the ditch.

Dismayed, she went to search the boxes for something to wear. She found a pale blue dress of crinkle cotton, free of wrinkles. The fitted bodice was low cut but not too revealing. The skirt ended at her ankles.

She completed the look with the gold locket, once belonging to her mother. It rested daintily on her chest. She seldom took it off except to bathe. She wore the beautiful heart as her mother always wore it. One of the few personal things her controlling husband allowed.

Tired, she reclined on the loveseat and gazed out the window. Was she ready to come back to all of this? Or, by coming here, was she hiding from her fears? Fears of finding a new job and being successful—or not. Fears of meeting new men who would be as depraved and contemptible as Mike. Could she trust again? Most of all, after all that happened to her, was she strong enough to tackle Adam for control—or whatever capacity he held?

She locked her door and dozed off only to be

awakened later when she heard the shower in Adam's bathroom. He was so close. She didn't think Adam was so low he would take advantage of her father, using his charm to embed himself into their lives. But he was older now and probably more cunning than the man she had known since childhood.

Besides, she was finding herself drawn to him, sexually, something she found disturbing, almost immoral. They knew too much about each other, too much history behind them: 4H events, rodeos, picnics and family get-togethers, and of course the constant ranch work.

Brooke knew she was a brat back then, trying new personalities, trying on adult behaviors. She recalled one time when Adam came to check on a pregnant mare for her father, who was attending a cattleman's association dinner. He found her making out in the hay loft with Sam, the son of the Farm Store owner. Soon after Sam skedaddled, her father arrived. She remembered grabbing Adam's shirt front with both hands and begging him not to tell. He shook her once and told her she needed to be spanked. He was so intense, she thought he would paddle her right there and then. He did give her a hard swat. She assumed he never told her father. Would Adam even remember?

During her entire life, he never caused her harm or discomfort. Not like the slaps, kicks, and outright madness she experienced in her marriage to Mike Boyle. She often thought he would kill her in a fit of temper.

Her heart quivered with the brutal memories. Just thinking of him disturbed her serenity.

She slipped on a pair of navy flats, checked herself in the mirror, and grabbed a light sweater in case the evening got too cool. Maybe, she mused, she could take her father and Mary into Laramie. They could eat at The Frenchman's Place and laugh like they used to years ago. She felt a great need to spend private time with her father. He seemed to be avoiding her.

However, dinner out was doomed when she saw Mary preparing a feast. A chocolate layer cake sat on a crystal plate at the edge of the counter.

"Can I do something to help? It seems we seldom have time to chat except here in the kitchen. I hoped the three of us could go out for dinner—my treat."

"Well, Adam is having a guest tonight." Mary smiled at the look on Brooke's face.

"And who is Mr. Wonderful having over for dinner?" She took a piece of celery and stabbed it into the onion-flavored dip.

"Kitty was supposed to come last week, but Adam had some fence problems and loose animals, not to mention missing ones. He had to postpone until tonight." Mary went to the stove.

"He's bringing that little tart here—for dinner?" Little wasn't the right word, she thought as she sliced a loaf of Italian bread—large slut would be better. Some parts of Kitty were not little at all, and all in the right places.

"You know, with the death of her parents, Kitty inherited the sprawling ranch next to this one and enough money to live comfortably her entire life if she were careful. Although she looks like a flighty redhead, she runs the ranch with the same iron will as her parents. But, unlike her frugal mother and father, Kitty lives life to the fullest—so I've heard."

Not only would Adam spoil her plans for the evening, but he was bringing the infamous Kitty as a guest. She had a way of making other women feel dowdy.

She continued to slice the loaf, sometimes viciously, until she felt his eyes on her.

"Are you making breadcrumbs for the chickens?" He taunted with a grin.

Brooke wasn't sure what cologne he wore, but she would have welcomed an invitation to put her head on his chest and .... ah, hell. Freshly showered, his skin glowed with good health. His eyes sparkled with animation.

Adam wore a white and navy pinstriped shirt and a pair of well-fitting jeans, encircled with an expensive braided leather belt and silver buckle. On his feet were soft, tan leather ropers.

Conflicting emotions made her hands flutter as she resumed her task, placing the slices in the napkin-lined basket. He moved over to the counter and helped her finish.

"You look really pretty. Are you feeling better? Any major bruises?"

"Thank you and I'm fine. Just sore."

She looked away from his inquiring stare and took the basket into the dining room. When she returned, he was opening a bottle of wine.

"Mary and I are going to have a glass. Would you like to join us?"

"No, thank you. Not right now."

He glanced up at her periodically. An easy smile crossed his features. "By the way, how's Buddy?"

She sighed, knowing he probably talked to Abe before he came in the house. But she decided to humor him in his small talk.

"Abe says he'll be fine in a few weeks."

His grin was infectious, and she couldn't fight the unwanted surge of turmoil his presence seemed to elicit. She gave up a smile, lightening her mood.

"I'm sure he will be fine. You certainly had a lot of daylight between you and the saddle, though."

She found an unusual gentleness in his eyes. "I feel terrible about him."

The doorbell rang, interrupting their comfortable exchange. He frowned. "Must be Kitty. I'll get it."

For Adam the meal was unsettling. His need to banter with Brooke was of a long standing but friendly feud. He hoped to find something needling to say to her, to goad her into an emotion. But for reasons beyond his understanding, the words never found an appropriate time.

She looked extremely feminine, a delicate angel. The long mane of hair flowed across her shoulders like golden gossamers of silk as the soft illumination of the chandelier spread over them.

Her eyes sparkled with energy whenever she spoke with Joe or Mary. However, the light disappeared whenever she glanced his way. The discord between the two women dated back to childhood. Kitty's parents spoiled her. Basically she was a brat. Brooke was her nearest neighbor and her favorite target for devilish behaviors and spreading nasty rumors.

However, he blamed himself for the stifled atmosphere in the house. He should have taken Kitty to dinner in town or cancelled for a better time. Nevertheless, Brooke had exceptional table manners and gave stiff but polite answers to Kitty about life in Los Angeles.

"Must have been great living in a big house and all?" Kitty sipped her wine and stared at Brooke over the glass.

"What do you mean?"

Kitty kept up her inquiry. "Well, I looked you up, your address, your husband. You were in the papers a lot. Beautiful clothes, beautiful cars, beautiful people to hang out with. Too bad, it's all gone."

"Don't believe everything you read in the tabloids, Kitty."

Finishing her glass of wine, Kitty turned her attention to Brooke once more. "I heard you took a fall today. Nothing was broken, I take it?"

"My saddle."

"I leave the physical work up to the men. A woman could even break a nail," Kitty responded with a wry smile. She extended her manicured nails and raised an eyebrow.

Adam knew Kitty had some meanness in her. Could it have been one of Kitty's men who severed the cinch and cut Buddy? He felt an odd twitch of disappointment when Brooke stood and gathered up her dishes.

"I think I'll help Mary get this all cleaned up. Adam, why don't you go ahead and do whatever you planned?"

Thinking of the evening ahead, he replied, "Abe won't be around tonight. Maybe you could check on your injured horse before you turn in. I may not be back until very late."

"Or," Kitty chimed in, "Maybe not at all."

CHAPTER SEVEN

*W*ith the kitchen cleaned up, Mary and Brooke joined Joe in the den. Her father's choice to watch television in the early evenings instead of being down by the arenas, or checking and fussing over his horses, hinted that something had changed.

Soon Mary began to yawn. "I think I'll leave you two to your mystery. I'm really having trouble keeping my eyes open. Some cake is left if you would like a snack later."

"Thanks, Mary. Sleep well," Joe offered easily.

The early nine o'clock news came on, but Brooke could not concentrate on worldly events. Her mind was in turmoil, filled with questions, aching for answers. Was it too soon to butt into his affairs? He never let her in on the daily running of the ranch before she left for college, why would he now? And why didn't Adam tell him the truth about her fall off Buddy?

She moved over close to her father, holding his worn hand. The many scars reminded her that her father had always been a very active man, unlike the way he was now.

"Is this house always so busy? I've been home two days and we've had company twice." She smiled to soften her question.

Joe chuckled but kept watching the television. "No. As a matter of fact it is usually tomb-like around here." He looked at her. "You look very lovely tonight. I'm glad you still wear your mother's locket. It was her favorite. I gave it to her when we were dating."

"Thank you. Mother's locket gives me comfort." Brooke placed a light kiss on his cheek. "You seemed quiet at dinner. Is something wrong?"

A smirk crossed his face. "The company didn't lend itself to any deep discussions." Looking at her, they both began to chuckle.

"Does Adam see Kitty often?"

"No. I think she is a diversion—if you know what I mean." He spoke as though he really didn't care for Kitty.

"Don't you go down to say good night to the horses like you used to?"

He patted her hand. "I haven't lately. Getting old and slow, I guess. Don't worry yourself. Adam is a big help. His work here gives me time to take care of office details and the oil well business. Only occasionally do I have to work outside or when I really want to. I do frequent the horse shows when they are close." He sounded accepting of the situation. "I think I'll follow Mary's lead." He kissed the top of her head, seeming anxious to leave.

Brooke watched her father amble from the room. His behavior distressed her, particularly whenever they discussed the ranch or him. Adam appeared to have a free hand in everything. Even her.

Joe was never forthright with her. He made his own decisions and never asked for her input. He had always been that way when it came to their relationship. Adam managed the ranch. She'd already been told that bit of information. Two days home after eight years away wasn't much time to start demanding answers about how he controlled the ranch and the horses.

Or was it too late already?

The local news was over. She turned off the television. As she wandered through the house, her fingers occasionally touched something of sentimental value. So many fond memories came to her. Little things, such as nicks in the woodwork she had accidentally made, endeared the home to her heart even more. This old well-built home was so much more than the modern, minimalist style she lived in during her marriage. This house had its own life, a living entity.

She padded through the foyer to the office doorway. A solid wooden desk sat on the far side facing the door. She relaxed on the brown leather sofa against the solid wall, facing the front windows and across from the brick fireplace. The room oozed masculinity with the smell of wood and leather as they mingled to create a comfortable workplace. The dark cherry paneling and the thick, red Persian rug added to the restful quality of the large room. When a fire crackled in the hearth the office became a quiet haven.

Brooke found some needed solace. She located a collection of photo albums on the bookshelves. Taking them down, she sat at the desk with only the brass lamp for light and looked through them with pleasure.

Pictures of her mother warmed her heart. She was so beautiful. Her 4H days were captured there as well. She found the pictures of herself and Steve as he awarded her the silver buckle. She smiled with the memories. Her anxiety grew with the increasing amount of Adam pictured with her father or a winning horse. Photographs of him in the recent books were more in volume than of her in the older books. He was photographed with an assortment of trophies, some with Joe and some without.

Had Joe included Adam because of the horses, or had they developed a much stronger bond? Little nerve ending of fear began to tingle. Was it fear or jealousy? Had he in the eight years she had been gone usurped her place in this home, in her father's heart?

Disturbed, she replaced the albums and turned off the light on the desk. As she mounted the stairs, she remembered that Adam asked her to check on Buddy.

Choosing not to change for such a quick chore, she vowed to herself she would be careful.

The night was beautiful, enchanting. The full moon bathed everything in beacons of silver. She could see the mares and foals as well as Buddy in his run. Because she loved the moonlit evenings at the ranch, she chose not to put on the outside lights and spoil the mood. Instead, she took a large flashlight from the mudroom.

As she walked across the yard, she noticed the foals as they hurried over to their mothers for protection from the unknown invader of their world. Wobbly legs carried them with incredible quickness to the safety of their dams. Kitty's car was still parked along the drive. Had they taken Adam's truck to town, to drink, to dance or whatever?

The sorrel gelding nickered to her in a call for attention. Brooke entered the stall, the first on the left inside the barn. Caressing his neck, she assured him he could relax. Turning on the flashlight, she checked his side for more bleeding, but she found no fresh blood or swelling where Abe sutured the wound. Buddy nudged her with his head to gain attention.

"Let me get a brush. Besides, you now have my dress covered in dust. Lucky for you it's washable," she crooned to the patient animal.

Bright moon beams coming through the door window made the tack room across the aisle visible. Trying not to disturb the pregnant mares, she proceeded across the way without turning on the lights. As her hand reached for the doorknob, she heard movement inside. For a brief time, she stood still and listened, fearfully remembering the discussion about rustlers and thefts. When she heard nothing more, she assumed the ruckus was merely a barn cat after a mouse. But she waited a moment longer, still feeling a bit spooked.

Finally, she opened the door and flicked on the light.

A gasp. No one moved.

Kitty screeched like an angry old barn cat. "Brooke, you bitch! Get out. Get out."

Adam reclined on the old leather couch with his shirt unbuttoned. Kitty, however, had little covering her buxom frame. Her shapely legs, exposed by her raised, denim skirt, straddled Adam's torso. Her blouse was undone, as well as the front clasp of her bra.

Brooke's face blushed profusely. "Sorry."

Adam chuckled, his chest moving up and down with each laughing breath. "I told you this was a bad idea."

"Oh, I don't believe this," Kitty ranted as her yes glared. She looked like a red-headed Medusa as her red fiery locks flared around them. Brooke was sure if she were capable, Kitty would have turned her to stone.

It all happened in seconds. Bouncing as Adam's chuckled, Kitty lost her balance, falling forward. Her arm stretched out to the wall and her hand tangled in a halter. With the groan of escaping nails, the rack in its entirety crashed down, spilling the load of halters, bits, and lead ropes. A cloud of decades-old dust billowed over them.

Brooke grabbed a soft brush on a nearby shelf and

backing out of the room she mouthed, "Sorry." At least, she thought, Adam was grinning, and the more incensed Kitty got, the louder he laughed.

Occasionally, as she gently brushed the horse, she felt a slight twinge of guilt for interrupting their private party. Then she heard them leaving. Standing behind Buddy, she concealed her presence. A heated discussion was in full progress as they walked to Kitty's car. Adam was still laughing. A good sign, she thought. Her name came up repeatedly. Would he accuse her of intentionally being rude and tactless?

After she finished brushing Buddy, she fastened the stall door and made her way across the wide aisle to the demolished tack room to return the brush. She opened the door, but before she could put on the light, hands of steel grabbed her throat and shook.

Grabbing the pinkies of both hands, she pulled hard and screamed to be let go. The hands released her, but the chain on her neck tightened and broke. She quickly plucked the locket as it slid down her chest.

A dire warning came in a deep whisper, "Go away."

With a vicious shove she was thrown into the rubble. As she landed, an exposed nail sliced open her upper arm, leaving a gaping wound. Blood gushed over her skirt.

Heavy footfalls crossed the floor. A cold knot of fear squeezed her heart, thinking her attacker was back. A waves of apprehension rose within her, nearly choking her. Holding her arm, she tried to stop the bleeding.

She gasped at the large shadow in the doorway. She hurled whatever she could in the dark, fearing her attacker had returned. A headstall with a long-shank bit landed squarely, hitting the person in the chest.

He flicked on the light and took in the bloody mess. "Brooke, stop. It's me."

She sat, crumpled in a heap at Adam's feet. Blood flowed from the open wound.

Leaving her momentarily, he went into the walkway and switched on the interior lights. Then he stooped down and gently examined her arm. His hands, cautious and gentle, lent a feeling of security.

"You'll need stitches. I'll wrap this for you, and we'll go in to see Doc."

Brooke didn't answer him. She watched his broad back as he rummaged around in the tack room. He turned with a first aid box.

Her heart raced, but she remained silent. Adam sat facing her, his hip touching hers. Carefully, he laid her arm in his lap. Neither spoke. He expertly butterflied the wound and applied a thick bandage, taping it securely. Her eyes constantly darted to his, looking for a reason to blame him. She was stunned, shocked by this unwarranted attack, a terrifying reenactment of her previous life, of Mike's irrational brutality.

"Fortunately, no one heard you or we would have had two nervous nellies on our hands." He smiled gently at her, easing some of her anxiety.

Adam took his handkerchief and wiped away the residue of blood. "Did you fall?"

Her voice choked. "No. Somebody pushed me. I thought *you* did it."

"Why would I want to hurt you?"

She dropped her eyes from his as she breathed deeply to garner her strength. "Maybe you don't want me back here," she whispered.

"Well, maybe you're wrong."

Adam helped her up and guided her to his pickup. Her skin was clammy, and tremors rippled over her. After securing her seat belt, he drove to Hank's trailer. Pounding on the door with more force than necessary, he explained the current situation.

"I need someone to examine the barn and outlying areas while I run Brooke in for stitches. She said someone pushed her into the tack room, and she has a deep cut on her arm. Be sure all the show horses and new foals are accounted for. Have an extra man watch over the herd we brought in. Sorry about the time. I'll check with you later."

"Is Brooke all right? Her homecoming has been a disaster."

"Yes, but the cut is bad. Call Doc for me and let him know we'll be at his house soon." He left Hank standing in the doorway.

On the drive into town his mind buzzed with

unanswered questions. Vandalism and rustling had intensified in the area over the last month. His was the only ranch that had not lost any expensive horses. The attack on Brooke made no sense. When he got back to the ranch, he would call Buck and report it. He was sickened by the thought the ranch could be a target.

"Who is out to get you?" His question blurted out with his inner anger.

"No one. Who would want to hurt me?"

He was now sure someone wanted her gone—first Buddy, now an attack on her. Black fright sailed through him. "I don't know, maybe someone from your past. Did you come home to hide, to escape someone? Were you or your husband into anything illegal that would bring danger to this ranch?" he barked.

With the same tone she fired back, "Adam, nothing is left. After his death, everything was sold or auctioned off to pay his debts. Everything was mortgaged, and taxes, and debts galore. All I have is ten thousand dollars and the car. I came home to gather my wits and to find some solid ground. Besides, why would I bring trouble to my father's house?"

Adam didn't answer. He was not aware of her dire situation, but she was right, he thought, she would never do Joe any harm.

"Whoever it was said to go away. Did you have one of your men try to scare me away? Maybe you're trying to get me to leave."

He laid his hand on her shoulder. "You can't believe that."

"Yes, I can.," she murmured. She leaned closer to the door.

The gash took a dozen stitches. Doc, a longtime friend, clucked as he worked. "I have sewn you two up so many times—and I'm always entertained with the excuses. This will leave a scar, but not a bad one. I'm not too sure you can save the dress though."

Neither spoke. After a tetanus shot for good measure, Doc gave out his orders.

"I want you here in about a week—unless Abe wants to take out the stitches," he mumbled. Doc moved his portly frame away from the table so she could get off. He ran his hand through his gray hair and yawned. Adjusting his glasses, he looked down his nose at her and pointed a finger. "If it starts to bleed badly, you get back here—and no jumping around for a few days." And to Adam, "You keep her quiet."

"Doc, I can take care of myself."

Ignoring her, Doc turned to Adam. "Make sure she takes these at least for tonight, or occasionally for pain. If she develops a fever, call me. Now get out of here so I can get my beauty rest." His gruff voice didn't intimidate either of them.

As Adam drove, he occasionally looked over at her

to be sure she was all right. But Brooke remained silent, leaning into the door.

Her voice was barely above a whisper as she strained to have him hear her. "Stop the truck. I'm going to be sick."

As the truck came to a complete stop, Brooke was out and, on her knees, retching. Adam knelt by her side, gently holding her long tresses from her face. When her stomach quieted, he went to the back seat of the truck and retrieved a box of tissues to wipe her mouth.

"I'm sorry."

"Don't worry about it. We'll wait here until you're ready." After a moment as if to try to lighten the moment, he jested. "Reminds me of the first time you snuck a beer. Only, as I recall, you didn't make it out of my truck in time."

A small chuckle rose from her misery. He had offered to drop her off on his way home from a neighborhood picnic. He didn't yell at her or have a tantrum. He remembered his own trek into alcohol. And here he was again, taking care of her.

He got a bottle of water from the pickup for her to rinse her mouth. She accepted his help into the truck, and even his comfort as he tucked her next to him the rest of the way home.

He saw her to her room and sat on her loveseat until she came out of the bathroom.

. . .

Brooke folded up the damaged dress and placed it across her tub. A blue nightshirt with short sleeves left the bandaged arm bare. She washed up and brushed her teeth. After running a comb through her hair, she sought Adam's help.

He helped her with the sling Doc insisted she use. She found his touch comforting as he carefully tied the strings to hold her arm in place. His nearness was unsettling. His familiar cologne still lingered. He was so devilishly handsome, the dark eyes, the sensuous face, his well-honed body. His fingers adjusted the sling to her shoulder. She forced her face into an unreadable mask, hiding her wandering thoughts.

He helped her into bed and settled the light blanket around her. After he brought her two of the pills the doctor sent for pain, he sat with her on the edge of the bed.

Adam stared at her. "You keep looking at me as though I'm the enemy. So, you really think I pushed you into the tack room?"

She looked away. "Someone did. Grabbed me by the throat and shook until I pulled on his pinky fingers and screamed. Someone wants me to leave."

"Why?"

"I don't know." A sob came out like a hiccup. "Maybe Kitty wants me gone."

"I don't. I kind of like having you here." His hand rose to caress her head and move a strand of hair out of the way.

Did he mean it, or was he just making small talk? Since she arrived, she had been seeing Adam in a different light, not the boy next door, not the insufferable task master, but a handsome man any woman would be proud to be with. But her traitorous body wasn't thinking friend.

"What's wrong with your hand? You've been clenching it."

She looked and opened it. "When the hands grabbed my throat, the chain broke. It's my mother's gold locket. Would you put it on the dresser?"

"Do you have another? I can fix it for you. I know how much it means to you." He took the locket from her and waited.

"On the dresser is an old jewelry box. Maybe you can find another suitable chain."

He searched the box and found one she could use until she went to town. He slid the locket on and sat on the edge of the bed while he fastened the chain around her neck. "Where did the chain go? Maybe it can be fixed."

"I don't know. Probably still on the barn floor. Thank you, Adam."

He pulled her forward and rested her head on his shoulder. His warmth and strength were so welcome. This was the Adam she remembered. His hands caressed her back until she relaxed, and the medication made her drowsy. Then he lifted her face to his and kissed her forehead.

"Rest quietly. I won't be far away."

Brooke awoke as the sun was peeking out over the hills. The deep salmon hue was more like a sunset as a spectrum of light spread from behind the hills.

A shiver of fear shot through her as she recalled the previous night, difficult to believe someone wanted to hurt her, here at home. Not once, but twice. Tears glazed her eyes as she recalled the torment and risk taking, she endured while Mike was alive. The fear she would one day die from his reckless nature or become physically broken from his temper tantrums was imbedded in her subconscious.

But Mike was dead.

She realized Adam was in her room, sitting comfortably on the love seat. From his weary appearance, he hadn't slept. His bare foot poked out from the leg of a clean pair of jeans and rested negligently on the small cherry coffee table. An elbow perched on his raised knee while his hand drooped freely. His dark brown curls were not neatly combed but ruffled as if he had run his fingers through them repeatedly. Longer strands in the back played teasingly with his chambray shirt collar. Noticing his weary slump, she assumed he spent the greater part of the night in her room. And then she blushed with embarrassment as she realized he was staring back.

"Good morning," she managed to squeak out, searching for an escape. "Did you sleep here all night?"

Adam leaned forward, resting his sinewy arms on his

thighs. He yawned as he spoke. "I felt someone should be here in case you needed anything. You had some bad dreams. Since no one else knows, I didn't seem to have any other choice."

They fenced with their eyes—questions, emotions, as if each of them held back their innermost thoughts. But when he spoke again his voice was warm and compassionate. "Does your arm hurt? I'll get you one of the pills, if you want."

"Yes, please. It's throbbing. What time is it?"

"It's after five." He got up and stretched before the window and then went into her bathroom for her antibiotics and pain medication. He sat on the side of the bed. "It would be a good idea if you slept for a while. I'll go down and investigate last night and talk with Joe. What shall we tell him? You know how he is about you."

"Have you been assigned the guardian angel?" Her voice was clipped and short and not what she wanted to say at all. She wanted to crawl in those strong arms. Tension suddenly mounted as he stared down at her, absorbing her sarcasm.

His response rang with censure. "Normally life is pretty quiet. We prefer it that way. And, in case you haven't noticed, your father is not as healthy has he used to be."

She had noticed, and it pained her to think he was getting older. He was not as strong as he had been, naps in the afternoon, more paperwork than time at the barn. Yes, she had noticed, and she worried.

"Tell them I fell in the tack room." She looked up at him and grinned. "I guess you will have to come up with some reason for the mess."

He smiled back. "I'll think of something."

The indefinable truce between them was almost pleasant, he reflected. Adam stifled the urge to go over and enfold her in his arms to rid her of the fear, plaguing those periwinkle eyes. She wasn't quite as brave as she wanted everyone to believe. The dreams disturbing her sleep weren't just nightmares. They were more of a reenactment, residual fear. Would she ever tell him what made her dreams so violent?

Later, he left the house and headed for Hank's. The bungalow sat sheltered among the trees just past the barns, bordering the drive that led to the various pastures. Hank seemed happy, living in the small home supplied by the ranch. He kept it spotless as if it were his own.

Hank's family ranched near Wheatland. They had little extra money to spend on frivolous things while they raised seven children. As they grew, the ranch became too small for all of them. A decade ago, Joe offered him a full-time job. Lately he was Adam's right-hand man, as well as a good friend.

Adam pounded on his door. Groggily he admitted his boss.

"Did you see or hear anything?"

"A junker of a truck up on the road sped away. It was

too dark to see the color, just the noise of the engine. I went out to check on the cattle. They seemed a bit restless about being confined. The tack room was a real mess, though."

Adam tried to explain the events of the evening and could not hold back a chuckle. Hank burst into tear-filled howling. "I'd bet on Kitty."

Adam took a glass of orange juice from Hank. "Well, someone apparently pushed Brooke. She's got a bad gash on her arm, and I was right in front of the house. Kitty had left."

"Are you sure the trouble was meant for Brooke?"

Adam shrugged negligently. "She was the only one in the barn. Besides, whoever it was told her to go away. I'll tell Joe she fell in the dark. She agreed. We told Doc that, too." He placed the empty glass in the sink. "I'll see you later."

Adam retraced Hank's search in the barn and the outside areas. But nothing was apparent. He would have blamed Kit outright, but he was watching her drive away when he heard the scream. Who would want Brooke gone? Did she pose a threat to anyone?

He knew she wanted to blame him. His mind rambled for answers as he covered every inch of the barn areas. He took a 4-wheeler up to the road where he found the tracks of the truck Hank heard, apparently in a hurry from the skid ruts left in the roadside. He remembered vaguely the old truck sitting alongside the road, but he thought it was broken down. His mind was on getting

Brooke to Doc. Finally, he returned to the house for breakfast.

In the mudroom, he removed his work boots, mindful of Mary's rule. Noticing Joe at the table, he came in quietly and poured himself a cup of coffee before sitting at the table. Joe watched him pensively.

"Well, are you going to tell me what's making your face all mean?"

"Brooke had an accident last night. She was slightly injured—but she'll be alright." He paused to drink from his cup, avoiding Joe's stare. "She has a cut on her arm. She tripped in the dark and fell in the tack room. I took her to Doc's. She has a few stitches, and he suggested she rest for a few days." He grasped the mug as though it were an anchor. He felt his integrity was at stake here, muffling the truth from Joe.

Joe didn't speak for a moment. "Is she really alright?" he murmured.

"Yes, she'll be fine."

"Maybe I should go up and see her, take her breakfast."

"No, Joe, I gave her a pain pill a couple of hours ago. She's probably out cold." He didn't want to explain all that went on the night before, especially after Hank rolled with laughter when he was told. "I was nearby when she fell."

Joe patted Adam's hand. "I'll wait a few hours. I wish the medication I take for my heart wouldn't make me sleep so soundly." Tears glazed his weary eyes.

Adam's own heart ached for the man across from him. He had once been the strongest and most competitive horseman he had ever known. Now he was a shell of his former self, aching to once again feel the thrill of competition. After a quick discussion about the daily work, he filled his thermal mug again and quietly left the house. Neither said a word as they ambled down to the barns and arenas. Near the cattle, men were waiting for instructions, some with horses saddled, and others on foot.

Adam eyed each man carefully. Could it be one of them who pushed Brooke? His voice held more authority, staring at each man as he gave orders while he wrestled with his feelings.

The cows and calves were now moved into the old outside arena with cattle chutes, and the tagging and vaccination could get under way. The ranch hands could manage the job on their own, and old Abe would be available for any medical emergency.

He and Hank headed into town for additional vaccines and basic supplies. Fear clutched his heart. Could he leave the ranch for even a short trip to town?

CHAPTER EIGHT

$\mathcal{F}$eeling the weight on her bed, Brooke assumed Adam had returned. Not Adam, but her worried father checking up on her. She was now wide awake, her pulses spinning. Sitting up further in the bed, she was momentarily speechless.

"Hello, sweetheart. I hear you had a little accident." He fiddled with the bow on the sling. "I waited to come up because Adam said you were sleeping."

"Yes. Doc gave me something to help me sleep." She wasn't sure what Adam told him, so she didn't offer any information. Did he tell him what she fell on? Did he tell him about the person who grabbed her, who told her to go away? Probably not. "But I'll be fine."

"You should be more careful when you wander around at night. It's a good thing Adam was around." He patted her hand and smiled at her.

Yes, she thought, it was a good thing Adam was

around. He must have frightened off whoever pushed her. And for just that fleeting moment, it was like old times, his confident self, getting her out of a jam. But he was running the ranch, living in the house, and it wasn't old times. She thought she could come back to find peace, to find herself.

Go away. Who wanted her to leave? Her head swirled with doubts.

"I chose not to put on the yard light. I didn't want to spoil the beautiful evening." Would the outcome have been a different if she had put on the outside lights? Adam would have seen the lights shining in the tack room window. Maybe then she wouldn't have interrupted their little rendezvous. Or did Kitty, always the exhibitionist, want her to see them together? Probably so, she mused.

"Look, Mary hasn't eaten yet. The sun is nice and warm now. We could eat on the patio."

"Alright. But no special favors. I'll be fine in a couple of days."

"Good enough." His face crinkled with a smile as he closed her door.

She took off the sling. With some difficulty she managed to get into her bra and panties. She slipped on a pair of well-worn jeans and carefully slipped her arm in a white tee. Over that she pulled on an oversized, white cotton jacket. With soft moccasins on her feet, she carried her sling down to the kitchen.

Joe and Mary were outside on the patio drinking

coffee. Mary jumped up. "Now let me help you with the sling. We don't want too much movement to open the stitches, and I'll get a comb to straighten up your hair a bit more."

Joe made her a cup of coffee. "Mary picked up some regular for you. I know you don't care for the decaf I drink. What would you like for breakfast?"

"Those muffins look good. And homemade butter. Yum." The situation with the two of them was hard at times. Throughout her life she wished she could somehow reciprocate all the wonderful things they lavished on her over the years. But the crux of the problem was that they wouldn't let her if she tried.

Joe sat down and explained his new idea. "You know the ranch has always had cow dogs for years to help with the stock, but we haven't had one at the house for a long time. I called Red at the K-9 center about a dog to have around the house, just for you. A dog would give you some protection when you are alone or when you're out riding."

"It sounds like you have already made up your mind." Back to normal, she mused. But she loved him for his thoughtfulness, anyway.

Joe continued. "Do you remember Red? He used to train horses for me."

"Yes. He always had a cast on somewhere." She chuckled as she remembered.

"Well, he decided to work with dogs instead. I told

him I needed something special for my special girl." Joe smiled with his secret as if it was Christmas.

Mary must have been in on the secret. She gave up a smile, too. "I think a dog at the house would be wonderful."

"You'll spoil it. Probably can't wait to make homemade dog biscuits." Joe smiled warmly and tapped Mary's hand. He excused himself from the table and set out for the horse barns. Brooke knew his paint horses were his life. He used to spend more attention to the horses, the cattle, and the oilwells than his time with her. Now apparently, times were different. He only seemed to go to the show barn in the morning.

The day grew beautiful, over seventy degrees and not a cloud to mar the blue of the sky. To Brooke this was like a holiday. From the amount of food lavished on her, she guessed Mary wanted her to heal overnight. She was stiff from her fall and from the stitches, and her residual Mike-induced anxieties kept her close to the house. The push was real, not her imagination. Twice in two days. So, who would want her away from the ranch and why?

A swift shadow of anger swept over her. She had no intention of letting others bully her into decisions affecting her life. Not now. She took a deep breath and let it out slowly.

Brooke reclined on a chaise lounge. Because of the heat, she changed into a pink plaid blouse with short, capped sleeves and matching shorts. She forgot how intense the sun could be in the hills of southern

Wyoming and generously spread suntan lotion on her exposed skin. If it hadn't been for the discomfort in her arm, she would have marked this as a nearly perfect day.

Male voices carried up from the barn, signaling their lunch break. Brooke watched the three men as they made their way across the large expanse of lawn. The vision was like old times when Adam and her father would be out organizing a road trip to a show—before, when Adam lived at home at Hightower.

"Hello, darlin'," Joe said with a soft, affectionate tone, giving her a gentle hug and avoiding her arm. Taking a chair next to her, he held her hand and patted it tenderly.

She could handle the affection lavished on her by her father, but it was Adam who made her uncomfortable and restless. Those deep orbs didn't have to focus on her to make her feel exposed, open to his scrutiny.

"Here. These are for you." Hank sauntered over with his confections.

"Hank, if I didn't know better, I'd think you were after my heart." She laughed lightly. "Here, sit down." She moved her legs to make room for him on the chaise.

She opened the gift with enthusiasm. Holding the box out to him first, she offered him a piece of her prize. "Have some?"

"Mm, I have good taste in chocolates." Hank laughed at his own words.

Adam slouched in a chair at the table. "Aren't you going to offer the rest of us a share in your fortune?"

"I thought you were concerned about your weight?" She grinned impishly.

Adam rose from his seat and zeroed in on the candy. "But you still could have asked." He chose a few. His eyes darted to her smiling face. "Besides, if I don't get some now, they'll be gone. I remember what a candy freak you are." His mouth turned up to one side in a mischievous grin. He gave her a wink, alluding to younger, happier times.

Mary came out with a tray loaded with food. She prepared a tower of roast beef sandwiches with dill pickles on the side. Dishes of raw vegetables and potato salad rounded out the meal.

During the afternoon, Joe allowed Brooke to sort papers in the office and explained as many questions as she asked. He was right, she mused, contemplating the many bills and records she handled that day. Running a ranch so large was more complicated than she expected. He had always made it sound so easy. However, if she wanted to send Adam back to Hightower, she would have to give it greater effort.

Adam returned from town with Hank and parked the ranch pickup near the main barn. The barn doors were open on each end for fresh air. Beyond the doors yearling horses were out in a paddock eating, running, playing. He went into the tack room and restocked medications for the brood mares in the small refrigerator. Abe was grumbling about having to put halters and tack back on their appropriate hooks.

"Here, let me help you with that." He gave in to the guilty feeling he had for the mess.

"No, I've got it all handled. You have enough on your plate." Abe turned to him while he separated a clump of lead ropes. The old man had serious tears in his eyes. "You take care of our girl. You are the only one who can."

Adam nodded as if to agree. But he had serious doubt that he would be able to control her activities. And that worried him. As he left the tack room, he found Joe checking on Buddy.

Joe came over to him. "I need to talk to you as soon as you are free."

"We can talk now. Hank is taking the extra vaccines out to the pens."

Together they meandered through the lush pasture, bordering the house lawn. For a while neither man spoke as they checked the new foals. Some were brave enough to come up for a friendly scratch, but then they would turn and gallop back to their mothers, kicking and whinnying at their bravery.

Joe paused and put his hands in his pockets. "Have you seen anything unusual on your rounds with the cattle?"

"No, everything is almost too quiet." Except for last night, he wanted to say.

Adam caressed one of the mares whose curiosity

made her investigate them. "I stopped by the sheriff's office while I was in town. Buck wants to place a man undercover here and one at Hightower if we have any more problems."

"So, he thinks this is all planned and by someone we know?"

Adam shrugged. "He seems to believe they are working out of one of the ranches, has to be someone who knows the area. Or someone who works the area and knows the movement of the animals."

He didn't want Joe getting paranoid and making his heart act up. The stress in his face told the story. Or was it more? Brooke's return, maybe that was stressing him.

Walking back to the house, Joe changed the subject. He explained about the dog he ordered. "I told Red I wanted special dog for Brooke, but one trained to protect."

"That's probably a good idea. She'll be gallivanting around the countryside before too long." He stopped for a moment. He couldn't play this game anymore. "Joe? When are you going to tell her the truth?"

"Soon, soon. I'm surprised you were around at all last night. You certainly had your hands full," Joe laughed, ignoring Adam's request.

He placed an arm around his partner's shoulder. "Will you do it this week?"

Joe sobered some and nodded his head. He put his hands on his hips and stared at the ground. "I'm afraid of her reaction. I know it's not fair for you to keep up the charade."

He understood Joe's concern, but he couldn't pursue his feelings for Brooke as long as the lie floated out there. She will probably hate me afterward, he thought, never believe that he loved her, had always loved her. "So, when does this dog arrive?"

Later, when the late news went off and an old western rerun began, Brooke questioned whether she should go to bed. Alone, she stood up and stretched. Deciding to give it up for the night, she turned off the television and the lamp. When she turned, she stepped smack into Adam's solid frame. He reached out to steady her only to have her thrashing him to be free.

"Brooke. Stop, it's me."

"Damn, you scared me. You look like a monk in that robe. Why are you sneaking around?" She pulled at the stain of peppermint tea on her polo shirt. "Now I've got tea all over me."

"I'm sorry I startled you. I showered and thought I'd watch some news." He released her but didn't move.

The sudden contact with his warm naked chest was disturbing. She looked up as her heart pounded. Clearing her throat, she stepped back. "Well," she murmured, "the news is over."

He studied her for a moment. He went to the sofa,

and after turning on the lamp, he picked up a horseman's magazine.

She left the den but noticed the sudden throbbing of her arm. Glancing at it, she realized the tea also stained the bandage. The pain, however, was from Adam's grip as he kept her from falling. No light showed from below Mary's door. Determined not to ask Adam to help her, she decided to change it herself.

From the walk-in pantry she took out the first-aid kit and sat at the table. Rolling her sleeve as high as it would go, she cut the old bandage away, revealing the stitches. With one finger, she applied the medicated ointment and stuck on a thick pad. The pad balanced as she carefully wound the gauze around her arm. Her awkward motions sent her elbow colliding with the metal kit. Crashing to the floor, the contents scattered across the floor. Surely, now she would have everyone in the house up.

But it was only Adam who came.

Assessing the situation, he padded over to the table to help her pick up the items. "What were you trying to do?" He threw the spilled contents into the metal kit with seeming impatience.

Her own clumsiness angered her. "When you spilled the tea on me, it stained the bandage. I thought I could handle the bandage myself," she muttered.

"Let me see." He pulled a chair close to hers and took her arm. With gentleness, he layered the wide gauze around her arm.

Aftershave wound around her senses, touching her

pleasantly. His presence ruffled her self-control. Attempting to resist any more renegade thoughts to intrude, she lowered her eyes.

"Does that hurt? Is it too tight?" he asked.

Brooke shook her head and looked down at the floor.

"You should have asked. I would have been willing to do this for you." He hooked a strong finger under her chin and checked her eyes. "Are you still troubled by the other night?

"Yes," she whispered thickly, and avoided his piercing look. Yes, and the fright she felt still wormed around her psyche.

"Anything else bothering you?" Adam replaced the tape and gauze.

"Nothing," she hedged, refusing to tell him what a traitorous body she had, or the heat running through her, or her heart that wanted him to care.

"I can see that. I know we have a lot of history between us, but if you have a problem, maybe I can help—or listen." His face held an impassioned challenge for peace, intensifying her already inflamed senses.

"The only problem I have is you living in my father's house." Brooke stood up to leave only to be stopped by a powerful hand, grasping her elbow, spinning her about.

Adam pulled her struggling form onto his lap, holding her as he forced her to look at him. "Well, I'm not leaving. Do you think you can be absent for nearly a decade and then come back into your father's life and take up where you left off? Don't you ever consider the wishes of other people, your father included?"

His accusations stung like Wyoming hail in a summer storm.

Adam released her with a slight shove. He scooped up the first-aid kit and thrust it into the pantry, giving vent to his anger. Without a glance, he left her and went up the stairs.

Turning off the remaining lights, Brooke wandered through the house and up the stairs. Later, she lay in her bed wretchedly recanting the words Adam threw at her. She could not decipher the changes, but she knew Adam claimed more than his share of authority. He wasn't just the ranch manager and horse trainer. He was much more.

CHAPTER NINE

*B*rooke lay stiff and weary after a restless night. An early morning rain left a measure of moisture in the air. The sky was as gray and sunless as her battered emotions. The breeze from the slightly opened window permeated her room with the flowery smells of late spring.

She pushed away the comforter and got out of bed. As she rubbed her arms from the cool chill, she bumped her wound, reminding her, even after a week had gone by, that Adam had not found out who pushed her. Nor did she think he would. The residual ache in her arm matched the ache in her heart as her plans to relax and start over was not happening. She hoped these were random incidences—Kitty maybe—and not a plan to get her to leave the ranch. Pushing down the unwanted cowardice rising within her, she decided to go to town, open a bank account, and see Bess. Time to get on with life.

Abe took out the stitches for her the day before and a bandage really wasn't necessary. She dressed in a pair of Levi's and a long-sleeved, peach colored knit top with a boatneck embroidered neckline.

She picked up her locket, handling the substitute chain carefully, and fastened it around her neck. A smile touched her face as she gazed at the beautiful details. The gold filigree designs glittered in the light. The heart reminded her of her mother. Wearing it kept the memories close to the surface, memories of when she felt complete. After her mother's death, she still had Joe, but in her father's own grief, he often left her out of his daily activities. When Mike was at his worse, the locket gave her hope she would be free of him some day. And now she could start over. Well, maybe. She tucked that insecurity away.

Grabbing her leather hobo bag off the dresser, she went in search of Mary. For all of Mary's loving attention, she felt she could at least buy her lunch in town. Reaching the kitchen, she discovered everyone gone, the dishes done, and the Keurig turned off.

After a quick bowl of cold cereal and a cup of coffee, she slipped on a pair of tan leather mules and tried to find Mary. Spotting Abe near the new foals, Brooke determined he would know where to locate anyone.

"Have you seen Dad and Mary around?" she called from the fence.

Abe rambled over to her on his arthritic legs, a smile of pleasure on his face. "Let's see. T'day is Friday and on Fridays Joe takes Mary over to Hightower. Mary and their cook, Connie, are makin' a large quilt to raffle off at the Children's Hospital Dance durin' the fair. She won't be gettin' back 'til later t'day. They said to let you sleep in."

"Well, has Dad come back?"

"Your father plays golf on Fridays after he drops Mary off, usually doesn't show up 'til after lunch. Guess he eats at the clubhouse. Adam might be in the new arena. Why? Is somethin' wrong?" Abe's face took on dark concern as he laid his weathered hand on her arm.

"No. I'm going into Bantry. I wanted to ask Mary to go with me to have lunch, maybe shop a little. You know —girl stuff. And I wanted to look up Bess. I didn't want anyone to think I was missing." She smiled lightly. "I'll have to go alone. Do you need anything?"

Abe didn't smile. "Are you sure ya should be drivin'? Do ya want me to drive ya, sugar?"

"No. Thank you, Abe. I'm sure you have plenty of work to do. I can handle a quick trip to town. See you later."

"Oh, by the way, sugar, I cleaned the dust out of your car for you. It's all polished up."

"Thank you, Abe. You didn't have to."

"Well, I never get to touch a nice car like that. I also went for a drive." He grinned like a boy who had succeeded at a prank.

Abe was very thorough. The car was spotless inside and smelled of leather polish and carpet cleaner. On the way she passed by Kitty's ranch, who's sprawling home sat far back from the gravel road. Who was ensconced in her "cat" house that morning? She hadn't seen Adam. Maybe he was with Kitty. She wasn't going to let Kitty or Adam ruin her day. When She reached the state highway, she accelerated rapidly, the empty road hers.

The car gave her a sense of freedom. Cattle grazed on both sides of the highway. She observed a herd of pronghorn antelope, their distinctive coloring and black horns setting them apart from the domestic animals. The land was so vast and so open, even after all these years, she was in awe.

Brooke slowed the car and stopped at an entrance to another side road, absorbing the silence. With the wide expanse of the land before her, she felt free, a feeling she hadn't had in eight years. In the far distance, over thirty miles away, the Medicine Bow National Forest formed a bowl where the city of Laramie rested.

When Mike was alive, they were hardly ever home. Going to a restaurant or on a trip to another country or to an island paradise held no magic for her. He often told her in anger that those were business trips. And they bought all the beautiful things she owned. And she should be grateful. But all those beautiful things did not bring happiness in an abusive marriage.

Her life had no substance then. Sometimes she wondered what had attracted her to Mike. He seemed so different from the men she knew, mostly ranchers or horsemen who worked close to nature and loved it. Mike Boyle was suave, sophisticated, but she soon learned he was more interested in tinsel and cold hard cash. He became more driven and more controlling. Brooke certainly knew what she didn't want in a relationship. But she was spooked, afraid she would find the same Jekyll and Hyde personality again.

She set the car in motion and before long the road wound down the valley into the sleepy town of Bantry. Martin Bantry set up shop in the late1800s, supplying the ranchers and miners as they came through the area. His small general store blossomed into this ranching community with a splattering of small working mines.

The town still preserved the flavor of the Old West with brick buildings. The upper floors were transformed into offices or apartments. The main street was wide where years ago buckboards and wagons were common.

She noticed the new grocery store and the new bank building, but everything had to remain in the same architectural style, saving the ambiance of the main part of town. Sidewalks replaced the boardwalks of old and most of the streets had been paved.

Brooke parked in front of the beauty salon, owned by her childhood friend, Bess. The shop had a brick veneer and lace curtains hung at the windows. She recognized the irrational need to be with someone she knew. She was alone for six months after Mike's death, clearing up his faulty business matters and healing her own self-esteem. Now she craved the company of others, and at times Adam's presence was welcome.

She entered the store through a new glass door with hair styling posters taped here and there. The smell of hair products filled the large salon. Bess struggled with a tiny permanent rod as she worked on an older woman's hair. Bess hadn't changed much, she noted. Her dark hair was always well done, and today it was pulled up and fell in long curls down her back.

On the counter next to the register was an old-fashioned brass bell. Feeling rather lighthearted, she smiled and childishly banged on the bell.

"Just a moment please." Bess tried to remain calm as the woman complained and the bell rang. Impatiently, she looked to the counter, hesitated for a moment, and then, with a whoop of joy, went over to exchange an embrace, leaving the roller hanging.

"I heard you were back."

"News spreads fast."

"Well, Kitty came in for a trim and mentioned she saw you." Bess wiped her hands in a nervous gesture as though she should have left out that last bit.

"Yes, I did see her," Brooke could only guess what kind of manure Kitty was spreading. Age didn't change some people. "Can you get away for lunch? I'll be in town for a while."

"I can't get out until noon. Can you find something to do until then? Please?"

"Sure. I have a number of errands to run." She smiled with encouragement.

Beth looked at the waiting customer. "I'll let Abby handle the few appointments I have this afternoon, and we'll have a long lunch."

"Great. I'll see you at the hotel. Does Mac still own it?"

"Yes, and the food is better than ever."

With a last hug, she left the shop.

The bank officer was glad to see her, but she was chagrinned at his fatherly attentions. To this seasoned bank president, she would always be Joe Montgomery's little girl. After the bank, she strolled through a few of the new shops. In one she found a pair of dangling, silver earrings she knew Mary would enjoy. Having time on her hands, she asked the cashier to wrap them and include a gift tag. Hopefully, she would be able to see her alone before the men arrived for dinner.

The Bantry Hotel was next. The large bar and restaurant were usually filled for breakfast, lunch, and dinner. Excellent food always drew many to eat, drink and dance. The interior had an ambiance of an Old West saloon where one would expect gunslingers and Marshal Dillon. On the right side as you entered, a large U-shaped cherry-wood bar took up a third of the room. The mirror behind the bar resembled a multi-paned window of beveled glass.

On three sides were booths, simulating individual stalls, stained cherry and distressed to look antique.

Hanging on the wall of each booth were shiny brass and crystal lanterns. The rest of the floor contained tables and captain's chairs.

The dining area had hand-carved panels and period crystal chandeliers and provided a pleasant place to eat or visit with friends. At night, the banquet room usually had a live band entertaining or a DJ, so patrons could use the dance floor and kick up their heels or snuggle close to a slow dance. She smiled, remembering the many evenings she and her friends moved to the music, flirted, and laughed, unjaded by life.

Brooke took a booth along the side wall. She sat facing the door and waited for Bess. She ordered a Margarita from the waitress. The complimentary chips and salsa eased the gnawing of her empty stomach.

Kitty, her red hair blazing as it cascaded down her back, sat with a man whose bearded face Brooke could not see. By the clothes he wore, she suspected he was from one of the ranches or maybe even worked for Kitty. Maybe her most recent victim.

Brooke stifled a giggle when she thought about her intrusion into Adam's little love nest. She swallowed down the bit of jealousy that always stung her when she saw him with a woman. Even when he was high school age and the heart throb of many, she imagined what went on between him and whatever girl he had on his arm. At the time, she discounted it as the mysteries of youth and immaturity. But now, she wasn't an inexperienced adolescent. And he was more stunningly virile than she remembered. She found her thoughts vaguely disturbing.

A male voice behind her ruffled her composure. "Welcome home."

Her hand jerked, splattering her drink.

"Oh, I didn't mean to startle you, Brooke. I'll get you another—on the house." Mack grinned down at her amicably. With a bar towel he wiped up the spill.

"Thank you, Mack. It's good to be back."

"Is Adam is joining you for lunch? I need to see him about a baseball bet he and I have." The owner of the hotel was single, fiftyish, whose last name no one could pronounce. Everyone called him Mack. He wasn't a large man, and gray accented his dark, brown hair. His happiness and good humor reflected in the comfortable atmosphere.

"Thank you, and no, Adam is not joining me for lunch." Her face turned pink at the insinuation.

Mack continued to smile, but with an apologetic look. "Apparently the rumor mill is running strong. According to Kitty, you and Adam are—you know—a thing."

She placed a finger on her lips to remind herself to be polite. With a long sigh, she explained. "We are not a thing," she replied with impatience. "I'm sorry, Mack. I shouldn't take my anger with Kitty out on you."

"Oh, I understand." He patted her shoulder lightly and smiled. "I'll be right back with a new drink, and you can decide if you want to order."

Why would Kitty spread a rumor like that? She wasn't the one nearly naked on top of Adam. Her heart thumped traitorously. Images of trading places with Kitty in the tack room passed through her thoughts a few times. But the thoughts were fleeting.

Bess arrived with bubbling good humor. "Hello, Mack. I'll have whatever Brooke is having. Thanks." After sitting down, she commented on Brooke's stiffness. "Have I interrupted something?'

"No." She spoke between sips from her large glass, cooling the heat from the salsa and chips she methodically devoured. "Kitty told Mack that Adam and I are ..." She scowled over at Kitty. "Kitty is obviously vexed over the other night. It's not my fault she strips at a moment's notice."

Mack returned with their drinks. "Would you girls like to order something now, or do you want to visit for a spell?" Mack's charm disarmed Brooke's tension.

She returned a smile. "I'll have the taco salad special."

"Yes, I'll have the same." Bess settled herself more comfortably. "I heard about the rumor, but I didn't want to jump to any conclusions." She grinned as she sipped from her drink. Her dark hair fell playfully about her face, lightening the mood. "Adam is quite the catch around here, you know."

Brooke swished a corn chip in the salsa. Everyone thought he was so wonderful. The jury was still out, she mused. People changed, and after eight years, she was sure Adam had some secrets of his own. And she didn't know what hold he held over her father.

"Many women—married or not—would trade just the rumor with you." Bess smiled with frivolity. She wiggled her eyebrows. "Even me."

"Adam has always been popular with the ladies." She knew he had always been a hot topic with the fairer sex.

"Where would Kitty get the idea that you had taken her place with Adam? He does date her occasionally. I've seen them together. It's never been a secret. But he does date other women, too. He even brought me here to dance a few rounds—nothing romantic. It was a nice evening and a kiss good night.

"Maybe Kitty thinks she can provoke you into leaving town." Bess offered as she filled a chip with salsa. "Well shoot, I hope not. Remember all the good times we used to have?"

Brooke chuckled. "I know what started all this backbiting. The second night I was home, I walked in on them in the tack room—and they weren't polishing leather. I'm sure Kitty thinks I interrupted their little party on purpose."

"Did you?" Bess smiled devilishly.

"No." She laughed. "I was checking on a wounded horse at Adam's request."

At Bess's urging, she finally explained the entire day. Explaining to someone she considered a friend seemed to lighten the situation in her mind. Deceptive calmness hid her battered emotions.

"Maybe the attack was reciprocation from Kitty for spoiling her fun?"

"Adam seemed to think the timing was wrong. He was with her on the drive by the house. I even accused him, but he denied having anything to do with it. Could have been one of her lackeys."

"Oh, I don't know. There's been a lot of strange things going on lately. Missing cows, horses. A few pickup trucks have up and disappeared. Besides, you ended up spending the rest of the night with Adam, not her." Bess wiggled her eyebrows.

Uncomfortable with the direction of her thoughts she changed the subject. "Let's drop this and talk about you."

As they ate and reminisced, Brooke noticed Kitty's departure on the arm of her cowboy. She would have to watch herself around the voluptuous, lady rancher, suspecting Kitty would pounce on any crumb to create turmoil for her.

"Tell me, do you miss the city?" Bess ate a chip and sipped from her glass.

"As a matter of fact, no. I've decided to stay here, help Dad with the ranch."

"I thought Adam was the head honcho." Bess looked up as she dipped another chip.

"He thinks so." She scowled. There had to be more, more she didn't know.

"Is the investigation into your husband's death over? You wrote you were going to keep working on it." Beth appeared interested in her past.

A little voice inside her head told her to go slowly. Just the investigation, nothing about the brutality, the imprisonment in her own home. No, her friend at this point just needed to know the basics, the end of that relationship.

"The crash, and then the explosion and fire destroyed the plane and the bodies. Not much left for them to investigate." Between bites of food, she continued. "He sure wasn't as business wise as I thought he was. He invested so poorly. I barely had enough to cover all his debts. The business was in serious financial trouble. The other plane, even our home, was sold to pay off everything. And then the FBI kept asking me questions as if I knew what he did or didn't do. Scary." Yes, she had really been afraid they would somehow connect her with his financial dealings and arrest her.

"But now you are back here with familiar faces and places. You can start over."

"Yes," Brooke took a fortifying breath and smiled through her fears. "That's what I had hoped for."

Over coffee and dessert, they reminisced and laughed. The medicine of laughter was good for both. Temporarily, she pushed to the back of her mind the war with Adam. The irritation from Kitty. The cut on her arm.

"Gosh, it's almost five. Talk about a long lunch. Where does the time go? I have to lock up the shop."

"Why don't you come for dinner?" Brooke urged.

"I have a date tonight," Bess smiled. Her eyes

glittered with anticipation. "He's really quite nice, but he lives in Laramie. He made reservations at a new Italian restaurant."

"Sounds serious—and a long-distance relationship."

"No. He's lots of fun, though."

She picked up the check. "I'll take care of this. You have brightened my day considerably."

They gathered their things and headed for the door. "I'll drive you to your shop. My car is outside. I need to see Mary before the men arrive for dinner."

CHAPTER TEN

*T*he white pickup with the Montgomery Ranch brand emblazoned on the door stalked down the street like a cougar seeking its prey. Brooke frowned. Now what?

Slipping into a parking space next to her roadster, Adam jumped from the truck, slamming the door on his way. His eyes glanced at Bess before they homed in on Brooke. His body barked with anger before his voice carried to her.

He spaced his words evenly. "Where the hell have you been? I've been looking all over for you." His hands landed on his hips.

Chilling fear raced through her. Involuntarily, her hand came up to rest on his chest. "Is something wrong with Dad?"

"No, it's not Joe. When are you going to learn a little courtesy? You could leave a note—or something. And why aren't you answering your phone?" he growled. "After all that has happened since you arrived, one would think you could at least stay in touch with someone."

The mention of her phone reminded her she had left it plugged into her car. He was looking for her. Fear rattled in her chest. "Is someone hurt?"

"No, everyone's fine." His arm spread in a wide arc. "I've been out over an hour searching for you, fearing the worst, and here you are out on a lark with Bess."

Brooke's color rose with embarrassment and anger. A nip of dread crawled under her skin. She hated the residual fear planted there by a violent monster. Adam wasn't a monster. With false bravado she asked, "So, what do you want?"

He pointed his finger at her. "Well, *princess,* if your father returns from his game and finds you gone, he'll probably think something else happened."

Silly from the drinks, and relieved that nothing dire happened, she began to chuckle, and with lots of gesturing and pointing she asked, "You mean you drove all the way into town to find me so I would be home for dinner? I'm sorry to worry you. You should have checked with Abe. He stays around the main barn during the day."

To her chagrin, she saw Kitty and her bearded companion driving past slowly. How embarrassing, verifying Kitty's new rumor by having what looked like a lover's quarrel right in the middle of town. She wanted to stomp all over Adam.

She turned her back on him and faced Bess. Her voice was syrupy sweet as she countered the anger boiling within her. "I'm sorry for his rudeness. Do you want a ride to the shop?"

"No ... um, I'll walk." Bess started down the street. "I'll call you."

Adam was less angry, his voice quieter. "Let's go."

Giving no further indication he existed, Brooke got into her car. She heard the impatient churning of the diesel engine as he waited for her to leave. As she left the fringes of civilization behind, she became aware of the intense shaking of her insides as she fought the overwhelming fear of his strength. His bellowing triggered memories, memories of beatings and humiliation during her marriage.

Would she ever forget? Could she free herself of the cowardice she felt whenever someone raised their voice? And what of Adam, would he also resort to violence when he discovered she wanted to replace him?

Adam cursed himself all the way home for making a scene in town. When it came to Brooke, he had no control over his emotions. She set off conflicts within him, causing him to do things out of character. Never would he have embarrassed a woman in public, but he did, bellowing like an injured bear. When he saw her eyes, the fear he had generated, even if it were only a second before she regained control, he wanted to hold her and tell her she was safe.

Running his long fingers through his hair, he recalled how frantic he was when he found her gone, the house empty. Anxiety knotted within him as he feared the worst, feared he would lose her for good.

Abe had left for the day, and he didn't even think to call him. Was he really concerned about Joe's health or was it Brooke's welfare? He knew the truth. What happened to his self-control since she arrived a week ago? She was constantly on his mind, visions of holding her, loving her, cluttered up his thoughts. Maybe, the pretense that he was merely an employee at the ranch irritated him.

Time for Joe to tell her the truth. Tonight would be as good a time as any.

After parking her car, Brooke raced to the house ahead of Adam. In a gallant attempt to hold his temper, he stood outside the door, his forehead leaning on the screen until he gained some composure. As he entered the mudroom, Mary informed him dinner was nearly ready. She wiped her hands on a kitchen towel.

"We'll be starting the steaks in a few minutes. Did you two have another *disagreement*?"

He knew Mary was asking out of concern for everyone's wellbeing. "Nothing serious. Just a misunderstanding. I'm going to shower before we eat."

His voice was tight with control as he made his way across the kitchen and down the hall.

Adding charcoal as needed, Joe tended the fire on the handcrafted, brick fireplace. Adam came out, freshly showered, carrying a large pitcher filled with iced tea and four glasses. He slumped into the largest lounge chair.

"What was all that grumbling about? Were you two trying to beat each other to the shower?" Joe turned toward the fire but not before Adam noticed the grin.

"No. she was gone when I got back this afternoon. With no note and no response on her cell phone, I got worried. So, I drove around trying to find her. Finally, I went to town to see if anyone had seen her. I guess I lost my temper, or something, maybe we both did," he tried to explain in circumspect.

"I knew where she was. Abe called me when he left this afternoon." Joe came over to sit at the table. "Thanks for your concern."

Adam began to soften around the edges. He felt like a fool. His fear caused him to ignore a simpler solution to finding her. If he had called Joe to find out where she was and if he didn't know, then Joe would get upset. Soon the subject was dropped for more mundane, daily problems. Brooke interrupted their discussion. She sat opposite him.

She sighed and looked off at the horses in the pasture, browsing on the new grasses. "Were you talking about cattle rustling when I came out?"

Before Joe could speak, Adam answered the

question. "Yes. Several heifers have disappeared from Hightower. Might be a good idea if you were careful about going out alone. They have been known to shoot at people, of course, unless you are the rustler, then you don't have anything to worry about."

Was she the rustler? Could she have sent someone ahead to rustle? She said she had no money. She was nearly broke.

Adam gazed into her eyes. She stared back at him with fire. Could she be commandeering the rustling? His heart didn't believe she would be involved, but his brain gave it a possibility. After all, what did he know about the Brooke who had been gone for years? He stared at her, while his heart ached with the thought that she could be part of the thefts.

The meal, though delicious, was conspicuously quiet. After a dessert of devil's food cake, Brooke gave Mary the earrings she purchased. "I wanted to buy you something for all of the things you did for me last week. It's a small token of my appreciation."

"They're beautiful. Thank you, but I really do enjoy spoiling you."

Although Adam regained his congeniality, his dark eyes hardened. Suddenly she realized her oversight. How could she have been so insensitive? Hadn't he bandaged her arm? And after returning from Doc's, he remained in her room all night to care for her. Maybe he was really worried about her all afternoon. Humiliation washed over her knowing she had snubbed him.

Before she could say anything, Adam turned pensive. His dark mood indicated he had other things on his mind besides the socializing at the table.

"I'm going down to the barn to see about the tobiano mare. She's way overdue. This might be a good time to explain to your daughter the changes made since she's been away from home. It's time we get everything out in the open," he suggested. "We can no longer pretend things are the same as when she left."

Puzzled by Adam's outburst, Brooke sat quietly. He called her "daughter" and not "princess." That alone sent a shaft of discomfort through her. He excused himself, sending an almost apologetic glance her way. His long purposeful strides emphasized his agitation as he moved away from them. Her eyes strayed to her father, finding a painful expression on his face as he watched Adam leaving. Mary sipped her iced tea.

Was Adam holding something over her father's head? What situation could have changed since she left? Adam's behavior was rather dominating, insisting on having his own way about things in general. All the employees did whatever he asked. She wanted this settled and to eliminate the look of despair on her father's face.

Brooke's desire for peace and solitude was becoming an obsession. She needed the calm and fortitude of her father. His strength of mind and body was her guiding force as long as she could remember. But he was hiding something.

"Let's go into the office. I will show you the paperwork to make this whole affair clearer to you. Would you like to join us, Mary?" Joe looked to his companion for support.

"I'll finish up the dishes. Besides, this is between you two."

She followed her father inside and further to the office, fearful of what he was going to tell her. The room was warm with its rich cherry panels and carved moldings. At that moment, it held a feeling of doom and darkness.

Joe quietly went to the desk and removed a large file from one of the desk's drawers. He brought the cream-colored folder over to the couch and sat close to her. He placed the file on the coffee table.

"Soon after you were married, I suffered a heart attack. Although the doctors said I would recover, I had to slow down and change my lifestyle. I cannot be as active as I was. He also suggested I find something to occupy my time besides work. That's why I play golf on Fridays with Josh. We both need the diversion and exercise. In the winter months I have to be content with a card game or chess with Josh and others I have known for years—a bunch of worn-out old cowboys." He chuckled, while his eyes held sadness. "I also have to use my gym set for an hour each day. It's set up in my bedroom near the windows."

Brooke knew he was rambling. She listened patiently, sensing an unusual nervousness about him, making him seem vulnerable. "Why haven't you told me this before now?"

Her insides rattled. She hurt. Why hadn't he told her about his illness? Didn't he think she would care? Did it go back to his not approving of Mike Boyle as a son-in-law?

Joe took her hand in his. His voice grew husky. "I didn't want to worry you unnecessarily. Besides, I wanted to let your marriage get off to a good start without stress."

"Well, that makes it more important for me to learn about the ranching operations so I can help you," she put in with much enthusiasm. In her heart she knew it wasn't so simple. Adam's words rang in her head: *Get everything out it the open.*

Joe's voice was sad and heavy. He didn't look at her. "It's not as simple as you helping out. You see, I had to sell off some of the ranch to pay the bills. I've never seen the need to have health insurance. The hospital bills were enormous. And we had a few rough years with severe winters, the drought, and all ... The ranch is no longer mine."

Brooke looked to him for further explanation. He took her hands in his. With a deep breath to fortify him, he explained.

"I sold half of the ranch to Adam, and when I die, he

will inherit the house, as well as the rest of the land, as I have stipulated in my will."

Brooke stood up with outrage. "How did he talk you into this? How could you let him have the ranch?" Screams of frustration lodged in her throat. A war of emotions raged within her. Now she knew why Adam had such an overbearing attitude toward her and the ranch. The Montgomery Ranch was his.

"Oh, Brooke, I am sorry. I've done what I thought was best and right. Please sit down and I'll finish."

Shaking with anger, she returned to her place on the couch. Under his scrutiny she couldn't think. Her heart thumped wildly, fearing the rest of his explanation.

"I've put aside two sections of prime land adjacent to the lake. It's yours as soon as you sign the paperwork. A lifetime of money is sitting in a trust fund for you. There is one stipulation. If you choose not to keep the land, you may only sell it to Adam at a fair market price. The ranch is not to be divided."

Silence permeated the room. She felt like she had lockjaw—the words in her head refused to come out. A trap door had opened under her, dropping her into an endless pit of denial. She couldn't believe her father had done this.

"Why would you give everything to Adam?" Her voice was a pained whisper.

Joe's voice filled with conviction. "Brooke, Adam worked for me for free for two years. Any funds came from his savings. He took nothing from me and saved my ranch. We had a few bad years and losses. Without Adam to help me with the animals, the horses, and the crops, we would have lost everything. I couldn't do the work. I insisted you have the land next to the lake, and you have access to the house until you decide your future."

With tears, he continued. "I didn't want to take anything from you, but I truly didn't think you would return here to live. You only came back to visit twice. And I don't want you to blame Adam. It wasn't his idea. It was mine. He bought his half when I was ill and needed the money. I have the option to buy it back. That was written in this agreement. However, I'm getting old and for everyone involved, I believe this is best."

She wanted to return, she wanted to come home. But being controlled through fear for herself and her father, Mike won. Had she been a coward?

When she didn't comment, Joe continued. "Adam sold out to his father and brother. He now has no holdings in the Hightower Ranches."

"I see." The strain to speak was nearly painful. She held his weary and scarred hands. "Well, we'll have to go out tomorrow and see my property. Maybe I should think about building on it soon. Adam won't want me to intrude for too long."

For a quiet moment they sat, absorbing all that was said. It didn't seem real. It all belonged to Adam. She had been wrong. Even by coming back to the ranch—she still had no place to call home.

Adam. She could feel the difference when she

arrived. Something felt different. Now she knew why. His attitude was due to his pretending for her father's sake.

Brooke's heart took on added weight, like a lead ball hanging in her chest. She was going to have to let it sink in before she made any decisions. Why didn't he ever confide in her? Why had he let this happen?

"Brooke?" Joe wiped a glistening tear from her cheek. "Remember, I still own the house." He placed a comforting arm around her. "I like having my girl around here again. You don't have to build if you don't want to. You can stay here. We love you very much."

"I'll have to consider all of this. I'm sure Adam will want his life back to normal soon." Her voice was a thought spoken out loud. To ease her father's concern, she stood and spoke as normally as she could. "I'll go to the lake tomorrow, choose a place to build."

CHAPTER ELEVEN

*S*leep was impossible. Tossing and turning, the bed became a place of torment. Hugging her pillow, Brooke wearily padded to the loveseat and curled up. The ache in her heart kept her from sleeping. Her head filled with if-only until she could no longer stand their echoes—if only Mike had allowed her to come home more often. If only she had been strong enough to escape her husband. If only her father had thought of her as more than a responsibility.

She felt drained. Her one sanctuary was gone, gone with a quick signature. All of it now belonged to Adam. How she wanted to hate him.

"Well, I won't have to learn about running the ranch to get him out of the guest room—he owns it. Damn. He doesn't own me. I won't stay in this house longer than I have to." she whispered bitterly. "But I will read all the contracts. Maybe he can still be bought out."

Red, puffy eyes stared at her from the bathroom mirror. She let the cool water run slowly to soak a washcloth, not wanting to wake anyone at such an early hour, especially Adam who was right next door.

Streaks of salmon and yellow were coloring the horizon. Being civil to Adam over breakfast or lunch would be nearly impossible. To avoid any confrontation, she would get away early before anyone else was about.

She slipped on a black two-piece bathing suit. A well-worn pair of jeans and a light-blue chambray shirt, tied in the front, covered the suit. Carefully, she placed her gold locket on the dresser, fearing she would lose it if she decided to swim in the lake.

Her lake—at least the land adjacent to that part of the lake—would belong to her. The property would put her between the Montgomery Ranch and Kitty, the Jones Ranch. All she had to do was sign the papers. Spending some time alone would help her decide what to do.

Whys kept haunting her as she dressed. Why hadn't he mentioned his heart attack to her? He never had communicated with her. At times she felt like an ornament, something he could show off as his flesh and blood. Did he feel closer to Adam than his own daughter? Would life as she knew it be different if she had been a boy? Would he have taught her how to ride instead of Abe? Would he have bought her fancy riding clothes instead of Mary?

Brooke stood before the large bedroom window,

gazing at the surrounding land. She had to get away from the house soon. She crept silently down the stairs.

In the kitchen she worked with haste. After packing a chicken sandwich, an apple and an orange, she helped herself to one of the chocolate bars in the pantry. In the mudroom she found an old knapsack and a canteen. She placed her lunch, a brush for her hair, and suntan lotion inside. She filled the canteen with water.

Brooke hurried into the office, and with the key from the desk, she unlocked the cabinet. She took out the small palm-sized pistol she always carried with her on backcountry rides, loaded it, and made sure the safety was on. She placed it inside the front pocket of the pack. She had always carried it with her in case of rattle snakes or aggressive coyotes. Adam had warned her of the problem with rustlers. Or had he made up the rustling to scare her? She relocked the cabinet and put the key back in the desk.

With her cell phone clipped to her belt, she wondered if she'd even have a signal that far out? She grabbed a light jacket and plopped a baseball cap on her head. She stuck a note to the refrigerator with a red cowboy boot magnet. "Gone riding," it said.

Brooke hurried to the large show barn and runs. Looking at the horizon, she frowned, knowing if she didn't stop wasting time someone would be up. With her emotions tangled, she needed no conversation, explanations, or recommendations.

A movement in the trees caught her eye. For an instant, fear gripped her. She gasped, coming to an abrupt stop. But then she recognized him.

"Hank, what are you doing out here at this time of the morning? Wearing a six-shooter?" She wasn't quite sure if he was up to something or not. A cold knot formed in her stomach. Were there more secrets she didn't know?

"Oh, it's my night to be on watch. And what are you doing up so early? You look like a kid, running away from home. Going camping?"

She would not let the tears start up again. No more tears. She was on her own. Make the best of it, her heart advised.

Hank glanced down at his boots, and up at the sky with an accompanying sigh. Finally, his attention came back to rest compassionately on her face. "Want to talk about it? I have a shoulder to lean on." He held out his arms in an invitation. "I'll keep my hands behind my back."

She refused the offer. A bit of anger surfaced. "So, you knew."

"I was here when Adam bought his share of the ranch. Adam is actually my boss."

She shrugged her slight shoulders. "Well, then, we've nothing to talk about."

Hank smiled at her with affection. "Everything will be all right, you'll see. Can I help?"

"I'm going to go up to the lake and think about the

possibilities and whether to stay or sell. I need a horse. I can't ride Buddy. He's still sore. Adam even owns Sly now. Another secret." She hiccoughed away a residual sob. "Is there a good ranch horse close in I can use?"

"I'll be in the sack shortly, so you could use my gelding. I won't be using him today. He's gentle for anyone."

"Are you sure?"

"I know you'll take care of him." Hank squeezed her shoulder with affection.

"Thanks, Hank." Brooke knew he would tell Adam. She had to get away, find herself, and decide what to do. Everything had pretty much been decided without her input. She just had to sign the papers.

He gave her a brotherly smile and held out his hand for her to take. "Come on. I'll help you get on your way. Take the hobbles with you. Then you can put him out to graze somewhere if you decide to rest. And you will only need a hackamore on him for your ride."

Silently they walked to the barn. Hank helped her saddle the palomino with equipment from the new tack room and looped the knapsack and canteen to the saddle horn. After mounting the gelding, she took a few turns around the arena to gauge his gates, waved to Hank, and left for the hills.

The county road led to the overgrown lane to the lake, a much shorter trip than through the fields and rolling hills. She decided to follow the slow-moving streams to the lake and to enjoy the beauty of the land the back trail would give her.

The streams, coming down from the mountain, were crystal-clear fingers, stretching their way down the hills and feeding the valley. Clumps of aspen provided some shade. Potentilla sat at the foot of the aspen, showing off their bright yellow flowers. From time to time, red splotches of Indian paintbrush decorated the water's edge.

For a moment she let the horse graze on the new growth around them. Sitting on a large boulder, she allowed an array of thoughts to pass through her, unable to concentrate on one. Everything jumbled into a tangled mess inside her head. Was she being too sentimental about the ranch and the many generations it had been in her family name? Or was Adam's strong presence in the house her real problem?

She watched her thumb as she ran it over the smooth leather of the loose reins. The familiar, hollow ache settled within her. The deep need to have someone care for her, to want her for herself, pervaded her senses. Her father said he cared, but he gave Adam the ranch. If he had called her when he became ill, she might have been able to come home to help. Maybe. And to get away from an abusive, dominating man. He didn't, and the abuse got progressively worse.

And what about Adam? He could have called her, informed her of her father's health problems. She had never considered Adam a conniver. But he now owned the ranch and the house or would one day. And would he decide later to buy back into the Hightower Ranch, make the Montgomery Ranch part of the corporation? Did he not call her on purpose?

Wearily Brooke gathered up the gelding and mounted, moving him away from the lush undergrowth he was enjoying. The thirty-foot span of slowly moving water eased itself down the mountain slope toward the ranches and the valley pastures. The depth of the stream didn't worry the well-used gelding as he crossed. At times the water splashed up on her boots or trailed lightly at her heels as it eddied around the legs of the animal.

Brooke followed the river to the base of the hill where she would begin her climb. The lake was at the top and the overflow dam created the river whose fingers spread out to nourish everything. This spring was good to the land. Some of the trail was overgrown with aspen saplings. Bluebonnets, larkspur, and daisies dotted the hillside, gathering the morning sun.

She picked her way up the hill. About halfway up she reined in the horse and listened. Not far from her she could hear the splash of water as other animals crossed the stream. She hoped it was grazing animals, but she remembered Adam's warning about rustlers. Concerned for Hank's fine horse rather than her own safety, she urged the animal up the hill.

At the top, the many rock outcroppings could be an advantage. She knew the horse was in excellent condition and probably could outrun the majority. He was winded from the rush up the steep hillside. The horse's sides heaved as he regained his wind, occasionally snorting from the dust. She patted his neck and loosened the reins.

She would have felt rather foolish if she hadn't spotted the two riders. They were obviously following her, picking up her trail at the stream's edge. She watched them searching for her prints. Icy fear twisted around her heart.

Old memories of physical abuse sent momentary panic welling within her, erasing her weariness, and replacing it with frenzied thoughts of protecting herself. Her heart raced, her breathing shallow. She gathered up the sack and placed it in front of her.

An abandoned mine shaft further on would give her shelter. She guided the horse into the opening, backing him into the shadows.

She waited.

Locating her small pistol, she held the weapon inside the sack, hoping she wouldn't have to use it. She could hear the labored breathing of the horses.

Her legs trembled with fear. Trying to decipher her indistinct cues, the palomino shuffled. She brought the horse under control, talking to him in hushed tones, and trying to keep her quaking legs away from his sides.

As they passed her hiding place, she recognized the riders as two of the young ranch hands on the roundup. She couldn't remember if they were from her ranch or another. One of the other horses gave her away as it nickered to the palomino.

One man turned back to the mine shaft, only to find her pointing a pistol at them. He raised his hands slightly. She hoped her quivering insides didn't make her hands shake. Her voice was steady. "Why are you following me?"

The other rider came to a stop next to his partner. Reluctantly, one of the men answered. "Adam sent us to keep an eye on you and get a new head count on the heifers up here. Sorry, ma'am, if we frightened you. Adam would have really been piss...mad if we lost you."

The second man seemed honest and even a bit embarrassed. "We were only supposed to keep you in sight, not have contact with you—unless you were in trouble of some sort."

She rested her hands on the backpack, holding the gun. "Well, you've completed your assignment and found me. Now go back and tell Mr. Tower if I need a babysitter, he should do the work himself. He doesn't need to waste the time of the employees."

The men tipped their hats and turned their horses toward the lake, presumably to take the road to the upper pastures to check the cattle. "Damn." Brooke heard one mutter, "Adam's gonna be pissed. You want to call him?"

"Nope." The cowboy squeezed his horse into a trot.

Brooke was assailed by a terrible feeling of bitterness. Her misery was so acute it hurt to swallow. Taking a big breath for fortitude, she patted the gelding's neck and ran her shaky fingers through his mane. She hated situations where she felt out of control. Now more determined than ever, she would set out to find a life for herself on her terms. She would have to sign the papers and move out of the family home.

She guided the gelding outside the shaft. She kept the men in sight until they moved around the lake and farther to the road. Making the same trip up the slight rise, she had a full view of the lake and the road.

Behind her, a small herd of cows grazed in the open pastures. She could see Kitty's house and barns about a mile away. Satisfied that she was alone, she rode down to circle the lake and check for tracks. On her way she chased away a few cattle.

At the natural beach a few hundred feet from the dirt road, she dismounted. She unsaddled the palomino. She took off the headstall but left the spare halter on. With hobbles on his front legs to keep him nearby, he immediately began to graze on the fine, spring grasses.

An old fallen tree trunk with branches served as her clothes hanger. She smoothed on suntan lotion and relaxed on a huge boulder in the now warm sun. This was her favorite spot when she was a teenager. The rock was large enough for her and her friends to lie side by side and sunbathe. She and Kitty, Bess, and others would pack a lunch and ride their horses from the ranch to the lake. After smearing on lotion, they sunbathed on large beach towels. They would giggle about boys, how to style their hair, or what to wear to the Saturday night dance. She smiled with the memories.

Relaxation, however, was evasive. Her fingers pierced and stripped the skin from the orange, working the peel as though she was exorcising some demon from the pulp. By the time she was finished she was covered in sticky juice. She climbed off the warm rock and caught a glimpse of the men riding back to the ranch via the dirt road. Without them to worry about, she decided a swim would be refreshing.

A wall of rock cradled the far side of the lake. She grasped a jutting crag to rest and float in the deep, clear water. She gazed up at the forested hills before her. At one time the area swarmed with over two-hundred hopeful miners, looking for one special vein. Silver had been taken from the mountains around her. Those endeavors were over a century ago. Now barely a sign of tracings from the abandoned tunnels was evident.

After a brief rest, she started back to the beach, forcing water away from her as she had in college competitions. The regular strokes of her arms and legs were soothing, the cool water sliding across her body. However, her injured arm felt weak from use, and she slowed.

She left the lake and headed for the large rock and her towel. A gun shot echoed behind her on the hill above, not too far away. Unease knotted within her as she looked around for any sign of the shooter. She recognized the sound. Her terror heightened when a herd of cows came at her at a fear-filled run. Rushing to the rock, she climbed quickly, the animals missing her by inches. Hank's horse bucked at the rushing cows until they settled nearby in a grassy field.

Brooke grabbed her backpack and slid off the far side of the rock. Taking the small gun from the front pocket, she scanned the far side of the lake and the hills. A small glint of metal caught her eye. She fired toward the open area of rock above the lake as a warning, knowing the bullet wouldn't even travel to the spot. The shooter might not know what weapon she had but would hear the shot. Her body shook with the same feelings of terror she felt with Mike. Only this terror was worse—a hidden threat she could not identify. Was Kitty behind it? Adam?

She sat against the large rock and tried to ease the dull ache of foreboding. She peeked around its edges on occasion to look for any sign of the intruder. Time lessened her acute panic. Intense fear still rioted within her. With a deep fortifying breath, Brooke left the security of the rock and walked quickly to the branch holding her clothes, constantly scanning the area for any movement.

Adam rose early with Hank's phone call. The last thing he wanted to do was confront her until she had time to contemplate the truth. He had been masking his inner turmoil from his employees and probably himself. Secrets. Why did Joe want him to keep such a large change from his only daughter? Joe did love her, but he never connected her to the ranch, never let her in to his innermost thoughts. Never told her he had heart troubles. Now he was the heavy, the bad guy in all of this, and he hated it. He had no idea how to mend these broken fences.

He sent a couple of ranch hands to keep an eye on her while they tallied the cows in the upper pasture. Then he exercised some young halter horses to ready them for an upcoming show. Those two ranch hands now stood with doleful expressions in front of him.

"What are you two doing here? You're supposed to be watching Brooke." Adam handed the lead line to one of his young trainees to bathe and rub down the tired colt. He held the reins to his working gelding, hands on his hips, waiting for an answer.

"She saw us when we crossed the river." The man hesitated. He raised his eyes to his boss who stood stoically nearby.

"Well?"

The cowboy dismounted, and kicking a small stone, he looked away nervously. "She said, if you thought she needed a babysitter, you should do it yourself, and not take us from our work—or something like that. I can't quite remember exactly what she said—she had a gun."

Adam said nothing. He could tell the men thought he would be angry. He tried to ease their concern. "So, she had a gun? Scare you, did she?" He smiled at them. "You two can go help Abe and the others doctor and vaccinate cattle."

Adam mounted his saddled horse and headed out the drive at a strong trot. Although a truck would be faster, finding her in the hills could be a problem if she didn't want him around. And he did want to find her. This emotion was new to him, a protective kind of anger. He wanted her safe. He wanted no more secrets between them.

On his ride to the lake, he grew pensive. Uncertainty knotted inside his chest. He knew the sale would strike a heavy blow. He could see Brooke feeling victimized. He often urged Joe to tell her, but he wouldn't, kept putting it off. She now knew he kept secrets, lied for her father, pretending to work at a ranch she assumed would belong to her. He wouldn't blame her if she hated him at this point. But he would never stop loving her.

Adam dismounted close to Brooke. Expecting her to rage at him, he was unprepared for the gun pointed at him. This was no false front. Holding the gun, her small, fine-boned hands trembled. Golden locks, wet and stringy framed her face and neck. She glared at him.

He put his hands up in a gesture of surrender.

"Well, do you have any more tricks up your sleeve?" Brooke stammered.

He kept his voice low and soothing as though he was talking to a panicked colt. "I sent my men to protect you. They were not supposed to have any contact with you unless it was necessary. You sure made them nervous."

"So, then who sent the cattle to run me down?"

"I heard the shots—I don't know. I thought maybe you were shooting at something. A snake, a coyote?" He stared at the far side of the lake and around the hills for a hint of what might have happened. He slowly stepped toward her, watching her all the while.

"The reason I came up here myself was to have a chance to talk with you, straighten things out some. I don't blame you for your anger. If I were you, I'd probably be as hurt. I wanted him to tell you from the start. He wouldn't. We need to get things out in the open. Please?"

"Do you always talk with a rifle?"

"I don't know what you're talking about." Adam's eyes never left hers.

"If it wasn't you stampeding the cows, then who was it?"

Who would be stampeding cows? Kitty? How would she know Brooke was up there? Maybe he had a traitor who kept Kitty informed. That thought angered him and brought a new level of fear to the surface.

"I'm going to let go of my horse so he can get over by the palomino. If you decide to shoot me, I don't want an innocent animal to be in the way." He removed the headstall and bit from the horse and released him to join the palomino with a resounding whack on his rump.

Adam turned quickly and grabbed her wrist, shaking the gun free. With his other arm, he pulled her against his broad chest, holding her easily. Heart-rending sobs wracked her body. He continued to hold her with a natural tenderness, his one arm around her waist, the other supporting her head. Finally, her head rested quietly on his chest.

His hand glided over her silken shoulders, nearly covering her narrow back. And when his fingers slipped beneath her suit, he quickly brought them to rest. His lips rested on the top of her head. Then taking her face in both hands, he kissed her lips tenderly.

Brooke didn't pull away, didn't reject his affection. His emotions whirled and skidded. His heart thundered. The feel of her, the smell of her was intoxicating. He wanted to tell her how much he loved her, had always loved her. Now, surely, she would not believe him.

She stepped away from his warmth. She wouldn't look at him. "Someone tried to run me over with the cows."

"I believe you, if you say that's what happened. I heard the shots. I never thought they were panicking this small herd." He sighed with exasperation. "Maybe it was someone trying to steal more cows. Maybe you stopped them." He caressed the side of her face and thumbed away a lingering tear.

She moved away from him and dressed. Something was obviously tormenting her. Was she trying to hide something from the family, he mused? For Joe's sake he hoped the cattle rustling and her return were purely coincidental. Was she up there to see about rustling part of the herd? If Brooke were part of the rustling, the truth would kill Joe. The man's heart would not be able to stand the strain, and neither would his own.

Adam didn't speak while she dressed. The way her tight, bottom slipped into her jeans did nothing for his overwrought emotions. He wanted her to stay. He wanted her with him forever. Her life was not as rosy as Joe was told. The death of her undeserving husband was a relief, knowing from an investigator that he was a control freak.

If he were to tell her how he felt, would she assume his feelings were a ploy. Would she assume it was just a way of getting more of what she felt should have been hers? He sighed.

"When you're ready to go back home, I'll ride along with you. We'll search the hillside together. Maybe we can see what spooked the cows."

"You mean back to your house?"

He paused a moment. "No, I mean our house." She was so quick to end the respite in their relationship. It angered him.

She sat at the base of the rock and pulled on her boots. "I'd like to sit here a while. There's a sandwich in the bag. You can have it if you want. Unless you need to get back."

He went over to her things and took out the lunch. "Thanks. I am a bit hungry. We'll have to get back soon, though. Joe said Red would be coming with your new dog. He should be here this afternoon." While he ate, he searched the hills for any sign of an intruder.

They adjusted the saddles and bridles and mounted.

Silence rode with them until they were across the lake in the area where Brooke thought she saw a glint of something metal. They found nothing but cow and horseshoe prints that could have been from his ranch hands and the palomino. Returning to the road, they continued home at a walk, the steady beat of the horses' hooves, lulling them into quiet contemplation.

Close to the house, Adam grabbed the reins to the palomino and gently pulled her horse to a halt next to his. "If you take the time to read the contracts, you'll find I have not taken advantage of Joe—or you. He's had every opportunity to buy me out, but he hasn't. I'm not the ogre you seem to think I am. You know, we did not grow up poor, dirt farmers all our lives. We both enjoyed the bounty of living and working here. I don't feel bad about the sale. It was the right thing to do at the time. I never wanted to keep it a secret. Joe did."

He turned his horse, so they faced each other. His hand rested on her arm lightly. "Look, I want you to stay. You belong here as I do. We could find a way to run the ranch together. Or if you find that unworkable and you want to set up your own place at the lake, I'll give you as much of my time as I can. You are free to stay at the house as long as you wish."

Or forever, his thoughts streamed. He felt a terrible ache inside. Would she ever trust him again? He wanted to hold her, love her, and make her laugh once again. He wanted to make those wary eyes glisten with happiness, make her mouth turn up in a bright smile.

Brooke stared at him. "Thank you. I'll try to decide as soon as possible."

They rode in silence. The slight reprieve at the lake had dwindled into the same awkward relationship. At the barn they unsaddled their horses and put the saddles and bridles in the tack room. Brooke took extra care to brush and bathe Hank's beautiful animal and to be sure he had not suffered an injury from the interlude with the cows. She had him cleaned up and shining like a gold coin when she returned him to his stall. She found a bag of fresh carrots and offered him a few. Reluctant to return to the house, she took her time, glancing at the rest of the horses in the barn and offering each a carrot.

Adam preceded her to the house. On the patio, they were having lunch.

"Would you join us for a glass of tea or a bite to eat?" Joe asked tentatively.

To refuse would only make things worse, she thought. She reluctantly sat across from Adam. "Yes, I am a bit thirsty. Iced tea sounds fine."

"Hank's palomino is a fine animal. Did he work out all right for you?" Joe asked.

"Yes," Brooke replied. "Hank's horse was the best part of my morning."

"What do you mean?" Joe's question held a note of concern and sadness. He worked on his salad while he waited for her to reply.

A boot prodded her shin. She glanced at Adam's glaring face. "Excuse me. I'm going to clean up. I'll be right down."

After showering and putting on cut-offs and a red tee shirt, she returned to find everyone gone except for Mary, who was outside on the patio, knitting a pink baby hat. She sat down and poured a glass of tea.

"Are you angry with your father?" Mary looked up from her knitting.

"That he didn't tell me sooner, yes. I'm so tired of everything, including Adam."

"Adam is a good, kind man." Mary's needles clicked away rhythmically.

"Well, he and I don't see eye to eye. He still treats me like I'm ten years old."

With a smile and a twinkle in her eyes, Mary paused. "When he looks at you, he does not see the child you were but a beautiful woman."

She didn't respond. She didn't trust herself to be rational. Adam wasn't the boy she grew up with either. Now he was a potent, powerful man whose kiss sang in her veins.

"I came back here to get my life together, only it seems to be falling further apart. I almost feel like an outsider now, a guest."

"The world is always changing. We can only look for the good in life and make it better. Adam's contract on the ranch let your dad stay here. He may have had to sell —that would have destroyed him. And Adam has the ability to make this place grow and prosper, and he has. So don't look at the change as bad, just different."

Mary always put positive points on things negative. And she was probably right about the ranch. At least they could all still live together, at least for a while. She dozed off with those thoughts in mind.

CHAPTER TWELVE

*M*ary gently prodded her. "Brooke? Red arrived with your dog."

"Oh, I must have fallen asleep. I guess I'm not very good company." She stretched and yawned. A smile turned into an amused chuckle when she saw the dog Red had on a leash. With bubbling excitement, she hurried across the lawn toward them.

"Hello, Brooke. You sure have grown up since the last time I saw you."

She smiled with a touch of embarrassment. "No more broken bones, I hope."

"No, not since I left here. Meet your new guardian. His name is Claude." Red handed her the leash. "Say hello, Claude."

The dog whined softly and extended his right front paw. Brooke accepted his offer of a handshake with a chuckle of delight.

"Now we have to teach you how to control him. Once he knows you are his, he will protect you from or warn you of any danger. All you have to do is give the correct word."

He spent a few hours, instructing her and visiting with Joe. She found it heartening that her father would buy her a black standard poodle. His cut was short and impeccably trimmed, and his white bow tie gave him a classy butler look.

Later in the afternoon, Adam came into the house. A bluish lump on his forehead required an ice pack. His banging around in the freezer aroused Claude's interest. Growling a warning, the dog left Brooke in the den and charged into the kitchen. He dared Adam to leave the area near the refrigerator.

"Brooke." His voice bellowed. "What the hell is that?"

Adam's loud voice did nothing to lessen the dog's threat. Claude bared his teeth and took bouncing hops in his direction. Laughing, she called the dog off. She located a cold pack, placed it in a small towel, and gave it to him. He shook his head and rolled his eyes. He took the ice. With a gentle hand on the back of her head, he placed a soft kiss on her forehead, and left for the barn. He was as erratic as a summer storm. Would they ever be able to work the ranch together?

. . .

Soft cotton nuzzled her neck as she woke to a sunny, glorious day. As though to further encourage her to leave her bed, Claude pulled at her arm with his groomed paw and whined.

"I bet you need to go out. You are such a handsome guy." She rubbed his soft head with affection. Brooke slipped on a pink robe over the matching gown and opened the door. Claude trotted down the thick, green carpet ahead of her and started down the stairs. As she approached the stairs, Adam's door opened.

"I need to talk to you now." Before she could issue a complaint, he pulled her into his room and shut the door.

"What are you doing?" she demanded. He held her wrist and leaned on the door to prevent her escape.

Having his mistress stolen from him, Claude whined and scratched, becoming more and more agitated at her disappearance.

"I don't want you to tell your father about yesterday." Adam spoke with real concern. "Knowing would cause him too much anxiety. His heart is not strong enough to be constantly worrying. He's been taking his nitro pills more often. Besides, Abe searched around and found casings from a rifle up on the hill. So, you were right, someone did spook the herd. You should probably stay around here for a while."

She struggled to get free and finally slipped out of his hold. Fear welled up within her. Would the next time be for real? How could she protect herself?

"Yes, fine. I won't mention it. Besides, Claude will

have everyone up with his complaining." Her voice was flippant to hide her nervousness, and she didn't want her father to find her in this compromising situation.

Adam was not immune to her sleepy look. He could ask for nothing more than to keep her there. The flawless, creamy skin lured his eyes to take a longer look. Full breasts covered in a thin cotton robe tempted his touch.

"Has Kitty been unavailable?" she taunted, stunning him with the outburst.

Angered by his own weakness for her, Adam pulled her against him, wrapping his arms about her slight frame. He held her in a tender embrace momentarily before he moved his head to look down at her.

"I don't want you hurt again," he grumbled, holding raw emotion in check. If something dire happened to her now, now that she was back, he didn't think his heart could bear it.

She didn't fight him. Soon her hands pushed lightly against him in rejection.

He released her. She didn't rush away from him. Her blue eyes scanned his face. She licked her lips nervously. "I have to let the dog out. He'll wake up Dad."

As she reached for the doorknob, he covered her hand with his. "Are you going to keep me here all morning?" she asked softly.

His gaze was as soft as a caress. "If it would keep you safe."

He opened the door and smiled. Claude wiggled and nudged her hand with relief.

But Joe came padding down the hall in his moose-hide slippers, worn jeans and a tee shirt. His gray hair pointed out in different directions. He stopped for lack of words and ran a nervous hand through his wayward locks. "I…ah…thought there might be a problem. Claude was whining and scratching."

Adam's voice behind her was almost believable. "I wanted to see if the dog has adjusted to Brooke. So, as she passed my room, I pulled her in here and closed the door. Seems he settled in fine. Now I'll have to refinish the molding." He patted the dog's head.

"I was going to let him out. He must be an early riser," she explained.

Joe cleared his throat, "I'll let the dog out for you if you want to go back to bed. It's still very early. I'll feed him, too.

"Thanks. I'll do that." She patted her father on the shoulder lovingly. Adam's eyes followed her. She left the door open a bit for Claude.

The men continued down the stairs to the kitchen. Neither spoke. Adam knew what Joe was thinking. He could read those thoughts in the man's body language. If they lived a hundred years ago, he would have a shotgun in his backbone and a preacher saying the vows by noon.

Joe let the dog out while Adam turned on the Keurig. They both moved around in silence as they prepared their breakfasts of cold cereal and cinnamon rolls.

Joe broke the silence. "I'm going to have Hank practice roping on Contender today and for the rest of the week. I think we can have a good round on him at your father's barbeque. Then we can see if he's ready to go on to the regular shows. He's a young horse, has agility and the conformation for an all-around horse. I'd like to consider not selling him, keeping him here as a stud if he can compete and if his foals this year are quality. Will Steve be back by then?"

"I don't know for sure. Dad has baby brother out looking in Texas for a new bull for their herd. I have some young hands helping me with the younger colts, so they won't be out with the men as usual. I gave them a radio in case they need help or need to ask about something. The calls will come in here on the kitchen monitor."

"Sounds fine to me. Have you noticed how Brooke has been working with the foals this past week? She should build on the land I gave her, raise some of her own. She always did like to help with the new babies." Joe became misty-eyed as he reflected on his daughter. "Next week is her birthday. Maybe I'll give her one she can develop into an all-around champion."

Adam didn't say anything right away. He appeared to be pondering the idea as he refilled their mugs. "I may have a solution, but I'll have to think it over first. You really feel guilty about the ranch and selling to me, don't you?"

"No." was Joe's immediate answer. His gray head came

up swiftly from his cereal. "No, I don't feel one bit guilty about the ranch. I have given her everything she has ever wanted. I even let her marry that misfit from California. I've worked too long and too hard to give this land to someone who loves this place for sentimental reasons."

Joe rose from the table and placed his dishes in the sink. With a troubled look on his face, he continued, "Brooke doesn't have the discipline to run a ranch this size, and she is too gullible. She can be talked into anything. Look what she married. She would only lose the ranch and then feel horrible."

"You never gave her the opportunity to be your partner. You always kept her separate, like the Montgomery princess locked up in the tower."

Joe paused, contemplating what was said. "I know. But I feel as close to you as I would my own son, if I had one. I know you have the same dreams and drive I had when I was your age. You've never married. Why don't you marry that daughter of mine?" Joe hurried before Adam could swallow and reply. "She needs you. I guess I was too sentimental about her mother, spoiled her."

"You still are spoiling her. You should have taken a paddle to her bottom at least once in her life. Maybe then she wouldn't have been such a brat." His reply came with a large grin, letting Joe off the hook.

Joe came back to sit at the table, coffee in hand. "Well, she wasn't too bad."

"Let's drop me for a while. Let's talk about you.

Have you told Brooke you and Mary have been sleeping partners for years now? Why don't you make an honest woman out of her?" He narrowed his eyes as he grinned at his partner.

"I've seriously thought about it. Maybe I will. What if she doesn't want to get married to some old man like me?" Joe grinned sheepishly.

"Don't go getting gloomy on me. Marriage won't be painful."

Joe put a crooked smile on his face and gazed out the window. "I've been living in this shell of memories far too long. Mary has been so good to all of us."

Adam rose and sauntered to the sink. He rinsed out a sponge and brought it back to the table with a kitchen towel. He wiped off his place and dried it. Far too long, he mused. He'd been living with hope. Their lives had become so complicated now. Would Brooke ever believe he truly loved her? "I'm going down to the barn. What did you want Abe to do today?"

"Yes, the shavings have to be replaced in the stalls in the foaling barn. And Buddy could be put out back in his own stall with the other ranch horses."

Adam was slipping on his boots in the mudroom when Mary padded into the kitchen. "Good morning, you two. Did you have breakfast, Adam?" Mary's face glowed with a smile. Her hair was pulled back and fastened with silver combs. She wore a blue running suit for her morning jog.

Adam let Claude in, and he went right for his bowl of food.

"Good morning, Mary." He threw on his tan canvas jacket. With deviltry shining in his eyes, he grinned. "Mary, Joe has something he wants to ask you."

Joe only needed a slight push to get him going, and this morning was as good as any. The thoughts of his own life penetrated his soul. He was his own man and didn't lean on anyone for support. But he had an empty void that could only be filled with the warmth of a good woman. He envied Joe and Mary and their comfortable relationship.

Mary made a cup of tea and sat down adjacent to Joe at the table. "What did you have to ask me? Adam seems a little strange this morning."

Joe took her hand in both of his and looked at her smiling face. "My dear, he thinks we should get married. I think he's right. Will you marry this old coot?"

"Oh, Joe, you old fool, of course I'll marry you." She rose and wrapped her arms around him and kissed his balding spot.

"Good." He laughed. "That was easier than I thought it would be. We'll go to town and get a license. How about it?"

"You'd better go before he loses his nerve," Adam called from the mudroom.

"I thought you left," Joe grumbled.

"I didn't want you to let this opportunity slip by."

Mary became pensive. "How do you think Brooke will take it?"

Adam wandered into the kitchen. "She loves you both dearly."

"Can't think of anyone I'd rather share the future with more than you," Joe murmured.

"I feel the same way." Mary smiled lovingly.

"Adam, this came up so sudden—thanks to you—I don't have a ring. You are going to have to handle things today while I take Mary into Laramie to buy one. And we'll go to the travel agency to plan a honeymoon. Where would you like to go?"

Adam interrupted his stream of thought. "Why don't you go until you get tired, visit people you want to see? Make the honeymoon my gift."

"I feel like a child at Christmas," Mary giggled. "Do you want to wait and tell Brooke when she gets up, or shall I?"

"You two lovebirds get going with your plans before he gets cold feet. I'll tell her when she gets up," Adam offered, before he realized the task before him.

Brooke sauntered into the kitchen with Claude at her heels. Adam sat nonchalantly at the table, slouched in his chair, a stocking foot braced on the empty chair next to him. He sipped from a large mug decorated with horses. Claude came over to him for a scratch behind the ear.

She glanced at him on and off as she prepared her

own breakfast of toast and homemade jam. "I would have thought you would be down working the horses." She fixed a cup of coffee and took a sip while she waited for her toast.

"I was." He wasn't sure how she was going to take the news. Maybe, he had taken on more than he should have. Would she feel he had again interceded, chipped away one more item in her life? He watched her as she prepared her breakfast. She resembled a sprite in her light blue caftan, her blonde hair flowing around her like golden silk. His gruffness was a poor cover for the surge of emotions she set off within him. He could still feel the warmth of her body.

He walked over to her and leaned his arms on the counter. She slathered a good coating of strawberry jam on her toast. "Mary's jam is so good. Isn't it?"

"Yes, it is. Do you have enough? Maybe you should dunk the toast." He smiled at her.

"It's a thought."

For a moment they stood, awkwardly, silently. Finally, he broke the stillness. "I have something to tell you."

"What might that be? Some other dark secret you don't want my father to find out about?" she taunted.

"No, actually, the information comes from Joe."

She bit into the toast, licking the excess jam from her lips. "So, what's the message?"

"He and Mary went into the city to find a wedding ring. They're getting married late Friday afternoon."

When she didn't immediately speak, he began to worry. "They only decided this morning over coffee and took off like a couple of kids."

When she did respond he worried, not knowing what she was thinking. "Friday." she gasped. She began to grin, breaking into hysterical laughter. "Mary and Dad? Oh, how wonderful." Without warning she threw her arms around him, giggling like a schoolgirl.

Instinctively, his arms came around to hold her. The feel of her against him sent a surge of heat. Involuntarily he grasped her waist and set her aside, denying the invisible web of attraction she spun. He moved away from her and poured a cup of fresh coffee to give him the space he needed. For a moment, a tense silence enveloped them.

Brooke began to smile. "You have jam on your cheek." She laughed and reached up to wipe the red glob away.

He smiled, then he moved over to the table and sat down, avoiding the torture of wanting to hold her and being so close he could smell her soft perfume. "I wasn't sure you would be happy about the wedding."

"Are you kidding? I've wanted them to get married for years. Now Mary will be my real mother— stepmother—and will legally be part of the family."

"After all that has happened, I thought you might feel a bit rejected by the idea."

"Adam, you don't know me at all. About the ranch— yes, I'm angry. I'll never own it, never inherit it. My children, if I have any, will never run through these halls. But about Dad and Mary—I can only wish them happiness. I wish they had told me themselves."

She took her coffee and toast and went upstairs, her black shadow trotting behind her.

Stung by the probable truth in her words, Adam left the house and pushed himself the rest of the day to keep his thoughts away from her. How would they ever spend the next few weeks alone in the same house?

CHAPTER THIRTEEN

The morning of the wedding dawned with a bright sun and a cloudless sky. Birds sang merrily as if they knew this was a special day. Trees rustled gently in the breeze, while the abundant flower arrangements delivered a pleasant bouquet. The caterers would soon arrive to set up the reception on the lawn.

Brooke awoke before the others and dressed in yoga pants and a worn tee shirt. She put on her running shoes and slipped her long hair through the back of a baseball cap. The horses with outside runs nickered to her, as she took a brisk jog around the barns and pastures. Back at the house, she rested in one of the lounge chairs on the patio and enjoyed the warmth of the sun.

"A rather doleful face for such a bright morning," Adam's deep voice broke the quiet.

Turning in her seat, she turned to the voice, coming from the bushes near the drive. "Doleful? Actually, I was thinking how beautiful the day was going to be, perfect for a wedding."

Adam sauntered over to the table and sat down across from her. He stretched his long legs as he settled in the chair. He was dressed in jeans, moccasins, and a navy-blue rugby shirt, opened at the neck. He fiddled with a toothpick.

"Are you still happy about the wedding?" Dark eyes stared into hers.

"I'm ecstatic about it. Why would I feel any different?' She didn't want to argue with him this early, particularly this morning. She hated the way he insinuated things about her, seeming to enjoy arguing with her.

"I don't know. Trouble has been following you." His voice was almost a whisper as though he were talking to himself.

"Maybe you're the trouble, maybe you're trying to scare me off, get more of the land. After all I can only sell it to you," she replied in the same whispery voice as his. She knew in her heart he would never hurt her. She'd been through hell while married to Mike. Would she ever trust any man? His dark eyes never left hers.

"If I were trying to chase you away, you wouldn't still be here." He studied her for a moment. The toothpick stilled in his fingers.

She looked back, momentarily rebuffed. Her heart thumped in her throat. He owned everything she reflected with bitterness. Yes, he could drive her away. But would he?

"Well, then, I guess I'd better take a look at those papers I need to sign."

Dark eyes caught and held hers. "You'll be a lovely maid-of-honor. Mary made a good choice."

Brooke could feel the sexual magnetism that drew other women. She knew he was arrogant, pushy, demanding. Damn, every time his eyes met hers, her heart turned over in an unwelcome response. He made no attempt to hide the fact he was watching her, waiting for a reaction. She concentrated on his open shirt front. "Thank you."

Joe and Mary came outside, interrupting their word play. Joe's voice rang with happiness. "I'm starved. Let's go."

They all rode in the Suburban, Adam and Brooke sat in the back close to their own doors. The table was ready for them at the hotel, and many good wishes came to Joe and Mary.

"Do you think you can hold down the fort while Mary and I are gone?" Joe asked as he forked his abundant breakfast into his mouth.

"Sure. Why not?" Adam buttered his biscuit and spooned marmalade over it.

"Well, the cold vibrations coming from you both, I thought I might have to hire a referee to stay at the house."

"We'll be fine. Won't we, Brooke?" He reached over and covered her hand with his in a show of camaraderie.

She was conscious of his warm flesh and the index finger moving across the back of her hand. The answer to his touch was a rapid thud of her pulse. She looked up and found his eyes sparkling with an indefinable emotion. Resisting the need to snatch her hand away from his touch, she smiled. "Yes, we'll get along fine."

But would they? Brooke had always felt comfortable in Adam's presence. He made her feel safe, always believing things would work out. Years have a way of changing a person. She changed. He must have, too. And even trying to reason out how the ranch now belonged to him, she knew her physical reaction to him had nothing to do with reason.

The ceremony was short and traditional. Mary wore a cream-colored lace dress with a matching jacket. Brooke's dress was a simple silk shift in pale blue. Her father and Adam wore black tuxedoes. The unusual formality for this part of the country came from Mary who wanted the figurine-on-the-wedding-cake effect. She'd never been married. She wanted her dream of a story-book wedding.

A smorgasbord of taste tempting foods and an open bar were handled by Mack and his staff from the hotel. The guests visited and danced to a variety of old and new favorites, most with a country flavor.

Steve Tower greeted Brooke with a giant bear hug

and swung her around with a joyful laugh. "How long have you been home?"

Adam's younger brother was three years older than her. He had the height of Adam and the same luxurious, wavy hair. However, his eyes twinkled with laughter, unlike Adam's.

"Over a month. Didn't you know? I would have thought your father would have mentioned it if Adam hadn't."

"I just got back from a long business trip. I cut short my trip to attend this wedding and our barbeque and rodeo. I've been visiting with friends and relatives and trying to find some good breeding bulls. Actually," he chuckled, "I've been doing more playing than working, but don't tell my father. He frowns on fun."

Sounds like Adam, she thought. "What happened to the career naval officer?'

"Well, I decided I liked the rolling gate of a good horse better than the roll of the sea and bucking ships. And my painting keeps me pretty busy." He stared at her for a quiet moment. "I heard you lost your husband. I'm sorry for you."

"Well, it wasn't a love-fest marriage. It does feel good to be home." She didn't know how much had been discussed through her father, and she didn't want to discuss the man and her sham of a marriage.

Steve changed the subject and amused her with anecdotes. This was a different Tower than the father and older brother. Both were so serious about life, but Steve was able to put work aside. Brooke was obligated to dance with various neighbors and friends of the family, separating her from Steve. Whenever she glanced back in his direction, he was watching her.

"Before anyone can steal you away again, let's go get a drink and find a quiet place to sit. We have a lot of reminiscing to do." Steve led her to the bar and then to a table on the far side of the yard near a group of shade trees.

She took a sip of wine and relaxed. "Are you prepared for tomorrow's contests?"

"I can't wait. I've had one of our trainers working Comanche while I've been away, so he'll be fresh. Are you going to compete?" His well-groomed hand reached out to touch hers in a warm caress.

"No. I haven't had the time to practice. I haven't thought about it much." She moved her small, delicate fingers from under his and guided a loose hair around her ear. She felt uncomfortable with the intimate contact. She always thought of Steve as a friend, playmate, not anything romantic. And maybe he wasn't being romantic, just familiar with an old friend.

Steve's eyes crinkled in the corners to accompany a roguish smile. "Good. Maybe I can win something this year besides second place." He laughed. "We really had a lot of fun when we were kids. Remember sledding down the hill behind my father's house? How many times did we walk up that hill, frozen to the bones? And riding out to Hightower Mountain, having picnics and pretending to be knights and ladies?"

"And all the fun we had at the lake swimming, snorkeling, doing dive bombs off the large boulders in the middle." She smiled and looked off in the distance with a chuckle. Her memory bubbled up with fond memories. "Yes. Desiree came with us when her aunt would let her get away from chores."

Steve ignored her inquiry about Desiree. They were so close then. What had happened to her?

He pointed at Adam who stood with another rancher across the lawn. "Do you remember when we were having a water fight with buckets, and Adam walked between us. Boy was he mad—all dressed up for a date."

She laughed until tears streamed down her face. "Poor Adam. He was always assigned to watch over us. Haul our butts to the 4-H rodeos, Little Britches, baby-sit us when our dads were away at conventions."

"Yea, poor Adam always had a girl in his pickup to keep him company. Kitty was the usual item," Steve recalled.

"We really did have a great childhood." She remembered what Adam had said on their ride back to the house. Yes, they did have a great place to spread their wings. She grew curious and decided to just ask. "Did you ever hear from Desiree? You two were so close."

"No." He frowned and looked off to the open pastures. "She never wrote or called. Her aunt said she moved to New York, lived with a photographer. The end.

Then her aunt and uncle moved to Colorado with Chip and Raven."

Brooke ended that conversation because there seemed to be an open wound still festering. "Your brother seems to have found quite a following," she commented. She noticed Adam with two women. The women were flirting, open invitations for sex, including Kitty who was draped around him.

"Yes, although, Kitty seems to be getting her share of his time. She's been chasing him since they were kids, forever envisioning herself as Mrs. Adam Tower. How are you getting along with him, living here and all?" He shifted in his chair and rested his arms on the table.

What could she say about the man who now owned her family's ranch? What could she say to his brother? "Adam and I tolerate each other. I'm not sure how long I will continue to live here. I may build on my property soon."

Steve nodded his head as if to agree with her. "He is very loyal to your father and to the running of this ranch now. But he's always felt protective of you, like a little sister. I suppose he hasn't changed."

"I don't know about little sister." Was Adam concerned about her welfare? Was that why he was always checking up on her? Selecting horses for her to ride? Having her trailed? Did he really care about her, or did he really believe she had some nefarious reason for coming home?

"Are you sure you're not mistaking his concern for

your father and the ranch for his grumpy behavior? He is very competitive, even with me and our horses." Steve tried to alleviate the concern on her face. "Speak of the devil, he's found us."

Adam interrupted their temporary seclusion. Nonchalantly, he guided his long frame into the barrel-styled, wrought-iron chair, stretching his legs before him. He'd removed his tuxedo jacket, and his sleeves were rolled up. Three studs from his neck down were missing.

"When did you get in?" He sipped from his glass of Scotch.

"Last night. How come no one told me our girl was home?" Steve's voice was casual. A touch of irritation rumbled just under the surface.

Adam gave her a cursory glance. He turned to Steve. "I guess it never came up."

Idle chatter about business and travel continued for a time between the two men. Brooke was eliminated from the discussion. When they exhausted their topics of interest, Adam stood. Brooke expected him to leave. Instead, he took her hand and eased her out of her seat.

Adam looked at Steve with a bemused glint. "You don't mind if I have a dance with our pretty matron-of-honor, do you?"

His hand was firm as he held hers, and when they danced, he held her close. She felt the length of his powerful body against her own. His chin rested near her temple, his warm breath in her hair. The scent of his expensive after shave mingled with the trail of Scotch on his breath. He was as accomplished on the dance floor as he was in the saddle, and he guided her around with grace. On the outside of the rectangle, he paused. They moved to the music while almost standing still.

Adam lessened his grip on her and gazed down into her face. He covered her right hand in his and held it on his chest. She couldn't read his face. Whatever he had on his mind was directly affected by the events of the day. His eyes were not sharp and arrogant but tempered to a soft, velvet brown.

"You look very lovely. I like your hair down and wavy. It's almost like gossamers of gold." He released her right hand to carefully lift and examine the locket she always wore. His touch was light, gentle. The feel of his warm fingers on her skin sent a flutter through her.

"Why do you always wear this locket? Mike is dead. You should put away the past. A locket can't salvage the loss. Don't live like your father did."

His speech was almost imploring. Had he forgotten the locket did not come from Mike? Did he really care about her, or was he making a comparison? Or was the Scotch he'd been drinking affecting him?

"Mike didn't give me this locket. Don't you remember? It was Mother's. Dad gave it to her. Mike had it repaired once."

He touched the locket with his finger. "How could I have forgotten? It is beautiful."

"My father loved my mother with a blind intensity.

My marriage held no similarity. I would have divorced him if it had been possible."

"I'm sorry you had to suffer that." His voice was a silky whisper.

"I think the music stopped. Miss Kitty is stalking you…"

He glanced quickly to see Kitty's approach. A frown touched his face.

"You're right. Thank you for the dance, madam." Her face felt small as his large hands cupped her cheeks. A spark of some indefinable emotion filled his eyes. She thought for a brief second that he was going to kiss her. Then abruptly he tucked her arm and covered her hand with his, as he led her back to her table.

Brooke's reaction was a rapid beating of her pulse. She couldn't deny the intense physical reaction he set off, and she wanted to blame it on the day. The nearness of him gave her comfort. Her inner turmoil was masked with deceptive calmness. A quiver of want sped through her veins. Yes, she wanted him to kiss her. It was an awaking experience that left her reeling.

She remained with Steve for the rest of the wedding reception. However, she could still feel Adam's rugged hands as they cupped her face. Little by little he was invading her senses, invading her thoughts. And what she was feeling was deeper, more intense than brotherly affection.

. . .

By nine the reception wound down to the family and the Tower clan. Abe was there, as well as Hank and a few of the old regular cowboys. The band was gone. Mack was sorting and storing his supplies for his trip to town.

Except to accommodate a few women who wanted to dance with the groom, Joe never left Mary's side. He held her hand constantly and seemed happier than Brooke could remember.

They made a handsome couple.

"You seem preoccupied, love." Steve's eyes held a note of concern.

"No. Not at all." She sat up and nodded in her father's direction. "I was thinking of how happy my father and Mary are right now. They should have married years ago."

He glanced over at them. "Maybe they were afraid or embarrassed. Their generation has a different perspective than ours."

Melancholy swept over her, exacerbated by the champagne and the celebration. "I guess I'm feeling some remorse for all the years they doted on me. I never asked them to do so much. If I told them not to, I know I would have hurt their feelings—kind of like a double-edged sword, if you know what I mean."

Steve nodded as he took her hand. "I used to envy you when we were children. Joe bought everything you wanted: silver saddles, show clothes, a shiny pickup when you could drive. Dad made us work for everything. Even with all the hands working there, he made us do every job on the ranch and work for the oil company on drilling rigs. I suppose all good things have a price."

A chafing voice accompanied the once well-groomed best man. "Tears, darlin'? Is my brother being mean to you already?"

"Adam," Steve reprimanded. "Those are happy tears."

Adam placed his hands up in a sign of surrender. An apologetic appearance diffused his boorish manner. He reclined in a chair but said no more.

She excused herself to get the few things she would need to spend the night in the Hightower Ranch's guest house. When she returned Steve took her bag.

"Where are you going?" Adam viewed her suspiciously.

"Your father is gifting me the use of his guest house next to the pool tonight so Dad and Mary can be alone. Ah, looks like Kitty is on her way over to see you, um, staggering. Without me around, you two could play in the tack room all night and not be disturbed." She chuckled and patted his shoulder. "Don't leave a mess this time."

Before he could get a word out, Kitty sat next to him, purring for attention. Brooke gave a wave of fingers and a large grin. He ignored Kitty. Her heart thumped as he studied her with curious intensity. It would be too easy to get lost in the way he looked at her. Entirely caught up in her own emotions, she was sad the day was ending.

Adam's hoarse whisper travelled to her. "Sleep well."

She didn't reply and masked her inner turmoil with deceptive calmness. Steve took her bag and she walked with him to his pickup. From the pickup she scanned the patio. Adam was standing, holding his Scotch, staring their way. She knew a deeper significance to their visual interchange. Like the gossamer web of the spider, a slender delicate thread was forming between them. She turned her head and watched as the road well-travelled seemed bumpy and rough.

Later, the pool water felt warm compared to the breeze coming from the hills. There in the hills the evenings always cooled off and a blanket during the night was often necessary. She remembered as a child she would stay in the warm water with Steve and Adam because getting out meant getting cold. After a few laps they held on to the shallow side of the pool and kept themselves immersed for warmth.

"Steve, thank you. I would have felt uncomfortable at the house tonight."

"It's a beautiful night to top off a beautiful day, and speaking of beautiful," he turned in her direction, holding her lightly by her elbows, "you have become one beautiful lady."

"I never knew you to be a flatterer." She blushed, uncomfortable with the divergent road they were traveling. She hadn't seen him in eight years. He still had a devilish manner, a quirk of a smile that always brought results, and a body as fit as they come. But they weren't children anymore.

"Just being honest," he whispered. Gentle fingers removed the wet strands of hair from her face.

She was torn from this need for warmth and kindness, and the fear that sex with this man would destroy in some way all they shared over the years. Her thoughts scrambled as she tried to find a way out of this situation without hurting their friendship. He was so dear to her, always her friend. Then he ended what could have changed their friendship forever.

Steve turned and rested his back against to pool. "Are you still in love with your husband?"

"No. I'm glad he he's gone." Her voice was harsh. "I'm sorry. I sound like a shrew."

"Don't be sorry. Just move on, build a new life." He kissed her cheek lightly. "I'll tell you what, we'll go in and change, and I'll make us a Kahlua laced cup of cocoa. Then we'll call it a day."

Brooke smiled and accepted his hand as he led them out of the pool. "Sounds wonderful. Besides, you have a busy day tomorrow."

After finishing the cocoa at the wrought iron table, she stood. Steve placed a gentle kiss on her cheek. "Sleep well, dear Brooke."

Quietly she left him and went to bed.

CHAPTER FOURTEEN

*B*right rays of sunlight lit up the room. The warm aroma of fresh perked coffee permeated Brooke's senses, arousing her from a deep sleep. She realized Steve was already up and about. Impatiently she pulled her thoughts together. She wasn't a teenager on a first date. But she worried about getting close to Steve too soon. Was it in his eyes or was she imagining an interest that wasn't there? It was the crossing of the thin line that would either strengthen a relationship or destroy it. Once the line was crossed, she feared there was no jumping back to what once was.

Brooke heard the diving board vibrate and Steve's nearly silent entrance. She could envision his early morning swim—graceful, powerful. Her insecurity about his feelings forced her to remain under the warmth of the blanket, postponing the encounter.

Soon she heard him stirring around in the kitchen.

She should probably get up, she thought. His footsteps crossed the small living room and even closer to the bedroom door. A navy bath towel wrapped his hips and tucked into the waistband of his suit. In his hands he carried two, giant coffee cups. Cautious silence filled the room.

Steve's face, however, held no animosity, just wariness. "Good morning." A tender, crooked smile touched his lips.

"Good morning." She smiled, sitting up and pulling the covers with her to fend off the cool morning air. Brooke took a big breath and drew her fingers through her hair.

"Sleep well?" He handed her one of the cups and sat on the edge of the bed. The nod of her head and a warm smile was rewarded with a warm kiss on her cheek. "Good. I think we both had too much to drink last night."

"Yes, I believe so." She replied softly. He appeared pensive, not angry. And here he sat, one of her dearest friends, and she didn't know him, not now, not as a man.

He ran his finger down her still red scar. "I didn't notice this before."

"Oh, I fell and cut myself on a nail the second night I was home. It's okay." She lied not yet up to telling him the whole story.

Steve didn't push for more of an explanation. "Can you smell the meat the men have in the pits, cooking most of the night? Are you hungry? I can make omelets up at the house."

"No. I'm really not ready for food. I guess I'd better get home and help Mary. She's probably been up since before dawn. She does love this shindig."

Steve slipped on a spare robe from the closet and returned to sit on the bed near her. "Your father and Mary make a nice couple. They always have."

"Yes, they do." Brooke fingered the blanket as she sipped from the steaming mug. "Why hasn't your father ever remarried? Josh has been alone for many years."

Steve shrugged noncommittally. "He never filed for divorce. We've never heard from her. He hired a detective, but she just seemed to disappear." He sipped from his cup. He shrugged. "Some women he's been fond of. I guess, like Joe, he couldn't find one who would let him forget my mother—or put up with him," he chuckled.

"Must be something. Loving someone so much that you decide to spend the rest of your life alone." Could she ever love someone that fiercely again?

Steve studied her for a moment. "It sounds like your marriage wasn't all you had hoped for." He watched her with intense curiosity.

"No. It wasn't." She looked into his warm, eyes and found reassurance and caring. "Now it's over. I can be objective. I didn't fit into his lifestyle, dressing to impress others, or to show how much money one has."

Steve kissed the back of her hand. "Let's get dressed. We have a big day ahead of us. Maybe I can even get you to compete in something—as long as it isn't against me."

A delicate chuckle eased her thoughts. "I haven't practiced. By the end of summer, I'll take you on."

Steve drove his black pickup to the back yard of the Montgomery house and parked next to the sidewalk to let Brooke out. "The horse competitions will be early, around nine before it gets too hot. The rest of the games and festivities will be after the food is served." He placed a hand on her elbow and kissed her cheek lightly. "Will you be rooting for me?"

"You're putting me on the spot. I do have to root for our ranch, too." Brooke squeezed his hand before she left the truck. She waited for him to turn around and waved as he drove by.

Adam watched Brooke as she walked to the patio where everyone was having coffee. He gripped his coffee cup.

"Good morning." She smiled brightly as she gave a kiss and a quick squeeze to Mary and Joe and hugged Abe, who was also enjoying breakfast there.

"We missed your smiling face at breakfast," Joe teased.

Brooke stared at Joe. "I made a decision. I'll sign the paperwork. I'm going to build on the land, maybe start raising some of my own horses—give you some competition."

"Well, that's great news. Hopefully my birthday present will be of some help. Of course, we won't be here." He smiled at Mary and patted her hand. "We'll be on a cruise to the Bahamas. Then we are going to wing it. Adam promised to see to the details."

"Sounds mysterious." Brooke's attention darted to Adam.

Just her physical presence sent his pulse spinning. The thought of spending her birthday with him came with conflicting emotions. The night before Adam couldn't stop worrying, fearing Steve would leave her alone in the small guest house. Although it wasn't far from the main house, it was far enough in his estimation. He drove to Hightower to make sure she was all right and ease his worry.

Panic nearly overcame him as he thought of what he could find. He still had no real idea as to who was tormenting her, and his fear for her welfare consumed every moment. On Scotch weary legs, he staggered down the hill to the pool and guest house. He slipped open the door and peeked inside. The only light visible was a night light in the kitchenette. Large towels were draped everywhere. Adam entered the kitchenette, following a trail of water to the telltale bathing suits still dripping on the hooks.

He stared for a moment at the mounting evidence and the bedroom door, slightly ajar. But he could not force himself to look inside. An unreasonable fury coursed through him as he envisioned his brother and Brooke curled skin to skin.

Morning found him in Kitty's covetous hold. A foul taste permeated his mouth. His head pounded to an offbeat rhythm. Adam felt as though he had lost something precious. Brooke and Steve had always been closer, in trouble together as teens, competing against one another. They had never been romantic. His thoughts ate at him. And here was Brooke, and he couldn't get out of his mind what he imagined had happened at the pool.

"How was my father's pool?" Adam's voice was slightly sarcastic and the word—pool—was exaggerated. An ice pack lay on his neck.

She turned her back on him and walked over to sit on the steps. "Great, very relaxing."

His eyes narrowed, challenging her.

After a pause, she turned the subject back to him. "Where did you sleep last night? I hope you left the newlyweds alone?"

"Yes, he left us alone," Joe interrupted with a smile. "He slept at the hotel."

She smiled crookedly at him. "Tell me, Adam, how are you going to ride a roping horse when you can't even sit straight in a chair?"

"Don't worry your little head any." He excused himself from the table and asked Abe to come with him. "Abe's talented fingers can work wonders on man and beast."

The Montgomerys and their crew arrived at Hightower Ranch around eight. Few had arrived early, except for those who would be in the horse competitions or those who were busy with the preparation. Tables were set out for salads and cakes. Josh paid some of his men to stay up most of the night, cooking a steer and several pigs in a large in-ground fire pit, covered to roast all night. Fried chicken would be available later.

This was an annual affair, a charity for the local medical center and free vaccines for children. Most came to compete in the rodeo.

One pasture was set aside for trailers and vans of friends and relatives who traveled a distance for this once-a-year shindig. The ranch resembled a travel-trailer campsite with vehicles of all shapes and sizes, taking up space normally occupied by horses and cattle.

Josh, like Joe, paid his men to help with the barbeque, except during the time they chose to enter an event. Ranch hands that chose to work the barbecue or at the ranch were paid double. Some preferred to simply have the day off and use their expertise to compete with the owners for the contest money. By eight, many were assembled at the arena to find a seat.

For once Brooke would be an observer and not a competitor. Kitty was there. She recognized the same bearded cowboy who accompanied her, the same one she was with at the hotel. As she waited, she saw Adam near the barns, walking Contender towards the arena. Pretty Sara Anderson, the daughter of a local rancher who raised Rambouillet sheep and Quarter horses, walked close to Adam. He seemed to be listening to her flirty chatter. She pondered how his head was feeling.

Brooke's probing thoughts were interrupted when two strong arms came to wrap around her waist. She stiffened in a knee-jerk reaction to the sudden embrace. Her pulse skittered alarmingly. She turned quickly, smiling when she realized Steve had arrived. A tick back to happier times brought old memories to the surface, and the comfortable, uncomplicated friendship they had.

"Sorry I took so long." Steve sat next to her. "I had some long-distant phone calls about one of my paintings and errands to run for Dad. I told him to tell you to meet me at the stalls."

"He didn't tell me. It must have slipped his mind with everything else to think about."

"Hey. Why don't you enter the barrel race? You used to be pretty fast." He nudged her with encouragement. "You're dressed for it—jeans and old comfy boots."

"I don't have a horse, and I haven't done any racing in quite a while."

"You can use my horse, the gelding. Come on, give it a try. It's for charity anyway."

He took her hand in his and pulled her in the direction of the stables. Brooke worried. She wasn't familiar with the animal's temperament. And she had no time to do some practice before the event. But it was all in good fun—and for a good cause. She just had to stay on the horse.

Steve squeezed her hand. "I would label him gentle and easy mannered. He's used for different jobs on the ranch and rodeo events."

She thought this one felt power packed, ready for any leg cue. It wasn't the animal's abilities she questioned—it was hers. Her doubts became a reality when she finished with a terrible score.

"I told you I'd lose." She laughed out loud at her own ineptness as she dismounted. Her breath was short from the excitement and the exercise. She felt alive and refreshed. This was what she needed, familiar activities to get her mind and body back in sync.

"So, you came in fourth in a field of five. At least you weren't last." He laughed with her as he took the reins from her hands. "Your timing wasn't too bad, if you take off the penalties for knocking over the barrels—two out of three."

They walked to the stable, unsaddled the horse, and put him in his familiar stall. Brooke threw him another flake of hay and patted his neck through the half door.

"Why don't you go find a good seat for the roping? It's going to get started soon, and I need to warm up."

From the stands Brooke watched Adam work as the header and Steve as the heeler. Backed into the chute, the horses were on their haunches and ready for the steer to be released. Within seconds, Adam gave the nod, the gate opened, and the steer bolted out of the chute. Adam easily swung and caught the horns, but lost time when the seasoned steer turned in the opposite direction. Finally straightening out the animal, Adam was able to turn it so Steve could rope the back feet. The horses faced each other, and their time stopped.

Brooke remembered how they always worked well together, and even though they put on a good performance with the wild-eyed steer, they took second money. Family winnings were always donated to a local cause.

The barbecue was served after the rodeo. Tables full of pot-luck salads and desserts were offered along with the barbequed meat. Steve insisted on filling her plate. He laughed at her light attempts at protest. "You're too skinny anyway," he taunted.

They located a quiet spot under a clump of aspen trees near the house, away from the crowd. She couldn't finish all he stacked on her plate, so she donated it to the ranch's Australian cow dogs. With bellies full, Brooke and Steve reclined against a thick aspen and lounged like well-fed puppies. The meal was so filling, and the sun so warm. She began to yawn. She rested her head against the trunk of the tree.

He cleaned up their area and came back to their tree. "Go to sleep for a while. I'll wake you in a little bit. Neither of us got much sleep yesterday."

Adam wasn't sure how Sara became his afternoon partner. She was pretty with peaches and cream complexion—and a slim, eye-catching body. Her light hair was as ever perfect as were her expensive clothes. As they neared the patio of the house, Adam swerved suddenly to avoid his brother's hand. A streak of jealousy ran through him, seeing Brooke asleep, leaning on his shoulder. Adam remembered how she felt as he kissed her at the lake, and how soft and warm from sleep her body was in his room—and how small she would have appeared nestled in the warmth of Steve's shadow at the pool house the night before. He couldn't shake the scene he planted in his own brain.

"Must have been a late night?" Adam asked pointedly.

Steve cocked his head slightly and grinned. "No, actually we only swam for a short time, and then we turned in."

Feeling like he had been kicked in the stomach, Adam looked down the hill toward the gathering. "Well, join me later when Sleeping Beauty wakes up."

For the briefest moment, Adam wanted to tell Steve he was at the guest house the night before. What a fool, he thought. To let his brother know what he suspected would make him look like a jealous suitor. Or make Steve look too incompetent to take care of her. The last thing he needed was an argument with his brother—or have her accuse him of interfering again. He moved toward the kitchen and took some aspirin.

Steve inadvertently woke Brooke when he tried to shift his weight. She yawned and stretched. "How long have I been sleeping?"

"At least four hours," he teased, brushing the hair from her face.

"Well, the sun isn't in the right place, so I know it isn't late."

"Just what I need, a female astrologer." Steve flashed a sparkling smile her way.

"Let's do something. No sense in wasting a beautiful day." Brooke sat up and slapped his thigh lightly. She still felt uneasy. Their old friendship was too dear to her to have it destroyed in a spur of the moment decision. Should she let it run its course? What if it turned out they were compatible, and they could have a wonderful life together?

Steve pulled her back against his chest. "Well, I would not call it wasting the day away. I don't often get to lie around under the shade of a tree with an old friend."

"Get up." Brooke forced a laugh and pulled on his hand.

"Well, what would you like to do?"

"We could get into the volleyball game by the barn."

He chuckled. "Are you good? I don't want to have the same results as your barrel racing."

"Yes, I love the game."

They sauntered over to the pit and sat along the sidelines until an opening occurred. As they waited, Kitty and her cowboy friend rode by on horseback.

"Where are you headed, Kitty?" Steve asked loudly.

"Oh, we're going for a ride along the river a spell.

It's so pretty this time of the year. Your dad let us borrow a couple of horses."

Wearing a full beard and sunglasses, the man sat like a lumpy greenhorn on the horse, staring at Brooke while he twirled a toothpick in his mouth.

"Let's be going," Kitty urged her mount forward, and the man followed.

"Strange," Brooke breathed. "He must be new, but he seems so familiar."

"Oh, she's probably headed for the old line shack near your property line, a little hanky-panky maybe?"

"Well, why doesn't she go home?"

Steve grinned. "Kitty is not very conventional. She likes things different."

Brooke stared at their retreating backs. The same ominous feeling she had when she first saw the cowboy rattled through her once again. Or maybe his connection to Kitty was the root of her discomfort.

"Well, here's our opening. Let's show them how to play this game."

The remainder of the day went considerably smooth. The guests came back time and again to fill their plates between games of baseball and volleyball. The waning sun called for the end of the festivities. By then most of the people were packing to go home. Children were ready for their beds and sleep. Sara left with her own family since Adam offered to take Joe and Mary to the Laramie Airport.

The Montgomerys and the Towers were the only

survivors of the long, exhausting day. They sat on the large redwood deck off the kitchen and family room. The oversized, pillowed chaise lounges were a welcome respite to their tired bodies.

A small crew of men worked quietly and efficiently on the cleanup, getting most of the trash picked up. In the morning the large items would be scrubbed and stored for the next year.

Talk was limited and weariness from the long day seemed to settle on all of them. Occasionally, she would catch Steve watching her. Twice he left them to take calls about a painting, the last one taking a good amount of time.

For Brooke, it was as well they were not alone. She did love Steve in a special way. However, she couldn't see anything permanent in their relationship. He was a free spirit, and his artwork reflected that, like the eagles he so loved to paint. Or maybe it was her. Maybe at this point in her life she was unable to give herself completely to any man.

CHAPTER FIFTEEN

"*B*rooke, wake up." Adam's hand shook her shoulder gently.

She stretched and took a sleepy look around. "Are they ready to go?" She sat up and pushed away the thick, woolen Afghan someone had spread over her.

"Actually, I'm just getting back. Joe saw you were sacked out. Since I was just dropping them off, he said to let you sleep." Adam sat on the edge of the chaise. "He sent you this."

Slowly she tore open the small envelope. Brooke was anxious as well as fearful of its contents. Joe had one too many surprises for her. The handwritten note told of his love for her and his desire for her understanding in the decisions he had made. He would help her get started with her own ranch if she chose to build on the land. Joe included their hotel names and destinations. He also pleaded with her to get along with Adam while he was gone.

So, her father couldn't wait one more day to help her celebrate her birthday. Screams of frustration burned at the back of her throat. She dropped her lashes to hide the hurt. She swung her legs off the opposite side of the chaise and got up from her seat.

"Where are Josh and Steve?" She realized the house had few lights on.

"Dad was in the kitchen waiting for me. I guess he went on to bed. He said Steve got a call about one of his paintings and must have gone to bed, too. I didn't see the lights on in the studio."

"I wanted to thank them, especially Steve. He was a lot of fun today." She looked up to find Adam watching her. "It almost felt like we were teenagers again."

He grinned. "Well, love, tomorrow your body will tell you differently."

An evasive silence controlled the drive to the ranch. He pulled the horse trailer alongside the open barn doors of the new stallion barn. They unloaded Contender and settled him in his stall with fresh hay. She poured his ration of grain while Adam put on his summer sheet.

Together, they walked through the show barn and up the gravel drive to the house, silence falling heavily around them. The moonless night hid their expressions from one another.

Near the mudroom door, she noticed a furry bundle. "Claude? Why are you out here?" She expected him to jump and run to her, but he merely lifted his head, his tail giving a thump of recognition. With a moan of fear, she ran to her dog. She knelt next to him, finding blood, dripping from the top of his head.

Following close behind her, Adam checked the dog's eye movement and the wound. "He has a head wound."

After examining the dog for any other injuries, he had him up on four legs. Claude licked his hand and gave a little wag of his tail. "I'm going inside. I want you to stay here in case someone is in the house."

"No." A wave of terror raced through her and gnawed away at her confidence. "I'm not staying out here alone." Before, the care and welfare of her dog had been uppermost in her mind. Now she realized they could be in danger. Someone could be watching from anywhere outside, concealed in the darkness. Clouds covered the moon. Wind whistled through the trees and rustled the shrubs near the house. The ominous hoot of an owl sent a shiver through her.

Concern made Adam impatient. "You have Claude here. He'll give a warning."

She stood her ground. "No, I'm going with you."

He led the way through the house, Claude at his heels. The dog seemed unconcerned. "I think whoever injured him is long gone."

The office had been severely ransacked. He checked for anything missing from the desk. He found nothing taken, including the cash box and the ranch checkbook. He continued to examine the disorder.

"Don't touch anything." He used his handkerchief to look in the drawer. "I'll call and have Buck come out."

"What do you think they wanted?"

"Beats me. Money's still in the drawer. Guns are in the cabinet." Adam stood there, tall and angry. His voice was cold.

Brooke stared at him, his stance dark and dangerous. Denial flew from her. "I have nothing, remember? I'm sure you had Buck check me out when I arrived." She turned away from his wrath and headed for the foyer.

She cautiously went up the stairs to look around. Standing in her bedroom doorway, she released a moan of despair. The room was trashed. She instinctively spun around looking for danger, looking for her ex-husband, expecting him to be there, smiling, leering, enjoying her terror. Raw, primitive fear raced through her.

The room reeked of perfume, bottles empty and splashed over her things.

Go Away was printed in red lipstick across her mirror.

With a moan of despair, she fell to her knees in the middle of her torn and shredded clothing. Claude licked her face.

Adam bounded up the stairs two at a time, handgun ready. He stopped dead still, shocked with what he saw. Not one piece of clothing was left on hangers. Drawers had been pulled out and emptied. Everything, including her underwear and shoes had been slashed.

Her jewelry boxes were gone—even the ballerina box from her childhood. Nothing glittered in the rubble.

He touched her lightly on her shoulder, and she flinched. "Let me take you back to my father's until I can get this figured out."

"No," she breathed. Claude nestled next to her.

Adam left her in the shredded pile to check the other rooms. Except for hers and the office, none had been touched. He took her by the elbow and escorted her downstairs to the den. He encouraged her to sit on the sofa. He sat next to her holding her hand. Chill black silence surrounded them. For some time neither spoke. His mind raced, trying to come up with a reason or clue to this new assault. Was she still hiding something from her past?

He ordered the dog to stay with Brooke and checked to see if the front door was locked. He put on all the outside spotlights and took a moment to assess the outside. Taking his pistol, he went to the main barn to talk with John who was supposed to be watching over the barns and the house. Inside the doorway of an empty stall, he found him, dazed from a blow to the head. After arousing him and checking for serious damage, he went into the tack room refrigerator and took out one of the ice packs.

"Adam, I saw a woman up at the door trying to pet the dog. He was barking and growling something awful.

As I came out of the barn to see who it was, someone hit me from behind."

John sat on a chair just inside the barn door, woozy and pale.

"I hadn't expected this. Why don't I get one of the boys to take you into Doc? Will you be all right here while I check the other barns?"

John merely nodded and rubbed the back of his neck. "I'll be fine. Hope none of the horses are missing."

Adam switched on the inside and outside lights as he moved from one barn to the other. He checked to be sure none of the show horses had been stolen or injured in some way. After turning off the lights as he moved through the stables, his worry turned to Brooke. He returned to the den, and for a moment, Claude growled at him, and then rushed over to kiss his hand.

"Well, old boy, you're one thing I don't have to worry about anymore." He stooped to caress the animal for some comfort of his own.

Brooke sat on the floor, leaning her head back against the sectional. Claude rested his chin on her lap as he snuggled close to his charge. She glanced up at Adam when he entered.

She was in no state to hear about John, so he bypassed the information for the moment. "I'm going to check on the other rooms and see if I can come up with any clues. Will you be all right?"

"Yes," she nodded. He noticed a glass of Scotch, sitting lightly in her hand.

"Are you cold?" He came over and put a pillow behind her head.

"No."

Adam stood there, angry that this last bit of vandalism directed toward her had now entered his home, his sanctuary. She was not her usual spit-fire self. Normally, in years past, she would have been out for blood. He surmised she had more history than she cared to divulge.

Sensing for a time she would be safe, he went upstairs. Nothing in the other rooms had been touched. Joe's jewelry drawer held many expensive items, including his late wife's necklace of heavy silver and turquoise. If it had been a robbery, then surely the necklace would have been taken.

Sitting on the edge of her bed, he sifted through some shredded items on the floor. At a loss, he got up and paced the room, examining the destruction. Finally, he sat on the love seat, furious at this new turn of events. Under what was once a green silk blouse, he spotted a dangling earring. Shaped like a quarter moon, it was enameled in yellow. Kitty was one of the few women he knew who wore flashy jewelry. He wouldn't put it past her to create this mess. Tortured with fear and anger, he hurried back to the den.

"Brooke? Is this yours?" He lowered himself to sit on the carpet next to her.

Deep in thought, she glanced up at the earring. She

responded matter-of-factly. "No. I've never seen it before. Besides, I have pierced ears. This is a clip-on."

He lost his temper, more from the impotence he felt than the destruction. He gripped her shoulders and made her face him. "Brooke. Damn it. Don't you care what has happened?"

"What do you want me to do, call up the posse? For all I know, you arranged all these events to drive me away. You could have done it before you picked me up." Her voice ended in a high-pitched tremor as she wrestled from his grip.

"What do you have that someone wants? People are getting hurt," he bellowed.

"The only person getting hurt around here is me," she replied testily.

"John. He was knocked unconscious in the barn. He was lying in an empty stall in this front barn, and we missed him." Unconsciously, his grip grew stronger.

"Stop, you're hurting me. Why don't you admit you want me gone from here—out of your life—and sell you the rest?"

"Because damn-it-to-hell, it's not true. Just maybe you are the one creating these scenes for some sick reason." His angry fear-filled glare met hers and held for a moment.

Confused by their shouting, Claude began to whine and poke his nose between them. Realizing his frustration, Adam released her. He resettled the pillow behind her head.

She accepted his attention in silence. When he was settled on the floor next to her, his legs stretched out and crossed before him, he took one of her hands and cradled it in his.

"I'm sorry for yelling at you. I'm not responsible for what has happened since you came back. I've called Buck. He'll be here shortly." He moved the hair away from her face. "I'm probably going to be with Buck for a while in the house and outside. Do you want me to have Abe or Hank come stay with you while he's here?"

Their eyes held, seeming to agree to a noncommittal truce. "Would you call Steve?"

He looked away from her and flinched. "I already called to warn them. Steve left for Denver over an hour ago." He saw the dismay register on her face. "Steve is not very organized, something about one of his paintings. Would you rather I call Abe?"

He wanted to hold her close, make her feel safe. But at this moment she didn't trust him. Confusion laced with anger as he stared at her.

"No, I'll stay here with Claude." She leaned her head on the soft pillow.

Even in the dark, Adam knew it was Buck, walking across the lawn to the back door. Buck Johnson was in his fifth year as sheriff. He wasn't quite as tall as Adam. His red wavy hair was his trademark. He was the center on their high school football team, and even now he looked the part. His brawny shoulders and thick neck gave him a look of power and importance.

"Got a problem, huh?"

"Yes, and it seems to be getting worse with each incident. I don't know if Brooke is as innocent as she claims she is, or if she has something to hide. Although, I think if she had something to hide, she wouldn't wear those looks of terror I see from her. I found this in the rubble. She said it isn't hers—she wears pierced and these are clip-on."

"Do you have any guess who?" Buck played with his pen, tapping it on his clipboard.

"Well, as far as tonight goes—Kitty. She wears this flashy stuff. The way she's always felt about Brooke, I wouldn't doubt her involvement."

"Or the way Kitty's always felt about you. It's no secret." Buck inserted. "Let's go up and look around." They spent close to an hour taking photos and looking through the things on the floor and the other damage to the room. Buck took fingerprints from the dresser and mirror and bagged the empty perfume bottles to take with him.

"I could pick Kitty up for interrogation, as long as I had someone else in the office with me. I don't trust her. No telling what she could dream up in that squirrelly head of hers. Besides, unless we have proof, I can't keep her."

Adam threw himself on the love seat and stared at the pile of shredded clothes. His shoulders and arms were tight with anger. A headache was forthcoming. The thundercloud hovering over them, spitting lightning strikes unexpectedly, bedeviled him. He hated ineptness, especially within himself. The stories she told about the gunshots while swimming at the lake were true. He had to believe her after Abe found bullet casings on the hill above the lake. Now he couldn't help but worry. At some point the game could become deadly.

"No, Buck, I'll go over myself. If Kitty is behind this, then maybe I can stop it."

"You're kind of edgy right now. Do you think it's a good idea?"

"I'll be all right. If something comes of it, I'll call you."

He escorted Buck through the house and outside. Buck put his worn Stetson atop his head and put his hand out to Adam. "Well, good luck. I'll fill out a report tomorrow. You can come in and sign it then." He turned. "By the way, you might want to know, the new vet in town has closed his book to Kitty and placed a hefty lien on her property."

"Thanks for telling me. I'll see you tomorrow, unless something else happens."

Adam watched the white Explorer leave. He called Hank and asked him to sit with Brooke. By the time he left for the Jones Ranch, his fury had cooled a notch. He parked in front of the house and headed for the front door. The foyer light was on. Trying the doorknob, he found it unlocked and knew where Kitty was entertaining. He headed straight down the hall to the double doors.

"Adam." Kitty gasped.

The bearded cowboy pulled the covers over himself and remained in the bed, watchful and arrogant. Kitty, however, was flustered and slipped on a pink lacy robe to cover her nakedness. She hurried to the door. Grabbing Adam by the arm, she escorted him from her room.

"Adam," she cooed. Her breathing was shallow. Her hands fluttered over him. "You really should have called first. You know I always make time for you."

He followed her to the living room. Her high-heeled mules clicked across the oak floor while the rest of her moved sensually in the dim light. She turned to face him. When she attempted to put her arms under his jacket, she quickly moved back. "Gees, Adam, you're wearing a gun?"

"This isn't a social call, Kitty."

"Oh?" She poured two glassed of Scotch and handed him one.

"No, thank you."

Kitty sighed audibly and put the extra glass on the tray. She reminded Adam of a cat, cool and cunning, always landing on her feet.

"You seem all tensed up. Did you and the little woman have another argument?"

He grabbed her arm and pulled her close. "Where were you earlier this evening?"

Kitty flinched at his anger but still held her

composure. She ran a finger around his neckline. "Why, darlin', I was here. We came straight here from the barbeque."

"When did you meet him? I haven't seen him around?" He let go of her arm and moved to the back of the club chair to get away from her.

Kitty flounced down on the loose-pillowed sofa, crossing her legs and letting the flimsy material fall away to expose her beauty-pageant qualities. "He's my new foreman, Junior Mason."

"And where did you meet him? Or did you pick him out of the personals?" Adam couldn't help letting his sarcasm show. He didn't feel up to word games.

"Adam." Kitty frowned at the insult. "I met him at the hotel. He was looking for work and had references. Besides, what do you care?" She pouted. "I haven't seen much of you since the little Montgomery bitch came home. Are you two playing house?"

He moved over behind her and leaned an elbow on the couch. "You don't have pierced ears, do you? I never noticed before."

She fiddled with the sash of her robe. "I never could stand pain."

Leaning out over her shoulder, he pulled out the earring and dangled it. "Yours?"

A flicker of apprehension flashed through her wide blue eyes before she answered him. "I could have. They're very common—the in-thing. You can buy them anywhere—even Bess has them in her shop."

His mind wandered. Could Bess, Brooke's best friend, be the vandal?

"Is this one yours?" he persisted.

"I don't know."

"Then let's go look." He took her by the arm to lead her back to her bedroom.

"Wait, Adam. I have tons of earrings. Why do you want to know if this is mine?"

"Did you wear this kind of earring today?"

"I don't remember. I told you I have hundreds of cheap earrings and stuff." She rambled on as he dragged her from the living room, her white silky slippers clicking on the wooden floor. The cowboy was now fully dressed and headed for the front door.

"Where are those hundreds of earrings?"

"Here." She hurried to her dresser and took out a large plastic box. Inside were matched and mismatched earrings of various sizes and colors. "I told you, hundreds."

"I'm only interested in one." He picked though them for a time, all the while holding Kitty's wrist. "Let's look in your bathroom."

She pulled out of his grasp. "I want to know what this is all about. You come in here and disturb me in my own house without a knock or phone call. You owe me an explanation." Her bravado seemed to be more for her benefit than to reprimand Adam.

"Since when do I need to knock?" Adam glared at her. "You were at the ranch today and shredded

Brooke's clothes. What were you looking for in the office?"

Kitty paled. "How do you know I was there? Could have been anyone."

"You are a lousy liar, Kit." Adam turned to go.

Her voice grew shrill. "You have always loved her, always. You could have me full time, but no, you must have Miss Perfect. You'll be back, you always do come back."

He stared into her pleading face. "You would enjoy that too much." He pulled her hands away. "I won't be back. You and your cowboy will pay for the clothes."

Defeated, Kitty nodded. "I'll send a check over in the morning. Anything you want. Just don't shut me out." She sniffled and followed him to the door.

Adam drove to the ranch, his mind buzzing. He sent Hank home. Too tired to do anything about the mess in Brooke's room, he wearily stretched out on the sofa, trying not to disturb her. An occasional whimper kept him awake. Finally, with throw pillows from the sofa, he made a makeshift bed on the floor. Curled up behind her, he held her, hoping to ease her fears. And with every jerk from a nightmare, he ran his hand down her arm to her hand and whispered that she was going to be all right. He prayed that she would be.

CHAPTER SIXTEEN

*W*hen Adam arrived at the Sheriff's office, Buck was sitting behind his desk. A pot full of coffee sat on the weathered counter. He hovered over a bag of sweet rolls.

"Morning, Adam. Coffee?"

"Sure. I need something."

Buck handed him a white chipped mug. He took out one of the rolls and then offered the bag to Adam. "These are still warm from the hotel's kitchen. Better eat one before I eat all of them."

Adam filled his cup and sat in the oversized, leather chair in front of the desk. "This was a good idea. I was going to take you out for breakfast." He took a hearty bite of a bear claw and washed it down with a good gulp of coffee.

Buck chuckled as he talked around the jelly

doughnut. "Breakfast. When have you ever bought me breakfast? You are so cheap. You would probably leave me with the tab."

"That's gratitude for you." He smiled and lightened the burning anger within him.

Buck grinned. "So, how did your visit with Kitty go last night? You didn't bring her in, so I take it you couldn't come up with any real proof."

"She did it. I told her she had to pay for the damage and return the jewelry boxes. Do you know anything about her new foreman?"

Buck rocked back in his chair and balanced his coffee cup on his huge chest. "Just a drifter from what I understand. He hasn't been in any scrapes here in town. I really haven't had any contact with him."

With the cup in hand, Adam wandered over to the window to watch the town come alive. "When did he arrive in town?"

"A month ago. Kitty sure goes through foremen."

He chuckled. "Yes, in more ways than one."

"Well, here's your statement. Sign it, and I'll keep it handy in case something new comes up." Buck placed the form on the edge of the desk and laid a pen on top of it.

He walked over and scanned the report before he signed. Rereading the events of the previous night renewed his anger and the impotence he felt. Suddenly, the musty, old office seemed stifling instead of comforting. Adam placed his half-filled cup on the desk and headed for the door. He needed some fresh air and some new angles.

"I'll talk with you later. I'd better not leave Brooke alone too long."

Buck sat up and tapped the phone. "Why don't you call the house?"

"Thanks, maybe I will. I left my cell phone on the counter this morning." He ran his fingers through is hair with the frustration he felt. He didn't like turmoil. He liked having his days organized. He set his hat on his head.

The phone rang only once when Abe's brazen, old voice answered, "Yeah, Montgomery's."

"How's Brooke?" he inquired quietly.

"Well, Adam," he whispered, "she's not herself. Just stares out at her mother's roses."

"Try to get her to eat something. I'm going to go buy something she can wear until I take her shopping. Has Hank got everything handled out in the barns?"

"You worry too much. Everythin's fine. We're not kids you know."

He chuckled, envisioning the fusty old rooster "I'll be back soon."

Bess was in her shop when Adam walked in. Impatience oozed from him, and when she smiled his way, he returned a tentative smile.

"Adam, what brings you to this place of feminine whiles? Not a haircut, I'm sure."

"No. I need your help for a minute. So, you sell

earrings like this one?" He took the earring out of his shirt pocket and dangled it.

"Yes, right here on the rack. I had dozens. Most have sold already."

"Do you wear pierced?" He looked closer.

"Yes, sometimes I wear clip-on if I can't get the one I want in a pierced style. Why?"

"I'm trying to match this one. I don't see a match. Thanks anyway. Oh, by the way, I didn't see you at the barbeque." He watched her face for any evasion. She didn't offer any information on the purchase of the earrings. If she did know, would she even tell him? Did she help Kitty with the mess? And she was not at his father's barbecue.

"Well, the shop was open for part of the day, and then I was tired and went home. I wasn't up for all the activity." Bess didn't look at him, just adjusted the display cases.

"Today is Sunday. Do you stay open every day?"

Bess chuckled. "No, I'm doing a wedding party today, so I guess I'm open seven days this week. Extra money is always good."

Adam smiled at her. "Yes, it is. Don't work too hard."

He walked to the General Store, open from early morning to late evening every day of the week. One could buy anything from breakfast to a wheelbarrow, even basic groceries. Someone from the area was usually there, sometimes old timers jawing over the old ways of doing things before they filled up their gas tanks.

They also had a small selection of clothes available. Before leaving the house, he went to Brooke's room and jotted down the sizes she wore. He chose a pair of jeans, two tee shirts—white and pink, a gray sweatshirt and matching pants, and underwear—three to a pack. Now, the bra size he forgot. Fortunately, those on the rack were stretchy, small, medium, and large sports-type bras he could choose from. Tomorrow was her birthday, and if nothing else dire happened, he would take her to Laramie and let her shop herself silly.

On his way to the checkout, he spotted a display of jewelry. Spinning the rack slowly, he discovered a heart locket similar to the one Brooke wore. It wasn't the same quality or size. For the moment it would do. Feeling awkward with his rash decision, he held the little box all the way home. Would she refuse this impulsive gift? Would she misinterpret its meaning? He felt like a teenager. He was not used to this emotional turmoil.

He parked his truck next to the back lawn. Anxiety filled him, unusually so. His stride was long and sure as he hurried without running to the door. There he found Claude, daring him to enter his own home.

"Hey, flea bag, is that any way to treat me?"

With Adam's voice, Claude dropped his guard. Jumping up on him, the dog renewed their friendship and trust. He checked the gash and scratched his ears. Claude walked back to the den and flopped down next to Brooke, laying his black furry head in her lap.

As he approached the den, he caught sight of her curled up on the sofa. She looked small and lost, like and orphan in a robe too large for her.

"Brooke," his deep-timbered voice rumbled softly.

Without looking at him she replied politely, "I'm all right, Adam. I need to sort this all out. This is not how coming home was supposed to be."

He went over to the sofa and sat next to her. "I had to go in and sign the report about last night. While I was in town, I picked out some clothes for you to wear. I hope they will be alright for now. We'll go to Laramie tomorrow. You can shop to replace what was lost."

She let out a sigh. Silently, she opened the package. Her eyes filled. "Wow, just the right sizes. Thank you for your thoughtfulness." Then she gave him a crooked smile. "I was waiting for the dryer to stop so I could change. Your robe is a bit large."

"Oh, I almost forgot." And he reached in his shirt pocket for the small package. "I saw this in town. It won't replace the one you had stolen. I know it meant a lot to you."

Taking the wrapped package, she slowly undid the ribbons and tape, exposing a small blue-velvet box. When she saw the gold-plated locket inside, hot tears slowly ran down her face. She swiped them away. One big sob was painfully swallowed. She took Adam's hand in hers and caressed it with her other hand.

"This was an unusual gesture on your part, and I thank you with all my heart. But they didn't steal my locket. I was wearing it."

Brooke pulled the gold chain and heart out of the robe neckline.

"Well, I can take it back when we go to town. You can pick out something else."

"No, Adam," she smiled through her tears. "I have to let go of the past. Tshis is as good a time as any. I've always worried about losing it. Besides, this one is much smaller and daintier. We'll put my mother's locket in the safe." She stood up. "Would you help me put it on?"

He got up from the sofa and stood behind her. She held her long hair out of his way. Clumsily, he worked with the clasps. "They don't make these for large fingers. Let's put your mother's locket in the safe now."

When the heart was tucked away in the safe, she turned to him. A big tear of frustration rolled down her face. Adam sat in the large, leather desk chair and pulled her onto his lap and held her. He tucked her head to his chest, holding it with a soothing hand. He rocked the old office chair gently, comforting both.

After a while she smiled up at him. "I'm sorry for all the nasty things I said to you last night. I know they aren't true—at least I hope they aren't true."

"I'm sorry, too. Maybe we need to join forces and find out who's tormenting us."

She rose from his gentle hold and turned to face him.

She took his face in her hands and planted a chaise kiss on his lips.

"Thank you. I think I'll take a shower and get dressed." She went into the den and collected her new clothes. As she headed for the hallway, Adam stopped her with a worried look.

"It's all right. I saw Abe cleaning up. He tried to get out of the house with the trash bags without my knowing what he was doing. And he was vacuuming. I have to get him something for being so kind."

"Oh, I forgot to tell you. Abe and Hank are coming for dinner. We can eat early after chores. Abe took out a few steaks. He's cooking. Maybe you'll be up to eating by then."

She smiled at him and continued up the stairs. Later, she came to the kitchen, barefooted in the new jeans and pink tee shirt. Hank was shredding lettuce while Abe fried potatoes. Adam tended to the steaks outside on the grill.

"Well, now, you look mighty fine in those new duds. Don't she, Hank?" Abe looked up from his frying pan and smiled a toothless grin at her.

"Yes, Adam has pretty good taste in women's clothes. Too bad he can't do the same for himself." Hank chimed in lightheartedly.

"You're breakin' that into too large a piece. Lettuce needs to be in smaller pieces, like this." Abe complained and proceeded to show Hank how he wanted it done.

During the meal, the men joked and made small talk

about the day's work and what needed to be accomplished the following day. Using the foals as a lure, they tried to get her involved with the discussions. However, all they received were monosyllables or a nod or a smile.

"Shall we have our coffee outside? The sky is clear, and the stars are like glitter." Adam made coffee for each of them in large white mugs. "Brooke?"

"No, thank you. I'll clean up the dishes and then go in and watch some television before I go to bed. You go on outside and finish your coffee."

After the kitchen was back to Mary's standard, Abe and Hank left for their own homes, complaining to Adam lightly about the early hour he wanted them out working the horses.

Adam, being the only one left, watched television with Brooke, something he rarely did, except for the news. He knew he should be in the office, keeping up with the paperwork and the bookkeeping Joe left in his hands, but he felt she might need some company—and he wanted to be with her. With the news blaring, and her head nodding, he suggested they go to bed. He took her hand.

"Tomorrow is your birthday. I promised your father I would do something for him. So, in order to get an early start, I think we should turn in, don't you?"

"Yes, I suppose so." She yawned. "Thank you for all

you have done. Please don't think you have to patronize me while Dad and Mary are gone. I'm fine. I need time to work out my life. Really, it's all I came home for ... Someone wants me gone. Probably Kitty."

"Not me." He turned off the set and followed her through the house. "I'm sorry these things had to happen. I should have believed you sooner. But then you thought I had something to do with the other events."

"Yes, I did."

"Oh, I forgot to tell you. Steve called me earlier. He said not to wake you. I told him what happened."

She turned on the stairs to look at him. The mention of his brother seemed to spark an interest. An odd sense of disappointment slithered through him. He wanted her to have that same spark of interest directed at him, not Steve. Was it too soon to tell her how he felt? To his chagrin, she searched his face for more information.

"He said he would see you when he got back. He wasn't sure when."

Brooke looked away, and she nodded with an acceptance of the information. Yawning, she turned toward her room, Claude at her heels.

"I forgot...to buy you a nightgown," he murmured as if he were telling himself.

She chuckled as she walked back to him and gave him a hug. "I can sleep in this tee. You did buy me two and the other clothes are now clean. Thank you."

He watched her until she shut her door. Sitting

heavily on his bed, he ran a hand through his thick, curly hair. His quiet, steady existence had been disrupted, his ranch turned into an armed camp. How was he going to keep them safe?

CHAPTER SEVENTEEN

The ringing woke Brooke from a troubled sleep, ringing and ringing until she wanted to slam the phone off the nightstand. She glanced at her bedside clock—barely six. The sun just touched her window. Where was Adam? Someone surely would answer the house phone, she thought, until she realized the ringing was her cell phone.

A hollow, empty feeling pervaded her senses. She thought about the past year and all she had lost. She rolled her head back on the pillow and stared at the ceiling. Marriage, at one time, was important to her. She chose a husband who made her life a nightmare. The dream was gone. The ranch she loved had slipped into Adam's hands.

Now all her beautiful clothes were destroyed. That Kitty would hate her so much seemed unbelievable. Someone wanted her to leave. Had Kitty been encouraged to terrorize her? And Steve, had he deserted her, too? He hadn't called again or left a number. That old saying, *you can't go home again*, certainly was holding true. Despondency kept her in the comfort of her bed—and the phone kept ringing.

"Damn phone." She sat up and answered. "What!"

"Ooh, testy this morning." The familiar, deep-timbered voice teased. "Gee, Brooke, I didn't think you would ever answer the phone."

Her voice rose above a whisper, remembering what he planned for the day. "What do you want?" She pulled the quilt up close to her face, snuggling in the safe warmth of her bed.

"I'm at the barn. I'll be up in a few minutes to fix your breakfast. You have about fifteen minutes. Be ready for a full day. Oh, by the way, happy birthday."

She didn't speak for a moment. "I'm not getting up yet but thank you anyway." She curled further under the covers. Claude jumped up to lie in the bend of her knees. She reached and scratched his soft black head.

"Yes, you are. Your father gave me written instructions for your birthday. Brooke, I'm coming up to the house now. If you aren't dressed and in the kitchen by the time breakfast is ready, I will come up to roust you out."

Adam tried to keep his voice gentle. However, he heard her indifferent sigh of refusal. He noticed Hank standing a few feet away, grinning and yawning. None too gently he threw the bridle at Hank, catching him in the chest. Unable to control smiles, they both began to chuckle.

"Brooke, I'm leaving now." He hung up the barn phone without waiting for a reply. Either she would be up, or he would have to drag her out of bed like he did when they were youngsters.

Hank shook his head and grinned. "Well, you are improving. I wouldn't hesitate to bet you will be screaming at each other before the day is out. Shopping is what you said, isn't it?"

Adam smiled, and then he became pensive. "You know, I'm really worried about her. It's more than the robbery. Whatever has stirred her up is deep. She acts like an abused horse. Their eyes carry the same inner fear and apprehension I see in Brooke's before she hides it.

"If Joe or Mary calls while we're gone today don't tell them anything. They'll want to come right home. Tell them everything is fine. If they really want to talk to us, then have them call on my cell."

"While you're here, you need to sign this order for the vet supplies."

Hank handed the clipboard to Adam, and after perusing the forms, signed them. "Thanks, Hank. Just work the show horses lightly today until I can get back on track." He strode up to the house, hoping no battle lines would be drawn.

Banging around in the kitchen, he prepared his favorite, western omelet. By the time breakfast was ready, Brooke arrived. He put his hands on her shoulders and stared at her for a moment.

"Happy birthday." He gave her a light, brotherly kiss on the forehead and then escorted her to her chair. "I hoped you would refuse my order and let me dump you out of bed like I did when we were children."

She smiled and then chuckled. "Yes, you did regularly, especially when we traveled to all those horse shows." She added sugar and fresh cream to her coffee and stirred. "Adam, thank you. You don't have to do this. I'm sure you have horses to get ready for the first show of the season, and more valuable things to do than shop with me."

He brought over the omelets, warm cinnamon rolls, and fresh cut melon.

Brooke had pulled her blonde hair up in a knot. The shorter hairs softly teased the back of her neck. She had applied only eyebrow pencil and a blue liner. She wore one of the tee shirts he purchased as well as a pair of jeans. Her feet were bare. And it was a pleasant surprise to see she was wearing the locket he gave her.

"Are you going to wear shoes today?" He stared at her bare feet.

She grinned between bites of food. "I only have the boots I wore to the barbeque. They will be too hot to walk around in all day. My other choice is a pair of old sandals out in the mudroom. They will have to do."

"Well, do you want an agenda for today, or do you want it to be a surprise?"

A smile wrinkled the corner of her rosy lips. "I think I have had all of the surprises I can handle for the moment. I need to buy a few things for now."

Adam smiled back at her. "First, we're going to drive into Laramie. It's a long drive, but there are more stores. You can shop wherever you choose. You can buy anything you desire." Her eyebrows shot up in a challenge along with a disbelieving smile. "Think of it as a birthday present, and a guilt release for not having enough men standing guard the night of the barbeque." His voice held an apology.

She didn't answer right away. She nibbled on her eggs and then, putting her fork down, placed her hands in her lap. She finally looked up, a sad smile crossing her lips.

"I appreciate what you are doing, but I will be fine with a stack of catalogs. You're really leaving yourself open. I might take advantage of you."

He couldn't blame her. The violence was directed at her. He recalled picking up the slashed sundress she wore the night Kitty came over for dinner, the one with residual blood stains. She looked like an angel in the dress, and he was beginning to feel the loss as much as she. He had to get her back to her old self somehow. He took her hand and rested it on the table.

"Sweetheart, I know things have frightened you badly. Kitty is a loose wire. And she probably brought that foreman of hers with her. You can't quit living and hide here in the house. If it will make you feel better, I'll wear a small pistol under my sport coat. I carry it with me when I travel with the horses. Alright?"

She looked out the window, and he saw tears clouding her vision. He took a napkin from the silver holder and gently wiped the tears on her cheek.

"We really need to get going. Your father would be angry with both of us if I don't make this a great birthday for you. He doesn't know about your clothes. He did tell me to take you out and to show you a good time. He'll probably be checking up on me." With one finger he turned her chin his way. "Patronize me, please?"

He wasn't going to take no for an answer, even if he had to carry her bodily everywhere they went. She looked up at him with a tentative smile.

"All right, I'll go. We can take my car. You drive." She smiled at him, awkward with the harmony between them.

A satisfied light entered his whiskey, brown eyes. "Good, I'm not much at patient persuasion."

"You didn't do too badly," she chuckled lightly as she worked on her breakfast.

They cleaned off the table and placed the dishes in the sink. "We'll do these later." He took her hand and led her to the mudroom. "Let's go before you change your mind."

As they walked to the garage, Adam pointed. "Those are the ugliest sandals. The first things we will buy you are shoes."

With his large body, the small car caused them to

bump arms. For a while she tried to sit closer to her own door. As they relaxed with the beauty of the land and the comfort with each other, their touching became less of an issue and evolved into a small warm comfort.

"I hope Dad hasn't conned you into buying something outrageous."

Her statement came so unexpectedly Adam seemed lost for words. "No, his gift comes from the heart." And from mine, he mused. Was Kitty right? Yes, he did love her. From the day her mother let him hold her in a pink blanket while he sat in the big club chair, he loved her.

"My father won't let me go. He is forever buying expensive things for me, always trying to buy my love. He doesn't understand I love him just as he is."

"I have often misread you, even when we were children. We were always battling about something, usually something unimportant. Your father is a hard man to reject. I can appreciate your predicament."

He had no intention of looking at those worn out sandals all day, so the first stop was at a western store. He personally removed the sandals and threw them in the store's trash. Brooke chose new sandals, and then he told her to pick out a pair of dress boots, English riding boots, and a pair of barn boots for every day. Even though she protested, he told her he would pick them out if she didn't.

"Let's see, my list says you also need jeans, a barn jacket, more tee shirts, shirts, and a few sweaters. And underwear."

"You made a list?" she laughed.

Adam became silly at times, and if she hesitated to shop, he took items and threw them on the pile. He kept those she would wear for a few days. The rest he shipped to the ranch.

Famished, he drove to a steak house he enjoyed. A sense of privacy was assured as each booth filled its own alcove, tall and separate from others. The tranquility of the restaurant and the quiet intimate sounds of silverware, ringing faintly around them, he hoped would give Brooke a secure, restful feeling.

Adam's obvious patronage was noted as many of the employees called him by name, his last name. The owner came out of the office and after a short visit, took their order and offered them a complimentary drink.

"No, thank you, on the drinks. As for lunch, we'll have your New York cut—medium, a Caesar's salad, no potato. Also, two raspberry iced teas. And do you still have the dark, fresh baked bread?"

Brooke sat quietly. When the owner took their menus and left, Adam asked, "What's wrong? Do you prefer something else? I'll go get him."

"No. For someone who has never liked me very well, you seem to know a lot about my likes and dislikes."

"We may not always agree on things, but it doesn't mean I don't love you just the way you are. And I do notice. And you didn't eat much for breakfast." He grinned. "Sometimes your behavior draws more than my ire. You've always known how to get into trouble, impish trouble." His voice was gentle and lacked criticism.

Smiling, she agreed. "Yes, I guess I do have a temper. So do you. I remember a time all too well when you walloped me."

"Maybe I was playing the part of a surrogate brother. Did you ever tell your father?" His eyes twinkled.

"No," she chuckled. "I guess I was kind of a brat. Did you tell him?

"I didn't. I guess I was a sucker for your big tears." He didn't report to Joe that he found her half-dressed, kissing a boy from town. He should have.

Even then she had a spell on him. He hated to see her cry, be unhappy, or lose a class at a show. His whole life he had waited, and then she was gone from him. Now she was back, but she came back with a lot of baggage. He wanted to believe everything she said.

"Your father thought marriage would kind of mellow you out," Adam teased.

After the plates were cleared away, he became pensive. "Did you have a semblance of a good marriage with Mike?" He had to know from her mouth. He knew what had been gleaned by the investigators. Personal feelings weren't part of the study.

Brooke fidgeted for a moment. Mixed emotions could be read on her face. "I was alone a lot. The people who were supposed to be our friends didn't appeal to me. They were always flaunting their most recent purchases and trading bed partners."

She stopped abruptly. She didn't look at him.

He let out a sigh filled with pity. "Look, if you don't want to talk about it, it's all right," he hedged. "I'm sorry I interfered."

Her voice was a bare whisper. "No. I did have to play hostess to his friends and business partners. They were appalling."

"Why didn't you leave him?" He sipped his tea and watched her.

"He would have come after me, and he did have a violent temper. I was never allowed to go out unless he was with me or the bodyguard, Mason. The doors had key bolt locks and they had alarms. I was not allowed a key. Even the windows had key locks, so I couldn't get out if I tried." She stared out the window for a time before she continued. "I never had a friend. Never bought my own clothes—he picked out everything. Even my meals were decided by him. My whole life was under his control. He threatened to kill Dad if I left him." She stopped talking, but the painful memories were revealed in her eyes, haunted as she stared out the window.

Adam had no idea how awful her life had been. Rage filled his chest. He clenched and unclenched his fist holding his napkin, wishing it were the man's neck. She had gone from pampered and spoiled to a prisoner. "I wish I had known. I would have come to get you."

"To emphasize his threat, he shot my beautiful thoroughbred in the head while I was still on her. She reared and landed on me. I broke my leg." Her face twisted. "Oh, God," she whispered out the painful memory.

"Brooke, I wish you had told someone." He reached over and took her hand in his. He placed an endearing kissed on its back.

"How could I live with the fear he would hurt someone I loved, or burn the house, or kill the horses?" A deep sob was absorbed in her cloth napkin.

He gave her a moment. "Are you glad he's gone?" He ran his fingers along her arm.

"Truthfully, yes. He was contemptible, dangerous." She stared out of the window at the distant mountains. She spoke as if she were detached, an observer. Her voice was a whisper. "He was into drugs. Sometimes when he had been out flying with some client, he would come home, not loving or gentle, often abusive. Most of the time, he ignored me. The first time I threatened to leave, he burned all of my clothes."

He wiped away the tear trickling down the side of her face. The destruction in her room sparked that fear, an old threat. "Brooke, who knew he burned your clothes?"

She looked up at him, and after a moment she took a deep breath, "I told Bess. She called to talk the same night, a few years ago. Of course, everything I said was listened to, and I was told what to say. You don't think she would have trashed my room, do you? What reason would she have to want me gone? Could she have pushed me into the tack room, too?"

"No, it's probably some weird coincidence. Kitty

admitted to the destruction of your clothes. You know how she is ... I'm sorry I brought it up. Besides, we came to shop."

For the better part of the day, they replenished Brooke's wardrobe. To the entire world they looked like a couple. Adam constantly touched her or held her hand, guiding her from one store to another.

He gave her free rein in the department store, ordering two of everything. Shoes, he insisted on four or five pair to match the dresses and suits she might wear to dinner or ranch parties. He bought ten of anything she wore underneath and three of each set of robes and nightgowns in different weights to accommodate the changes in the weather.

He asked for the department store manager and requested he send by currier anything she did not take home with her. The little car's trunk would be quite full.

"I'm sure this will only touch lightly all you originally had, but it is a start. At least you won't look like Raggedy Brooke tomorrow. And these clothes are from me." He tapped her on the nose gently. "Besides, it's worth it to see you smile again."

She noticed a warm brown replaced his usual glare, and the hard panes of his face softened as he gazed down at her. He provided her with a very pleasant, revealing day. She expected him to be more impatient. He wasn't.

He was kind and considerate and fun. She felt a sense of pride being with him.

She was not, however, insensitive to the way other women openly admired Adam, or how the store clerks and owners zealously hopped to produce whatever he asked. The young woman in the western shop flirted outrageously, ignoring the fact Brooke stood next to them.

Pangs of insecurity often stung. Was she part of a play, a character in her father's birthday plans?

And what about Steve? He hadn't bothered to call to talk to her, just left without a word.

"I know this is out of your element, and you would probably be more comfortable at home. So, if you want, we can get back to the ranch now. You are a very good friend to do this."

Adam squeezed her hand and then pulled her close. She stood quietly as he spoke in her ear. "It was my pleasure, madam. If you want the truth, I have enjoyed myself. A little western bar down the road a spell has great Marguerites and a country band. You need to dance on your birthday."

Fear showed its ugly head. She looked around nervously. "Maybe we should go. They may need you for something."

Adam turned her by her shoulders. Close to her face he whispered, "It will be all right. I promise. My cell phone hasn't rung once. I'm sure they're fine."

Taking her hand, he guided her into the car. They ate

a small dinner of tacos and burritos, did a little two-stepping, and then journeyed home.

At the ranch, she accompanied him as he checked with the two men posted around the barns. Outside lights lit the darkness. Claude met them as they came through the kitchen with her packages. He licked and whined and wiggled with delight. She gave him a giant chew bone.

On the counter, in a domed, crystal cake plate was a fudge cake. Multicolored sprinkles decorated the top. Small pink candles stood at attention. The note, leaning against the plate, simply said, "Happy birthday." Abe signed his name in his familiar scrawl.

Adam lit all the candles and had her blow them out with a wish. She took plates from the cabinet and found the cake knife. She cut two large pieces and carried them over to the table.

"How about some milk?" she added.

"What else goes as well with chocolate cake? It looks homemade." He took a generous bite. "Abe is always full of surprises."

They ate in silence. Then she remembered the gift she purchased for Adam to thank him. She found the small box among her packages and hurried back to the table.

"What's this?"

"Something I bought to thank you." She stood nervously waiting for his response.

Inside the box was an expensive hand-made silver, belt buckle. Wordlessly, he put it on his belt. "This is beautiful, but it wasn't necessary. I truly enjoyed today … I'm almost glad someone broke in here. If your clothes hadn't been ruined, I would not have had a reason to take you shopping. Besides you wouldn't have come with me." His smile was devastating. "When exactly did you have time to buy this?"

She chuckled lightly, "When the perky little salesgirl gave you the come-on."

He leaned over and applied a warm kiss on her cheek. "Thank you." His eyes tarried too long on hers. He stood quickly, picked up the dirty dishes, and put them in the sink. Then he came over to Brooke and took her hand, urging her from her seat. His face held an endearing smile. "Come. I have to give you your birthday present."

"More? This is too much."

"Now it's time for your birthday. We have to go down to the barn."

Brooke was puzzled. Was her father giving her one of his foals as a gift, maybe the little filly with the four, white stockings she often groomed? She was excited, but hollowness entered her being as this was another expensive gift from her father. But she would take in all in stride, and not take out on Adam her reluctance to accept her father's gift. She would have preferred that he and Mary stayed another day.

Inside the barn, near the tack room on a portable rack, stood a silver show saddle, a pink ribbon and a card adorning it. The card was from her father and Mary.

"This is beautiful. He must think I will be showing again."

"Well, even if you don't show, it's a fine saddle to ride in."

She ran her fingers over the silver and the embossed designs in the leather affectionately. Then she threw her leg over and tried it for fit.

"We're not done yet." Adam helped her off and led her down the end of the barn where another pink ribbon decorated a stall door. She knew Sly used to be stalled there. Hand-in-hand he pulled her along, down the long aisle to the waiting stall.

Adam stopped before the stall and turned to her. Still holding her hand, his face held an enigmatic smile. "I thought this would be an appropriate gift to go with the saddle Joe bought for you. Here." He pulled a large envelope off the stall door and handed it to her.

She opened the enveloped and read the card. Then she scanned the registration clipped inside. It was Sly's. And the ownership transfer was in her name. She thought the mare was lost to her forever when she found out Adam really did own her. She stepped into the stall, her throat tight with tears, and stroked the silken neck of her favorite horse. "Oh, Sly."

After a short time, she turned and left the stall. She closed it and secured the latch. Then she purposely went to Adam and slid her arms around his middle. Heartfelt tears left tracks on his shirt. "Thank you, Adam. But she is far too expensive a gift."

"No, she belongs to you and always has. I've far too many other projects, and Sly is too old now to be shown and worked hard. She needs to be loved."

Emotions swirled through her as he carefully held her as he would delicate porcelain. She always knew Adam was special. She had never experienced this intimate side of him. Theirs had always been a close friendship—not this warmth she wanted hold on to forever.

"Tomorrow we will go for a short ride, or you can get reacquainted in the arena. It's getting late. We probably should clean up the dishes before Abe comes in the morning and grumbles at us."

"Yes," she said in a near whisper. She walked back to the bars of the stall. "I'll see you tomorrow, Sly."

They travelled through the barn and back up to the house in silence. This new bond between them made talking unnecessary. Brooke put the plates and glasses in the dishwasher and cleaned up the crumbs. Adam locked the door and checked the phone in the office for any messages. Claude raced ahead of her as she approached the stairs.

He came from the office. "Joe must have called while we were at the barn. He wishes you a happy birthday. He said he would call tomorrow."

"I hope they are enjoying themselves. He hasn't gone on an extended vacation ever."

"I know. It will be good for them." They ascended the stairs in quiet contemplation, and as she got to her door, she turned to face him. Her eyes darkened with emotion.

He walked the few feet between them.

Brooke took his hands in hers. "Thank you for everything. I cannot remember a more wonderful birthday."

"You cannot hide, sweetheart. Hiding only makes things harder in the long run. If you feel like riding tomorrow, I'll try to fit in some time to trail ride with you. It probably would be good for some of the young horses. And of course, Claude has his job to do. Just don't hide."

His voice was soothing and comforting, giving her a sense of well-being and strength.

"Don't tell my father what I told you. Please?" Her eyes probed his in a heartfelt plea.

She didn't resist when his arms wrapped around her, cradling her in his warmth. He tipped her chin up to meet his. His lips covered hers in a surprisingly gentle kiss, dessert for her ravished soul. He held her close, resting her head on his chest. Caressing her back softly, she felt his deep sigh.

Brooke was at odds with her thoughts—the thought of his large, hard body wrapped around hers, snuggled under the covers safe and warm. If he even hinted at sleeping with her, she would not have refused him.

Stepping back, he guided her delicately into her room. His voice was a mellow whisper, "Sleep well, princess."

CHAPTER EIGHTEEN

For days after her birthday, Brooke spent most of her time alone. Although she craved peace and quiet, now her days seemed rather solitary. Claude was always there for companionship. In the morning, she rode Sly lightly in the indoor arena or worked with the crew halter-training the new foals, guiding them around with halter and a lead rope.

Although Abe was busy polishing the silver tack for the next show, he was constantly checking up on her. She supposed Adam had some influence in Abe's rounds. She didn't mind. Adam had become her champion when her world seemed to be falling into ruin again. He showed none of the physical affection he displayed on her birthday. But when had she stopped suspecting him of inciting some of the attacks?

Was he corrupt? No, her subconscious whispered, not

Adam. And the trashing of her room was assigned to Kitty. He assured her of that.

She knew that many machines seemed to be going on strike around the ranch. Adam was constantly absent. He and Hank were kept busy most of the day and into the night coaxing the metal monsters back to work or trying to keep up the training on the horses. The new John Deere tractor had starter problems. And while Hank and Adam tried to doctor the monstrosity, another man was sent to Laramie for parts not available in town. Haying was a slow process with the old, less powerful tractors.

She sat on the patio, polishing her old, silver show halter. The halter looked beautiful on Sly with her dainty chiseled head, and although she wouldn't be able to show her, she hoped another horse would have the same qualities.

The sound of the four-wheeler interrupted her musings. Adam parked the new red machine at the edge of the lawn. He plodded up from the barn, no smile forthcoming. With grease everywhere he no longer looked the part of the well-groomed trainer. His tanned face and arms were beginning to burn from the intense heat of the mountain sun. His open shirt exposed his muscular chest covered in dark wisps of hair. Even filthy with grit and dirt, he radiated a vitality that drew her like a magnet.

He slumped down in one of the black, wrought iron chairs, lines of weariness and frustration etched his face.

He sighed with fatigue. His dark eyes softened as he grinned at her. It was easy to get lost in the way he looked at her.

"Would you please get me an iced tea. I am just filthy."

"How about lunch while you're here?" She got up and headed for the door, pausing to wait for his answer.

He looked up for a moment from the notes he was jotting down. "I may as well. I'll need the phone book, too."

Although she knew he was frustrated with the machinery and the training time he was losing on several colts, he was congenial with her. The lack of turmoil between them was welcome. He got up to take the book from her at the door.

Brooke made his favorite roast beef sandwich on rye bread with pickles, and melon slices on the side. She also made one for herself. Grabbing a couple of red-plastic plates they used outside, she arranged their lunches and added two chocolate chip cookies. After placing them on the picnic table, she went inside to get a pitcher of iced tea and glasses.

From his conversation, she concluded the bailer had broken down and it, too, needed a repairman. He placed his phone next to his plate, and sipped his cool, drink. "You really do surprise me. I didn't know you could cook. I assumed Mary did everything for you." And then he winked at her and smiled, a little devilishness entered his eyes.

She grinned. "Mary is a good teacher."

"I can see that. If you continue cooking like you have the past few days, I'll have to go on a diet." He patted his flat, rock-hard stomach.

"Well, since Wednesday you haven't had much rest. Food, at least will keep you going."

"After we eat, would you do me a favor?" He didn't look at her when he asked and seemed preoccupied with his lunch.

"What would that be?"

"I need to go over to my father's and borrow his bailer for today and tomorrow. He's done for now, and by the time he needs it, mine will be fixed. You can drive behind me on the way back with the flashers on."

She was shocked with the word 'mine' more so than the thought of driving to his father's house. The fact he really did own the ranch and all it entailed struck a sad note in her heart. A sigh of despair did not go unnoticed.

"You will be all right." His voice was firm with a note to inspire confidence.

"I know." She smiled lightly.

"I wouldn't ask, but everyone is involved with one thing or another. You're the only available person. It seems we have been cursed with machinery gremlins."

His phone rang. Since he had taken a large bite of sandwich, Adam indicated with a nod of his head for her to answer it.

"Well, Buck is this pleasure call or business call?"

"A bit of both actually. How are you getting along?" he asked.

"Just fine." She tried to keep her voice light. The scene of her room in total ruins surfaced in her mind with Buck's question. She bit down on her bottom lip as a wave of residual fear wash through her. She knew the overall conclusion was that Kitty ruined her things and stole her jewelry. And Kit did give her a substantial check to cover most of it. But why did Kitty shred them like her dead husband would do? Or was it a coincidence?

Buck continued with his always positive spin on life. "It's probably jealousy and not something to brood about. Some people are just mean. Get yourself busy with some project and not worry on it, hear?" His western drawl was comforting. "I do need to talk to Adam if he is around, or you could leave him a message to have him call me soon."

Adam took the phone, and although it wasn't a long conversation, it did seem to be one sided. He merely made negative or positive grunts. He placed the phone on the table.

He fiddled with his napkin, staring at it as if it could give him some answers. His voice held a thin edge of irritation. "I forgot about a meeting I promised to attend with Buck tomorrow night. I'll have Abe come up and stay with you. I'll try not to be too late." He took a last drink of iced tea and got up from his seat. "Are you ready? We'll be back in no time."

She left the dishes on the table and followed him to the pickup. She wondered what Buck said to provoke him. Neither spoke on the drive to Hightower. When they returned, he acknowledged her help with a simple thank you.

"Adam, I have to go into town for groceries."

He stared at her for a moment, his mouth working on a toothpick. "Damn. I wish someone was free to go with you. We're all swamped."

"You said not to hide, remember?"

"Yes, I did. Don't take the car. Drive your father's new pickup." He paused for a moment. His brow furrowed. Then he said, "You could also pick up some Oreos for me." He smiled, but it didn't reach his eyes. "Call me when you get to town. I may recall something I need by then. Sign for whatever you buy at the grocery store, and the bill will come here."

"All right. I'll bring Claude with me. He probably would like the ride."

He touched the back of her head with two, grimy fingers and pressed a warm kiss on her cheek. "Be careful." He walked a distance away and stopped, turned to look at her as though he wanted to say something, and then continued to the barn.

Adam spent hours after dinner in the office, working on record books and invoices. He kept the room dark, except for the brass lamp illuminating the large antique desk.

Brooke brought him a tray of milk and Oreos. He thanked her, but his voice told her his thoughts were elsewhere.

"Is something wrong?"

He looked up at her. His face still held a bedeviled look. "No, nothing for you to worry about. Just ranch business, your father is much more patient with this."

"Do you want me to do some of the bookkeeping until he gets back?"

Almost too quickly he replied. "Oh, no thank you. I've about finished." He shuffled papers, clearing off the top of his desk. "I was contemplating some things."

He pushed the sleeves of his white, cotton sweater back to his elbows, exposing the bronzed skin of his arms and chest where the 'v' of the neckline lay open. He inhaled an Oreo and then a gulp of milk to wash it down.

Brooke watched from where she stood across the desk. He was so very handsome in the dim light of the lamp. She had a desire to go over and sit in his lap, feel the comfort of those strong arms like she did the day after her clothes were ruined. She felt safe at that moment. He made it clear she was a responsibility until she established her own place. Was his gift of Sly a hint for her to get started?

"Well, I'll see you in the morning." She headed for the door.

"Brooke, thank you for the cookies and milk. Sleep well."

"You're welcome. Good night."

She sat up with a stack of pillows and tried to read a book she had picked up at the store. Her wandering thoughts kept going back to Adam. He was soothing to her battered soul. She heard the water of his shower through the wall of her bathroom. Visualizing him naked with the warm water, the soap bubbles caressing his body. Damn, her feelings for him had nothing to do with reason. Long into the night she wondered about the future.

Adam came up from the barns around five on Saturday to shower and dress for the evening. His eyes touched on her repeatedly as he removed his boots in the mudroom and continued through the kitchen. Abe would be coming up to have dinner with her.

Apparently, Brooke thought, he prefers a more distant relationship. His attitude had changed, and now she felt like a little sister once again, a border in his home. The realization stung some. She was sure it was better this way.

She picked up a few catalogues of house plans when she went to town for groceries. She agonized over the time she was spending alone without anyone near. A sudden burst of cabin fever struck her. However, she didn't feel compelled to call Bess or anyone to keep her company. And she couldn't very well expect Adam to feel he needed to keep her company.

She took two pork chops from the refrigerator for herself and Abe and placed them on the counter. Agitated, she tore open the tape on the white butcher paper and placed them on a platter. Her gloomy thoughts were interrupted by the sound of Adam's boots as he sauntered through the foyer. Pensively, he came into the kitchen, fastening his expensive gold watch. She was taken by the handsome figure he presented. Her thoughts seemed hers alone until she noticed he was watching her.

"Is something wrong? Wrong color combination?" His eyebrows shot up with the question as his arms spread to afford her a better view.

She swallowed nervously. "No. You look fine." Her words were almost a whisper. Embarrassment flushed her cheeks.

His black pants were well cut and accented the length of his long legs. His white shirt, open at the neck, was striking against his darkened skin. A tan leather blazer finished off the ensemble. He should model for men's wear, she marveled, but kept silent.

"I'll try not to be too late." His boots tapped their way across the kitchen.

Brooke stood, immobilized for a time, feeling temporarily rejected. Then she silenced her fears. Neither of them needed to account to the other. No matter what happened earlier in the week, they were still adversaries on certain points. He was acting out a part for the benefit of her father, she mused, nothing more, a responsibility, a way to ease his conscience, he said.

Later, as she and Abe were about to sit down outside with their meal, a black Suburban pulled into the yard The Hightower monogram decorated the driver's door. Steve was driving. Bess and Hank were with him. Steve seemed to leap from the vehicle and in no time, he was swinging her in an embrace, giving her a large smacking kiss before he set her down.

"Welcome back," she giggled at his enthusiasm. "Would you like to join us? I can take out a few more chops." She had been angry at Steve. Why hadn't he even called? But did he have to? She weighed the whole structure of events. A tumble of confused thoughts assailed her. She forced herself to produce a stiff smile.

"No, thank you. If Abe doesn't mind my stealing you from his company, I'd like to take you to town with Hank and Bess to have dinner. I sold one of my paintings to a large resort in Steamboat. They're going to use it in their logos. We are going to the hotel to eat and then kick up our heels a bit. The band in town has everybody talking. And, I know you haven't been out with anyone. I checked with Abe. So, what do you say?" Steve rambled on with the assurance he was going to have his own way.

"Get goin' Claude and me will share this here meal of yours," Abe offered as he forked a piece of pork chop in his mouth.

She chuckled. "I'll have to change first. Just stay put."

Rustling around in her large dressing-room sized closet, she found a pair of new jeans and her new red boots, also a fitted blouse, loosely knit with a low neckline. After removing the tags and getting dressed, she checked herself in the full-length mirror. She found the small shoulder bag that matched the boots. Pulling her hair back, she secured it with silver combs.

She left the dressing room and reached for the gold heart that Adam gave her. It wasn't on the dresser where she placed it. Could it have fallen behind her dresser? After a quick search, she decided to look for it later, probably nestled behind the dresser in the thick carpet. Then she thought, wouldn't it seem indecent to date one brother and wear the jewelry from the other?

The Bantry Hotel was full of people when they arrived. Bess had the forethought to reserve a table. By the time their dessert came, Brooke had relaxed a bit and was trying to have a good time. She watched Bess surreptitiously, wondering if she really had something to do with destroying her clothes. Or did she and Kitty have some pact? She was no longer the free spirit who left Wyoming years ago. Now she even suspected those around her of heinous acts. Needing a moment alone, she excused herself from the booth and headed to the restroom to freshen up.

Adam couldn't believe what he was seeing. Brooke was there. He worried all night, worried over how she felt about being left alone, feeling guilty about going out and leaving her at the ranch. And here she was, bold as brass, dressed for a night out, and wearing the new clothes he purchased for her. He suffered the dull ache of desire when he watched the appreciative glances she was getting from the men in the room. Anger filled him.

As she came out of the lady's room, he grasped her arm. The cold fury of his eyes left her temporarily speechless. He led her away from the crowds at the bar. The tension of his grip belied the smile on his face. "What are you doing here?"

She pulled her arm out of his painful hold and rubbed at the soreness. "Steve came out to the house with Hank and Bess. They insisted I come with them. So, here I am."

"Oh ... Steve didn't mention it," he frowned. His gaze never left hers. "Well, let me walk you back to your group." The statement was more of an order than a request as he followed her to her table in the back room, his hand keeping contact with the small of her back.

Brooke slid in next to Steve.

Adam remained standing. His voice hid whatever thoughts his eyes betrayed. "When did you get back?"

"A few hours ago. I did get one painting sold for what I was asking. Now if Dad will give me some time, I'll get started on another one." Steve reclined in the booth nonchalantly, perfectly in tune with the woman sitting next to him.

Adam jiggled some coins in his pocket to keep his

hands occupied. His shoulders were tight. He wanted to stay with them, but at the same time he wanted to escort Brooke back to the banquet with him and away from his brother, or maybe home.

"It was nice of you to take Brooke out tonight." Adam watched her solemnly, swimming through a haze of feelings and desires. She glanced up at him in spurts.

"Can you sit a while?" Steve made a gesture with his free hand.

"No, I'd better get back to the dinner. If I can escape early, I'll join you for a drink."

Bess spoke up for the group. "Great, Hank and I are going to hoof it up a bit, right Hank?"

"See you later." With a nod of his head, Adam walked away, knowing he wanted to be with them instead of with Buck's spinster sister. She was one of the most boring women he had ever known. Her constant stream of chatter and questions nearly drove him crazy.

His thoughts tormented him. Steve was no good for Brooke, he mused. He could not give her all of himself. Only one woman held a place in Steve's heart—Desiree, and she was long gone. He was a free spirit and always would be, unless Desiree miraculously reentered the picture. Brooke was a pleasant diversion for Steve, he tried to convince himself. But she was a grown woman. She'd already survived one marriage. She would have to make her own decisions.

At the double doors, a flashy redhead stopped him. Kitty smiled as her hands danced over his upper torso.

Another unpretentious, overweight woman approached them, and they moved into the banquet room.

When Adam had enough socializing, he excused himself, using an imagined workload for the next day, even if it was Sunday. Only one light was on in the house when he arrived. He assumed Brooke was still up. Maybe, he pondered, he could share a nightcap with her, or a snack. With a blow of disappointment, he discovered Abe and Claude snoring as the television blared to accommodate his hearing loss.

"Hey, Abe, television keeping you awake?" He shook the older man's shoulder gently. Claude barked a warning. Then recognizing Adam, he went back to his bed.

"Adam," he mumbled half asleep.

"Did Brooke get home yet? I didn't see them in town when I left."

"Well, she's not here. She's at Hightower. Seems there's some new movie Steve picked up they're watchin'."

"Well, she should be safe enough over there." The side of his mouth twitched once as if he had been pinched. An awkward silence settled between them. He hated to consider how seriously Steve would watch out for her. He recalled his imagined scene at the pool house. Were they back in the pool? He gritted his teeth with angst.

The day they spent in the city he found a new person hidden under all the pain. Brooke looked so bored when he left for town. He almost invited her to the banquet with him.

Abe nodded his head to acknowledge Adam's statement. "I'll sleep here in the den and take off early for my own place in the morning. Don't wait too long to ask her," Abe grumbled.

CHAPTER NINETEEN

*T*he phone rang once before Adam tore the receiver from its holder, unable to tolerate the sound of a second ring. The clock flashed an early six o'clock. Irritation at being awakened on a Sunday morning suddenly switched to concern. Brooke could be in trouble.

"Yes," he rasped.

"Adam, did I wake you?" Joe asked with innocence.

"It is six, and it is Sunday."

Joe chuckled. "I thought I'd better call while I have the chance. Our plane is leaving here shortly, and I don't know when I would find the time to let you know of our plans."

"You're leaving for the islands?"

"No. I met an old, roping buddy, Mitch, down here. He owns a spread in Texas, north of Dallas. Mary and I are going there for a while. I'm borrowing one of his horses to rope on at an Old Timers Rodeo in Fort Worth this weekend."

"Sounds like a plan. Are you having a good time?" He sat up straighter on the bed and ran his free hand through his hair.

"Mary's buying me into the poor house. We're shipping home some of the things we bought, so we won't have to carry them around. Is everything all right there?" Joe's worried tone came through to Adam.

"Yes, the cattle have been sent off. We've had some machinery problems." He yawned as he forced himself into a sitting position on the edge of the bed. He stretched his bare feet along the thick carpet. The night was long, and he felt as though he hardly slept.

"I wasn't referring to the ranch. Have there been any more incidents?" Joe insisted.

"No." He lied for the benefit of his friend.

"I'd like to talk to her. Get her up if you have to."

"Joe, she is not here." He hesitated for a fraction of a second before he continued. "She spent the night at my father's."

"Have you two been at each other's throats again?" Joe's voice accused.

He forced some sincerity, knowing Joe and Mary would cut short their vacation and be on the first flight home. "No, it's nothing like that."

"Well, then why isn't she home?"

"Joe, she went over to watch old John Wayne movies

with Steve. It got late and she stayed the night. Nothing more."

His head began to throb. Impatiently, he ran his fingers over his scalp, combing through the dark curls. He couldn't envision why it would be 'nothing more.'

"Well, then, do you think we can spare the extra week away, Mary and I will keep traveling."

"Fine, Joe. Call and let us know where you're going to be—and have fun for a change."

"Thanks, Adam. I'll try again in a few days."

After replacing the receiver, he stood up. He reached and stretched his muscles to get of the stiffness out, but the crick in his neck remained. He put on a pair of soft worn jeans and a chambray shirt, leaving the buttons undone and his shirttail hanging out.

He shuffled down the stairs and into the kitchen barefooted where he saw Abe sitting in the mudroom putting on his boots. The aroma of freshly brewed coffee filled the kitchen. The Keurig was on, and its reservoir was filled.

"Naw, not really. It's morning and time to move anyways." Abe pulled on the other boot. "I'll have to go over and feed my critters, then come back and get started on the chores. Which of those halters do you want polished for next week's show?"

Adam couldn't think of work right then. He went to the cabinet and took two aspirin.

"The new one, I guess. Joe called a bit ago. They're going to Texas for a spell and then on to Hawaii. If Joe calls and I'm not here, take a message. Don't tell him about the vandalism. I don't want him worrying about problems here. They need to have a good time."

"Just when are you going to take care of that other problem?" Abe replied pointedly.

Before he could reply to Abe's hinting, the discussion was interrupted as the problem entered the house. Brooke smiled at Abe as he finished with his boots. "Good morning, Abe."

"Well, good mornin' to yourself," he acknowledged with a toothless smile. He headed out the door, but not before he waggled a finger at Adam.

Adam sat at the table with a glass of orange juice and a cup of coffee. Brooke noticed the dark curls on his chest, exposed by the unbuttoned shirt. His bare foot was propped on the empty chair where she usually sat. He stared at her with what she assumed was hostility.

"The social butterfly returns. What would bring you home so early—or is it late?" He shifted in his chair and sipped from his cup.

She didn't trust herself to reply. She went over and made her own cup of coffee and sat down in her father's chair, avoiding any battle with his bare foot.

"Must have been a very long movie, or did you need to go for another swim in Dad's pool?"

She let out a deep sigh and stared out of the window.

The last thing she wanted was to revisit the conflicts between them. She realized Steve was not what she would want in a permanent partner. She had no feelings for him other than as a dear old friend. No sparks to cause her heart to flutter. However, the lost affability with Adam saddened her. She really did enjoy his company the week before and the easy rapport between them.

"Since my absence from this house has caused you to be sarcastic this early, here's the play by play—your brother and I watched old John Wayne movies. Your father came home from his poker game and sat in the den with us. We must have all fallen asleep because the television was still on this morning when we got up to take Josh to the airport. They dropped me off on the way."

She took a sip of coffee and then quickly offered, "Oh, and so your sordid mind doesn't have anything to feed on, I'll confess nothing happened—no sex." Her voice became quiet, almost a whisper. "Now you have the facts."

He did not respond, nor did he look at her. He fiddled with the corner of the placemat. She picked up her coffee and headed for the hallway. She couldn't stand to sit at the table with him, looking like every-woman's dream, but his voice stopped her.

"Your father called this morning. He wanted to talk to you. They are going to Texas for a few days and then on to Hawaii. They'll be gone a few weeks."

"Well, at least they sound like they're having a good time. You didn't tell him about my room, did you?"

"No, I didn't think it was necessary at this point."

She continued to her bedroom. A hot shower and some clean clothes were in order, and maybe she could get a small nap. She finished stripping and slipping into a robe when the house phone rang.

On the fourth ring she picked up the receiver. Adam had beat her to it. The caller identified himself as a detective from Los Angeles. Adam was investigating Mike. What was he up to now? He had everything. Adam couldn't take much more from her. Or was there?

Brooke hurried downstairs. Adam was still in the office when she entered. Ending the call, he hung up the phone slowly and sat on the edge of the desk. He tapped a newly sharpened yellow pencil on his knee.

When Adam finally spoke, his voice was softer without an edge. "You were listening."

"Not on purpose. Why are you investigating Mike? I told you there isn't anything left." Her voice sparked with anger. "If you want to know something I probably would be able to tell you. Instead, you go behind my back."

"Brooke, I am sorry you had to find out this way. I should have told you. I have no devious intentions." He walked slowly over to where she stood. "After we talked last week at the restaurant, I thought how terrible a life you must have had with him. It occurred to me he may have held things from you, and you were entitled to anything they found. Land. Stocks. Apparently, he wasn't an upright citizen, but nothing of monetary value was discovered." He looked deep into her blue eyes, mellowed since her outburst. "I was only trying to help".

"Why would they call on Sunday?"

He leaned his shoulder into the doorjamb. "They called this morning because I told them I would be here to take their call."

She didn't reply immediately. She stood her ground in the doorway, one hand pressed on the jamb. Maybe he was just looking out for her. She took a step back, back away from the temptation inches from her. Why after all these years did she now find herself drawn to him? She had to fight her own battle of restraint. He needed his life back to normal. She needed to rebuild.

She looked up, and her heart jumped uncomfortably. "Adam, I've decided to build on the property. Apparently, my presence here—your home— is causing you anxiety. I need to find a new life for myself, one with some peace and self-satisfaction. Last week while I was home alone, I found a house plan I like. I've sent for the plans and ordered a survey to be done on the site. It might be best if I move out now. I can live in a motor home at the lake while the house and barn are being built, and you can go on with your life as before."

She turned and quickly ran up the stairs, her heart lodged in her throat. The suddenness of her disclosure left her frightened. Could she protect herself? Did he even care? He didn't stop her. He didn't say a word. Maybe he would be glad to have her gone from his life.

Brooke curled up on her loveseat and stared into the openness beyond. Her life seemed so muddled and unsettled. She did not want to leave this beautiful house with all its memories, its feeling of solid security. Home. Too much of her life was here. But things had changed. They were out of her control. She would have to go on and make the best of it.

Adam threw the pencil viciously onto the desk and watched it skitter and fall to the floor. He didn't want her to move out. This was not what he expected. After making scrambled eggs and toast, he found he had no appetite. Claude was enthusiastic about the remains.

He cared a lot what happened to Brooke. Protective, a feeling he only sensed in himself with Joe. Now it was Joe's daughter. Somehow the Montgomery clan got into his blood, and he could not shake them off.

He had learned a lot about Brooke since she came back. His previous impressions of her were just that—impressions. Most of their lives they bickered and argued about the most mundane things. Usually, it was his need to have his own way, while she fought like a hellcat to stand her ground.

Their age difference was probably at fault. He left high school even before she finished elementary school. He attended college and all the wildness those years entailed, including co-eds who wanted to experiment with alcohol and sex as he did. And when he came back to Hightower to help work the ranch, Brooke was still competing in high school rodeos. She had spirit then, now she was frightened and fragile. Even as she told him she was leaving, he could see reluctant fear slip into her eyes.

He wanted her there permanently. She finished off the ranch and his life. She belonged there more than he did. He had the ranch, the house, and Joe's respect. He was a nationally known breeder and trainer of fine horses. Success had come easy, along with hard work. But it wasn't enough to complete him.

Slowly he got up from the table and placed his dishes in the sink. They had to talk. She needed him to protect her and to keep her safe. He needed her to fill his life, make all his hard work worth more than a hefty bank account. And, Abe warned, "Don't wait too long." Maybe he had already. He knocked on her door lightly.

"Just a minute," she called.

A few seconds later she opened the door with a question planted in her eyes. "What do you want now? I was going to shower."

"You didn't ask who was on the other side. It could have been anyone."

For a moment she considered his statement. "Well?"

"Brooke, we need to talk." Impatient with himself, he let himself into her room, staring at her as she moved to the windows, out of his reach. He recognized the silky, white robe she wore, one he purchased for her on their shopping trip. The front was closed tightly, hiding her soft skin.

She waited, anticipating what he would say. The house phone interrupted again. Irritably he picked up the receiver next to her bed. He listened for a few moments and then handed it to her. "It's Buck. I'll take it in the office. Would you please hang up after I get there?"

Without waiting for a reply, he raced down the stairs to the office phone. He was hoping Buck had some positive news for him. Adam waited to talk until he heard the click. While he tried to absorb the dire news from Buck, the front door chimes sounded twice. Claude barked at the unknown. And, before he could finish his conversation with Buck, he saw Brooke in the foyer opening the front door.

"Kitty, what would bring you out so early?" Brooke' voice was sugary sweet.

Adam saw the red-headed hussy brazenly push her way into the foyer. She had on a pair of tight jeans, black high-heeled boots, and a leopard print knit top, low cut and revealing.

"I'm looking for Adam. He has something of mine." Kitty threw Brooke a hateful look and turned to scan the office.

He met her at the doorway. Leaning his shoulder into the doorjamb, he frowned. "Hello, Kit. It's rather early for you to be up and about, isn't it, especially on a Sunday?"

"Well," she cooed, "I couldn't sleep. I thought I'd drop over and pick up my earrings and maybe share a cup of coffee with you."

Kitty looked back at Brooke and then to Adam's open shirt and bare feet. "Oh, dear, am I interrupting something?" Sarcasm oozed from her. Her green eyes flashed with anger.

"I don't have your earrings." He interrupted. He sensed what she was up to, and her antics could not have come at a worse time. He didn't need Brooke standing there watching Kitty's theatrics. He really wanted to spin her around and send her out the door.

Kitty fingered his shirt front, running the back of her hand down his chest seductively. "Why sure you do. Don't you remember? I gave them to you to hold for me. They were pinching my poor, little earlobes something terrible. You put them in your jacket pocket, during one of those slow dances."

He glanced over at Brooke, who was studying them with amused curiosity, arms folded. Claude perched next to her, watching.

"I don't remember you giving me your earrings.'" Irritably, he brushed her hand away.

"You did, love. Why don't you go up and look? Or I could come up with you and help you? Please? They are very expensive."

Brooke grinned, eyes twinkling with amusement. "I can go up and look for you."

"No." He threw Kitty's pawing hands from his shirt.

"Stay here," he growled. "I'll be right back." He left the women alone and took the stairs two at a time. He could hear the words coming fast and catty from the foyer.

"You two look awfully cozy. Here alone. Half dressed. All by yourselves. I wonder what tales the walls could tell. I bet there are all kinds of lustful things going on in these rooms. Lots of rooms to play in."

"I hope those images keep you warm at night." Brooke fingered the overlap of her robe.

"Oh. So, you do have claws. Adam is mine, and I will do anything to have him."

"So, what's kept you all these years?" Brooke countered.

"Oh, Adam, did you find them?" Kitty smiled, honey dripping from her lips as she heard his footsteps.

"Yes," he said irritably. At the bottom of the stairs, he handed Kitty the earrings.

She slipped her hand in the crook of his arm. "I knew they were there. They're so old. I'd hate to lose them. How about a cup of coffee, cowboy?"

Adam loosened her grip and stepped back. "No. I have to go to town."

"At this hour?" Kitty mewed and ran her fingers up his arm.

He took her wrist and turned her away. "Yes, at this hour. Now why don't you take your earrings home and put them away before they get themselves lost again?"

He opened the door, indicating she had no choice.

"Well, if you must. Please call." She smiled, running

her hand in a caress along his face. He didn't miss the venomous look she threw at Brooke.

He shut the door and leaned his forehead against the doorframe for a moment. He secured the bolt lock and turned toward Brooke who was already at the stairs.

"Kitty said you are hers. She seemed pretty serious," she sang devilishly.

She stood nearly level with him on the first stair. "I'm going up to the lake—alone—to plan my new place."

Without thought, he gently took her face in his hands and kissed her soft lips, then rested his forehead on hers. Adam sighed with impatience. "I have to go into town to see Buck. It's important. Please stay in the house until I get back."

CHAPTER TWENTY

*B*rooke let out a small sigh. Her pride kept her true feelings hidden. And she reveled in the feel of his warm length against her. In an uncontrolled surge of want, she wanted to cry, because she guessed he wasn't feeling the same ache of desire, just brotherly love.

His reactions were the same as when she was young, the peacemaker. This big, powerful man wore the look of a woeful hound, sad and worried. He kissed her as though those instances were natural to them, as though he always had—as though she had always let him.

And she had let him. And every time he kissed her so tenderly, her heart swelled with feelings she had thought were long gone. Would she stay if he asked her to? Adam never married. Maybe his idea of a relationship was having women available when he wanted to play.

"Well?" he asked softly.

"I guess. Maybe." Nervously, she turned and quickly mounted the stairs before her heart overtook her fragile emotions.

She watched from her window as he sped out the drive. Adam seemed so unusual that morning, so unpredictable. He let Joe believe all was well there so not to ruin their honeymoon. Something was bothering him. He would eventually tell her.

She decided to drive up to the lake. Who knew when he would be back? The morning sun was already warming up the land. Having Claude with her, she would feel relatively safe. She would take her small pistol along. Besides, it was time to get on with her own life. She would decide where she would build her house and how she should place it in relation to the lake.

Adam would have his freedom from her—and his ranch. And maybe, if she left there the problems would cease. If Kitty was the one trying to drive her away, then Adam would be available. She was haunted by the sad, almost pleading expression, burning in his eyes moments ago, when he suddenly planted a kiss on her lips, so spontaneous, so natural to their life-long friendship.

She struggled with the uncertainties cluttering her thinking. Adam had been her champion since she arrived at the ranch, always there, taking care of her problems. He suddenly became distant, as though he didn't know what to do with her presence in his home.

Maybe, she thought, she was the one who needed distance. Distance from the ranch itself. Building her own place would give her space and something to keep her mind busy, a creative project in which she could immerse all her energy. She came home broke and broken. At least the land and her trust fund would give her the opportunity to start over.

Adam knew by the look on Buck's face something dire had happened. His instincts suggested it had to have connections to the rustling and maybe Brooke.

"Thanks for coming. I didn't expect you here so soon." Buck sat back in his old wooden chair and rubbed the sleep from his face.

"I was awake anyway. So, what's this about a murder?" He eased himself into a captain's chair opposite Buck's desk.

"Well, a man was found this morning by two families who went to camp on the national forest land across from your lake. The teenagers were out running around with their dogs when they came across the body in a deep ravine. They don't seem to be involved. They flew into Denver and rented a small camper and drove out here on a whim. They'd never been camping before. Said they were going back to Rocky Mountain State Park and find a safe campground." Buck frowned and sipped from his endless cup of coffee. "Whoever did this took no cash or jewelry. I looked around but didn't find anything of significance."

"How did he die?" Adam sat up and leaned on his knees.

"Someone bashed his head in. Looks like the body was dumped there, been there a few days. Animals have been at it. Not pretty at all." Buck grimaced with the statement.

"Was there any identification?"

"Driver's license from somewhere in Texas. Here, you can look at it." Buck handed Adam the document.

Adam stared at the picture for some time, knowing where he had seen the man. "Junior Mason, if that's his real name. This is the man Kitty hired as her foreman. I found him in bed with her the night I went to see about the earring."

Silence hung heavily over the two friends.

"If he wasn't killed for his money or jewelry," Adam thought out loud, "then possibly he was involved in the rustling. Could be a partner in crime got too greedy. Any more reports of rustlers? It's been rather quiet around our place."

"No ... While we wait for Doc to get his old bones moving, why don't we go over to the hotel and get some breakfast and kill some time? I've been here since it got light out."

Adam's stomach turned in knots. "I think I'll pass on the breakfast. Maybe I had too much beer last night." He worried about Brooke being in the house alone and hoped she wouldn't be stubborn and go up to the lake by herself.

Pensively, he looked at the evidence, lying on the desk blotter. Someone had been killed close to his home. That someone was connected to Kitty. A cold knot formed in his chest.

Buck ran his fingers through his red hair. He put his cup down with an exasperated sigh. "His wrists have rub marks. He may have been tied up at one time. No ropes were found on the body. Maybe it was some drunken cowboys on Kitty's ranch who got out of control and dumped his body, thinking that only a coyote or a cougar would find it."

"So far out of town? And he worked for Kitty. There has to be a connection to all of this." His face clouded with uneasiness. Why would his body be dumped there? Just bad luck on the part of the campers to have come across the body, he mused. The location was so far off the beaten path it was unlikely that the body would be found until hunting season, or never. Did Kitty have him killed?

Buck turned silent. His voice was cautious when he finally spoke. "Adam, the rustling started a few months before Brooke arrived. And odd things have been happening to her. Could she, well, be involved—maybe even the ringleader in all of this? I have to look at all angles."

Adam stared at his friend in disbelief. "You can't be serious."

"Just a thought. Is it possible you are so connected to

the Montgomerys you can't be objective? Where was she last night?" Buck spoke quietly, not too accusing.

The silence of the office was only interrupted by the ticking of the old school clock on the far wall as it monitored the hours of the day. A dusty old pickup moved slowly down the worn pavement of the main street. The office smelled of paper and ink and stale coffee.

He found it hard to breath. He knew Buck was only trying to help, trying to do his job. If Brooke were involved, then her father's life would be in danger by her very presence. "Brooke was at Hightower with Steve. She's not involved in anything—at least knowingly. She wouldn't have come back if she were."

Buck forced a smile. "I hope you're sure."

"Yes, I am. Brooke loves her father too much to put him in danger—or Mary."

"I thought being close to them, you may have noticed something I didn't." The gentle giant rocked back in his chair. He gave his hand a wave of dismissal. "It was a thought. You did say she was out all night."

He frowned and looked away. "She was with Steve."

"Steve in town?" Buck picked up a pen and jotted on his yellow legal pad.

"No," Adam countered. "He went to Laramie to drop dad at the airport." He moved over to the window and wearily leaned his hand on the windowsill. "Brooke wasn't the only one up and about last night. Kitty showed up this morning while I was talking to you. She planted a pair of earrings in my jacket pocket as a ruse for coming over."

"I noticed how clingy she was last night. What makes you think Kitty's involved?"

He turned to face Buck. "I don't trust her. I guess I never have. And where the body was found isn't too far from her house."

"She sure has gotten around in her lifetime. I bet she knows more scuttlebutt about the people in this town than anyone else." Buck sauntered over to the window and placed a comforting hand on Adam's shoulder. "We'll get to the bottom of this. Oh, thanks for escorting Eleanor last night."

He nodded his head and grinned without comment. He turned to check the clock. "Well, most of the morning is gone. I'd better get back home before anything else happens. I'll call you later to see if anything new turns up."

"I think I'll go out and visit with Kitty a bit. Want to come along? I'd feel safer with someone else with me." He smiled. When Adam didn't offer to accompany him, he continued. "It will take a while for tests to come back. I'll let you know what the results are."

Wearily Adam closed the door to the office and headed for his pickup. Buck's insinuations bothered him, not because they were directed at Brooke, but because for all he knew, they could be true. His mind swirled with facts and hunches. Was that why she let him kiss her, even a natural kiss on the cheek? This morning was sweet and heartwarming, and she didn't stop him or pull out of his hold.

No, not Brooke. Even when she blurted that she was moving out, was going to live on her property alone in a motor home, she had fear in her eyes, a paranoid fear he had come to recognize in her. And he damned her dead husband for what he had programmed in her over those years of abuse. Her stare let him know she wasn't as brave as she wanted him to believe.

From his pickup he called the ranch on his cell. No one answered. Then he tried Brooke's phone, but she didn't answer either. Maybe she realized it was him and refused to answer. Hopefully nothing else happened while he was gone.

Anxiety welled in him. He raced back to the ranch to reassure himself. When he arrived, he found the house empty. After an examination of his home, he ran to the barn to locate Hank.

Adam was out of breath and his speech rushed as Hank walked over to meet him. "Where is Brooke? She's not in the house."

"She took the Explorer and the dog and drove up to the lake. She said she wanted to decide on a place for her house, thought she might swim for a while if the sun warmed up." Hank eyed his boss speculatively. "I did send Dan out with a four-wheeler to watch her from the ridge just to be safe. He has a two-way radio to call with if something is amiss, or he'll come in if he sees either me or you."

He let out a sigh of relief. Unconsciously, he was holding his breath, waiting for Hank to finish. "Damn woman, she never listens. I told her to wait. A man was found inside the national forest land not far from the lake this morning—dead." He glanced out at the far hills behind his ranch. "He was Kitty's newest foreman. I want to step up the number of help we have on an around the clock system. I think I'll call a company in Laramie and have surveillance cameras installed everywhere."

"Probably a good idea, especially if they can be hidden from sight. Maybe Kitty wore the guy out." Hank offered with a smile.

"Actually, someone smashed his head in."

Hank's worry showed on his face. "Hmm, well, that's not good."

"I'm going up to the lake now. I have to talk to her." Adam turned to go and stopped. "You were in town last night. Did you see anything or anyone new hanging around?"

Hank cleared his throat and grinned. "I didn't stay at the hotel long."

He smiled and headed for his truck.

The lake began about a hundred feet from the road, hidden by brush and trees. He parked his truck next to the Explorer. As he walked down the path, he could see her sitting on the large rock outcropping on the north edge of the lake called Grandpa's Lap.

The boulder, the size of a small garage tumbled down the hillside eons ago and landed along the edge of the lake. On its way, a huge crack caused a flat area the size of a large table and about as high. Water lapped over the flat area, cooling the rock, and made for a comfortable place to sit and dangle one's feet, or to lie down and let the thin layer of water cool one's sides on a hot summer day.

As she doved from the rock, he watched her lithe, willowy body break through the water with dolphin-like grace. Recognizing him, Claude did not bark a warning. Adam located the man Hank sent and waved him off. Then he sat on a large, boulder with the dog and watched over her as she swam.

CHAPTER TWENTY-ONE

$\mathcal{W}$ith a residue of fear from her last visit to the lake, Brook constantly reminded herself that Kitty had been behind the clothing fiasco and probably the other incidents. At least that's what Adam claimed. And Kitty did pay her for the clothes, so she had to believe that was true.

She forced herself not to envision anything and to concentrate on her purpose—the building of her own ranch. She and Claude wandered around the areas nearest the road, trying to get an idea of where she would place her house and barn. She wanted a view of the lake and pastures from her kitchen and patio. The barn would be to the right of the house so she could view her horses in their runs and pasture.

A more modern home would be best—not traditional one like the homestead. She ordered plans with long, wall-like windows to let in the sunshine and to provide her with the comforting views of the pastures. Still, she could barely hold back the ache in her chest when she remembered Adam owned her family home. Her throat tightened when she realized that his children—not hers—would run through those halls, filled with her memories.

To alleviate the negative thoughts, she swam, and kept swimming until fatigue released her tension. To relax and recoup her strength, she floated and recalling being a child, watching the clouds as they formed different pictures in her innocent mind. She couldn't have envisioned then how her life would have evolved.

Whenever she thought about her marriage, anxiety gripped her. Living with Mike was like being a slave, a prisoner with little love or affection. Sex was violent and quick. No satisfaction. No loving endearments. No caresses. And now her sanctuary from the world, her home, the one thing she considered her anchor was no longer her heritage. Sold.

She was on her own.

Brooke heard the splash, and with the fear of her last experience fresh in her mind, she began to swim. Terrorized, she pushed herself to get to the beach, her lungs nearly bursting. In shallow water she began to run, forcing her legs to pull through the encumbering water. She had to get to her gun.

Claude, sensing her fright, barked, urging her on, and ran into the water to meet her. Through her waves of fear and Claude's barking, she heard her name.

"Brooke, don't go."

Adam. She fell on all fours on the edge of the beach, gasping with anger—and relief. Claude licked her face, checking to see if she was alright. She rose and faced her monster.

"Damn you, Adam. You scared the hell out of me."

"Don't be angry." He chuckled. Adam stood waist deep in the water. "I'm sorry I frightened you. I like the suit."

She wore the blue bikini he bought for her on their shopping trip.

He gave her a thumbs up. "Nice suit. Come out and swim with me."

Brooke eyed him anxiously. Her heart told her to hurry to him, while her mind stayed suspicious. "Why should I?"

"We'll swim, and then we'll have that talk I wanted earlier."

And there he stood, devilishly handsome, his muscular chest covered lightly in wet, dark curls. She considered his request for a moment and then shrugged. What exactly did he want to talk about? He had everything.

Brooke sent Claude back to the rock and started toward Adam cautiously. When they were even, they swam slowly with even strokes to the other side of the lake. They hung on to the crevices of the rock wall, forming the back side of the lake, and rested.

Neither spoke. She was aware of the curious but intense

stares she was getting from him. He made no overt gestures toward her. She sensed something was on his mind. His temperamental behavior the past week puzzled her.

Wasn't he insolent and rude early that morning, only to turn gentle when she announced she was leaving? Hadn't he barged into her room, demanding to talk, only to leave abruptly after Buck called him? And now he wanted to swim. She gazed at him with curiosity and found him watching her, studying her. She cleared her throat and looked away, pretending not to be affected by his nearness.

After a few moments of rest, they started back for the other side where Claude sat waiting for their return. As they approached the edge of the lake, where Adam's legs could touch bottom, he maneuvered close to Brooke and drew her to him. Anchored to the bottom, he held her gently by her waist, allowing the buoyancy of the water to keep her even with his shoulders.

"Let's go over to Grandpa's Lap."

With an arm wrapped around her, he carried her over to the rock and sat her on the flat ledge. The water licked at her thighs. Slowly, seductively, he scanned her face, as on the night he kissed her after their trip to the city. She sat facing him while her calves dangled on the outside of his thighs. His arousing good looks tempted her to reach out and stroke his face. She waited, hoping to learn what was on his mind.

"I thought you wanted to swim?" With the warm

touch of his legs next to hers, her heart thumped in her breast.

"We did. Now we have to talk without your dog interrupting." He spoke softly, his voice a bit strained. His eyes touched her face ever so gently, covering each hollow and curve.

"Apparently, your disposition has changed since this morning. If you are trying to convince me to stay at the house—it won't work." Brooke tried to sound convincing, but she was distracted by his firm hands as they held her hips casually, his thumbs nearly coming together on her stomach, moving ever so gently down and over her smooth skin, inches from a building core of arousal.

"Why not?" He smiled with a caress.

Her emotions whirled and tingled. She pushed gently on his thumbs to try for a release. "I don't need another father."

Adam chuckled lightly and brought his hands up to hold her head. "Brooke, listen to me. Look at me." He tipped her chin to see her face. "I need you, more than anyone else. I want you to stay at the ranch, be my wife. Marry me."

Stunned, she studied his face and tried to assess this new challenge. Never had she seen him so vulnerable. She could feel the hardened tension in his forearms as he waited for her to reply. Uncertainty crept into her mind, clouding her thoughts.

"Marry you?" she struggled out, wanting more of an explanation to this sudden proposal.

"I love you, Brooke. I have always loved you—even when you were a little brat. I haven't been able to think of much of anything else all week. When you left for California, it nearly broke my heart." He put his forehead to hers for a moment and then moved back to stare into her eyes. His face lit with his thoughts. His mouth curved in a smile. "When I saw the little car coming down the drive the first day you came home, I was overjoyed. And even if I had to watch you and never be part of your life, I felt it would be tolerable. And then, when you didn't come home last night, I couldn't hide my feelings any longer."

She didn't answer him but continued to study what he was saying.

"Actually, I was afraid to ask you before now, afraid you would reject my offer—like now," he confessed.

For a few minutes she stared at him, hardly believing her ears. When she spoke, her soft words were full of accusations. "How do I know you aren't asking me to marry you so you can have my land?"

"You can give this damned land to the government for an animal refuge if you will marry me." His hands gripped her shoulders tighter.

Adam pulled her close, and finding no resistance, his lips claimed hers, cradling her as if she were a priceless possession. His hands slipped around her tight bottom and slid her closer.

Adam never played games, never pretended. She studied his face, taking in all he said, and remembering all the things they shared and confessed the past few weeks. She could feel the tenseness in his body and his hardness against her belly as he waited for her to answer.

Her eyes began to twinkle as she smiled at him. "Why did you choose here to ask me?"

"You chose the spot. I told you to stay home. Remember?" Adam cupped her face in his hands. "I would never hurt you. You and I may play word games with one another. Neither of us would intentionally cause the other pain, serious pain. You know as well as I do." He gently grasped her head with both hands and forced her to look at him. "You know I wouldn't say I loved you if I didn't mean it."

Yes, she knew. She also knew he had the inner strength she could depend on. She always felt safe with Adam, safe from whatever lurked in the shadows. And he was man enough to admit when he was wrong.

"I didn't want you to leave the other night," she confessed as she ran a finger around his furry chest. "I felt hurt you were leaving me with Abe and acting so distant."

"I didn't want to go. Buck's sister must have a recessive gene dating back to the Neanderthals, but I did promise him weeks ago." His grin was disarming.

"What about Kitty. She took up more of your time than Buck's sister."

"Forget Kitty. She has a way of making things look

the way she wants them to look, for her benefit—like this morning."

Brooke rested her cheek on his chest, letting her hands roam over his back. Then she grinned up at him. "You're in your underwear, like when we were kids."

He chuckled at her discovery. "Say yes," he whispered.

She knew this was right. Had always been right. Her hands touched his face. "Yes, I will marry you, Adam."

His lips covered hers hungrily. He pulled her closer, tucking her curves tight against his. His hands explored the silken skin of her back and shoulders, as she explored his. Her fine hand slipped inside his waist band.

A whispered moan rumbled from his chest. "We either have to finish this or stop now."

His answer came when she moved her hands under his waistband and slid it passed his hips and further to slide to his ankles. Her legs wrapped around him as her hands held his face to kiss him with soft, lapping kisses, turned urgent and delicious as the storm flooded through her. The heat of him pressed hard against her stomach.

Adam untied the neck of her suit and let it slide to her waist. He laid her back gently to lie on the flat stone. As the water lapped at her sides he caressed and kissed each globe, searching for pleasure points, while his hands toured her bared flesh. He untied the bottom strings and let the suit dangle from the ledge as his lips did a lust-burning exploration of her ivory flesh.

Brooke melted beneath his touch. Her delicate hand

guided him. Matching motion for motion, they moved in harmony until waves of ecstasy washed over her. She reached a height of passion she had never felt before, shattering the hard protective shell she had so carefully built.

His breath came in surrendering moans as he found his own release. He continued to caress her as though he were mapping a place in his heart.

She sat up, and they held each other tenderly, quietly, filled with an amazing sense of completeness. Brooke would have stayed there all day, locked together, right there in his arms, his safety, his love.

Adam lifted her head and kissed her lightly. "Yes, it's perfect. This was so sudden. I forgot a ring to make it official. I seem to be as impulsive as your father. We'll have to go on another shopping spree."

"I can wait. Let's stay here a bit longer. I'll never look at this old rock in the same way ever again."

"I don't want you to come up here alone." he murmured, almost like an afterthought.

"Why shouldn't I come up here?"

Adam held her away from him and stared into her face. "A man's body was found near here last night, near the forest service road. I'm not letting you out of my sight anymore."

CHAPTER TWENTY-TWO

*E*njoying their newfound bliss, Brooke helped Adam get ready to haul to Fort Collins for a three-day American Paint Horse Association show. She saddled and warmed up the horses, so he could work on the training. Afterwards, she brushed each horse and made sure they had some paddock time to play or brows on grass.

He noticed her pause as she ran a soft brush down the shiny, back of a beautiful black and white two-year-old mare. She stared, and he wondered what she was thinking. Buck had no leads on the man found in the forest. Still, he worried. She still had sleep tremors, disturbing quakes to her serenity. He wanted to help her forget, keep her safe.

Adam stood a few feet away on the other side of the horse. "Your arm stuck?" Smiling, he came over and gave her a warm hug. "When you're finished, we have shopping to do."

They drove to town and purchased food they would store in the living quarters of the horse trailer. Adam seldom let her out of his sight, and he enjoyed the hugs and sexual play she sent his way during the day. After a quick dinner, he scanned his to-do list, things he knew he would need for the care of the horses while they traveled. Most of the list had been checked off by Abe as he loaded the trailer with their saddles, tack, and horse supplies.

On the table, he had a portfolio, holding the registration papers of the four horses he would be hauling to the show. Brand inspections for each horse were also kept there in case they were stopped by the state police for some reason. He was meticulous about all he did, and the same nose for detail followed him into the show ring.

"Why are you smiling?" He grinned up at her.

"I forgot what a job it is to prepare for a show. You really do work hard. I can tell you really like what you do."

"Thank you." He smiled back and kissed her lightly on the lips. "I forgot one thing though," he murmured as he pulled her on to his lap.

"What?" She pressed kisses on his neck and earlobe.

"A ring for your finger. When are we going to tell your dad and Mary that I'm stealing his daughter away?"

His hands worked their way under her shirt and slickly unhooked her bra.

"Have they called to say where they are?" She squirmed and chuckled at his play.

"Not yet. He said he was planning to compete in an old timer's rodeo, so maybe they're travelling. He'll have to borrow a horse, I guess."

"We have to tell your father and Steve." She turned and looked into his face.

"As a matter of fact, I did. Dad called to see if we heard from Joe, and I told him. He said he couldn't think of a better person to call his daughter-in-law and wanted to know how long it would be before he had a grandson."

A mischievous look came into his eyes as his hand roamed her breasts. Adam didn't mention Steve. She assumed he didn't want to create a problem that wasn't. He re-hooked her bra and stood her up.

"We have to stop this, or we will never get finished." He grinned. "Let's get our bags out to the trailer, and we'll be done. I guess I'm going to have to make a space for you. Usually, it's just me and maybe Hank if I take two trailers full. I don't sleep with Hank—I usually get a motel room for him. I stay in the trailer so I can get up and check on the horses regularly. Waking up in the morning with a soft body next to me will be nice."

Adam roused her before the sun came up and hustled her through her routine. By the time she was dressed and in the kitchen, Adam had breakfast made and a thermos of coffee ready.

"I like to get an early start. It's hard on the horses as it is, so I try to get them settled well before the show the next day. If we can get them stalled, registered for classes, worked once or twice, and bathed, then you and I can go get a great steak in the city and get in the sack early."

"It sounds to me like you are more interested in having sack time."

Adam sipped his coffee and grinned at her. "I need my sleep if I'm going to have a good ride and win. I think I have you on my list of things to do, too." He kissed her for emphasis.

Brooke felt an excitement to all the work involved in getting the horses cleaned and shined, to have them exercised but not overworked for their classes. Most of the people at the show were new to her, except for some of the old trainers and breeders who were still in the business. Most of all she enjoyed Adam's company, this new freedom between them.

It was when she was in the wash rack, and up to her elbows in blue shampoo bubbles, and as soaked as the white filly she was bathing, she became aware of Adam's popularity. Just outside the wash rack, he sat in a foldable director's chair with the ranch logo embroidered on the back. He kept her company while he checked and planned the schedule for the following day. Without warning, a tall willowy woman with a black flowing mane of curly hair seated herself in Adam's lap.

"Hey, cowboy, I know a private party we can go to later." And she proceeded to caress his face and hair with a possessive flair.

Trying to be polite, Adam stood up but seemed to be unable to disentangle her arms. Helplessly he glanced at Brooke, seeming embarrassed by the whole experience, while the woman fawned over him. Taking her hands gently, Adam made introductions. "Julie, I want you to meet my fiancé."

The floozy stopped abruptly and glared with open rudeness. Brooke felt frumpy with her hair soaked and stringy along with her clinging, wet tee shirt. Julie flipped her black hair behind her ears and settled her hands on her hips.

"Julie, this is Brooke Montgomery, Joe's daughter. Brooke, this is Julie Moss, a trainer and breeder from Nebraska."

"I didn't know Joe had a daughter," Julie commented and looked Brooke over as if she was the worst horse left in a sale.

Brooke grinned at being ignored by this 'breeder.' She apparently put a damper on this woman's idea of a great weekend, probably a yearly date.

Adam seemed amused and came to her side, sliding a possessive arm around her and wiping soap suds from her cheek. "Brooke and I grew up together. We have a long history. We're nearly finished with all the bathing and banding of manes. You know how this first evening is—always so hectic. At least we'll be able to get to bed early and be rested for tomorrow."

Deflated, Julie wished him luck in the show and walked off. He gave Brooke an extra squeeze for reassurance. "As soon as we get these last two horses banded and blanketed for the night, we can go get something to eat." He kissed her gently on her temple.

They worked for another hour before the horses were finished. Brooke's fingers hurt from the many mini rubber bands she stretched to fasten each pencil-thin strand of mane. Adam trimmed the main to the correct length to accent the beauty of the animal's neck. They placed stretchy nylon hoods over on the horse's heads and neck to save the perfectly, banded manes from being ruined during the night. Light blankets went over the horses' bodies to keep them clean from manure and stains. Their legs were wrapped in polo wraps, and extra bedding was placed in the stalls to absorb any moisture. Then Adam meticulously placed the equipment in the tack stall next to Contender and locked it up.

He took her elbow and turned her towards him. "You look like you could use a steak and a hot shower. And I know just the place."

"Don't you usually camp out in the trailer?"

"Yes, but we are not going to cook. Let's go get cleaned up, and I'll buy you dinner. We do have to get back here early so we can get a good night's sleep," he hinted.

. . .

"It's time to rise and shine. Show starts in two hours. I bet you forgot how much work all this is. I'll run over and feed and water the horses if you'll get breakfast going. Abe usually stocks basic supplies in addition to the food we bought. Coffee should be the first thing."

"Gosh, I feel like I just got to bed," she moaned as she turned into him and placed her hands on his warm chest.

Adam kissed her lightly and sat her up on the mattress. "I'll be back in a few minutes."

After he left to tend to the animals, Brooke rustled around the small refrigerator and started the Keurig. She wasn't awake enough to cook, so breakfast was cereal and milk and the ever-present sweet rolls. She sliced bananas on the cereal. While she waited for Adam, she readied herself for another exhausting day.

She helped Adam by riding the young filly, while he exercised Contender. The stallion was a high-performance athlete and difficult in the morning, so Adam kept him moving in order to work off some of his pent-up energy.

Julie was there, exercising her mare. She chose to ignore Brooke, possibly out of embarrassment, except for one time. She rode her horse close to Brooke. Her foot shot out and kicked Brooke in the calf. Brooke had shown horses for years against heavy competitors before she left for California. Not one of the spoiled brats ever pulled a stunt like that.

"Apparently Adam hasn't shown you the proper

etiquette in a show ring. Try to stay out of my way," she spat. Julie stopped her insult when she saw Adam.

"Morning ladies," Adam greeted them as he rode up next to Brooke.

"Hi, Adam," Julie smiled sweetly at him. "Good luck today," she called back to him and rode off.

Adam leaned over and gave her a warm kiss. "I saw what she did. I'm sorry. She's kind of a prima donna. And, I must admit, a bitchy competitor." He stayed with her while they rode at a walk to cool the horses.

The remainder of the day was successful with two wins and placings in each of the other events. Brooke watched from the stands and recorded the judges' scores on Adam's rides.

When Adam wasn't riding, old timers wanted to visit with him or laugh and joke about the competition. Many were women of all ages. He was well liked by most, she could tell. Afterwards, they wearily ate hamburgers at a food stand on the show grounds and later fell asleep exhausted, comfortably entwined.

On the second day, while Brooke was rolling polo wraps to put away, Adam pulled her from her chair in front of the stalls. "Come with me. We need to get some clothes for you to show in."

"What do you mean 'show in'?" Panic rose in her throat to think he was serious.

"I don't have time to get Contender ready. He's hot today. If I'm going to get him to rope well tonight, I'm going to have to get him worked down more. I need you to ride the young filly—she's push button and just needs to be told what to do. She knows verbal commands, too."

Holding her hand, he pulled her toward one of the mobile shops present at every show. Everything was outlandishly expensive. Adam didn't seem to care. She was outfitted in black leather chaps with a matching vest. A bright blue silk blouse went underneath. He purchased a silver brooch and matching earrings and a silver buckle for her belt. A black western hat with a silver band and a pair of black boots finished the outfit.

With haste Adam helped her saddle the filly with saddle pad colors to match her shirt. He rushed her outside to get a fifteen-minute ride in the exercise arena to get her further acquainted with the animal's responses. He posted her number on the saddle pad. Then he hurried her to the show arena for the junior class. Adam had her so busy she forgot to be afraid. She hadn't competed in over eight years.

"You will be fine. Even if she doesn't get a win, she has to get the experience."

He pulled her down for a quick kiss for good luck and with a pat on her thigh sent her into the arena. He watched from the sideline and gave her thumbs up as she passed. When the class was over, she was amazed to have placed third.

Brooke saw Adam waiting at the gate on Contender with a large bouquet of red roses. She smiled at the gesture. But the announcer's voice held her attention.

"Would all of the riders remain in the arena? A Judge

has a question about a rider's tack. Would number eight-eleven move forward a few steps please?"

Her number was the one called. Curious, she moved the filly forward a few steps out of line and waited for one of the three judges to come to her. She realized it was a big rush to get her ready and maybe they forgot something, and she would be disqualified. No judge came.

However, Adam rode in at a lope with the roses, leaving her really confused. When he pulled his horse parallel to her horse facing her, Brooke's heart grew giddy with delight. From his pocket he took out the clearest diamond she had ever seen and placed it on her finger.

"Now it's for real." He took his hat off and sealed his vow with a kiss.

"Ladies," the announcer hooted, "the one and only Adam Tower is now officially taken. Sorry, girls. You'll have to set your cap for some other free man. Oh, by the way, I'm available," he joked.

Adam gave her the roses, and they slowly trotted out of the arena to the applause and greeting by many, wishing them well. Brooke knew in her heart he wanted everyone to know—no more Julies to explain. She was also amazed at the size of the diamond he purchased for her, almost afraid to keep it on.

When they were back at their stalls and the horses unsaddled, he pulled her into the tack stall for a private embrace. "I love you so much, Brooke Montgomery. I want everyone to know how happy I am."

"So, where did you get the ring?"

"Well, remember when I told you we had a break, and you could go take a nap? I drove downtown and bought it. Then I went to see Jimmy, the announcer today, who I have known for years. He helped me set it up and even got the judges to participate. I'm glad you didn't refuse to show today. You could have ruined all of my plans."

Brooke looked at the ring. "It's beautiful." She was more dazed by the thoughtfulness he showed her by arranging the whole scene.

"I'll take it out in trade," he smiled.

They arrived back at the ranch late the following night. Brooke felt she was gone for longer than four days. They unloaded the horses and settled them in their stalls. Abe had the stalls cleaned, bedded, and feed ready for them. The trailer would be cleaned out the next day.

Hank stayed in the house with Claude until they arrived and gave them a hand. He inquired about the show and was pleased it went so well. "Let me see the ring Adam said he bought on a whim ... wow! Quite a whim, but it looks great on you." And with a big hug, he wished them happiness.

Nothing unusual happened while they were gone, and the ranch slept in peace for one more night. And even in their exhausted state, the sweet agony of love, pure and explosive still warmed them. Too emotion-filled to speak, Brooke snuggled against his naked form, never wanting to leave this little bit of heaven.

CHAPTER TWENTY-THREE

*E*xcept for the necessary duties for the daily running of the ranch, Adam spent the next week at Brooke's side. Almost daily they rode up to the lake, now their favorite niche, never tiring of the place or the memories.

For the first few days Adam guided them further on to the national forest land and sometimes to the BLM land he leased for pasture. They both wore small pistols attached to their belts. His saddle held a rifle, secured in an easy to reach scabbard.

"Are you still looking for clues to the body they found?"

He looked out toward the horizon where miles of open space before them could not be patrolled regularly. He only sent his men out to check on the cattle in selected areas. That still left a huge amount of land, often wild in its isolation.

"It worries me there have been no clues. Buck said Kitty wasn't any help. When she wasn't crying, he said she was trying to climb his bones." Adam stopped his horse and turned to her. He held out his hand to take hers.

"Let's postpone the survey for now. We can take our time and find the perfect house and barn plans."

"Sure, if it's what you want to do. We do have to plan a wedding first." She smiled.

During the night, they slept in her oversized bed, made comfortable with the homemade, down filled pillows and comforters. He held her close each night, reluctantly letting go of her each morning. Brooke, however, had many ways of convincing him to remain a little longer. And he thanked the lord daily for bringing her back to him.

She rolled up on his chest and stared into his smiling face. "It's Sunday. Remember? We are supposed to meet Steve in town for breakfast."

"Oh, yes. He's buying. Get up or I'll have to throw you in the shower—with me." Adam smiled as he rolled her over. He made no attempt to get up or to leave her warmth, his body blanketing hers.

"Can't you call him and tell him we're not hungry?"

"That's not polite. He's planned the engagement party for tonight at my father's." he reminded her as he dragged her from the feather pillows. "Besides, he was a good loser."

"I didn't know you two were in a contest."

"Well, you two were pretty tight, always close. I thought maybe you had something serious going on. I was kind of afraid to butt in."

"You've grown rather smug. All this happiness could make you intolerable."

He pulled her up to stand next to him as he sat on the edge of the bed and held her warm body next to his. "Well, then, we'll have to be intolerable together." He planted little kisses on her neck and shoulders. "We have to find out when Joe is coming home so we can plan for the wedding."

"I think he will be happier giving me away this time than the last."

"I think he has good taste. Besides it was his idea anyway." Adam tapped her on the nose with his finger.

"What do you mean?" She leaned back from his hold.

"Don't get so defensive." He chuckled. "I didn't mean it literally."

He drew her back into his arms and enjoyed the feel of her breasts on his naked chest as his hands roamed down her spine.

"He told me I should marry you when I was complaining about your behavior. I told him you needed a trip to the woodshed."

"Is that so?" She grinned and cocked her head, sending a shiver of delight through him.

Laughing, he picked her up and tumbled them both

onto the bed. "I think I can find other ways to keep you busy."

Steve was on his third cup of coffee when the couple meandered into the restaurant. "Well, I thought I was going to have to order lunch instead of breakfast."

"We got busy with a few things." Adam put his arm around Brooke to pull her close.

"I hope you don't mind. I took the liberty of ordering Mack's platters—and champagne." Steve said as he smiled at them. "I heard you had a tack problem at the show. Let me see the problem." He reached for her hand.

Steve examined the ring. "It looks really good on your finger. You may have to wear a sling to keep it from wearing out your hand." He leaned over and kissed her lightly. "Welcome to the family, not that you weren't always part of us."

The meal was huge. As they were on final bits, the sheriff walked in.

"Morning, everybody." Buck removed his hat. "I hear congratulations are in order?" He leaned over and kissed Brooke on the cheek and shook hands with Adam vigorously. "I saw your truck outside. This is probably a bad time, but I really need to talk to you, Adam. Can we go outside?"

"Sure." He stood. "I'll be right back. Ask for another refill of coffee."

Brooke felt Steve's eyes on her after his brother departed. His constant staring made her grow uncomfortable. "Are you sure you made the right decision?"

"Yes." Brooke replied quietly.

She looked away from his troubled face. Steve was still the playboy he always was, lots of carousing in his life, lots of travel, lots of women. Since Desiree disappeared years ago, he didn't seem to be able to settle for just one woman.

"Adam didn't pressure you into it, did he?" Steve took her hand and massaged it between his own.

"No. If that were the case, don't you think I would have come to you for help? I really do love your brother. Don't ever doubt that."

"I needed to know. I'll still be here if you ever need me for anything, anything at all." He kissed her hand lightly.

"I know," her voice was a strained whisper. "Thank you."

Brook saw Adam enter and head for the table. Their hand holding was marked silently. He slid into the booth next to her and took the same hand Steve held, declaring ownership.

"What did Buck want?" Steve inquired, dismissing the episode.

"It was about the dead cowboy they found up by the lake." Adam stared into his empty coffee cup as if the left-over dredges had answers.

Brooke pulled her hand out from his and turned to him. "What did they find out?"

"His driver's license is false. He's not from Texas. Buck sent his fingerprints and DNA off for identification. He said it might take a while."

For what seemed a large amount of time, no one spoke. Each had his or her own thoughts about the murder.

"Buck wants you to stop over at his office before you leave town. I think he needs a date for his sister." Adam smiled.

"I'd better be on my way. Come out as early as you can. You don't have to wait for everyone." Steve pushed his Stetson far back on his forehead and started for the door.

The party began about seven. Steve invited about thirty people including his father and many of their close friends who lived close by, including Kitty. Mack catered the party with a barbeque to go along with the beer and wine, a toast with champagne, and a cake.

The night was clear with a crescent moon and stars like glitter on the navy-blue ceiling. Evening the air was warm, unusually so for that time of the year. By ten most of the excitement and playfulness wore down to an intimate group of friends, chatting and laughing over drinks at tables around the pool. The pool was now empty, and the tennis court was quiet. A light breeze ruffled the leaves in the surrounding trees. Coyotes called in the distance.

From her table, an inebriated Kitty called to Brooke, "You haven't opened your gifts yet. Let's see what's in those packages."

Adam sat next to Brooke at the gift table. She let him unwrap some. Most gifts were practical in nature, while others were a bit lewd.

When they thought they were finished, Kitty staggered close to them and remarked, "Isn't there one more under the table?"

Under the table was a small box. No card and no one at the party claimed it as theirs. The box was wrapped in shiny gold paper. With wonder, Brooke opened it. Inside was the locket Adam gave her a few weeks before. She remembered putting it on her dresser. On that Saturday, while Steve waited for her to dress, she went to put it on, and it was gone. She didn't tell Adam for fear he would be offended by her negligence.

Her heart pounded with fear, now knowing someone had stolen it, had taken it right off her dresser. Under the locket was a small card. Her hands shook as she read the card in a whisper, "Oops." It was signed with two x's and two o's, the way Mike used to sign his notes.

Panic gripped her like an iron band. Her whole body felt assaulted. She could barely breathe. *Could he still be alive? Was he the one tormenting them? Would he hurt Adam to get to her?* She crumpled the note in her hand and stood up.

"Brooke, tell me what's wrong. What does it say?" Adam turned her to look at him, trying to gain a sense of what happened.

"I have to get out of here," she wheezed.

"Must be jewelry from some other man," Kitty taunted, staggering over to the table close to Brooke. "Let's see. Show it off."

"Did you do this, Kitty?" She stared at her nemesis. Could Mike still be alive, watching, waiting to hurt someone she loved? Was he joyfully enjoying her fear? Fueled by Kitty's taunting, she pushed, sending both Kitty and Adam into the pool.

And then she ran, still gripping the note. She raced to her car before anyone could stop her. She accelerated down the dirt road with this new fear chasing her. Whoever was doing this could have her, but she had to protect Adam and the rest.

The Wyoming night was pitch black, the country road curvy and dark. She was near the Montgomery Ranch Road when it happened. She had no brakes. She pumped and pumped the brake pedal to no avail. She tried downshifting, slowing the car. She thought she had slowed enough to attempt a wide turn on the ranch road. Making the turn and realizing the gate was wide open, she breathed a sigh. She tried to decide where she would let the car come to a stop or maybe a bush she could use, when a dark figure jumped in front of her and slapped the left side of the windshield. She swerved to the right. The front wheels hit the culvert. After rolling once, the small convertible landed up right. The air bag opened and threw her back.

Adam couldn't remember being as terrified as when he stopped behind the little car. He prayed, begged Brooke would be alright. He couldn't lose her now. The door was jammed, her face bloody. And as he frantically pulled and pushed on the door, she turned her head, her eyes filled with fear.

She moved the air bag out of her way and tried to help. Pushing on the door as he pulled, the creaking hinges gave. They held each other, falling on the grass with shear relief. "Let's get you in the house. I'll call for an ambulance."

She stood on shaky legs and held on to his arm for balance. "I'll be alright. Just get me inside. See if Doc can drive out."

Inside, she cleaned the blood from her face. Adam made an ice pack and settled her in the den. "I'm going to go upstairs and change. I'll be right back."

His heart didn't stop racing until he had positive news. He sat next to her on the den's sofa and stared at her battered face. He kissed the bandage on her forehead. "You're going to look like you were in a barroom brawl tomorrow."

Fear stared back at him as she started to speak. He silenced her with a reassuring kiss. "Shh. Don't say anything yet. I'm sorry I yelled at you. I'm not angry with you, just the whole situation."

Her lips quivered slightly. She swallowed hard and released a long breath. "I didn't have any brakes. I pumped on the brake pedal, but the car kept going." She put a hand on her aching forehead. "Someone jumped in front of me and slapped the windshield. I had to swerve to avoid hitting whoever it was."

"Are you sure it was a person? Could it have been a coyote or deer?" Could she have seen John who was on guard at night?

"I'm sure someone walked right in front of me ... all black. Slapped the car. I swerved and ended in the ditch. And I heard an eerie laugh, evil. Then I saw your headlights."

Adam held her gently. They had all been drinking. Could she have imagined the laugh, an old reaction to fear? "Don't worry about the car, right now. Tell me what this note means."

"Mike used to sign his gift cards the same way after he hurt me or was abusive in some other way. I'm so afraid." She reread the crumpled note. "Could he still be alive? Were the inspectors of the plane crash wrong in the examination of the site?" She looked up at him bewildered. Her eyes pooled. "I'm so fearful he is alive and will hurt you."

"Did you lose the locket somewhere? Can you remember?" He carefully moved a strand of hair from her face.

"Adam, the night you attended the banquet, and I went to town with Steve, is when I noticed it missing. I didn't know they were coming, and when Abe said I should go with them, I came inside to change." She looked out the window as she remembered. "After I got dressed and did my hair and make-up, I went to get the necklace off my dresser. It was gone. I looked all over for it. It was just gone." She blew her nose and sniffed. "I didn't want to tell you I lost it. I was so touched by your thoughtfulness when you bought it. I thought you would think I was careless with your gift." Tears blinded her. She placed her hand on his chest.

"We'll get this figured out," he murmured, not sure how he would. Someone had been in his house. Someone took the locket. But why?

Later after a thorough examination, Doc closed his medical kit. "Well, young lady, I don't think there is anything serious for you to worry about. You have a nasty cut on your head, and some bruises. You will have a headache for a day or so. All your vital signs are good.

"However, Adam, I want you to wake her every hour or so to make sure she doesn't have a concussion. If you can't wake her, call me and get her to the hospital in Laramie—but I don't believe it will be necessary." Doc spoke in his usual efficient tone. "You two are getting married, I hear from the very, efficient grapevine." Doc held out his hand and his face lit with pleasure.

Adam's worried face brightened then, and his mouth turned into a wide grin. "Yes, as soon as Joe gets home, maybe even before. I guess we're lucky you still make house calls."

"I sure hope any children you have are not as accident prone as you two have always been." Doc chuckled as he left.

Adam pulled an Afghan around them as he held her. When she fell asleep, he carefully got up and called his brother.

"I can't believe this. She said she had no brakes?" Steve shouted over the phone.

"We'll have to check out the car tomorrow. I'll call Buck in the morning."

"Fortunately, he was still here. He took the necklace with him. He said he wanted to see if he could pull a partial print off the smooth back, maybe give us a clue," Steve told him. "Do you want me to come over and trade shifts with you during the night?"

"No, thanks. She's asleep right now, and as soon as I finish up here, I'll wake her and get her into bed. Could you make a list of everyone who was invited and everyone who came to cater with Mack?"

"I can make a list. I'll see you in the morning, and we'll check out the car."

The day dawned bright and sunny, lighting up the bedroom with the early splendor. "Morning." He yawned and stretched. "How do you feel?"

"A bit stiff. Tired. I'll be alright. I need you to hold me for a while."

"I think I can work that out for you." He gently

pulled her against him and held her close to his chest, avoiding the cut on her head. He lifted the hair away from her face and caressed her cheek with his thumb.

After a while his stomach began to growl with hunger. "I think I should go down and see about breakfast. Steve will be here soon to help pull your car to the garage. And Buck will be out. He wants to talk to you about some things and examine the car."

He shifted away from her and resettled the blanket around her. "Stay here and rest as long as you want. I'll be up later to check on you." He kissed her gently and left for his own room.

In the kitchen Adam let the dog out before he started the coffee. He noticed Steve and Hank walking across the lawn.

"You two are up pretty early." He smiled as he watched them approach.

"Got coffee made? I really need some." Steve followed Hank and Adam into the house.

"I was getting started on breakfast."

"How's Brooke this morning?" Steve helped make the coffee while Adam got the eggs and bacon out of the refrigerator.

"She's a bit stiff, will probably look like a prize fighter for a while." He grinned as he put bacon in the pan.

"Well, we towed the car in earlier to look at it. A good body shop may be able to restore it. However, it's not the most important thing—her brake lines are cut."

Anger permeated his brother. He threw a hand towel on the counter after drying his hands. "Even the emergency brake was tampered with!"

No one spoke as they pondered the glaring facts. Brooke was a target. And one glaring element could not go unnoticed. Someone was watching them. Someone knew what was going on in their lives. But which someone?

He hated the thoughts cluttering his mind. *Could Steve be involved? And what of Hank? Could he still trust him?* He knew the answers to those questions. He was so tired and so distraught his mind buzzed with possibilities.

"I feel so stupid. Just as I let my guard down—I thought everything was settled, over." He growled as he broke the silence. His muscles were tense to a point of hurting. He wanted to strike out at something or someone. Weary lines etched his forehead as his eyes darkened dangerously.

Steve commiserated with his brother's pain. "Adam, you can't blame yourself. Who knew some devil would pull something like that? Did you ask her about the card?"

"Yes, apparently her ex used to sign his cards the same way. I guess it scared her to think he may still be alive." He poured a cup of coffee and sat at the table while the bacon fried.

"Buck told me about the body they found. I can't believe we've all been under surveillance. Or at least our ranches are." Steve sat at the table with a warm mug of coffee in front of him.

"Yes, meaning she is either part of this cattle-rustling and drug smuggling or she is unwittingly holding answers someone wants. Someone wants her away from here. Why? Maybe we need to make a list of people she knows, likes, and hates. Whatever."

Adam got up and started scrambling eggs for everyone. "Did you make a list of everyone at the party?"

"I have the list of guests at the house, and I'll call Mack today to get his list of employees. He didn't bring many with him." Steve got up and put bread in the toaster.

He poured the eggs into the pan, "Hank, I'm going to have you work some of my younger horses. Have the young kid who wants more training hours work with the halter foals and the halter mare. I'll still train Contender and the filly. I'll have more time to be with Brooke. We need to solve this soon."

"I'll be fine, Adam." Startled they all looked to the kitchen door where Brooke stood, dressed in a dark blue robe. Her hair was undone and hung loosely around her face.

"You should still be in bed, my dear." Adam stared into her eyes.

"I'm fine. And I'm not going to hide, and you are not

going to stop what you are doing to baby-sit me. I won't be a victim anymore."

She walked over to the coffee pot, made a cup, and went over to sit down next to Hank at the table. "Let's have breakfast, and you can fill me in. Something we all know is missing, like a puzzle piece. The first thing I want to know is why I had no brakes." Her fingers came up to touch her forehead where the pain pounded.

She looked at all of them as they stood speechless.

Adam smiled and went over to gently kiss her, anticipating her reaction. "Someone cut the brake lines on your car. Someone wanted you to crash. Someone didn't know what a good driver you are."

She didn't speak for a moment. "Well, maybe they are out to get you. You could have driven the car home."

"I guess you're right," Steve chimed in. "Could have been directed at both of you."

"It doesn't really matter. I'm not going to cower in this house waiting for the next attack. We have to find out what they want. I could even put you three on the list—after all Adam, I can only sell the land back to you, or if I die before we are married, my father gets the land back and you still win. Steve will inherit anything from your death. And Hank, I don't know how you fit in, if you do. So, you see, I could be the victim of anyone."

They all stopped what they were doing and stared at her until she grinned.

Adam and Steve brought over the eggs, bacon, and

toast. Adam also poured orange juice for everyone. "There, I hope I didn't forget anything, did I?"

"Napkins and eating utensils?" She smiled at the men in her life.

When Steve and Hank left, she helped with the dishes. Adam insisted on doing the pots and finishing up the cleanup while she finished another cup of coffee. His worry for her emanated from him, and she wished she could ease his constant fear. But she didn't know how. She stared out at what used to bring her immense comfort. Her thoughts weren't on the beauty and the horses. They were on her fears for Adam.

His voice brought her back to their problem. "Who do you think took your necklace?"

"I really don't know. Kitty comes to mind because she made it clear she wants you and hates me. And Bess was here with Hank and Steve the Saturday it came up missing. I'd hate to believe she would have some reason to want to frighten me and try to ruin our party—or even kill me—or us."

She gently stroked her hands down her bruised face and pushed straggling hairs behind her ears. Adam took one of her hands in his. Befuddled, they both sat silently until the phone rang. He put it on speaker mode.

"Hello, Buck. Anything new?"

"Not much. Steve told me about the brakes. I'll be out a little later and see if we can come up with a print on the car. Don't touch it more than you have to. I did find a partial print on the back of the locket and I'm sending it out for identification. Maybe we will finally come up with someone."

"It would certainly give us some help. I really need closure to all of this."

"Why do you think they would steal the locket and then return it?" Buck queried.

"I don't know. Maybe between us, Brooke and I can come up with a reason." He looked at Brooke as she sat listening.

"Have you seen any small planes late at night in your area? We've had some sightings of planes, at least once a week. Never on or near the same ranch. Randall found four-wheeler tracks in one of his empty fields. And four-wheeler tracks were found not far from the man's body in the forest. Just keep a look out."

"Maybe I'll send someone out to browse around, try to follow the tracks. I'll let you know what they find later when you come out."

Adam hung up the phone and momentarily stared out the window. *Maybe her husband was still alive. If so, what does he want?*

"Brooke, let's go look at your mother's locket. Maybe they took the wrong one."

Excited by the possibilities, he opened the safe. "I know what the vandals were looking for the first time. They were looking for your locket. Apparently, Kitty doesn't know about this safe. Your clothes were ruined. Nothing was stolen except for your jewelry boxes."

He knelt in front of the desk and released the latch to

the false front. Lying behind the top drawer, a safe, large enough to hold important papers and her mother's jewelry, had been built into the panels of the hand-made cherry desk.

"When they didn't find it in your room, they tried here. That's why no other rooms were damaged."

He took the locket out and placed it on the blotter of the desk, staring at it as if it was a magic charm to exorcise the demons from their lives. As he studied it, he realized how beautiful it was with its filigreed gold applications. The locket was artistically created, not molded.

"This is very beautiful. I'm sure your mother must have loved it very much."

Brooke smiled down at the piece. "Yes, I always remember her wearing it. It always reminded me of her and her love." She sat on the arm of the chair and put an arm around his shoulder for balance.

He carefully opened it and found a frame for a picture, but no picture was inside. "You didn't have her picture in here?"

"No, it was ruined when the chain suddenly broke and fell into a puddle. I never got around to getting another made small enough to fit in there. And then Mike's plane crashed, and my life was turned into turmoil."

"You mean living with him wasn't turmoil for you?"

"Yes, this was different. After the crash I had so much to clear up with his debts and the government. FBI agents came often, trying to get me to tell them things about his businesses I didn't know about. I was so tired after everything was finally auctioned off, I wanted to come here and regroup."

He put his arm around her and kissed her lightly. "I'm glad you did. I can't tell you how much I missed you those years you were gone, and I want you to stay safe so we can grow very old together."

With his penknife he gently poked around the frame where a picture should be. Unexpectedly, the insides of the locket fell apart. "I'm sorry. I'll have it repaired."

As they stared at the pieces, they realized it was two hearts in one. The solid heart had numbers and letters engraved in its back.

"Did you know this came apart?" He examined the locket as it lay in pieces.

"No." She picked up the large heart and stared at the engravings.

He watched her faced as she examined the locket. "What do you think these numbers mean?"

"I don't know. Maybe it's the artist's way of identifying his work. It is a custom piece." She handed it back to Adam, puzzled by this new turn of events.

"You said the chain broke. Who fixed it?"

"Well, Mike said he would have it repaired and wanted to have the locket cleaned and examined. It was during one of his kinder moments." She stood and gazed out the window.

"When did you say you broke the chain?" He held the heart in his fingers.

"About two months before he crashed. He told me to wear it all the time and not worry about it. He had purchased a new gold chain for it and had all of the hinges and clasps adjusted."

"Could they be numbers to his safe or maybe an account number?" he puzzled.

"I never had anything to do with his business. I do know he could open the safe without a cheat sheet. I saw him do it numerous times."

Adam took her hand. "Do you think he could still be alive?"

The thought of his evil still existing registered on her face, making her head throb to a point she felt faint. She shivered and touched her bandage. Sitting on the leather sofa, she put her elbows on her knees and rested her head in her hands. She looked up at him.

"Adam, I don't know. I would like to believe he died in the plane crash, but no body was recovered. They said the explosion and fire incinerated everything."

She leaned her head back on the cool leather. "This renews all of the horror he put me through. It's as if he is still alive—haunting my every move."

Adam sat next to her, and let his fingers gently graze her forehead. "I think it's time you went back up to your room and rested—no excuses. Patronize me. Let me be your nurse." He took her face in his hands and pressing his lips to hers, caressed her mouth.

After seeing she was settled in bed, he left Claude with her and went out to the barns. Buck arrived and was doing his dusting job on the car and taking prints as he saw fit.

Adam had the locket with him. "I think the first time they broke in and wrecked Brooke's room and the office they were really looking for this. The one at the party was one I bought her because I thought this one had been stolen. Look inside. Does this look like a code of some kind?"

Buck examined the locket for a while. "Well, it looks like an account number. Some countries have bank accounts with specific numbered accounts. They are used by people trying to hide or launder money. I can't say for sure if this is the case. The engraving is rather new for such an old piece."

"Why don't you write it down? Or take a picture. I'm going to put it back in the safe." Adam wasn't going to let it out of his sight.

"I guess that means you don't want me to take it with me?" Buck asked with a grin.

"You're right. This may be the puzzle piece we need. Did you get the print results from the back of the other one?" He took the locket back from Buck and dropped it in his pocket.

He shook his head. "No. Does Brooke have any thoughts on this?" He put his equipment away and put evidence in labeled folders.

Adam stared at his friend. "She thinks her ex is still

alive and tormenting her. I haven't told her about Junior Mason."

"Here," he pulled a picture from another folder. "This is the most current photo of the man. Ask Brooke if she knows him. He was into some heavy drug dealing— maybe he was the reason for all the small planes sightings, using Kitty's place as a base."

"Wouldn't she know? Wouldn't he need a horse or four-wheeler to get to the drop sight?' Adam wondered aloud.

"Well, if Kitty knows, she's not telling. She's a pretty tough cookie." Buck plopped his hat on his head and headed for the door. "I'll be in touch."

CHAPTER TWENTY-FOUR

*A*dam placed the picture of Junior Mason on a shelf in the tack room of the main barn. His shoulders stiffened just looking at the photo. Junior's body was found near Brooke's property not far from Kitty's ranch. Had he conspired with Kitty to hurt Brooke?

The picture would have to wait. He had work to do. He took a four-wheeler to the new barn. In the office he listened to messages from prospective buyers or those interested in breeding a mare to one of the stallions. He made notes of the caller's names and addresses. Later, he would send them information about each specific horse and a contract. He also checked the training schedules and assigned each horse a specific daily workout with the appropriate handler.

After he called the feed store to order feed and bedding to be delivered, he took the four-wheeler to check the back pastures. He then checked on how the hay cutting and bailing was progressing. By then he began to worry about Brooke. As he walked through the main barn, he stopped to grab the picture. He hoped she would be awake by then.

"Are you ready for lunch? It's almost noon." Brooke stood by the kitchen counter with sandwich makings spread out. Barefooted, she was dressed in new jeans and a blue chambray shirt, left untucked and the sleeves rolled up. She moved around the kitchen, fixing lunch and setting the table.

Adam greeted her with a husky whisper, "What are you doing up?" Before she could answer he kissed her softly, trying to avoid any bruising.

"I couldn't sleep any longer and my mind was buzzing with questions, so I thought I'd make my favorite cowboy a sandwich."

He studied her face for a moment, judging her emotions. "What kind of questions?"

"Oh, things like who cut the brake lines on my car, why would they, what's with the locket numbers? Stuff like that." She finished making the sandwiches and put them on plates. She added potato chips and a pickle. She handed one to him and carried hers to the table.

"Does your head hurt anymore?" Adam put his plate on the table and went to the refrigerator for milk and glasses.

"Not much. I'll be fine. I'm not as swollen as I was.

I've been keeping hot and cold packs on it. What do you think?"

He fingered her chin lightly and tilted her face one way and then the other. "I think this need attention." He slowly kissed her lips.

She chuckled and began munching on a potato chip. "What did you bring with you?"

"Well, I didn't know if this would be the right time. It's a picture Buck was able to acquire. He wanted you to look at it, hoping you would recognize the man. He supposedly worked for your husband."

He went over to the mudroom to get the photo. He sat down at the table with her, and with keenly observant eyes, he handed it to her.

For a moment she didn't respond. "This is the person who was found up near the lake?"

"Yes. Do you recognize him?" She was so still. He placed his hand on her arm. He could feel her twitch with anger.

She leaned back in her chair and gazed at him. "Yes, he was Mike's right-hand man. Did whatever he was asked to do, even keeping me prisoner in our home. If Mike flew out of town, Junior was there to make sure I didn't leave. He never touched me. He was always there. Junior must have been with Kitty at the barbeque, and that's why he stared at me. He wanted to see if I recognized him with a full beard and long hair."

"I'm sorry this dredges up bad memories for you." He grasped her hand and gently squeezed it for reassurance. "We are going to solve this. I want my girl back, sexy, and smiling."

"I want us back, too, Adam. Whoever is trying to drive me away is going to lose. I would miss 'swimming' at the lake and stuff like that." She smiled and wiggled her eyebrows, but the frivolity didn't reach her eyes.

"I'm sure Buck will let us know what he finds out. He's more concerned, I think, about the FBI tracking people to our area. They've even mentioned you as a suspect."

She stared at him with a flash of impatience. "Yes, after all I had to deal with to clear his accounts, his losses —yes, they probably still think there is more I haven't told them or given them. How I hate him."

Adam pulled her over to sit on his lap and held her. She let her head rest in the curve of his neck. She was quiet for a while, then she turned to look in his eyes.

"I still hate him. But I do love you so very, very much." Brooke took his face in her hands and pressed her lips to his. She rested her head once again on his shoulder. She felt a momentary panic as fear rose from her subconscious. Her thoughts raged as anger rippled up her spine. Could Mike still be alive? Or was Mason the only survivor? But why would he come there? How did he meet Kitty? For a time, they sat as one, their minds caught up in the turmoil before them.

"We'd better eat these sandwiches. If we stay here

much longer, I may have to carry you upstairs. Then I'd never get any work done." Adam lifted her and sat her in her own chair. He went to the pantry and returned with chocolate syrup. He generously poured it into his glass of milk and then into hers. He shrugged his shoulders with a smile, "Comfort food."

"Dad called. I filled him in on the engagement. I didn't tell him about the car. They're coming home on Friday."

"What did he say about us getting married?" Adam asked through his bite of sandwich.

"He wants to plan a big wedding."

"Do you want a big wedding?" he murmured.

She could read caution in his voice. "I don't think at this time it would be a good thing. An extensive plan would give our demon something to use to torment us or hurt someone. Maybe a small and quiet wedding. Then we can get on with our new life." She took a small bite of sandwich. After a moment she said, "I'm probably being selfish, but I would be just as happy at a town hall."

"Your father won't go for that." Adam smiled at her. "Maybe we should plan this thing for Saturday. Then Joe and Mary won't be able to get their hands in it. We'll call a few friends, music from a cd, and a cake. What do you say?"

Brooke reached out to take his hand. "I think it's very romantic."

"Oh, by the way, Bess called to see how you were. I

told her you would be fine, and I wasn't going to let you out of my sight." He grinned and then grew serious. "She kept asking about the car. I told her you made the turn too fast and crashed. Buck doesn't want anyone else to know about the brakes until he does some more sleuthing. He's very good at this job."

"I won't tell anyone. I want to know myself—so I can get even."

During the dark of night, Brooke eased out of bed so as not to wake Adam. She had to do some investigating on her own. He would be angry, but something had to be going on at the Jones Ranch. Kitty was probably up to her neck in it. Mason had been with her. The question was why? Why wasn't he dead?

She took a 4-wheeler from the main barn and slowly left the ranch and headed toward the Jones Ranch. Leaving the road not far from Kitty's, she travelled to a high ridge overlooking the area. She parked the vehicle within the trees. Pulling up the hood of her navy windbreaker, she tied the strings under her chin. Her phone was on vibrate, should Adam try to call her. Reaching in her front pouch, she made sure the gun's safety was on.

Brooke knew she only had a few hours before people would be up doing chores. Kitty had only a small crew to help her, and she wanted to stay out of their sight. The night was bright and glistening with stars, a slither of moon.

Traipsing through the forest to get a view of Kitty's

house and open fields made her heart race. She knew night animals, such as cougars, were always on the hunt. The darkness of the forest floor made it hard to move quickly, and she found going from tree to tree was the most efficient way to travel. She could hear coyotes in the distance and the creaking of the pines in the mild breeze. And she worried there might be guards or even the government watching now that everyone knew Mason had been living with Kitty.

Brooke finally sat on a knoll, near where she left the cover of the trees. She took out her small binoculars. As she perused the windbreak for the cattle, she noticed a large, newly dug area at the edge of the trees near the house. It wasn't in an area where one would find a garden or where a pipeline would have been repaired. *What could she have buried there?*

Although she was deep in thought, her instincts took over when she heard a snap of a small, downed tree branch behind her. Stealthily, she unzipped her pocket and gripped her weapon. She spun to her feet, pointing her gun at the intruder.

In a quick whisper he ordered her, "Put that down, it's just me."

She whispered back. "What are you doing here? I left you a note."

"Let's go before anyone spots us. This is Buck's job." His voice was filled with irritation.

"If my ex-husband is still alive and here with Kitty, I will kill him myself." Brooke gave no hint she didn't mean every word. "And a spot over by the windbreak has been dug up."

"Maybe it's a garden ..."

"Kitty doesn't get dirty, let alone have a garden," she barked.

He came over to her then and put his arms around her. "I know you want answers, but we cannot allow it to take over our lives. Buck and the FBI are working on this. Let them."

She put her head on his shoulder for a moment. Suddenly she stiffened. "Do you see that?" Brooke pointed to the wide, open fields beyond Kitty's house.

Adam pulled her behind a stand of trees, holding her by her shoulders. "A signal, maybe a flashlight. There's a plane. Buck was right about the planes."

They stayed at their position watching for any other movement around the house and barns. All was quiet, not one light was on in the house. As they watched, the plane turned and headed away from them. The sun was creeping up the horizon.

"Brooke, it's time we get out of here before someone sees us or sees the four-wheelers in the trees." He took her hand and without a response from her, pulled her further into the forest toward their vehicles.

"Alright, I'll come. But I know somehow Kitty is responsible."

Neither of them spoke as they entered the house. Adam called Buck and told him what they saw and Brooke's recognition of Mason. He went to his room to change into his work clothes. She was sitting at the table, sipping from a coffee mug when he came downstairs.

Without a word, he filled an insulated mug with coffee and grabbed a protein bar. His voice was cold and exact. "I'll be at the arena most of today getting the horses ready for the show. Please don't go out without telling me." Without a kiss, he left for the barns.

Screams of frustration lodged in her throat. Emotions gathered like a bad storm. Everything happening at the ranch had to do with her. What did they want? She was sure Kitty was involved somehow. But it wasn't Kitty who caused her to crash her car. She was at the Hightower Ranch. So, who was it?

Later, on the patio she worked on her theories, jotting down notes and flow charts of possible suspects. She could see the men who worked for Adam. Old Abe would be cleaning tack in the doorway of the barn. Another man would be bathing one of the recently exercised horses. Adam made it obvious he was keeping a tight surveillance of the house.

The iced tea cooled her parched throat. The sun was warm, the air dry and still from the lack of rain. She dressed in jeans and a tee shirt as well as her lace-up boots. Later she would go down to the barn and brush out Sly.

The sound of scrunching gravel on the drive interrupted her thoughts. As the small pickup came into view, she recognized Bess. Claude barked once as a warning and with a word from Brooke, he laid back down beside her. Bouncing with energy, Bess came over and sat in another lounge chair.

"Would you like a glass of tea?" she offered.

"Sure. I'll get it." With more reserve and less enthusiasm, Bess prodded, "Have you found out anything knew about your car?"

"No, it's getting repaired. Then I think I'll get something more suitable." She sipped from her glass and looked out to the horizon. The sun was warm on her denim covered legs.

"Hank said you and Adam had a tiff." Her eyes twinkled with interest as she prodded.

She didn't respond to Bess' obvious need to know firsthand what happened. The paper she wrote on was conspicuously turned over, her hand resting on it possessively.

"You seem to be down, more than I expected."

"I just have a lot on my mind." Brooke sat up straighter with a defiant gleam in her eye. "You're right. We still have some things to discuss."

"Would you like to walk with me to find Hank? His sister was in the shop yesterday and left her sweater there. She said I could give it to Hank, and he would bring it to her on Sunday when he goes home to visit his mother."

"No, I have some things to work on here." Brooke tapped the paper under her hand. What if Mike was alive and killed Adam for spite? Her heart ached with the possibility. And now he was in a tiff because she wanted answers.

"Well, all right. Say, is this the locket that caused all the commotion at the party? I guess I missed out." Bess put her glass on the table as she pointed to the small heart on Brooke's chest.

Her voice was quiet when she spoke. Then she remembered...*Bess was not at the party*. "Yes, it's the one Adam bought for me when the house was vandalized. He thought my mother's locket was stolen— I almost wish it had."

"What's so mysterious about the other one?" Bess probed.

Bess's question struck a sour chord. She didn't know why, except the heart, which once meant so much to her, had become a malevolent presence.

"I don't know."

"Well, I see Hank's coming now. Stop in the shop and we'll have lunch."

Brooke watched Bess walk down the lawn to meet Hank.

The locket mystery—it sounded like a Nancy Drew story without any well-placed clues for her to figure out. Maybe, she thought, I should put an ad in the paper and tell the person interested to call and set up a drop-off time. As absurd as it sounded, it would probably work.

As Bess' truck pulled away, Hank strode up the lawn in her direction, carrying the blue sweater. He sat down on the edge of a chair nonchalantly and swung the sweater lightly between his legs as his arms rested on his knees.

"Would you like a glass of iced tea? I seem to be the local hostess here," she asked, trying to act gracious even though she knew he had firsthand knowledge of their dispute.

"Yes, thank you. I came up to visit for a minute," he replied with slight unease, his charm showing some nervous cracks. He laid the sweater across his knees as he took the glass from her.

"How is Contender doing?" Brooke tried to keep the conversation away from her and Adam. However, the ranch was Adam and everything on it wore his brand.

"Fine, Adam worked him on some cows earlier." Hank sipped from the glass and paused, contemplating his next words.

Hank didn't look at her but gazed down toward the open barn doors. "Adam told me when he found you gone, he was frantic, worrying he wouldn't find you." He shook his head remembering. "Trust him, Brooke. He loves you. He's a good man. I know you did what you thought was for the good of all of us. If we had to, we would fight Martians for you—as you would for us. Don't forget. You're not fighting this alone."

Then he gave his usual charming smile and asked for more tea. Holding the glass up in a toast, he said, "To all of us."

"To us." She smiled as she tapped his glass with hers.

"Would you like to go down to the arena and watch

the new cutting stallion? Adam thinks he could be a winner. He may show him at a cutting futurity this summer." When she didn't answer he continued. "I'll go with you. One of you two stubborn people has to make the first move, right? Besides, what's the worst thing that can happen—have another argument?"

"Maybe I shouldn't provoke him more. I know I hurt his feelings, bruised his ego. I don't want anything to happen to him because of me—and the damned locket."

"Come. It will be all right." Hank took her hand and helped her up from her seat. "I'll walk with you."

Her nervousness made her eager to talk. "How are you and Bess getting along?" Surreptitiously she placed the piece of paper in the back pocket of her jeans.

"We see each other occasionally. Bess is pretty independent, and she likes her life uncomplicated."

They continued through the main barn and out the to the new barns. They walked through the stallion barn to the doors of the large, outside arena. They stopped next to the tall, white metal gate and watched as Adam urged the horse through its lesson. A couple of ranch hands rode their mounts to act as hazers, keeping the rest of the steers in a confined area so the younger horse could pay attention to its job.

She could tell the young, tobiano stallion was coming along well. Somewhere down the line he would win big and make a name for himself and Adam.

She loved to ride cutting horses and the feel of the controlled, muscular power under her. They were so intelligent. They could almost do the job alone. Joe would occasionally let her ride if the contest was not a money-maker, and as a child she did well in the win column.

Adam noticed the two almost immediately upon their arrival. His legs tightened unconsciously, sending the horse jumping too quickly and missed the steer's sudden turn back to the herd. Irritated, he instructed the men to put the animals back in the holding pen and to take a break. It was close to lunch—he had been working the horse for a while, and this was as good a time as any to give him a rest.

He walked the horse ever so slowly over to the gate and dismounted. Holding the reins, he took off his gloves slowly—finger by finger—more for his own needs than for its purpose. He needed time. It was hard enough, sparing men to keep an eye on her and the property, but with her impetuous nature, it was near impossible to keep tabs on her.

Damn. He could understand deep down within himself her need to find things out. If someone was threatening him, he would probably be looking at all options. Unless it was someone they knew—anything was possible.

He avoided her most of the day against his own best judgment. Her face was like a threatened, wild cat when he found her in the forest, pointing her pistol at him, again. His anger was too strong—too strong, for him to give in to the relief of seeing her and knowing she was unharmed. And so, he ignored her pleas for him to listen to her.

He wasn't as angry. His greatest worry was he wouldn't get there in time—he would be too late to save her. He wasn't sure he would be able to handle losing her. And, yet he acted like a scorned schoolboy.

His eyes were soft where they touched her face. Just as quickly they darted away. Nor could he find words to start a conversation. "Would you like to try him?"

His sudden address of her took a second or two to sink in. Hank nudged her with his elbow from behind. "I, yes I would."

Adam haled the last man leaving the arena and directed him to leave one steer. He gave her a leg up and began to give her the incidentals about the horse's temperament and training. The brief contact as he adjusted the stirrups reconnected the tangible bond between them.

"There, you're ready." His eyes probed hers briefly. The desire for release was there, but neither offered to break the gossamer thread to end the stalemate.

As he watched her and admired her skill, a voice broke the silence behind him. "How long are you going to punish her for thinking of you?"

Without looking around, he replied sullenly, "What do you mean?"

"She's hurting inside because she is afraid whoever is causing the upheaval around here will hurt you—she doesn't even see the danger as her own, or she overlooks it. Maybe she is too much woman for you, Adam. After all she's been through, are you having second thoughts about getting married to someone as spirited and independent as Brooke. Someone who will stand up to you. If you don't want her, well, maybe I'll throw my hat into the ring."

He spun on his heel to face Hank. Anger emanated from him like an enraged bull. Hank's smiling face negated any fury he felt, realizing he had been bated. "You're lucky we're friends."

"I think I'll go saddle the two-year-old next on the list." He grinned at Adam as he sauntered away to the barn.

Adam turned and watched her ride. She had always been an independent spirit, and he was trying to control her to keep her safe from harm. He could only imagine her life in California, nearly imprisoned in her home, treated with as little respect as any of Mike's other possessions. His heart ached for her. She was trying to save everyone she loved. His heart squeezed with anguish with the thought he could lose her.

He watched from the rail, keenly observant of her. The horse was quick and an excellent ride. She seemed to thoroughly enjoy the exercise. She returned the horse to Adam at the gate. Dismounting quickly, she handed him the reins. "Thank you. He's quite an athlete."

The honesty in his response was unmistakable. "I forgot how talented you are."

"Thank you." Her voice nearly a whisper.

Instead of the reins, he took her hand in his. The warmth of her hand sent a vibrant chord through him. She closed her eyes to his. "Brooke, I'm sorry about last night. I wish you had come to me with your thoughts, and we could have handled them together."

He pulled her close and pressed her head to his chest. His hand rested lightly on her long, golden mane of hair. They stood locked together for some time until the tug on the reins brought them to reality. He wrapped his arm around her shoulders as they walked slowly to the barn.

After tying the horse to the ring outside the tack room, he gathered her in his arms and tasted the lips he craved. Their soft sweetness and the feel of her willowy body on his bedeviled his senses. Suddenly a wolf whistle, coming from the end of the aisle, restored reason.

Slowly Adam looked up from Brooke's flushed face to see Hank whooping it up with encouragement, a broad grin lighting his face. "Here, you can unsaddle this horse and clean him up. The boss has a long lunch on his agenda."

CHAPTER TWENTY-FIVE

*A*s the wee hours of the morning approached, Adam turned away from Brooke. He propped the up pillows and rested against the headboard. He hadn't slept well, and now he felt groggy and listless.

Brooke rolled his way as the coolness of the morning brushed across her skin. Automatically, his arm reached out and pulled her close, finding pleasure in her soft curves against his warm skin. Her hand rested on his chest as her leg entwined with his.

He studied her face, slightly golden from the sun. Her long eye lashes lay fragile on her cheeks. At rest, he thought, she looked like an angel—but he wondered if she was the angel he wanted her to be. *Did she know what the code in the locket meant? Had she gone out the other night to meet someone near Kitty's?*

During his restless night the thoughts nagged him. He

went over everything in his mind, even the way she held the gun on him when he found her.

"Adam?" She sat up, leaning an arm on his chest. "Is something wrong?"

Feeling he had been caught thinking aloud, he quickly looked out the window. "No, what could be wrong after last night?"

"You seem angry just now."

He could feel the rapid beating of her heart where his arm rested. "I didn't sleep well. I wasn't frowning at you," he lied. He kissed her forehead and with his hand, he pushed her head back down on his chest. "Be still a while. It's early. Besides, it's too pleasant right now to think of getting up." He ran his hand down her arm to her hip, and then cupping her bottom, pulled her closer.

Later, while Brooke straightened up the bedroom and bath, Adam went down to the barns to check on the horses and his men. Afterward, they drove into Bantry for breakfast.

Since they were late for the normal crowd, the hotel was nearly empty. A few, old farmers, who gathered there daily to gossip and talk of old times, sat in the far corner. It seemed to be their table for they always sat in the same place, gauging people as they came through the door. Mack greeted them warmly, and after taking their order, left them alone. "Maybe we should tell Dad and Mary to take an extended honeymoon." Brooke hinted.

"We are supposed to get married, remember?' Adam prompted her.

Her face brightened perceptively. "I feel married to you already."

"Well, if last night is any indication of what our life together will be like, then I am overjoyed at the prospect." Adam smiled and took her hand.

Brooke reached across the small table to touch his arm. She couldn't deny her curiosity. "I know you have learned things you are not telling me. I want to know. I don't want any secrets between us."

"Are there any secrets between us?" His body stiffened as he challenged her statement.

"No, I'm an open book."

"Then don't worry your pretty little head. I planned our wedding for Saturday as you agreed. Your dad and Mary agreed to be home by then. Oh, good. Here's our breakfast. I'm about starved."

Brooke sat stoical and watched him dig into his meal. He *planned* their wedding without consulting her. "You could let me in on your thoughts on occasions." The mood was gone. Resentment took the place of bliss.

In between bites of food, Adam told her of his plans. He could be ordering feed, she thought, as she listened to him.

"Steve agreed to be best man, and Bess said she could be maid of honor, unless you want someone else. I thought we could have the reception on the back lawn with only our best friends and relatives who can come on short notice, a buffet, and a cake, of course."

Brooke didn't speak for a while and didn't eat the

steaming plate of food before her. Finally, Adam looked up only to be met by her heated glare.

His eyes crinkled disarmingly. "We can have champagne, too."

"I wish you would have asked me first. It is my wedding, too." Her voice came out like a whisper, strained and breathless.

"I'm sorry. And you are right. However, everything, including the cake, has been ordered...besides, I think we should get married as soon as possible before something else comes up to spoil our plans."

Brooke didn't reply. They ate in silence, giving them time for thought. She sat quietly and held her coffee cup as if it could give her strength. He was much like her father. Strong willed, hardworking, and most of all giving.

Adam suddenly asked with a wry smile, "Do you want me to have some placards made up so you can march up and down the street at the unfairness of your fiancé?"

"No, I want to be your wife, equal in every way. I don't want to feel I have to get your permission to do something, or you need to have mine. Our wedding is different."

The grin on Adam's face was checked. A note of irritation carried with his voice. "Does that include running off in the night?"

She didn't reply.

"Brooke, I do love you, and I do want to marry you

on Saturday. Will you go with me to get the license today? Oh, before you answer, there's one more thing I forgot." He fished in his shirt pocket as his eyes twinkled merrily.

Brooke was speechless at the matching rings he pulled out. He never failed to surprise her. She knew his reason for a quick wedding was because of her. Everything he did lately had roots in her problems, her danger.

"If these don't fit your idea of a wedding ring, we can take them back and choose something else. They do go with the ring I gave you in Cheyenne." Adam got up from his seat and knelt next to her. Taking her hand in his he said, "Will you marry me on Saturday, fair princess?"

She smiled and choked out a whisper. "Yes."

Hoots and whistles came from the table of old timers. Adam rose and sat across from her.

"What if Mike is still alive? That note must have meant something?" she worried.

"No one has come up with any proof he is alive. The whole business has been closed by the authorities. Whoever wrote the note wanted to scare you, as he—or she—has been doing for months now. I won't let anyone hurt you again. If I knew who it was, or how to contact this person, I would sacrifice it, no questions asked."

"I'm afraid someone we love will get hurt because of this. I don't know what to do about it?" She sighed and poked at her remaining egg.

"No more of these negative thoughts. We're going to

Laramie and find some new duds for the wedding. We'll need to clean up the house before your father and Mary get back. She might want to take a broom to both of us if we don't make some attempt."

"Brooke, what does Mary use to polish this desk in the office?" Adam called from the bottom of the stairs.

"Paste wax. There's probably a can in the storage cabinet," she called above the roar of the Hoover as she vacuumed the upstairs hallway.

They shared the cleaning of the house, starting from the upstairs bedrooms, which Brooke dusted and vacuumed, to the bathrooms that Adam cleaned and polished.

Brooke despised housework. She turned off the vacuum and sat on the edge of her bed. She stared blindly at the floor, flicking the feather duster up and down. She didn't hear Adam approach until he was standing in the doorway with a can of wax in his hand. Brooke startled when she noticed him.

"It's me. Did I scare you?"

She smiled and noticed what was in his hand.

"You want me to wax the whole desk with this?"

Brooke nodded her head. "Apparently, the business of house cleaning isn't one of your favorite pastimes either." Feeding off his disdain for the job, she elaborated on her answer. "Mary always keeps it up, very shiny and lustrous. She sometimes works an entire day polishing the desk."

"I bet she does. You better take advantage of this while you can. I'm not going to do this every week after we're married," he grumbled.

"Oh? And who is going to clean every week?"

"Woman's work." He grinned.

"Well, not this woman." She protested and lunged at him with a feather duster.

One retaliation led to another. They chased each other through the house as a diversion from the work. The kitchen took the brunt of their play. A water fight ensued. Adam's white tee shirt clung to him like second skin where she showered him with the faucet's spray.

Finally managing to grasp hold of her, he forced her head in the sink and drenched her with the same sprayer until she agreed to call a truce. Claude found it exciting, and recognizing it as play, jumped and barked at the two of them.

"Is this a new premarital ritual?" a familiar voice called from the mudroom.

"Dad?" Brooke rushed from Adam to hug her father. "We thought we were supposed to pick you up at the airport tonight."

"If you don't let go, we will both be wet." Joe chuckled.

Brooke went into the small bathroom and wrapped a towel around her soaked hair.

"Apparently you two love birds are getting along. I

think." Mary smiled at Brooke, pointing at her wet but happy appearance.

"We are cleaning." Adam grinned as he rubbed a kitchen towel over his wet hair. "How did you get here?"

"Hank offered to pick us up, and we took him up on it. He thought it would be a nice surprise," Joe informed them brightly. "I called the other night, and Hank answered the barn phone, and we decided to do it this way. Our flight was earlier than we thought. Hank, get in here with those rolls so we can have some coffee."

Hank came in with his charming grin, his dimples punctuating his expression. "You are supposed to wash the floor and stuff, not yourselves."

After Joe and Mary relived their extended honeymoon with dozens of pictures, Brooke suggested they go to town for groceries.

"I'd also like to stop and talk with Bess." She glanced at Adam. "I understand she is to me my maid of honor."

"I need to get to the store myself. Traveling can become tedious and inconvenient after a while," Mary agreed.

"Why don't we all go in for lunch? I'll buy." Adam's offer was almost too sudden.

"I suppose that would be fine, if you gents don't mind waiting around while we shop," Mary replied.

"Just so no one gets worried, I've got the help scheduled up to next week," Hank spoke up. "I'm taking

Adam's workload, figuring he had to clean house and get used to being married."

"Efficient, isn't he?" Adam smiled.

"Do you really think it's going to take much time for him to get used to the idea?" Joe teased while patting his shoulder.

"Yup. And plenty more." Hank jested and laughed at Adam.

"Well, in that case, you men clean up the dishes while Mary and I get changed." Brooke helped Mary out of her seat.

The table grew silent after the women left. Joe was the first to break the pervading quiet. "What happened while I was gone? You act like a mother hen around Brooke?"

"Well, we had a few mishaps. Brooke rolled her car and had some bruises—she was mad at me and took off before I could catch her," Adam hedged.

"What else?"

Looking to Hank for support, Adam told Joe about the locket and Junior Mason.

"So, does Buck have the locket, is he looking for answers to this problem?" Joe demanded.

Adam placed his hand on Joe's arm. "Joe, you will have to settle down. Don't get yourself riled and flustered now. The locket is in the desk safe. Buck has pictures of it and the numbers." He took a quick glance at the doorway. "The women will be down in a minute. This needs to be a happy time—especially for Brooke."

He wanted so much for his life to get back to its steady beat, quiet and efficient. He felt angered and frustrated, feelings that could leave him off guard.

"Maybe you're right. We can talk about this later. I stopped for an extra day in L.A. and talked with our investigators. They had nothing more to tell me than what they told you. Maybe we are looking in the wrong place." Joe became more absorbed in his own thoughts as they fussed about in the kitchen.

Adam mopped up the rest of the spattered water. "Let's not dwell on this now. I'm getting married tomorrow, remember?"

Joe laughed. "I really can't believe it. After all these years, you two are now getting married. I can't say I didn't hope for it."

"This mess is finally cleaned up—we really soaked everything." Adam grinned as he slipped on a clean shirt from the dryer. "Let's go down to the barn. I want to show you my wedding gift to Brooke."

Joe approved of the gift as soon as he opened the stall door. Light gray, with four white stockings and the look of a soft kitten, the mare was exquisite. Trained for the show ring, and gentle for anyone, she came to the door and nudged to be petting and given a treat.

"She will love her." Joe commented. He let the horse nuzzle his hand and pockets as he caressed her neck.

"That she will." A rasping voice came from behind

them. Abe held the new bridle, trimmed with silver, which Adam purchased for the new mare to wear. "He's had me running all over the state."

"You old geezer, how are you?" Joe exclaimed as the two old men bear hugged.

"I'm good. How were them beaches and those bikinis? Aint you getting too old for that sort of thing?" He smiled a toothless grin.

"Not as long as I'm breathing. Women are a gift from God." Joe replied with a chuckle.

"We had better get out of here before the women come." Adam warned as he quickly shut the stall and pushed them all forward to the open barn doors.

The drive into town was a feast of discussions. Most of the talk was about the places Joe and Mary visited. The subject of Brooke and the apparent attacks on her were shelved.

Brooke touched Adam's arm. "If you will drop Mary and me off at Bess's, we can walk back to the hotel. You gents can go do whatever it is men do in town."

"I suppose it will be alright." Adam didn't want her to be alone. Even in the small confines of the town, tragedy could strike. He loved her more than life itself.

"Be careful," he advised as she left the car.

Brooke kissed him lightly through the open car window. "Don't worry. We'll be fine. See you in a little bit."

. . .

"Well, have you girls bought out the store?" Joe jested, grinning with adoration as they sat down at the table.

"Not quite. We left some items for you to purchase." Brooke poked him in the arm.

Adam helped Brooke find a seat and a place for her packages. "Let's eat. With so much cleaning, I'm starved,"

He wasn't as starved for food as he was the sight of her. If she could always look as happy, he would be pleased. But he feared danger lurked out there, waiting for them to slip up.

"Bess should be along any minute now. She wasn't feeling well this morning and didn't come into the shop," Brooke informed the men.

She took her napkin and laid it on her lap before she fixed the coffee Adam had poured for her. He felt obsessed with the need to touch her, even to simply lay his hand upon hers. He didn't want anything to interfere.

Mary's attention shifted to the door. "Here's Bess now."

"Ah. Our maid of honor," Adam greeted her and held a chair for her to sit in.

Bess smiled and deposited a kiss on everyone. To Adam, Bess seemed drawn and pale. He hoped she would be well enough to attend their little wedding. She had been Brooke's closest friend for years. However, he was sure Mary would welcome the idea of standing in if Bess was unavailable.

"Hank tells me you have a new beau," Adam hinted as they ordered lunch.

"Um, yes, someone I met while I was in Laramie one day. I literally ran into him in a doorway." Bess tried to explain. "Where is Hank?"

"He's working," Adam chimed in. "When are we going to see this mystery man? Can you bring him tomorrow?"

Too quickly, she responded. "No. I mean, he'll be out of town on business."

Brooke tapped Bess' hand. "I hope Adam didn't make you feel obligated to be in the wedding—if you have something more important to do, I'm sure Mary would be able to step in. I don't want you to feel you have to change your plans on such short notice,"

"Not at all—I'd love to be at your wedding tomorrow. Adam hasn't told me what time?" Bess smiled with more enthusiasm.

"If you got to the ranch around eleven, that would be time enough," Adam spoke as he finished his mug of coffee. He shot her a penetrating look. Could Bess be behind the attacks on Brooke? Would her best friend turn on her? Best to keep your enemies close, he thought.

Joe's enthusiasm broke the tension. "Well," Joe's face lit up with deviltry before they again grew serious. "Tomorrow Adam will no longer be a bachelor. I never thought I'd see the day. I can't think of anyone I would want for a son-in-law more than you. I know my girl will be in good hands." Joe put his arm around Mary and gave her a hug as she nodded in agreement.

Later, near the main barn, Adam noticed a brand new, black truck with the familiar Hightower brand adorning the door. Steve and Hank grinned ear to ear as they sat on the open tailgate. The cans from a six pack of beer littered the bed of the truck, the creation of their jovial spirit.

"Well, here comes the groom." Steve bantered. His eyes darted to Brooke's in spurts.

"Watch your step." Adam wrestled with his brother in a pretend fight. "It creeps up on you like a cougar in the bushes." He wasn't immune to the affection Steve always had for Brooke. "Not me. That's for fools." Steve put his attention to swirling his can of beer. "Anyway, we are here to invite you to your bachelor party at home, last night of freedom."

"Bachelor party, huh?" Adam would at one time thought of a bachelor party as a rip-roaring good time. Now he hoped for an excuse not to go.

"You can let her out of your sight for a few hours. Besides, you're not supposed to see the bride until tomorrow," Steve insisted.

Joe came around and put his hand on Brooke's shoulder. His wizened and caring grey eyes touched Adam gently. "She will be alright with us, Adam. You go along and have a good time of it. However, before you go, I need to talk to both of you in the office, privately."

Joe's gaze traveled to Steve, and with a slight nod

from Steve, he took Mary's hand and slowly made his way to the house. When they gathered in the office, Joe motioned for Brooke and Adam to sit on the couch. He took Mary's hand and leaned on the large, antique desk.

"I have a wedding gift for you, that is, if you want it. Maybe you will decide against it. It will be yours if you accept the terms." Joe spoke quietly and slowly, appearing somewhat cautious in his explanations. "Because Adam will own all of this someday, I have made a decision. I will trade you your lakeside property, a life estate, if you will. The same rule about the land still stands. No parts will be sold separately to outsiders. The ranch is to stay in the hands of family members."

No one spoke for a while. Adam looked at his boots and crossed his legs as he adjusted his sitting position. Brooke said nothing but stared into her father's face.

"Aren't you happy with the change?" Joe asked curiously.

"Why can't we all live right here as we have been? You love this house so much. It's a big part of you, of us. I don't want to take it from you now. You should stay here and let us build on the other property," Brooke declared. "How do you feel about this, Mary?"

"Brooke, I love this house, too. Joe is right. It's not as if we would be moving to Texas. We will be just down the road a bit." Mary's voice was calm and composed. "Besides, Adam does all of the ranch work and training. He may as well be here where the work is rather than having to drive back and forth. And your father and I may want our own privacy." She smiled and kissed Joe on the cheek.

Getting up from his perch on the desk, Joe placed the paperwork on the desk and went over to Mary, took her hand, and walked to the office door. "I'll leave you to ponder this. We will accept whatever you decide."

Adam remained silent. He knew he would one day have the large house and the ranch itself. He hadn't expected Joe to do this. It really wouldn't be difficult to drive over there every day, but he would let Brooke decide. However, he couldn't see her happy in any other house. "Well, my dear, have you decided?"

"Do you think my father still feels the presence of my mother in this house even after all these years?" She took his hand in hers to gaining his full attention. "Do you think this is his way of having a new home for himself and Mary?"

"Yes, it's possible. If they build up by the lake, there's a problem."

"What's that?" Brooke turned her body so she could look at his face.

"Well, we won't be able to go skinny dipping and have sex on 'Grandpa's Lap' because they would always be there." He grinned at her as they remembered.

Chuckling, she kissed him. "We will have to encourage them to go on more vacations."

Joe mentioned grandchildren. She really would want her children raised in the house of memories, in the house she grew to love deeply, Adam mused.

"You never mentioned anything about our future together or what you want. What about a passel of kids running through these halls?" she asked.

Taking her in his arms, he gently turned her to face him. Smiling, he gazed into her bright, blue eyes. "We have to have at least one son to carry the Tower name and to continue on when I'm too old, or a tomboy like her mother.

"Why don't we let them live here until they are ready to go to a new house? I really think you are right in thinking Joe needs a different surrounding with Mary. This has always been your mother's house—even the rose garden. They should have a place of their own. And they won't be too far away when we need them—like to baby-sit."

Brooke's eyes darted to his. Her heart smiled with the thought of him as a father, playing pony, riding a toddler on his shoulders. She kissed him quickly and got up to look at the papers on the desk.

Joe came in a few minutes later to stand next to her at the desk. "Well, have you decided, or do you need more time?"

Steve stood in the doorway waiting.

"Oh, all right, if it will make you happy. I don't want you to leave in a big hurry, take your time." Brooke signed her land over to her father.

"Steve, you can do your notarizing now and everything will be legal. I'll take all of these to the county clerk on Monday."

After Steve signed and stamped each document, he gave them to Brooke and Joe. "Good. Now, Adam, you have to leave for your party. The three of us are going to have a special dinner all alone. Why don't you send Abe up here to join us?"

Brooke walked outside with Adam as he joined his brother and Hank. He stopped on the patio to kiss her good-by. His eyes were clouded with uncertainties.

CHAPTER TWENTY-SIX

The day dawned bright with a beautiful full sun to compliment the nearly naked sky. Wispy clouds dotted the deep blue of the heavens to break up the solid background. Joe rented a wedding arch, covered with white flowers. White chairs were set up on the lawn and filled with invited guests. The ceremony was simple, traditional, and included the traditional vows and ring exchange. And with the *you can kiss the bride*, wishes and good cheer rose from the attendees.

"Excuse me, big brother, if I don't get to kiss the bride now, I know I'll never get another chance." Steve stepped before Brooke and took her by the elbows. The kiss was brotherly and proper. The air became tight with anticipation, and although Brooke knew Adam was watching intently, Steve continued to hold her at arm's length.

Steve smiled. "You remember what I said about

caring for her." His words were directed at Adam, although his attention was on Brooke. "If he doesn't treat you right, come to me. I'll set him straight."

Adam grinned. "Actually, I think you should be worried about me. I'll probably turn gray the first year." The light-hearted remark abated the tension. He let out a big sigh and patted Brooke's hand. "Can we have this dance, love?"

Later, after the dancing and the enormous spread of food had been grazed over, Brooke found time to sit while Adam enjoyed talking with some old friends, some of whom drove a great distance to share his wedding. Bess, too, needed a rest from the dance floor and found an empty seat next to Brooke.

"I don't think I told you how beautiful your dress is." Bess' compliment sounded honest.

The cream-colored silk had a low neckline with a covering of fine French lace. The fitted bodice gave way to a slightly shirred knee-length skirt. Brooke's satin, sling heels were of the same shade as the dress, as were the sheer stockings. Her mother's locket adorned the neckline.

"Thank you. I fell in love with it when we went to Laramie. I saw it in Darby's window.

Are you feeling better? You look tired." Brooke stared at her. Bess was not her usual carefree self. She feared something was seriously wrong.

"No, I'm fine. I got in a little late last night."

"Oh, yes, that new flame of yours. You should have brought him with you. He would have been welcome."

"He isn't available today, some business." Bess's hand appeared a bit shaky as she sipped at her glass of champagne.

She eyed her curiously. Her overall manner seemed overwrought and nervous. "Too bad, I hope this is serious?"

Bess smiled. "Well, time will tell."

"Thanks for being my maid of honor on such a short notice. I was angry with Adam because he made plans without asking me. I often get the feeling life with him is going to be bumpy sometimes. I do love him, and he is good to me."

"Adam is his own man," Bess murmured.

She watched her husband, amazed at how different two men could be. She grew up with Adam but never perceived him as the sexy, generous man he really was under his tough-man exterior. Back then, she regarded him as a brother figure, a neighbor, older than her. He was always stunningly virile, and females vied for his attention.

Mike, she had known for less than a year before they married. Good looking and sophisticated, compared to the cowboys she knew. Maybe that's what drew her to him. Someone different. He was generous, too—as long as she played by his rules.

"I didn't see Kitty here. Maybe he didn't invite her."

"I called her a week or so ago because she missed a

hair appointment. Her housekeeper said she was on a vacation in Mexico. That's all I know."

"Well, it would have been uncomfortable if she had come. She certainly knows how to stir up the pot. She always has, even in school."

"Kitty was always different." Bess downed the rest of the wine.

Around four, most of the guests had left, many to attend to chores or to pick up children. Some had lengthy rides ahead of them. The reason Adam chose an early wedding was the time factor, the distance between ranches and towns was great. Those who stayed were the usual close friends and relatives, including Josh and Abe. Steve sat with some locals who rodeoed with him, laughter coming often from that table. Hank assumed a spot next to Bess where they chatted amicably.

Slipping up behind her, Adam slid his arms around her waist. "I want you to go in and change into something you can ride in," he whispered.

"Now?"

"Yes." Adam smiled. "I'll give you fifteen minutes."

Reluctantly, Brooke gave in to her husband's wishes, not wanting to leave the small group. When she came back, everyone was clustered near the barn doors. As she neared the barn, Adam led out a beautiful gray mare. She could tell Abe had cleaned her up for the occasion, making her white stockings gleam and her white mane and tail brilliant in the light of day. The saddle and bridle were the set her father had given her for her birthday.

Brooke's voice seemed stuck in her throat as she recognized the mare they had seen at the show. Adam gripped her hand and with a beaming grin, he offered her his gift.

"Adam, she is more beautiful than I remember." Brooke took his face in her small hands and kissed him warmly, regardless of those standing nearby. The mare recalled for her all his kindness at the show and his surprise engagement announcement in the arena. She took the reins and stroked the horse's muzzle gently.

"Let's go for a test ride. You wait here while I go get Contender."

Joe came over, and beaming with pride for both, he hugged her warmly. "I'm so happy for both of you. I think this time you can truly be happy, and I hope for a very long time. Things seemed to work out the way I hoped."

"So, you think you had it all figured out, huh?" Tears blurred her vision. Yes, she could believe she was happy.

Brooke rode the mare out to one of the paddocks and studied her reactions while she waited for Adam. The mare responded to the slightest amount of leg pressure and was finger responsive to the bit.

She now felt guilty she had no time or even considered a gift for him. Adam had been determined to marry her. To order a saddle and matching bridle would have taken some time. Even the cheek piece of the bridle had the mare's name engraved on a silver plate.

Adam joined her, and they took the ranch road out to

the county road and toward the lake. Neither of them had much to say. A blanket of contentment draped over them —except for the ever-present gun Adam wore whenever he was far from the house. Nevertheless, whenever, she looked his way, he was smiling gently, warmly in her direction.

A few cow and calf pairs grazed in the lush grasses bordering the lake area. The animals were so content in their feasting, the horses and riders didn't bother them. They continued munching with an air of indifference.

After dismounting, Adam drew her from the saddle and crushing her to him, kissed her slow and thoughtful. He wrapped an arm about her shoulders as they walked to the water's edge.

As they ambled about, Brooke noticed the many imprints of horses' hooves in the soft dirt. "Adam, have many ranch hands been up here on horseback?"

"No, they have been working the hay fields on the south side." He also noted the many fresh tracks.

"Let's go see where these tracks go."

"Do you think we should?" Brooke hesitated. She still feared a phantom of sorts, lurking in and around every tree.

"Well, if we wait and the predicted showers arrive, they will be gone. Besides, it's probably some kids up here necking anyway. Isn't this where you always came with your boy friends?"

"Were you jealous?" she taunted, her eyes glittering with mischief.

. . .

Adam hugged her close. "I never liked the thought of you up here with skinny, pimple-faced teenage boys," he replied with a grin. He never liked it when she and Steve made the rounds at horse shows or fairs, laughing and teasing each other, either. Even back then, his heart refused to believe what his mind told him. He had always loved her. And he kept that secret in his heart for ever. But he didn't have that to worry about any longer. Now there were other pressing problems, endangering the many ranches around there.

They mounted their horses. Without confusing their tracks with the foreign ones, they rode around the lake. On the far side, one horse departed from the other and headed in the direction of the Montgomery and Hightower ranches. The tracks followed the river as it took its life from the cold mountain lake. The other horse rode off in the opposite direction.

"Apparently, this one came from one of our ranches. I'll have someone check the old shack again. Could be we have another resident."

"Maybe this is just a trysting place."

He grinned and nodded in agreement. They followed the tracks until they came to the road. Flattened grass indicated a vehicle had parked there, probably a horse trailer. The heavier imprints were those of the pickup.

"Here's where one of our riders left. Do you suppose

we have an over-worked imagination?" Adam suggested as he stood by her horse. His smiled, warming her.

Why would a rider from their ranch need to meet someone secretly, and on the afternoon of their wedding? If it were a ranch hand, they could have had their riding partner just drive into the ranch and park.

Adam reached over and squeezed her knee reassuringly. By the time they rode into the yard, the sun had fallen below the hills. The glow of a salmon-colored sky still decorated the ridge.

Only Abe, Josh, and the Montgomerys were still hanging around the patio when they returned. Hank took Bess home earlier and was planning to meet some friends at the hotel.

"We thought you two were going to camp out up there, newlyweds and all," Abe taunted amicably.

"Thought crossed my mind." Adam threw back with a broad smile. "We were investigating horse tracks we found. Seems like a rendezvous took place up by the lake sometime today," he added, giving his father and Joe a meaningful look. "Apparently one was headed for one of our ranches." He spoke as he helped Brooke dismount.

Brooke tapped Adam on the arm. "Could have been a romantic tryst."

Joe looked out at the barn. "We'll, have to check that out. Anyway, I think I've worked up an appetite. Anyone else hungry?" He turned to Brooke. "The air has really cooled down with the storm coming in. I'll put this gorgeous animal away. Then you can go in and help Mary rustle up some sandwiches and coffee?"

"Well, I suppose we could rustle up some chow," she mocked with a grin.

"I'll put the horse away." Abe spoke up quickly in his usual gruff but loving tone everyone came to recognize." He ran his hands down his front. "Hope you don't mind. I borrowed your jacket. It was just lying here, and it got a bit chilly." He shivered mockingly.

"It's pink." Adam chuckled at the old man. Abe was so slight of build most of Brooke's clothing fit him. On many occasions in the past, he recalled Brooke wearing Abe's clothing while out on a cattle drive to keep warm while he insisted on shivering in the cold.

"The horse won't notice, and even if she does, she won't tell the others." He took the reins from Brooke and started moving toward the barn.

Adam followed Abe to the new barn and the mare's stall. He continued through the show horse barn and out to the stallion barn attached to the arena. The tracks at the lake troubled him even though he tried to tell himself it was probably nothing. The lake had always been a quiet place for lovers to meet over the years. However, the business of the cattle rustling was not settled. He couldn't help feeling they were being watched.

Contender wasn't too sweaty from the ride, so putting him away didn't take as long as usual. He took off the saddle and placed it nearby.

Adam was aware of how peaceful he felt, content as

he had hoped he would feel someday. He knew the rest of their lives would not be as fine as this day, for he knew Brooke had a will of her own that he feared he would not be able to break, nor would he want to. He loved her spirit, and maybe the mercurial energy was what he always found desirable.

As he entered the barn, he noticed the gray mare wandering the aisle of the barn. She seemed content to munch on a stack of fresh hay stacked against a wall. Then he noticed a body sprawled in the front of the mare's stall. He ran to Abe who was moving slightly. He knelt next to the old man and helped him sit up.

"Abe, are you alright?"

"Adam?" Abe groaned quietly as he tried to focus on the person before him.

"What happened?"

Abe sat up against the stall and took off his baseball cap. He rubbed his white head. "I don't know … I was taking the mare's halter off and then ever' thin' went black. Ooh, I must a hit my head."

Adam looked around quickly. He caught the mare by her lead rope and led her inside the stall and took off the halter. He eased the stall door closed and secured the latch. After fastening the halter to the blanket bar, he turned his attention to Abe.

"Let's get you up to the house and get some ice on it before you have to wear a larger hat size."

When they returned to the house, Mary and Brooke

fussed over their old friend. Adam's insides railed with frustration and concern about this latest incident.

"I have to get back to the barn and put the saddle away. I'll be right back. See he's taken care of. Maybe the mare bumped him. I think it will take more than a lump on his head to hurt this old geezer," Adam jested, trying to put some levity in his voice. He gritted his teeth.

Was this meant for Brooke? He worried. Had Abe been mistaken for her in her pink jacket? At the barn he looked for any sign of an intruder. They were all sitting outside. Was he going to have to hire an armed guard service?

Frustration ate at him.

With Adam's returned they gathered for sandwiches and coffee. He tried to make it sound like Abe had fallen from too much drink.

Joe insisted. "Abe, I think it would be best if you stay here tonight. Josh and I will go over and feed your animals and check on your place. You can sleep in Mary's old room here next to the kitchen."

"Steve is sleeping in there," Mary reminded him.

"No, he isn't," Brooke spoke up. "I was in there to get this blanket. No one is there. Are you sure he didn't go home?"

"I thought he went in to sleep a few hours ago. Of course, he could have left through the front door. He did park out front today with all the cars and trucks about,"

Mary offered. She went to the front door and confirmed his truck was indeed gone.

Joe patted Abe's shoulder. "Well, that settles it. You will stay tonight. Come on, Josh. Let's go feed Abe's stock."

After they left, Brooke tried to behave as though it were in fact an accident. Deep inside, she was all jelly with fear. She knew whoever hurt Abe was trying to get to her. He could have easily been mistaken for her in the evening shadows. Besides, he was wearing her jacket. Now a dear friend was injured, and she was sure it was because of her.

Could Steve have had something to do with it? Would he hurt her? He was always around, and apparently, he left the house without being seen. And what about the tracks they found at the lake? Were they from someone at the ranch, someone with orders to follow? Brooke felt she was becoming recklessly paranoid. Soon she would have everyone she cared about on her list of suspects.

Coming back to the table, Adam sat down next to her. He put his hand over hers and gently squeezed. She drank in the comfort he provided, hoping they would find the answers before it was too late.

CHAPTER TWENTY-SEVEN

*T*he next few weeks as man and wife were spent doing chores or training the horses for the show circuit. Contender won his class in the major roping event of the early show season in Denver. Brooke competed in western pleasure with her new mare and placed in the top three spots each time.

On this day, Brooke awoke with sunbeams bounding off the wall of her bedroom. "Noon. Why didn't he wake me?" Sitting up, she discovered an unusual feeling of grogginess. Besides the lethargy, headaches brought her inside on two different afternoons—and the nausea.

Moaning with wretchedness, she decided to get up and see what everyone was doing and find out why she was left to sleep so long. After pulling her robe together, she headed downstairs to find Mary, humming and baking pecan rolls for Joe.

"Well, sleepy head, would you like some breakfast—or lunch?"

"Yes, thank you. A roll and maybe a cup of coffee." Brooke replied, yawning still as she ambled over to the table. Outside, she spotted Adam out in the mare's paddock, caressing and holding the new foals—those brave enough to come to him. He was gentle and kind as he stroked and scratched them, getting them ready to wear a halter.

"You know, Mary, I never sleep this late," Brooke commented, her eyes still glazed with sleep.

"Well, I know why. You see, Adam has been worrying about you. He gave instructions to let you sleep. Claude's been fretting all morning, running up and down the stairs. He, too, likes his daily schedules."

"Adam does take charge, doesn't he?" Brooke fondled the furry head in her lap.

"Doc called and said he had an opening for you. It's about ten, I think. I wrote it down. If you want, dear, I'll get Abe drive you to Doc's," Mary hinted. "I have bread rising to bake for the senior lunch."

"I'll see if Adam is busy. Maybe we can have lunch." But her phone just went to voice mail. "Is Adam still out with the foals? I can't get a hold of him."

"Adam said he was going to be riding out to the back pastures with the men. He said he would be going out to check on the cows there and take a head count in each pasture. If he rode out with the men, then he won't be in range." Mary pounded a slab of dough.

Brooke looked to Mary. "I think I'll drive into town alone and stop by to get my hair trimmed. I'll only be gone a short time. Unless you want to come and shop." Brooke explained.

"No, I don't mind—be careful, though. Call when you get there."

"I'll do that. I keep a small pistol in the Explorer." She tried to reinforce her own bravery. Fear raised its head. Would she be followed? Would she be attacked on the road, run into a ditch or shot at? Get a grip, she thought. She couldn't live in fear. Her head thumped like a drum.

"Don't you miss your beautiful car? I would have thought you would want a new one after the accident." Mary brought over a plate of warm, sticky rolls.

"Actually, the Explorer is better around here. Besides, the car represents a life I would like to forget." Yes, the car represented a life she would never want again. Just thinking of those abusive years made her heart ripple with fear. And now his go-to-guy shows up there dead. The implication stabbed her with the possibility that Mike could still be alive. Had they somehow staged the plane crash?

After finishing her roll and coffee, she went upstairs to change. She slipped on a pair of white jeans. Over the jeans she put on a loose fitting, light-blue flowery blouse, hanging free in a smock style.

Adam hadn't let her go to town by herself, and she understood his concern. She couldn't hide anymore.

Nothing related to her, or the locket, had occurred since the wedding. And nothing indicated the incident was even related to the others. The horse could have accidentally bumped him as he put her in the stall, or Abe could have passed out and hit his head. He was elderly. Maybe too much champaign.

Until the day after the wedding, both suspected Steve had some part in the attack on Abe. The suspicion was fueled by his lack of discretion in telling anyone where he had gone.

However, Josh had found him later that night in his pickup near their house. Because of his inebriated state, he was unable to drive all the way to the garage and humbly parked his truck on the back lawn of his home. Aided by his father, Steve managed to get in the house and to bed.

Brooke parked her Explorer near the hotel and walked to the doctor's office.

Doc stood next to the table. He gently tapped her hands folded on her lap. "I don't think the headaches are from the accident. Maybe stress is causing them. Or, you may have an allergy or a deep sinus infection. We'll take some tests just in case. I'll give you a mild prescription for allergies. If it doesn't help or the headaches get worse, call." He stared at her for a moment. Then he grinned. "How does Adam feel about children?"

"A baby?" Brooke hadn't even thought about it.

Doc smiled at her. "Well, headaches, morning nausea … Tests will tell us something."

She could be pregnant. Her heart welled with the joy of it. A baby. The thoughts of tiny clothes, sweet little boots. The smells of baby powder and baby's breath. She smiled. Then reality hit, and she would wait for the test.

After Doc's she headed for Bess's salon to get her hair trimmed. The shop wasn't busy. With a full-time beautician working for her, Brooke hoped they would be able to chat a bit.

"Can you get away from here for lunch—my treat?" Brooke offered.

Bess kept trimming the back of Brooke's long hair. "No, not today. I have a full calendar. And I have to leave early."

"We should make a date to spend some girl time." Brooke suddenly felt uncomfortable with Bess's cold responses. Was it her or something else?

"Yes, we should, soon." Bess untied the plastic sheet and brushed away any loose hair. When Brooke opened her purse to pay, Bess put up a hand. "We'll catch up later." Bess smiled and took the sweeper to clean up the area around the chair Brooke had just vacated. Her actions were more of a dismissal.

With mixed emotions, Brooke walked to the hotel and found a most welcome, smiling face of the day. "Brooke. How have you been? Is Adam joining you? Jalapeno burgers are the special today." Mack's beaming face was refreshing.

"I'll have the small chef's salad and a cup of tea, oh, and some of those whole wheat crackers. And, no, Adam is not joining me. Thanks." She smiled through the ache in her temple.

Sitting alone, she had time to think, time to piece together why someone might want her necklace. Attempts to get it had stopped. Was it a code, a bank account someone needed, either a partner of Mike or Mike himself? Had he faked his death? Trying to resolve her mixed thoughts took all her concentration until a body slipped into the booth opposite her.

"You don't look well, sister dear. Has Adam been treating you all right?" Steve's voice was soft and casual.

Brooke's heart gave a shudder. "I didn't expect you. You gave me a start."

The last person she wanted to see then was Steve. He had always been a comfort to her in the past. The sight of his handsome face and the familiar smell of his aftershave carried her to simpler times, youthful times.

"I was having a cool beer at the bar when I saw you. I thought Adam would be with you." He had his glass with him and sipped from it, methodically surveying her. He put the glass down and stretched his long legs under the table. "And where is your keeper? I'm surprised he let you out alone."

Brooke sat up straighter and moved her leg away from his. "I had some errands to run. Adam is working out in the fields." Her eyes were like pinballs as they bounced to and from his.

"What are you afraid of? You act like a cornered filly."

"I didn't expect anyone. And I'm always worried with all of the things that have happened." Brooke let out a sigh before she continued. "Actually, I thought you were Adam. He hardly lets me out of his sight."

"Then how come you're out alone?" His eyebrow on the left raised with the question as his eyes twinkled with mischief. "Adam is as protective of you as the guardian of a treasure, and I don't blame my brother one bit. I felt the same way years ago when Desiree and I were a couple. I don't know if I can ever give myself to someone to that same degree ever again."

Steve's charm and his smile were hard to resist. His constant staring made her uneasy. "Does anyone know you're in town?"

Her voice was cautious as she spoke. "Yes, Mary knows. I've had headaches. Doc says they're probably allergies."

"Don't be so defensive. I was concerned about your welfare. I was going to follow you home." He reached over and took one of her hands in his. "You are part of the family now. Besides, even if you are my brother's wife, I still enjoy your company."

Blushing uncomfortably, she asked him to stay for lunch. He accepted her invitation and in a short time the pretense was shattered, and they were once again laughing openly. Even as children, she recalled, he could make her laugh or simply smile no matter how sad or depressed she was. At the time, Steve was the right tonic to bring her out of her doldrums.

As their lunch ended, something caught his eye. He sat up abruptly, staring at the door.

"Steve?"

Before he could answer her, Adam filled the space next to her. "Is this a private party, or can I sit in?" He was in his work clothes, and his stained chambray shirt smelled of oil and hay.

Her heart thudded within her chest. How would she explain this? "We were just finishing lunch. Would you like something? Mack said he had smothered burritos."

"No, actually I came in to get supplies, and low and behold I find your Explorer." Adam's voice was measured and cautious.

"Mary suggested I get out for a bit. Doc called and said he had an opening and could see me about the headaches."

"So, are you done with your errands? Or are there other things you need to do?" Adam tapped his fingers on the table.

"Yes, I'm done, but I need to use the restroom before I leave."

Adam let her out of the booth and sat down to wait.

Steve glanced at the check and left cash on the table to cover it. "Brooke looks a bit haggard, Adam. Is she coming down with something?"

"I don't know. She's had headaches. What are you doing here with my wife?" he asked without anger.

"Actually, I'm not with your wife. I was having a beer with the old timers when I saw her come in for lunch and came over to sit with her. She's very jumpy— of you or something else?"

Adam didn't answer as he saw her coming back to the booth. "Are you ready to go now?"

"Yes. Goodbye, Steve. Thanks for the company."

"Anytime." A gentle smiled lit his face.

He was quiet as he followed her out of the restaurant. "I'll follow you home." He held open the door of her Explorer and closed it firmly.

Adam hadn't been looking for Brooke when he left for town. His sole purpose was to get veterinary supplies. He assumed she was still in bed resting. And there she was—with his brother, smiling, obviously pleased with his company, and seeming very chipper. The sight of her small hand resting under Steve's stronger one brought unbidden memories to the surface, nearly freezing him in his tracks.

The image of them lying side by side, Steve's strong form folded around her smaller, softer body sent chills of fury through him. Why had he even gone over there that night? If he hadn't, the misery he was feeling wouldn't exist. He had gone over to the pool house, and he still believed what he hadn't seen.

Words could not express the lack of control he sensed, and the foreboding he might lose the one thing he cherished over all else. The time it took to drive to the ranch was even more unsettling as questions unwanted and uncalled for seemed to flow steadily through his head. *Were they planning something together? Had they met like this before? Or worse, were they lovers? Had they been lovers?* Brooke was right when she reminded him their courtship was short. *Had she agreed to marry him to simply get back what she felt was rightfully hers?*

Adam hated himself for the pictures he painted. His insides were like a coiled snake. If she tried to explain now, he wouldn't be rational enough to answer her without striking out at her with words he probably wouldn't mean. He wanted to take her by the shoulders and shake her, exorcize the fears he held of her and Steve. Instead, he gripped the steering wheel and drove until they reached the barn.

Her voice stopped him as he threw himself from the truck. "Adam, it's not what you think."

"You presume too much, my dear wife. If you are so enamored with Steve, then why in hell's name did you marry me? Or was it to get your beloved ranch back?"

His words struck her in rapid succession, leaving her speechless. As Adam stomped away, she closed her eyes, her heart aching. Would he ever believe she and Steve did not have a lunch date?

Heavyhearted, she walked slowly up to the house. Claude's barks of pleasure could not dent the wall of despair around her. As she walked through the house,

Brooke met Mary coming out of the office with her hands full of cleaning supplies.

"Are you all right? You look so sad. Did Doc find out what's bothering you?" She put down the tote and came over to Brooke.

"Oh, Doc thinks allergies. Adam is so overprotective." She skipped over their one-sided argument.

The turmoil in Brooke was almost a tangible thing, and she knew space and time were needed to resolve whatever problems had arisen that day. Sighing deeply Brooke said, "I think I'll go lie down. Doc gave me a prescription for these headaches, something in the air."

The stairs seemed to be twice as long and her legs twice as heavy. When was she going to find some peace of mind? Adam brought her security and unquestionable love. But he was stubborn, and now he hurt with imagined crimes. What would he think if she mentioned a baby?

She slipped into a comfortable robe, took one of the pills, and crawled miserably on the bed. Despondently, she closed her eyes and didn't feel the handkerchief that later wiped away the escaping tears.

After a few feeble tries to focus, Brooke was able to read the clock on her bedside table. Twelve midnight. Still dressed in her day clothes, she reached over to Adam's side of the bed only to find it empty and cold.

"Damn." A tight pain of tension welled up in her throat, threatening to choke her.

Her sadness turned to fear as a weight settled on the edge of the bed. Instinctively, she pushed away the intruder, but her hands were taken without effort and treated to the feel of soft, warm lips. Realizing it was Adam and not her ever-present demon, she relaxed until the recent events of the day stirred her memory.

"Adam?" She said his name more for herself than for a reply.

"We need to talk. Are you feeling all right? I'm really concerned about these headaches and fatigue." His voice was deep and comforting. His large hand came up to remove the hair, hanging in her face and wound it about her ear.

"Just sleepy." She murmured cautiously.

"I wish you would have told me you needed to go to town. I'd have come in early to take you." He helped her adjust the pillows behind her head, so she was sitting up and facing him. The only light was from the full moon.

"I called you to let you know Doc was going to see me. You must have been in a canyon or something. Check your phone." Her voice was a bit touchier than she wanted. Her throat hurt with impending tears. Why didn't he want to believe her?

"Did you have a date with my brother?" His grip tightened subtly on her wrist, but his voice remained relatively calm.

"No, he sat down unexpectedly. He had been at the

bar having a beer. I invited him to have lunch with me, and then you came." She tried to see his face. The near dark prevented her from discerning how he responded to her reply.

"Every time I see you and Steve, it reminds me of your father's wedding." His hands began to caress her arm.

"Why?" she sighed.

"I suppose I need to be honest with you. You see, I wanted to apologize for being such a surly oaf at the wedding. When I got to the pool house and looked for you, I saw the wet bathing suits and assumed you two were sleeping in the bedroom. I couldn't bear to look inside."

"Well, if you had, you would have seen only me. Steve slept outside on a lounge chair. Nothing happened between us."

All this time he thought she and Steve had sex in the guest house. So much tension over something that never happened.

His lips claimed hers. As his tongue played give and take games with hers, his hand slid under her shirt to her roam intimately over her smooth skin. He whispered into her hair, "I love you, Mrs. Tower, and I'm really sorry."

Claude began to whine, apparently worried about the tension he sensed. With an order from Adam, he settled down on his pillow.

"I worry when you are out of sight."

"I went to see Doc."

"And?"

She felt the tension in his hand. His body shifted slightly. "I was worried about the headaches. He said they could be allergies. He took some blood tests ... I could be pregnant."

Adam wrapped his arms around her and pulled her close to his chest. His soft terry robe was a pillow for her face. He ran his fingers through her hair and further down her back, settling them to gently caress her.

He released her and watched her eyes in the moonlight. "A baby? I couldn't think of anything better."

Shedding their clothes, she worked her magic on him, while he was able to caress her willing flesh. When their barriers of control shattered, his hands reached to grasp her bottom and pressed her even closer to his own fevered response.

Her shower was barely large enough for the two of them. Neither spoke as the warm water showered over their bodies. Their motions played in slow motion as each in turn lathered the other. With large white towels they tenderly removed the droplets, glistening in the light. Neither spoke as each contemplated this new road of life.

They slept undisturbed until early the next morning. She woke before the morning sun, enjoying the drowsy warmth of her bed, Adam's warm body, and prayers for the future. In her heart she knew the day of reckoning was still to come.

CHAPTER TWENTY-EIGHT

*T*he mountain mornings were crisp and cool, a counter to the hot sun. The air near the house was full of rose scents and the abundance of flowers finally in bloom.

Their lives evolved into a natural rhythm. Days fell into the time frame of the ranch, the animals, and the crops. And the prospects of a baby.

Both families attended the Paint Horse World Show in Fort Worth where Contender's points gave him a reserve high point for the show. The designation would give him the recognition necessary to bring a larger fee for breeding outside mares and brought the name of the ranch and Adam further national attention.

The fourth of July occurred during their stay. They celebrated together along with other trainers and breeders they had long known in the industry. Steve came to their table with a woman Brooke recognized as one of the competitors. She was tall with long, dark hair and well dressed in expensive jeans, a yellow silk shirt, and silver jewelry.

"You all remember Raven McKay? Her family used to work on our ranch many years ago. She's got a few hours before they leave for Colorado." Steve found her a chair.

Brooke smiled at Raven. This was Desiree's younger cousin. She tagged along often when her mother was busy cleaning the Tower home. A question rolled out of her mouth. "Has anyone heard from Desiree?" Then she realized she may have overstepped. "Oh, sorry, Steve, I didn't mean to be nosey, just concerned."

Raven glanced at Steve. "No one has heard from her since she went to New York."

Steve grimaced. "Well, that seems like a lifetime ago."

"Yes, it has. I can't believe we've been working for the widow lady for nearly fifteen years. Time does fly."

Adam smiled at his brother and handed him a glass of beer. "Raven would you like one?"

Raven looked around as though she wanted to leave. "No, thank you. I really have to get back. It was so nice of Steve to bring me here to see you all once again. Have a safe trip home."

Raven left and the table became deadly quiet. Steve put down his glass of beer and took a seat at the table. "I didn't expect them to be here. I guess the old lady rancher they work for wanted her horses in the show. Well, she had no news about Desiree. Seems strange that she just disappeared." His face reflected his disappointment. Then he turned his attention to those at the table. "This must be your year, brother, a fantastic win with your horse and a wife and a baby on the way," he joked, "If my bridle hadn't broken on the poles event, I could have caught up with you—given you a run for your money and had a win for Hightower."

"Supposed to check your equipment before a class, aren't you? Well, maybe next year. We do need to give the other competitors something to shoot for." Adam grinned. "You did have a successful sale of some of your paintings."

"Yes, finally I get to have one on the cover of next year's sale catalogue." Steve beamed. "And someone from New York bought one of the originals, a pair of bald eagles in flight."

Josh chuckled at his sons. "Well, Joe, I guess we've done all right. It hasn't been easy with this group, but I think we are going to survive them."

"I'll drink to that," Joe quipped as he offered a toast.

During July, Mary began to can for winter whatever fruit or vegetable came in season. She didn't have to. They could afford to buy whatever they needed. Mary felt an obligation to the men and their families who worked on the ranch.

Their appreciation came at different times during the year. Sometimes she would receive an award-winning rose bush or discriminating gifts would be found under the Christmas tree.

The counters were full sparkling jars of berry jam, crabapple jelly, and choke cherry syrup. The kitchen smelled inviting and sweet. However, Brooke abhorred domestic chores, and although she enjoyed Mary's company, sorting berries and standing over kettles steaming with fruit and sugar was not her forte.

She always enjoyed being active to a point of exhaustion. Now the jams were finished, and she decided to get outside for a while. Wearing a pair of older jeans to accommodate her vanishing waistline and a gray tee shirt she walked down to the barns.

"Come, pretty Fancy, I need some exercise." She slipped the leather halter on the mare and led her to the cross ties near the tack room.

The mare stood patiently as Brooke groomed and fussed over her. The gray coat glistened in the light as the brush was liberally applied. Brooke slipped the breast strap over the horse's neck and settled it in place. She positioned the green plaid saddle pad and then the English saddle. The deep brown of the leather was a good contrast to the color of the mare.

Brooke strapped on leather gaiters over the calves of

her jeans instead of looking for her riding boots. She knew the leather straps from the English saddle could pinch the skin off the inside of her calves if she were to ride without the protection. Removing the horse from the cross ties, she put on the headstall and bit. Taking the reins, she headed for the back door of the barn and the outside arena.

"Hello, Hank," Brooke smiled as she saw him coming through the open overhead door of the barn.

"I take it Adam isn't back for lunch yet?" He grinned. "Adam asked me to work around the barns while he checked on the movement of cattle and the hay stacking. A strong storm has been predicted."

Brooke continued walking toward the arena. "No, he hasn't called to check in either."

Hank walked closer to her. "You know how he is. He is a hands-on kind of man and wants to know first-hand what has to be done. I'm sure he'll return soon … Why don't you wait until he gets back?"

"I cannot sit in the house all day. I feel as though I'm going to burst with so much domestic activity. It bores me to death."

"Mary really likes all that stuff." Hank smiled as he tapped the door framing.

Brooke could sense what was on his mind. Hank was a loyal, hardworking, and talented employee. The reason he wasn't out on this two-day round-up was because of her. Adam left him behind to watch over her and the barns. His military stint made him the man for the job.

The small pistol attached to his belt was not for snakes, she knew.

"I know he doesn't want me to do much of anything, Hank. Pregnancy isn't a disease."

"He's only doing what he feels is best. I'm sure he worries even more—especially with all that has happened lately."

Brooke knew in his own way he was trying to be helpful. She dropped her eyes from his. Adam was a worry wart about everything. But she couldn't hide from everyday life, not to things bringing her happiness. Years of oppression taught her well.

"I know. Why don't you get a horse to work, and you can ride with me? Give me a half an hour and I promise I'll quit."

She rode with Hank while he exercised one of the well-seasoned show horses. After thirty minutes, his watch began to chime. "Your time is up, Mrs. Tower." He smiled at her cautiously, hoping she would keep her word and quit the ride.

"Thanks, Hank." Brooke rode over to the gate and dismounted.

In the barn she hooked the mare to the crossties and unsaddled her, leaving the saddle and tack on the floor. After a quick brushing, she walked the horse back to the paddocks where she placed her with two other mares. She watched for a moment as the horses cavorted around the fence, their tails waving like flags. She smiled and returned to the barn to put her saddle away, a sense of gratification filled her.

As she entered the barn, loyal Claude, who followed her outside and waited while she released her horse, growled a warning. Adam stood next to her saddle, arms akimbo. He glared at her. The dark clouds on the horizon indicated an impending storm not unlike the one about to begin there.

The aisle way seemed unduly long as she endured his glaring stance. Straightening her shoulders, Brooke strode purposely to the tack room, disregarding the show of temper she knew would soon show itself.

"You could get seriously hurt out here messing with a horse." he barked in a tone tediously familiar.

"I could fall down the stairs. I could have a pot of hot jam spill on me. I could be struck with lightening." She tried to get by him to put away her saddle. "Why don't you just make up a padded room for me?"

Adam grabbed her upper arm to halt her pace. Finding more resistance than he anticipated, she was able to break free of his hold. She hurried to her saddle and proceeded to put everything away. His form filled the doorway, his hands propped on the doorjamb.

"Now that we are going to have a baby, you need to be careful, not out riding around. What if she spooked and you fell off?"

"Give me your phone," she demanded and proceeded to punch in numbers viciously. "Sally, this is Brooke Tower. I need to talk with Doc now if he is available.

Thank you … Doc, would you tell my husband what you told me about exercise. He doesn't think I should ride my horse … Thanks."

Brooke handed the phone to Adam who listened with very little response. When he turned off the phone, he looked at her. His voice was softer. "I love you more than I can put into words. I have been a bit overwhelmed with all that's been happening. There are too many ways you can get hurt out here, seriously hurt."

Brooke moved to sit on the leather couch in the tack room and took off her gaiters. "Well, you are going to have to change, because I will not be imprisoned in my home. And if I feel like coming down here to ride a bit or to see my animals, I will. I'm not trail riding or training, and you have no right to stifle me this way." Her emotions were at a high pitch as he stood there watching her.

Adam stared at her silently and without expression. His shoulders sagged under the strain. He hooked his thumbs in the pockets of his jeans and eyed his dust covered boots.

"What do you want of me?" he inquired quietly, his brown eyes touching her gently.

Her words blasted at him as Brooke tried to explain her side of the issue. "Ever since the rustling started up again at your father's place you won't let me go to town alone, or even with Mary. More planes hovering around, probably drug drops. And until the locket situation is resolved, I'm a prisoner. Now with the baby, I feel like you want me in a padded room. You are never around, and I haven't been to town to shop in weeks. And what about a nursery?"

Adam's sigh released some of his stiffness. He sat next to her. "I am sorry I have made you this angry. I don't know of any other way to ease my mind." A frown of remorse accompanied his hand as he gently touched her cheek.

Adam took her hand and ran his thumb over the back. "I need to explain a few things to you. Buck wanted it kept secret, but you need to know, and we can stop arguing. The new hand, Curly, is a federal marshal. He is one of the men who has been investigating the planes we saw. He and I have been riding out, looking for signs of any activity. Dad and Steve lost ten cows last week. We feel someone knows what's going on out here. Maybe the rustlings are a diversion to keep us looking in the wrong places.

"We suspected Kitty. She hasn't been around for over a month. Juan says she took a vacation, a cruise he said. Curly is going to work undercover with Dad for a while. Someone working for him may be part of all this."

Adam pulled her to sit on his lap and held her head on his shoulder. "I'm no longer sure of anything. I'm almost positive the men working for us are loyal. Many have been working for us for many years. Leaving you alone takes the joy out of my work. Fears mount with each passing minute until I'm home with you again."

He took her face in his hands. His brown eyes

mellowed and fell on her softly. "Sweetheart, let's go to Laramie tonight, just the two of us, a nice dinner?"

Brooke studied him for a moment. He had been under a lot of stress lately. She could tell by the fitful way he slept. He seldom rested, and she knew she was the cause of it all. The training, breeding of the horses, the cattle, and the hay production, all of it took time and effort without the added fear of an attack on the family.

Adam held her close. "Why don't you go in and freshen up? I'll be along as soon as I talk to Hank."

"Don't go blaming Hank."

"Blame Hank? If I can't control you, how could I expect poor Hank to stop you from doing what you want?" He grinned.

"Well, he did try. I felt sorry for him." she chuckled. "Are you hungry?"

"Yes, and pack a lunch for Joe. He said he was staying out until they had the cattle centralized. Joe and my father are both using those fancy new four-wheelers. We've been making them stay with the herd while we scout out the ones in the trees. I need to unload the bay gelding and let him rest. I guess I'll get the sorrel Hank usually rides to finish the day—and no you can't come help." He smiled.

She returned with a gunnysack of bagged lunches including candy bars they liked.

"I'll be back as soon as I can. Hopefully, many of the

animals will be in a central area by evening." Adam kissed her affectionately and held her, seeming reluctant to let go.

He left her to get back to the men rounding up the cattle. But she knew the dark clouds on the horizon would only mean trouble.

CHAPTER TWENTY-NINE

*M*ary entered the kitchen, from the hallway. She pulled on and buttoned a white wool cable-knit sweater. The house had grown cool with this latest spring storm. After pouring herself a cup of tea, she came to sit down at the table with Brooke. "You look kind of glum."

Brooke stabbed her fork into her salad. "I wish he would let me help. He did offer to take me out for dinner tonight."

"Well, he's worried about you being pregnant. He gets a big grin every time the baby is mentioned." Mary brightened and tapped her hand. "Wanting to go out for dinner is a good thing, isn't it?'

She sighed. "I have this gut feeling something will come up. Now a big spring storm has been predicted. You know how dangerous they can be. Lightning. Hale. Wind."

Mary's reading glasses rested precariously on her nose. She gazed up at Brooke. "He doesn't mean to disappoint you. This has been a different year."

"I know." Brooke got up from her chair and began to wash the lunch dishes. "If he would let me out there with them, I could help get the cattle in before it arrives."

Changing the subject, Mary gazed over at her. "Look, I have to go over to Hightower to help Connie bake pies and cakes for the church bazaar this weekend. She fell and injured her wrist. Some are going to be raffled off at the bingo game tonight. We thought we'd also bake up some chocolate chip cookies for the guys. Come along. Adam can pick you up later. Connie has been asking about you."

"No, thank you, anyway. Maybe I'll go lie down on the couch and watch a movie until Adam gets back. Maybe he will get back early."

"But aren't all of the men out with Joe and Adam?"

"Hank is in the barn. Don't worry. I'll be fine. I have the small handgun Dad bought me, and Claude is here. You go on and have a good afternoon."

Brooke followed Mary to the door and locked it. She waited and watched as Mary left the mudroom and heard the familiar slam of the screen door. Then, she travelled through the kitchen and into the den. She turned the television to the classic movie station, and after an hour of boredom, she dozed off into a fitful sleep. The slamming of the screen door woke her.

For a moment, she felt adrenalin rush through her

like hot acid. Claude didn't bark or growl. Instead, he whined and panted with his tail freely wagging. Brooke cautiously crept to the door and peaked out through the sheer curtains hanging there. The vision before her was of one tired and wet cowboy. With a crooked smile, she opened the door.

"Looks like you forgot your slicker."

"Brooke, would you get me a set of dry clothes? Ask Mary to get your father a set as well. The rain has been pouring for over an hour and it doesn't look like it will let up soon."

Adam began to strip off his sopping clothes in the mudroom. He hung them up piece by piece on hooks normally used for winter coats.

"Hmm, are you sure you don't want to stay and let me get you warmed up? All that naked skin."

"I wish." He smiled back at her but worry held in his eyes.

She left and returned with towel and clean, dry clothes. She put her father's clothes in a thick, plastic sack. After offering Adam a towel, she made him a hot cup of coffee to take the chill off. As he rubbed his wet hair vigorously, he came over to stand next to her. Putting a strong arm around her he held her close.

"I'm afraid we will have to postpone our trip until tomorrow. The reports from the men on the upper pastures aren't good. The rain has been coming down so rapidly the lake and the streams are filling up fast. Radar shows a large cell coming right over us. We may have a dangerous situation brewing."

Brooke didn't speak. She gazed past him out the window to the torrent of rain. "It looks really bad. The front pasture is now a pond."

"We have to get the animals back to higher ground near the Hightower formation before tonight. With all the rain they've predicted, the dam could be compromised. The cows and calves are in direct line if the dam should break. You know what happened last time. I'm sorry, believe me, Brooke."

She recalled one other time when the dam broke, during the same kind of storm. Spilling tons of water down the valley, the flood destroyed scores of animals from both ranches. Adam was aware of the danger. She wished he would let her come out there with them to help. She always had in the past. Now she could only allow her imagination to get the best of her.

"I, too, looked forward to going into the city, for us to have some time alone."

Brooke's voice was a whisper. "I believe you. I wish you would let me come out to work. I feel so useless sitting here while you are out there and knowing I could help."

He took her face in his hands and kissed her. "While I'm gone, why don't you and Mary make a list of things you need to buy in Laramie? Baby stuff."

"Mary isn't here. She's over at your dad's helping

Connie with pies and cakes for this weekend's church bazaar and for the bingo tonight."

His voice held disbelief. "Damn. Then you're alone?"

"I'll be fine, Adam. I have Claude, and I'll keep the doors locked."

"You didn't look too brave when you peeked out of the window," he accused, his voice becoming angered with his fear.

"Hank is down at the barns. I'll be fine."

"Hank is out with the crew. I guess you'll be alright for a few hours. If we lose power, the generator will come on. Your cell phone will work in case the lights go out—at least you'll have contact with Buck. I'll call you every so often to check up on you."

"And who is going to check on you? What if you're out of range? Then I worry." The thought tore at her insides. Could she bear it if anything dire happened to him? She shivered with anxiety and gritted her teeth at the vision of him injured. In the mud. Rain pouring down on him.

"I'll be around others. You lock this door." His kiss was hard and searching. He broke off the kiss and held her close. Placing his hands on her upper arms, he kissed her again and turned to leave. "Lock the door."

With Adam gone, a niggling fear shattered her bravado. What if someone did come while she was alone? Claude was her first line of defense. Besides, Adam didn't need to worry about her now. He needed his attention sharp and timely to get the cows and calves out of harm's way.

Her temple throbbed, and to keep herself busy, she made sandwiches. After wrapping them she put them in the refrigerator. With her small contribution, she went back into the den and sat in front of the television. As she settled in and became comfortable, the mudroom door swung open.

Real fear filled her. Her hand was firm as it held the little pistol she would use in her defense. But Claude again didn't show any sign of distress. Stealthily, she looked around the door jam. "What are you doing back? You scared the hell out of me."

"You can't stay here alone. Hank is out with me helping. I'll drive you over to my father's house. You can stay there with the women and maybe help a bit. And they both know how to protect themselves. Please, don't argue with me now. I'd feel much better about you being over there."

"I could drive over by myself."

"No, I want to know you are there——."

"I'll go if it will ease your mind. I don't want you to worry about me and take your mind off a dangerous situation." The rain, mud, angry cows, and tired horses equaled danger.

"I know, love. That's the way I feel. Get your slicker and boots. Let's get going before your father thinks I came back here just to be alone with you ..." He smiled devilishly but his eyes were dark with worry.

. . .

Mary showed some surprise, seeing her stepdaughter come running in out of the pouring rain. Brooke hung up her wet things and came to sit at the table with the women. Snug and safe, with the enticing smells of homemade cakes, pies, and cookies, the kitchen provided a refuge from the problems in her life.

"Adam brought me over. He's such a worrier."

"I'm glad you're here with us. I'll make a cup of tea for you."

Two hours passed quickly as she helped chop nuts and fruit for the batters. Mary noticed the flush on Brooke's face. She placed her hand on Brooke's head. "Are you getting tired, dear?"

Brooke sighed lightly. She was more anxious to hear from Adam than she was tired. However, she had been feeling anxious the entire afternoon. Probably stress.

"I am a bit weary. They shouldn't be much longer with all the men from both ranches out there. They are supposed to bring all of the cattle here to the Hightower plateau and sort them out later when the weather clears."

The mudroom doorbell interrupted. Connie got up to answer it, wiping her hands on a dishtowel as she went. Why anyone would be out in such weather? If Adam had come back, he wouldn't use the front door. The hairs on the back of her neck stood on end to signal her ever present fears. She suddenly remembered that as Adam hustled her out the door, her pistol was left on the table next to the sofa. To her relief, the intruder was Bess. She came over and gave everyone a light hug.

"I drove out to pick up the bake goods for the church. While I was there setting up for bingo, the pastor came down with the flu. Seems to be the new strain. They asked me to drive his van and bring these goodies to town. Some will be sold at the bingo tonight, if the weather lets up," Bess told them brightly as she nibbled on a cookie.

Brooke hadn't seen Kitty for a while, and she didn't attend their wedding. Maybe Bess had heard from her. "Has anyone been in contact with Kitty? Adam said her cows were mixed in with his."

"I called to talk with her. Old Juan said she was on a vacation, a cruise or something," Bess nibbled the cookie.

Brooke stretched and yawned. Her face felt flushed.

Mary put a hand to her head once again. "Brooke, you really should go lie down. Maybe you're coming down with the flu like the pastor. And there is the baby to worry about. We'll wake you as soon as we hear from Adam. He's about due to call."

Bess lit up. "You are having a baby. Oh, how exciting."

"Yes, it is. We were supposed to go shopping for the nursery today. The storm took precedent. Mother Nature doesn't care about plans."

"If you want to go home, I can drop you off on my

way to town with the baked goods. I'll be driving right past your place," Bess offered.

"I would really like to go home and take a warm shower and crawl under a nice warm quilt. Adam doesn't want me there alone." Brooke ran her fingers through her hair, massaging, and then wrapped a section behind her ear.

"How long do you think he will be?" Bess finished her cookie.

"Probably a few more hours. The last time he called he said they were out of the valley and out of danger, so it shouldn't take much more to get them all in the upper-level pastures. They'll sort the cows out when it's safe again. He said it was slow going with the mud."

Brooke tried to call him, but he didn't answer the phone. So, she left a message.

"I could stay with you for a couple hours. These cakes and pies don't have to be at the church until later. With this downpour, I doubt if there will be a bingo at all. The roads will probably become flooded or mudded out." Bess worked on the windowed pastry boxes she had brought from the church.

"Well, have another cup of tea and sample some of the luscious concoctions these ladies have baked. We'll have to see if Adam returns my call."

Brooke didn't want an unnecessary argument with Adam. She knew he was only thinking of her welfare, and she loved him for that. Always her hero. Another hour passed as the women talked and baked and wrapped individual items. She enjoyed the visit with Bess who was distant the past few weeks. "How is that new romance? Are you still seeing the same man?"

Although Bess didn't mention his name, she was open about her new love affair and their plans. "I may be leaving the area very soon. He has some business here to finish."

"Where will you be moving? I hope not too far away." Brooke rubbed the back of her neck and fluffed her long hair away from her head. Her forehead throbbed.

"Let me take you home and get you settled. I'll stay with you until Mary gets finished here, or until Adam returns," Bess cajoled.

"I don't know, Bess." Adam would go through the roof if he found out she left.

Mary urged. "Actually, there isn't much more to do. We have a few more batches. Bess has enough now for the bingo. The rest can wait. I'll be back soon."

Bess pulled out her phone and walked toward the mudroom. "I'm going to make a few calls to let them know where I am. I'll stay with you until someone gets home. I'll let Abby close for me...Really, I don't mind. And—you don't look well."

Mary chimed in. "Go ahead, Brooke. If Adam gets upset, I'll tell him I sent you home."

Brooke messaged on Adam about her plans to go home with Bess.

CHAPTER THIRTY

*P*otholes created hazardous obstacles for the church's old van to negotiate. What was only a short drive seemed like hours. Bess maneuvered through the muddy ruts. Flooding caused small rivers to wash across the road, claiming territory, and making the going treacherous.

Approaching the drive to the Montgomery Ranch, Brooke felt a sense of relief, for even if they were to get the van stuck, they would still be able to make it on foot to safety.

"Park next to the sidewalk, and we'll run into the mudroom from there," Brooke suggested.

She left the van and rushed to open the screen door. "Let's hang these things here."

Bess helped Brooke with the wet coats. "Boy. It sure is a bad storm. We haven't had one like this in years. I may not get to the church after all. People won't be able to get into town. They will have to cancel."

Their sopping shoes were placed on a wire-mesh shelf to dry. She took her key and opened the inside door. Claude met her, and then refused her offer to let him out in the rain.

"There are sandwiches in the refrigerator I made for Adam and dad, if you're hungry," Brooke spoke absently as she turned on the Keurig. *'Shouldn't be here'* kept echoing through her head. She placed her hand on her forehead. Her eyes burned. She felt quite flushed. At the sink she poured a glass of water. The drink cooled her throat.

"I'm not hungry after all of those cookies." Bess sat at the table, leaning back into the curved arms of the dark pine chair. "Mary spoke of you and Adam being on the outs lately."

Brooke looked at Bess as she searched for an answer. She really didn't want to respond to the question. Her relationship with her husband suddenly seemed more personal than the talks they used to have as young girls gossiping over a Saturday night date. Pausing, she wet a cloth and applied it to her forehead.

"We've had some disagreements over my activities. For the most part, I suppose he is right, and I am wrong. I certainly would rather be out there with him gathering the cattle than sitting here worrying about him."

"I suppose that could be a real problem for you. I

would love to be able to sit and do nothing—as you are. You are rather lucky, Brooke."

Brooke brought a cup of tea over for Bess. She had nothing for herself. She watched her surreptitiously. Something was on her mind, but Brooke could not pinpoint its source.

She began softly, "With your new friend, maybe things will work out for you, too."

Bess smiled then. "Yes, maybe I, too, can relax for once in my life."

Quiet pervaded the breakfast area. The air seemed thick with anticipation. The heavy rain slashed horizontally, tapping on the windows. Spitting lightening occasionally. Claude, too, sensed Brooke's unease and sat close to her with his head lying softly in her lap.

"This constant rain is beginning to wear on my nerves. I wish Adam and the men were back with those cows and in here safe and dry." She rose from the table and searched for the bottle of aspirin in the kitchen cabinet. After downing two tablets, she said, "I'm going to go up and wash up and put on a set of sweats. Maybe I'll feel a bit better afterward."

"You go on upstairs. I'll make myself another cup of tea. If there is wood inside, I'll build a fire in the den." Bess pushed Brooke in the direction of the stairs. "I'll need to contact a few people."

"A fire would be nice." She stopped and turned back to Bess. "Thanks, Bess."

"What are friends for?" Bess motioned with her fingers for her to go.

Before Brooke made the climb up the stairs, she double checked the front door to be sure it was locked. She could not alleviate the unease consuming her all day. Was it the pregnancy stirring up her senses? Was it the waiting for news and for Adam's safe return that gnawed at her? Or was there something else, maybe just the wind and rain making her edgy?

Brooke was never very good at reading mysteries. Often as not, she would read the last few pages to solve the riddle. Too bad, she thought, she couldn't find the last page to this day's scenario. If she knew everyone would be safe, then she could rest comfortably. Until then, she would wait and worry.

The water cooled her fevered face, and she enjoyed the cool washcloth as it sat on her neck. She put on a set of navy-blue sweats. The cotton knit was comforting against the cool dampness of the day. When she came out of her bathroom, her guardian was lying on her bed, wiggling with delight at the sight of her.

"Claude, you are a silly boy. I'm so glad dad bought you. You are so adorable, and the most unlikely guardian. You certainly do your job." Brooke hugged him and scratched behind his ears as he squirmed to help her find the right spot.

The wind, in its riotous force, slammed a tree limb against the side of the house, shattering one of the panes of glass in her room. Brooke froze. Claude barked frantically as he looked for an intruder. When he found none, he sniffed and eyed the broken glass on the floor.

She pulled him away from the damage, fearing he would cut himself and settled him on her bed. The rain splattered here and there as the force of the storm sent errant water beads into the room. Brooke stuffed a towel into the small opening to keep the wet out. She sat on the bed with Claude, holding him tight to settle her racing heart.

Brooke slowly traveled down the stairs with Claude. The dog began to whine with worry and crowded her. For a moment she thought she heard voices but brushed it off as the television. If Adam had returned, she mused, he would have sought her out. The closer she got to the den, the more she became aware they were not alone. Someone was in the den talking with Bess.

"It just can't be," she wheezed. She could hardly get a breath. Shock and anger at his presence in her home was almost more than she could bear.

"I think our Brooke is overwhelmed by such a wonderful surprise. Is that so, my pretty wife?" He spoke from the large wing chair where Adam often sat near the fire. Casually, and in control, he chuckled with meanness, humored by her reaction.

Brooke was speechless. Her fear was now tangible.

Mike was back. He hadn't died in the plane crash— he had been the one haunting her all these months. But now, she had grown to hate him, wishing he had perished in the plane crash.

Her greater fear was what he had on his devious mind. The treachery of his sick brain was well known to her. And the physical abuse—as well as the mental anguish.

Claude perched on tip of Brooke's feet as she stood apprehensively in the doorway. He whined quietly as he watched the man across from them, sensing danger. His body sat upright, ready to play the knight in shining armor for his princess.

"Make him be quiet," he warned. His green eyes were a bit glazed. He was probably under the influence of one of his favorite drugs. Without them, he was basically a coward. However, while under the influence, he exuded confidence. She knew what he had come for.

Would he let them live?

"Be silent, Claude." Had he not been holding her small pistol, she would have ordered Claude to attack him—the bearer of unwanted memories and fear. "I suppose you have come back for the locket—and whatever it will buy you. The locket is what you want, isn't it?"

"Yes." His refined features were an unfortunate parody of nature. "It has taken a great deal of time and energy. Your husband has made every turn difficult for me. It seems the weather will finally be my ally," he sneered. He grinned at her from under long, lazy eyelashes.

Her heart pounded with uncertainty. Needing time,

hoping someone would come before too long, Brooke tried to keep him talking.

"You were the one who injured my horse the first week I was home, weren't you?"

"Yes," he chuckled with mirth, "almost too easy. Kitty's idea. Thought it would be such a joke on you. Great makeup, don't you think? You never recognized me. I thought the gelding would throw you, and I could get to you first. You wore the locket so openly. I lived with Kitty for a time before you came back. I knew you would, such a Daddy's girl." He grinned insolently. He paused to take a few swallows. He licked his lips. "Bess, would you refill this?"

"What about the rest?" Brooke searched for ways to protect herself. She tried to keep him talking. Always so conceited, he liked to talk about himself, brag about how clever he was, how winning was the only way for a game to end.

"Oh, Junior was the one who pushed you in the barn. Stupid man. Thought he could just rip the locket from your neck. Then he began to cozy up to Kitty. Well, I needed her more than he needed a tussle in her bed. After all this time, I had to get rid of him. I thought the animals would dispose of him."

Mike eyed her for a while and took another sip of Scotch. "The cows were Kitty's idea. She was incensed with your return. She wanted Adam. She wanted some of the money to keep her expensive lifestyle going—and wanted you dead. She should have listened to me. Too late now though."

Brooke now knew Kitty wasn't on vacation, knew the turned dirt she saw was a grave. Fear of him took her breath. She had to take deep easing breaths to keep her senses.

His casual voice brought her back to the present. "Your husband stores excellent liquor." He swirled the Scotch in the crystal glass and held it up to the firelight. "You've caused me much trouble, my dear. I'm about out of funds. If this weather hadn't happened along, I may have had to come in and taken it. Then I would have had to eliminate the lot of you."

"So why didn't you?" Brooke's hatred for the man began to ooze into a strong fear.

"Well, then there would have been the state looking for me—the Montgomerys and the Towers clans are prominent citizens around here. But you already know that. I couldn't afford to have them chasing me and have my name in the papers."

"Why? Are you over your quota as a murderer?" she threw back his way.

Brooke had to find a way to make him leave before someone she loved was killed. An uncomfortable silence filled the room. Mike filled his glass once more from the crystal decanter and took a long hard swallow of the amber liqueur.

"No, actually there may be more. You see, I planted a charge at the dam. I should be hearing it at any time—

kind of a diversion." He chuckled obscenely, his eyes grinning with the fear he saw in hers.

Brooke was stunned by his admission. Terror and anger filled her as her mind searched for a weapon. If the dam were blown, the water would flood the valley and kill everything in its path. Adam said they were now on high ground away from any flooding. Mike didn't have to know that. "Bess, how can you associate with him?"

Their eyes held for a moment before Bess looked away. *Did she see some confusion there?* Maybe Bess wasn't as sure of things now. Or maybe she really didn't know her at all.

Bess replied, sounding brave. Her body inflections weren't as sure as her words. "Could be it's the only chance to have something better in life. You've always had everything you have ever wanted—including men. I have had to work, and work hard, for every dime. Oh, you try to be obliging and friendly, but you could never see I had nothing."

Bess paused a moment, and then as if she needed to say more, she continued. "Mike has promised to take me around the world if I would help him get the locket from you. So, please go get it."

Bess behaved in a manner totally uncharacteristic of the woman she knew. Brooke felt, for the first time, she probably didn't know Bess at all.

Her reply was heated with fear. "Do you really think this hollow shell of a man will keep his promises? Did he keep them with Kitty? He never kept them with me."

She rose and headed for the office to the safe where the locket was stored. Claude rode close to her heels.

She continued. "Has he beaten you because he felt like it? Threatened someone you love if you told him you wanted to leave? He threatened to kill my father. He shot a beautiful horse out from under me in a fit of temper. Still want to hang around this slime?"

Sadistic joy colored his tone. He chuckled. "Enough! Just get the locket my dear, and we will decide what to do with you in the meantime. Maybe, I should have one more go round with you before I leave. I did miss those 'parties' we used to have."

Brooke shivered with the thought of him touching her. She tried to stall. "I don't understand why someone who seemed to be smart would put account numbers as important as these apparently are in this locket."

"Well, I only thought of it as backup since you always wore it. You see I was on my way out of the country and out of your life forever. And then a funny thing happened. When Junior and I got to the airport, we were robbed at gunpoint by some thugs. They took the car, the briefcase with the account numbers, and our wallets. I couldn't call the police and hang around because our identities were forged. Junior had stolen the car and switched license plates. And the government was on my tail. So, I had to get back to you." Waving the pistol at her he finished, "Now go get it wherever it is. And any cash around."

In the office, Brooke tried to bide time and to think of

a plan to get out of the house alive. She knew Mike had already killed twice to get the information he needed. He certainly wouldn't let her go free.

Claude still followed her, staying close to her side. She might have to use him, she agonized. Sacrifice his life if it came to that. The realization brought a lump to her throat.

"Bess, is he your new friend?" Brooke spoke, trying to change the tone of her voice to one of indifference.

Uncertainty filled Bess' eyes, while her voice continued with bravado. "Yes. He's told me how ungrateful you were for everything he gave you. You were never satisfied. He said you were always cheating on him with his friends and associates when he was out of town. He said he found out you and his partner had hired to have his plane crash. He turned the tables on you," Bess rattled on. She seemed more nervous than before and appeared to be trying to convince herself of his worth.

"Is that why he allowed himself to be declared dead? And is that why he needs this locket so desperately—a locket he had secretly engraved? He's a thief and a conman. He's a murderer. Kitty? Junior? He is in the business of selling drugs. He takes them himself and becomes vicious and cruel—he's probably on them now."

For a moment the women stared at one another. They dared the other the look away first.

Bess broke first. Her hand motions filled the air

around her. "I have worked all of my life, even before I got out of high school. Everything I have I've worked and saved to get. I'm tired of squeezing pennies. This is my chance to have something other than hamburger or chicken soup for dinner. I'm not going to let you stand in my way."

Brooke opened the desk safe. "Here. Take it." Brooke shoved it at Bess, her eyes blazing with disgust for the woman and the lost friendship.

She heard Mike call them from the hallway. Her hatred now blazed for the poor excuse of a man who stood negligently in the doorway watching them.

Bess seemed worried. "Let's get out of here. If Adam comes back …"

"Yes, you're right. We will have to get going in order to make our flight. The islands are so nice this time of year—don't you think? All the money, just sitting there waiting for me." He looked at Brooke with a leering smile. "I'm not sure. Should I take you with us for insurance? Or should I just kill you now and make it look like a robbery?"

He came towards the desk. She moved to keep a distance from him. His menacing attitude recalled the abusive beatings and other humiliating acts during their marriage, melting away some of her bravado. Her knees began to shake.

"Bess says you are having a baby. You would never give me a child. I might have felt differently about our marriage." His glare held her captive. Moving around the desk, he searched the drawers for cash or other useful items.

The resolve to be angry rather than frightened jogged her brain. Her heart raced and her legs shook with fear.

"You're still the little prima donna." His sneering tone was accompanied by the slam of the desk drawer where he had found a small stash of cash. "Silly of me to think I should bring you along. You were too much trouble last time. I think I'll have to get rid of you after all."

Mike raised the gun slowly and fired.

A scream echoed in her head as Bess' body fell to the floor with hers.

"Bess," Brooke screamed. Bess had thrown herself as a shield. Blood splattered her front where the bullet exited Bess's neck. A dark pool was forming on the carpet.

Claude needed no order and jumped across the desk, overwhelming the offender of his home, tumbling both to the floor. Seeing her chance for escape, Brooke pushed Bess off and got up. Her mind covered many options as she thought like a trapped animal.

She couldn't chance going over to where Claude was fighting for her to get the gun Mike still held. And she had no time to get the gun cabinet key from the desk.

Abe kept a Colt 44 in the tack room for varmints. She would have to get there.

In the foyer, she threw open the front door. If Mike

escaped the dog, he might take the bait. Extra time. Get out through the mudroom and to the barn.

As she raced through the kitchen, she was brought up short by a gun shot and the simultaneous yelp from Claude. Her heart squeezed. She hoped precious Claude would survive. However, she could not chance her life to check on him.

Keeping to the row of lilacs for protection, she slapped barefooted through the thick and oozing mud. The battering rain, coming through the trees, hid some of her noise. The only place she would have to worry was the fifty feet or so from the tree's edge to the barn doors. They had been left open on both ends to allow drainage. The water streamed through the barn following the center aisle groove. Even in the barn he would be able to see her as the yard light lit the area and the inside lights lit the aisleway. She held her breath and ran.

Stealthily, she slipped into the tack room. Leaving the light off to stay hidden, she felt around for the gun. Panicking, she forced shallow breaths. Her heart pounded against her rib cage. She searched, knowing he would indeed kill her if he found her. He had the locket and the numbers he needed. Her legs were so shaky she could barely stand. In the dark she could not find the holster holding her only hope. Blindly, she groped. Finally, she located her objective. Under Abe's old denim jacket hung the Colt.

A shadow crossed the window, illuminated by the yard light. Brooke froze. Unlike her racing heart, her actions seemed slow and clumsy. Finally, taking the gun from its holster, she opened the cylinder and felt in the dark for bullets in the chambers.

Just one.

She had killed rattle snakes and coyotes—even a cougar—over her lifetime. This animal was much more dangerous. Could she kill a man?

Brooke eased opened the tack room door ever so slowly, enough to see out. Her body shook in nervous spasms. Her breath came quick and shallow. From her position, she first heard and then saw a rider, approaching quickly from the opposite end of the barn.

Adam. Just as she recognized his shadowed form, a shot rang out. His hands flew up to his head, and he fell off the horse backwards. Startled, the horse spun around and raced through the back of barn. An animal like wail poured from her. Her greatest fear had now become a reality.

Throwing the door wide, she saw her enemy.

"Oh, there you are my dear. Let's stop this cat and mouse game. We'll go inside and talk, and maybe play on your brass bed. Maybe I'll take you with me." Mike's voice was soft, mocking, the silken tone of insanity.

Without forethought, she raised and fired the revolver. The bullet hit him in the face, knocking him backwards beyond the barn door. His arms flailed for a moment. He staggered and fell on his back, his arms outspread. Rain washed over his still body.

Her heart squeezed with anguish. Brooke walked

with firm purposeful strides to the man who had terrorized her. Numb with rage and shock, she pointed the gun and began firing and firing the empty gun. Strong arms surrounded her.

"I think you got him," Adam's deep voice whispered. He removed the gun from her hand and tossed it to the ground. She turned in his arms and with great wracking sobs she held on.

Brooke stared out from inside the barn doors as the paramedics removed the bodies to the silent ambulance. Little could be said to lessen the pain and rejection she felt. A bit of her heart had been cut out by the duplicity of her old friend. After so many years, it was hard to believe Bess conspired with Mike. But then, she, too, was once deceived by his performance.

Buck came to stand inside the doorway with the man named Curly. "I have to take this gun with me and the locket. I sent Hank up with Curly to see about the explosives. They didn't find anything. Besides, it may have gotten wet. Let's hope he was playing with your mind."

Brooke felt numb, emotions on hold. "Thanks Buck. I guess there will be an investigation. You know about Kitty?"

Curly spoke up. "Yes, we'll look into Kitty's disappearance tomorrow when it gets light out. Old Juan will have to explain some."

Brooke was tired, feeling emotionally shaky. "Doc is in the house with Adam and Steve. I guess Abe is doctoring Claude. Poor thing. I need to get inside now."

Steve met her in the mudroom and enfolded her in his arms, holding her head against his chest. Taking an extra kitchen towel, he wiped away the rain on her face and blotted her hair.

"This has been one scary day." He turned her in the direction of the den. "Doc says my brother has a hard head, and the bullet grazed him. We'll all have to remember not to piss you off." He smiled, trying to lighten her mood as well as his own.

"I doubt you could make me that angry. Maybe now we can all find some peace."

Steve held her at arm's length. "Yes, it is sad. Devils are like that. I am going to be an uncle. That is something to celebrate." He kissed her forehead. "You better go in and see my brother before he comes out looking for you."

As she got to the kitchen, Doc was on his way out of the den. "Let Adam rest for a while. Just a deep furrow. He has a new part in his hair," he joked. "I want you to sit down here at the table so I can check you out." After taking her vitals he asked. "Do you have a headache from all this stress? I can give you something to help you sleep."

"No. As a matter of fact, I don't even feel the tightness working up my neck."

He smiled. "Maybe your headaches were from stress. Headaches are also an early sign of pregnancy." He grinned. "And I'm going to want to see you and Adam tomorrow."

Brooke hadn't expected Adam's head to be covered in bandages. A raised area of bandages on the right side indicated where Doc sutured the wound. The rest was wound with gauze to hold the bandage. He looked like a mummy. Sitting next to Adam on the couch, she welcomed the warmth of his arm around her shoulders.

Her voice was a whisper. "You knew he was alive, didn't you?"

"When you came here, I actually thought you might have been part of some scheme to get money from your father. When everything started to happen to you, I knew that couldn't be."

"I don't understand." She rested her head against his shoulder.

"Curly found out that the locket holds a password to a bank account in Aruba. Funds he stole from his partner and money he got from drug smuggling. He had to hide, dispose of his debts, and get rid of his partner. You came in handy."

Steve entered with a tray filled with cups of coffee and a basket of muffins. He placed them on the large square coffee table. "We have to be honest with you, Brooke. Curly is the one who decided you had no knowledge of Mike's illegal operations. They did know he landed on Kitty's ranch a few times before you came back." He sat in the oversized, wing-backed chair.

"Poor, stupid Kitty." Brooke shook her head in disbelief.

"She tried to kill you, my dear." Adam shifted to fix his coffee and grinned at her with wonder. "How could you feel sorry for someone out to harm you? Bess, on the other hand, has been under suspicion for weeks. Curly has photos of her at Kitty's on days when Kitty was supposed to be on vacation. Her partial fingerprint was found on the back of the locket the night of our engagement party, although, she denied it."

"If you suspected Bess, why did you want her to be my maid-of-honor?"

"We weren't sure, so we didn't want anything to look out of the ordinary. I was scared to death when I called, and Mary said Bess had brought you home." Adam gave her a gentle embrace to let her know he understood the pain she was feeling.

"Well, she must have had second thoughts. Bess saved my life." Brooke wiped away an errant tear with her napkin.

Abe arrived with a limping Claude whose shoulder and leg were bandaged. The dog was drowsy from the tranquilizer and nearly collapsed in his bed near the fireplace.

Abe tapped Brooke on the arm. "He's gonna be all

right. The bullet went through the soft tissue of his shoulder—he'll have a slight limp."

"He'll always have a home here. He gave me time to get out of the house."

Steve sipped from his cup. "I called Hightower. Joe and Mary are going to stay at the house with Dad until morning. I guess some of the road has washed out by the flooded stream."

"Well," Adam grinned, "I guess we will all have to party here tonight."

Brooke settled in his embrace. Her hand rested on his chest. She could feel the steady rhythm of his heart. Recalling her reasons for coming back to the ranch, she realized she had finally found her place, even if the going would be rough and tumble at times. But more important was the living heart of gold beating so steady and lovingly next to her.

THE END

ABOUT THE AUTHOR

Judith lives in Florida with her husband and canine administrator, Toby. In between golf and MahJongg, she writes. She called Colorado home for most of her adult life. When she bought two horses for her children to ride, she didn't realize it would grow to a herd of registered Paint horses, lessons for herself, and training for her horses, not to mention lots of travel to shows. Driving to Wyoming to visit family and enjoying the wide-open land was the creative inspiration for the fictional farm community called Bantry and the mountain formation Hightower Mountain in SECRETS OF THE HEART.

The second book in this series, RETURN TO HIGHTOWER, is in progress and focuses on Adam's younger brother Steve Tower and his lost love, Desiree Lorde. Both novels are stand-alone reads. I hope to have it out by summer.

Thank you for purchasing SECRETS OF THE HEART. If you enjoyed the story, please leave a review on Amazon.com to let others know. You can contact Judith at

judithluke.author@google.com

Made in the USA
Las Vegas, NV
25 August 2022

53884781R00233